Hell Money

Hell Money

Stefan Kanfer

Creators Publishing
Hermosa Beach, CA

HELL MONEY

Copyright © 2018 Stefan Kanfer

Cover art by Peter Kaminski

CREATORS PUBLISHING

737 3rd St
Hermosa Beach, CA 90254
310-337-7003

Library of Congress Control Number: 2017962922
ISBN (print): 978-1-945630-75-0
ISBN (ebook): 978-1-945630-74-3

First Edition
Printed in the United States of America
1 3 5 7 9 10 8 6 4 2

For Lea and Aly, an encore

China Town
Van Halen

Headless body in a topless bar.
Warring clans in lowered cars.
A buck is still a buck in Shanghai,
and a buck is all you earn.

A great night for all concerned.
Steel fingers play a deadly song.
Whole lotta Shakespeare going on and on and on.

It's all happening downtown.
You painted daughters of the Tong underground
don't mess around.

Welcome to China Town.
Well, you're in our town now.
Welcome to China Town.

Heroes aren't born; they're cornered.
And this corner is where we write the story.
Two tribes warring
downtown after hours.
The best to you each morning.

Can't survive and think to win.
Drugged into sin.
Next episode begins and begins and begins and begins.

It's all happening downtown.
You painted daughters of the Tong underground
don't mess around.

Welcome to China Town.
Well, you're in our town now.
Welcome to China Town.

It's all happening downtown.

****

Ang Chun was still working the crowd as the general led him off in handcuffs. The major turned on Lew Chun. "Your father now, Boy Chef," he warned. "You tomorrow."

The other soldiers and policemen were red-faced, hostile, intimidating. Not the major. Ang used to call him *Fēngxiàngbiāo,* the Weathervane, because he had survived three administrations, moving in whatever direction the Great Leaders wanted.

The major never raised his voice, never sweat. "Forget the hotblooded ones," Ang Chun used to advise his son. "All threats, all bluster all the time. It's the cold soldiers cause the grief. These are the dream killers."

The Boy Chef shouted at the officer's back. He even called him Weathervane. The major didn't turn around. Lew Chun wouldn't have cared if he did. It was June. He was 23 and famous. Both of his parents were alive. His paternal grandparents had died when he was in the crib. The Boy Chef had never been to a funeral. He knew nothing of sorrow — and less of fear.

These things he was to learn very quickly.

But right now, Tiananmen Square was where Lew Chun wanted to be, the scene of posters, slogans, speeches, demands for freedom, chants, music and smoke. He had watched a grim-faced man called Meng facing down a row of tanks as the cameras whirred. Then the army moved in on foot, collaring men here and there. No pattern to their arrests, no reason he could see for their being selected. Ang Chun disappeared into that sea of green uniforms. As he did, he dropped a torn piece of paper. It swirled at the Boy Chef's feet. He bent down and slipped it into his pocket.

A half-hour later, more tanks came, throwing long shadows, groaning as they moved forward. This time, the army cleared the square of students and demonstrators, with soldiers knocking down the Boy Chef, trampling on his stomach and chest, tossing the kitchen staff around and then pushing on. There was no place to sit down, nothing to lean on. There were no chairs, no pillars, no trees. The chatter of rifles and the clouds of tear gas made it impossible to stay, even on the periphery.

He and the others ran until they reached the Western Lake restaurant two miles away. His sides ached, but basically he was sound.

He had a key, and they went to the main room and sat at the dining tables, set with white cloths and gleaming glasses.

Here the Boy Chef had spent his childhood and adolescence, amid tidal aromas from the ovens and stovetops, garlic and black pepper and blue cheese saturating the air, bouquets of fermented mandarin fish; Peking roast duck; pond snail and chicken; lamb soup; honeycomb noodles; Harbin red sausage; *yang za sui tang* — sheep entrails soup, far more appetizing than it sounded; red braised pork belly; barbecued yak ribs; and his favorite, "Buddha jumps over the wall" — said to be so delicious that Siddhartha Gautama himself had vaulted above the barricades of his castle to consume this amalgam of shark skin, abalone, sea cucumber, ginseng, scallops and rice wine.

He looked at the framed picture of his father on the wall and saw himself. No one would have mistaken the Boy Chef for anyone else's son. Ang Chun had married late and fathered his one government-allotted male child, but for two decades, he continued to look 20 years younger than he was. Lew Chun was a Xerox of Ang Chun — wiry, black hair, rimless glasses, a steady stare, inexhaustible. Ang was fearless in the kitchen and, as it happened, in political life. On the wall over his bed, carefully lettered by a calligrapher, was the proverb, "When fate throws a dagger at you, there are only two ways to catch it: either by the blade or by the handle." His wife was forever getting out of the way of fate; Ang was always trying to catch it by the haft.

Everyone in downtown Beijing knew him as a valorous man — and funny, in his indirect way. The diners often made him retell the story that was supposed to explain all of Chinese history:

A peddler from the outer city of Urumqi was selling mushrooms on the street. A merchant bought a cartload of them and took the fungi to a big market in Yinchuan, where he sold them to a wholesaler. This man took the mushrooms to a big vegetable dealer in Wuhan. In turn, he sold them to a major distributor in Hangzhou, and that man unloaded them on a restaurateur in Shanghai. The mushrooms were served in a soup for the emperor's dinner.

And everybody who ate it got deathly ill.

An enormous fuss was raised, followed by a furious investigation. First the Shanghai man was interrogated. He blamed it on the salesman from Hangzhou, and back it went, from Wuhan to Yinchuan, until finally the emperor's squad found the original Uighur peddler.

He stared at the men, unbelieving. "You *ate* them?"

They nodded.

"But those mushrooms were not for eating! They were for buying and selling!"

To Ang Chun, this was the soul of the true China, despite the years of Marxism and re-education squads. Citizens of the People's Republic were still merchants underneath — traders, bargainers. It didn't matter what the merchandise was, wearing the hairs off their legs going forward and back; they were forever buying and selling.

Mushrooms were to change his son's life in other ways, ways neither of them could have known then. The Boy Chef was too busy trying to cherish what he could of his father. He remembered Ang's lessons and recalled his strange and compelling loyalties.

There was, for example, a neighbor, Fen Hsaio, known to be a dealer in hallucinogens. In China of this period, when such traffickers were arrested, they could be subject to capital punishment. One night, word got out that Fen had been arrested. Even though Ang held Fen in contempt, he visited him in jail. With him he carried a container of shark fin soup. It was to be the man's final meal.

Also, Ang was an encyclopedia when it came to mind-altering substances, knowing every detail of Britain's victories in the Opium Wars and how the Chinese were enslaved and humiliated by a fatal combination of military might and the juice of the poppy. Once, when the Boy Chef's adolescence had begun, he was taken to a place in the Eastern City, just past the 4th Ring Road.

He remembered the makeshift three-story brick building opposite a high-rise with a doorman and guards. No toilet except an outdoor privy, clouds of iridescent green flies everywhere. An arrowy white-haired man appeared at the door. Ang slipped him some money. Father and son followed their guide to a large room illuminated by a couple of low-wattage incandescent bulbs. These dangled from rubberized cords nailed into the plaster ceiling. Packing crates sat against the walls, with rough wooden planks laid across them.

About a dozen men were in evidence, varying from Lew Chun's age to one grasshopper-like gentleman well past 70. The smokers sat on the planks nodding out or mumbling to one another. The conversations were incoherent. The Chuns were about to take their leave, when the Boy Chef stopped in his tracks. He had recognized a former schoolmate. The name Wei meant big and clever, and in school the student was both — tall, quick to learn foreign tongues and an accomplished calligrapher. But troubled. Wei's mother was judged insane after she took an overdose of sleeping pills three separate times. She was warehoused in a mental hospital, and there she managed to do away with herself by stealing a plastic bag and putting it over her head. The family fell apart. Wei dropped out of school. It was rumored that he got a job downtown spray-painting cars. Maybe then; not now. Lew Chun looked at glazed eyes that didn't recognize him or anyone else. "Persistent cough," Ang whispered to his son. "Tremor in the hands. A death wish in brown muslin."

They moved on.

"Mao thought he would extinguish the drug business by executing the sellers and jailing the users," Ang remembered. "These people don't need prison. They need help."

"And if they're past help?" his son asked.

Ang turned to him: "Nobody is past help. *Nobody*."

The Boy Chef didn't agree but said nothing.

Now that Lew Chun had been exposed to the effects of illegal substances, his father thought him old enough to learn about his mother's shame. It had been kept from him all these years. Her cousin Hsu Dong was a high-level criminal, a fence for stolen goods, a smuggler and black marketer. Quick on his feet. Arrested only once, and that for a minor crime.

He had left China in the 1970s, abandoned his wife and two daughters, gotten himself smuggled into the U.S., nobody knew how, and made his way to New York. There he had prospered under his new name, Shawn Lin. Nobody quite understood what he did for a living; he was said to be in real estate.

Lew Chun had seen Shawn Lin's name in the paper now and then but never made the connection. Twice a letter had come, covered with bright U.S. postage stamps. The upper left corner was marked Col. S. Lin, 238 Mulberry St., New York, NY 10012. For Lew Chun, that address was a cause of great fascination. The leaves of the mulberry tree are the main food of silkworms, and he wondered whether there was an American species at work on the streets of Chinatown. The envelopes were addressed to his mother, but his father threw them unopened into the fireplace.

An official eye was kept on the restaurant from the day Ang Chun visited Fen in jail. But nothing happened — not until he had made clear that he was on the side of the protesting students. Now the officials had their opening. Now they had their rationale.

But the Chuns still had the Western Lake restaurant — at least for a few more hours. Here everything was calm and clean. In the kitchen, steel pots gleamed on the stove; woks and ladles dangled from overhead racks; bamboo cutting mats and knives caught the light. And the friendly, pervasive aroma of sesame hung in the air like a feminine scent. Lew Chun stood there and inhaled for a few minutes and then went back to the sea of tables covered in starched white cloth. He and the staff sat down and drank some green tea, and he read his father's message aloud as the listeners craned their necks to hear.

It seemed a parody of the sayings in Chairman Mao's Little Red Book: "The mantis stalks the cicada, unaware of the yellow bird behind them." But one of the cooks said, "No parody, Lew Chun. It speaks of survival and murder." The Boy Chef didn't believe him then, but he turned out to be correct. It *did* speak of survival and murder, that yellow bird. Survival for him, murder for his father. That morning, orders had come down for Lew Chun's execution.

****

Over the next few weeks, conflicting stories rumbled through the shops and streets. The soldiers had used lead bullets on an armed populace; no, the soldiers had used rubber bullets. More than a thousand had been arrested; only a handful had been detained. Thousands had been executed; fewer than 100 had died, almost all by accident.

No one in Beijing ever learned the complete truth. Lew Chun only knew that 223 men never came back. One of them was Ang Chun, owner of the Western Lake restaurant, leading chef, his professor, his boss, his father. Ang's body was claimed after a week — dead, it was reported, from internal injuries caused by a fall. Lew Chun wanted to stay at the restaurant, face the police when they arrived, but the staff wouldn't hear of it. Over his objections, Ke Han, the wide-bodied headwaiter who had taught him so much, guided him to a safe house.

His mother felt she was being watched, so she didn't dare to visit. Her parents were in a village outside Shenyang; Ang's parents, now deceased, had lived in the south. His remaining relatives were too infirm — and too afraid to travel. They mourned him from afar. In those weeks, time seemed to go in reverse. Mao's words came back to haunt them. "Is there famine? Is there disease? Perhaps it is necessary. Some of the people must fall and fertilize the soil."

After two weeks, information was leaked to Ke Han.

"I have one friend on the police," he told Lew Chun.

"Only one?"

"One is all I need." He was in no mood for sass. "The government looked upon your father as an agitator. He had many chances to change his tone. He never did. You know this."

Lew Chun conceded the point. For well over a year, Ang Chun had been ammonia to the authorities' nostrils. He was loud in support of movements to end censorship and take down the "re-education centers" — concentration camps in the guise of schools. For several weeks, he had joined the students' hunger strike; the irony of a chef's starving himself was not lost on the generals. But Lew Chun was only a few steps behind in his beliefs and gestures.

"So," Ke Han continued. "You're Ang's heir. Once, this signified cuisine. Now it means politics, Boy Chef."

That was indeed Lew Chun's title — and had been for 11 years. Well before entering adolescence, he had created new taste delights, dramatic chicken and beef dishes that were featured on state television last year and written up about in *Paris-Soir*, which first dubbed him "Le Garçon Cuisinier" — "Boy Chef," as the *Daily Express* headlined it.

Lew Chun used to revel in the celebrity because it impressed girls; now he hated it because it put a target on the back of his tunic.

"Neither your youth nor your reputation will save you, Lew Chun. They want the Boy Chef in custody. Once in prison, you will never emerge."

"Except horizontally."

"Just so."

"Then what am I to do? Hide here, waiting to be sold out? You know I will be, Ke."

"No doubt. If not this week, then the next."

"So where do I go?"

"You know what a snakehead is?"

"Of course I know what a snakehead is." The label was attached to traffickers in human beings. One of them ate regularly at the restaurant. Word got around. Ang snubbed him, and Lew Chun never spoke to the man. Of what use were such people to the Chuns? The family was prosperous — at least as prosperous as you could be in the People's Republic. Cooks came to consult both father and son. Lew Chun learned conversational French and English. American tourists were forever teaching him their idioms and slang.

"Tomorrow morning, you will be met by a snakehead. His name is Yao."

"Yao what?"

"Just Yao. He is short and ugly and trustworthy. You will be taken to a boat and from the boat to an ocean liner."

"To Hong Kong?" Lew Chun had always wanted to go to the chef's paradise.

"I don't think so. The government has operatives there. You could be abducted, sent back."

"Where then?"

"No idea. Yao will know. Here."

He handed Lew Chun an envelope. Inside were a bunch of $100 bills in American money. So, Lew Chun reflected, I'm going to the Gold Mountain after all.

"There's $2,000 in there. Tell no one about it. Not even Yao."

"How am I going? By sea? By plane?"

"Yao will know."

****

Yao knew. As Lew Chun lay under a canvas tarpaulin at midnight, he gave orders to the men who operated the oars of the dinghy. Finally, he turned to the Boy Chef.

"You will be taken aboard the Clementine Bartel. A sailor will guide you to a place next to the engine room. Do not give him money. He has been well-paid for his service. You will stay in that room. Food will be brought to you until you arrive."

"Arrive where?"

"A place you never heard of."

Infuriating bastard, Lew Chun muttered inaudibly. "Try me."

"Humboldt Bay Harbor, California."

Not only had Lew Chun never heard of it but also he would have been unable to find Humboldt Bay on a large-scale atlas of the United States.

"Someone will meet you, Boy Chef. He will tell you your next move."

"That someone have a name?"

"Names! Always names! You make me crazy with names. How do I know names? You're the one who talks American. Whoever it is will find you. These are my instructions."

The two men didn't speak the rest of the way. There was no sound but the splash of little waves against the hull and the oars dipping in and out of the water. Despite Yao's in-your-face attitude, Lew Chun was aware that he owed him his life. So he whispered some words of thanks as he ascended the rope ladder to the deck of the Clementine. Whether Yao heard them or not was impossible to tell.

A few moments later, a French seaman guided his passenger to a small dark place in the back of the ship. The door was dark green, the walls a lighter shade of the same color. On it, three words were stenciled in black: *Salle de Stockage*. Storage room. Lew Chun surprised him by translating the sign in French, but the seaman continued to point at things as if he were talking to an illiterate Chinese laundryman.

There were more permissive times, long past, when Ang and Lew Chun obtained permission to study the cuisine of four-star restaurants in Paris, Berlin and the Hague. But those were flying visits. This was the first time Lew Chun had ever been in a seagoing vessel. Twice a day, the matelot brought a tray of biscuits and consommé. These Lew Chun ate and drank. The small portions of meat and fish were cold, ghastly stuff, not at all French. More like animal feed. These he left untouched.

They arrived a week later — at night, as Lew Chun expected. The sailor pointed down.

"You have money?" he asked.

Instinctively, Lew Chun lied: "They didn't give me any."

The man muttered flatly to one of his companions; what do you expect from a *jaune*, a yellow man? He pointed again at the water. A black sailor was waiting in a rowboat. Lew Chun descended the ladder and, on the instructions of the oarsman, went into the water.

"*Nager vite*," came the order. Swim fast. Lew Chun sidestroked silently as the prow headed for shore. A Coast Guard vessel flashed a powerful searchlight on the boat and picked out its contents — a few rags and a six-pack of Rainier beer — and kept going. So did the rower, until he was 30 yards from the shore. They floated in under the lights.

A voice whispered in the Beijing dialect of Mandarin. Sand and rocks crunched under the keel. Lew Chun stepped from the water and onto the land. He followed his guide in a fluid crouch until they arrived at a beat-up brown truck.

On the side was a picture of a large golden pig and a legend: Raymond Bros., Hog Butchers to the World. The guide jerked his head toward the passenger side of the cab, and Lew Chun clambered in. A towel lay on the floor. He dried himself off as the trucker loudly changed gears and drove away from the shore. In carefully enunciated English, Lew Chun asked where they were going. He received a curt answer: "Des Moines." He thought the man was replying in French, but he didn't understand the reply. The man added a third word: "Iowa." No amount of prodding could get him to say anything else.

After just over an hour, they pulled up at a small airport. An old-style monoplane was waiting, sitting at a slant, the propellers turning around slowly and then more rapidly as the plane's lights blinked on, off, on. Lew Chun was escorted to the ladder and told to climb aboard. The seats were filled with Chinese — no doubt smuggled the way he was, on a ship. No one said anything. Apparently, the flight had been held for the last passenger. Ten minutes later, they taxied down the little runway and took off.

The plane seemed to hit every air pocket from the West Coast to Iowa. Some of the passengers were terrified; others were sick. Six hours later, they set down in what appeared to be a cornfield plowed down to hard-packed dirt. Another truck marked with the hog butcher legend waited a couple of hundred yards to the west. The Chinese piled in the back, the doors slammed in their faces, and they bounced around in the dark for another hour.

Sometime after midnight, the driver deposited his human cargo at a whitewashed stable converted into a barracks for farmhands. Lew Chun could tell the conversion was recent because it still stank of horses. The other hands were sleeping when the truckload arrived. They were tossing and mumbling, unconscious in the way of sleepers, breathing evenly and heavily, occasionally talking nonsense. With the use of a big dry-cell flashlight, the driver indicated a row of cots. At the foot of each one was a gray T-shirt and undershorts, denim bib overalls, a bar of soap, a washcloth, a small towel and a toothbrush in a plastic case. The newcomers were to dress in those work clothes in the morning when one of the bosses came to wake them up.

He went away. Five minutes later, Lew Chun was asleep on top of the covers. At dawn, a man with the build of a sumo wrestler appeared at the door. At his feet was a pit bull, barking repeatedly. The man was Asian, his head closely shaved except for the part that grew a ponytail. Nothing about him was moderate. He kept shouting "Up and out, up and out," in Mandarin and then in English, but he didn't have to. The dog would have been enough to get the laborers going.

As soon as Lew Chun heard the orders, he rolled out of bed and went to the big wide-open bathroom, with its row of toilets and a wall of shower heads. He hung up his old clothes on a nail in the unpainted pine wall, put his overalls on the neighboring nail and planted himself under one of the showers. As the other workers began to stir, Lew Chun guarded his uniform, making sure no one touched it as he cleaned up. He dressed while the others showered, palming the small envelope of money and transferring it to his trouser pocket.

There was no time to socialize. The boss introduced himself to Lew with one word, pointing at his broad chest. "Sam. You?" "Lew Chun," came the wary response. Sam grinned wickedly. "Ah. I know you. I tried once to get a job at the Great Western. Your father turned me down. Whatever you were in Beijing, here you are just an executioner. Follow me. I will teach you how to slaughter hogs." So after all the promises and assurances — *Yao is short and ugly and trustworthy* — the Boy Chef had been sold out. His assault on the Gold Mountain had begun.

****

Sam was greatly disappointed to find that the Boy Chef knew all about slaughtering. Ang Chun had wanted his son and heir to learn everything that went into the running of a restaurant — cooking, baking, chicken plucking, animal butchery, all things that were clean, all things that were bloody. No secrets.

Lew Chun remembered the day he was taken to a hog farm, where in a state of shock he watched the progress — or was it regress? — from sty to slaughterhouse. A weary and pitiless old butcher said the fate of a pig was pretty much the same all over the world. China, America, Europe, Africa — it wouldn't make much difference. Each hog would be treated like a pet — fattened, coddled — until the day of betrayal. At that point, a front leg would be tied up, forcing it to walk on three limbs, disoriented, fearful, tugged along mercilessly.

To Lew Chun, pigs seemed very intelligent, even more so than dogs. The pigs recognized the signals of their last day on earth. As they got closer to the place of death, the hogs began to squeal and bellow, "Not me! Oh, no, not me!" Or so it sounded to his ears. Two men grabbed the other leg, exposing the throat. The victim screamed in a higher pitch and struggled helplessly against its holders. The killer inserted a thin sharp knife in the animal's throat, and the blood gushed out in a furious stream as the cries sank from piercing to piteous to inaudible. Life drained from the animal.

The corpse was covered with hay and set afire. Then it was covered with more hay and ignited again — and perhaps a third time — so all the hair could be scraped off. His eyes were plucked. More blood got drained out. Then came the men with long thin knives who cut the animal up for ham and pork and sausages and soup and lard...

Lew Chun was the wielder of the knife that first day on the Bannock farm near Des Moines, and he was for many days thereafter. The slaughterhouse was scrubbed down daily, but it never lost its stench of manure, blood and chlorine. Hardly anyone talked to the Boy Chef, except to call him by the new title of Executioner or demand an implement or order him around with a curse. It occurred to Lew Chun that the obscenities were as stupid as the bosses who said them. In China, he had heard — and used — inventive schoolboy slurs, such as "speckled son of a white ape's abortion," "spawn of camel dung." Here it was just fuck you, fuck off, fuck this, fuck that.

On the fourth day, an older man with a Sichuan accent broke the silence.

"I'm Wen. I know you," he said, half in English half in Chinese, when they were washing the animal matter from their hands and arms.

"I don't know you."

"I don't mean I know you personally. I know who you are."

"That was in Beijing," I responded. "Here I'm the Executioner."

"Yes, I heard what they call you. Say nothing. Don't give them satisfaction. We're all the same. All hopeless."

Lew Chun asked why hopeless.

"No money. No one to help. I paid the same snakehead more than $1,000 American. He said he would get me a job in the Napa Valley picking grapes. But the job fell through. This is all I could get."

"How much do they pay here?"

"They didn't tell you?"

"I didn't ask."

"$30 a week. Maybe."

Lew Chun knew very little about the American economy, but he knew no one could live on $30 and said so.

"Of course they can," he insisted. "You get food, clothing, shelter."

"But never save enough to move on."

"Move on where? No papers, no money, nothing. Just a bunch of Chinamen. Who would hire?"

The water was splashing so loudly they didn't hear Sam until he was upon them.

"Listen to what he says, Boy Chef. You stay here until we let you go. Maybe never."

Wen slipped away and hustled back to work on the hog carcasses. "You can get out faster if you oblige," Sam grunted.

Lew Chun didn't understand what he meant by oblige.

"You have seen meth?"

"I have."

"And triads?"

"I am familiar with what they do."

He knew the whole process, how drugs were made, how they got around. Some of the information he had gleaned from waiters chatting on their off time, smoking on the back steps of the restaurant. Some he saw when he accompanied his father on visits to those places where addicts lived in hiding, places where Ang Chun brought leftover food.

Early on, Lew Chun had learned that the chemicals for methamphetamine were exported by Chinese gangs — the triads, they called themselves. The business had been going on for years, decades. Sell to citizens of the People's Republic and you were airbrushed from the page. The family might not be able to find your grave. But peddle the stuff to the nation's Western enemies, weakening them and making money in the process — that was different. From the 1980s on, the government had turned a blind eye to the triads, let them operate through Mexico, where there were factories to turn methylamine and pseudoephedrine into batu, glass, quartz — whatever they were calling it now.

Why did Sam select me of all the workers? Lew Chun wondered. He decided there were two answers. One, he was younger than the rest.

And two, he was smarter than they were. Had to be; his Beijing title said as much. The Boy Chef could be useful to such an operator. Very well, Lew Chun would return the favor. He would have to be quick-witted — but not so quick he would call attention to himself — while he waited for the chance to make money outside the $30, break out one night, acquire fake ID somehow and get going. But to where? In this vast country there were how many people? What did they teach them in school — 250 million? And he didn't know anyone to ask for help. Not a soul.

****

For immigrants, North America was a magnet in the 19th century and an illusion in the 20th. The vast plains, the snow-covered mountains, the long blue rivers, the limitless forests and the open skies were a part of a mythic — and now unwanted — past. In its place were the big cities of the New World. The foreigners felt displaced and uncomfortable in raw nature. Paved streets and buildings of concrete and metal were the objects of desire. The lumber yards and rural farms meant oppression, ignorance, poverty. *Stadtluft macht frei* was the way the Germans had it. City air makes freedom. It was a phrase Lew Chun had first heard as he and his father were taken on a tour of Hamburg. It came back to him now as he walked on a real street with real tar for the first time since he left the city of Beijing.

"The way it works is this." Sam was laying down the rules to all three operatives. They bent closer as he whispered. The man to Lew Chun's right was a small cheerless moron. The other had some intelligence in his narrow face. He may have been bright as a child, but now, at what could have been anywhere from 35 to 50, he was nervous and spacy. Lew Chun recognized the symptoms, the drumming fingers, the restless leg, the repeated words. A typical addict between highs. Sam referred to them by their street names: Ketamine One and Ketamine Two. He addressed Lew Chun by his new sobriquet. He, too, was named for a drug: Ecstasy Eddie. Ketamine Two wore a black shoulder holster under his khaki field jacket.

"You wait at this corner." Sam called down directions from the cab of his truck while the trio stood outside. "Pretty soon a guy will drive up. Pravda, he calls himself. He'll be Russian, short, white hat, carrying a Nordstrom shopping bag. Got that? Nordstrom."

They chorused Nordstrom.

"He gives you the bag. You count the money. Seventy-five G's in there, you give him this." He handed Lew Chun a metal box painted white and marked with a red cross and the words First Aid.

Sam took off. It was late spring, raining lightly but not cold. His employees huddled under the eaves of a five-story office building. Fifteen minutes dragged by. Twenty. A half-hour. Pravda showed up 45 minutes late, behind the wheel of an anonymous black Buick. He was not alone. Two men with dark shiny eyes peered from the back but didn't get out.

Lew Chun stepped forward as instructed. Pravda handed him the Nordstrom bag. He counted the bills. The sum was all there. Ketamine Two gave Pravda the box with the red cross, and the Buick drove away. Lew Chun had seen the bootleg TV shows from America and expected weird and deadly stuff to happen. But there was no hustle, no guns, no trouble. It was as simple as that.

Twenty minutes later, Sam materialized. Lew Chun gave him the money. Sam counted it out deliberately, bill by bill. Satisfied, he doled out an envelope to the first Ketamine and another to the second. They walked away rapidly and disappeared around a corner. Sam motioned Lew Chun into his vehicle. When they were underway, he handed his passenger a $10 bill.

Before Lew Chun had a chance to react, the driver challenged him. "What do you want? All you did is hand over some powder."

"And what did the Ketamines do for *their* money?"

"They took a bigger chance. They have prison records. You're clean."

"So when I get caught and sentenced, when I get out of jail I'll get paid more? That it?"

"You don't accept, you can always go back to pig sticking."

Lew Chun made a show of hesitation. Then: "I accept."

"Be at the front gate tomorrow morning, 10 sharp."

"How will I know when it's 10?"

Sam shrugged. He drove back to the farm in silence. When Lew Chun debarked, Sam thrust his hand out the window. Something metallic gleamed in the air. Lew Chun caught it in his right hand.

"A present," Sam announced with a sharp smile. "On top of your salary."

Lew Chun examined his gift — a wristwatch with a fake leather band, white dial, black numbers and a red sweep second hand. The back bore an imprint. Lew Chun squinted but couldn't make it out. Sam knew what it said.

"Made in China."

"Weren't we all," replied the Boy Chef, and then he walked away.

****

Lew Chun learned many invaluable street truths during the two years working with Sam. If a squad car was three blocks from the drop-off locale, for example, it was a decoy. You were supposed to relax when you saw it; it was too far away for the police to see what was taking place. Actually, the real narcs were close by in an unmarked vehicle, circling the area and waiting to pounce. So whenever Sam spotted an official PD vehicle, he didn't wait around for confirmation. The deal was immediately canceled and then rescheduled for another time, another locale.

One week, after a third postponement, Sam let the Boy Chef know there was a leak somewhere in his organization. He didn't accuse anyone outright, but Lew Chun was the new man, and several times he caught the boss appraising him in a sidelong manner. Sam's attitude was mimicked by the Ketamines, Taken together, their moves meant he was on trial, possibly for his life.

There was no way out. Lew Chun knew what they would say if he maintained his innocence and if he pointed out that he was a new arrival in the Gold Mountain, an illegal who wouldn't dare call attention to himself by addressing a cop. They would call him a sellout trying to save his ass. And if he didn't say or do anything? Probably, their judgment would be the same.

Yet they said and did nothing to him. Sam vanished from Lew Chun's life. There were no drop-offs. No threats or intimidating gestures. Just silence. Indeed, none of the men talked to him openly, at night or at meals.

Once more he was assigned to pig slaughtering. Then on a Friday, Sam abruptly showed up and made a motion toward his car, and Lew Chun got in the back with the Ketamines. He thought perhaps he had been reinstated. Sam drove silently to the edge of a wood bordering on Route 9, exited, came around to the back door and ordered the passengers to follow him. When the road could no longer be seen, he grabbed Lew Chun by the collar and threw him to the ground.

The Ketamines watched approvingly as he kicked the Boy Chef in the ribs. They were smiling now, exchanging remarks; Sam the Man knew how to work over a mook, kicking the shit out of him but just missing the vital organs and the breakable bones of the shins and wrists. An amazing talent. Look at Ecstasy Eddie, doubled over. "Man going to be Sam's bitch very soon," Ketamine One said, and Ketamine Two giggled through his runny nose.

Sam lifted up the Boy Chef by his shirt front and smacked him on the left cheekbone. Lew Chun tasted blood, and when Sam did it a second time in the same place, he couldn't hold back a hard yelp of pain. The witnesses laughed louder. At that moment, Lew Chun sensed that he wasn't going to be killed. Sam was going to provoke the maximum amount of pain and let the blood run down the white shirt, but he wouldn't cause permanent damage. Because somehow he needed all three men for those drop-offs. This was a lesson in intimidation, as much for the goons as for the Boy Chef.

He bloodied Lew Chun's ear, caused some contusions, kicked him a few more times in the ribs, expertly avoiding a simple fracture. Then he dusted his hands off and withdrew. The Ketamines carried their semiconscious burden back to the car, opened the trunk and stuffed him in it. Lew Chun came to inside the metal coffin, convinced that he was wrong about Sam's intentions, that he would never last the night. But the car suddenly stopped, and Sam opened the trunk and threw Lew Chun out.

"I got trouble," he said, looking down. "If you're the one who made it, Boy Chef, you get stuck like one of the pigs."

They left him in the dirt at the edge of the slaughterhouse. The next day, aching but in one piece, Lew Chun was back to killing hogs, listening to their pleas and screams, wondering whether there was an exit from this inferno of pain and filth. After two nights of incessant brooding, an idea came to him. Every evening when the work was done, the men were required to put their knives in a magnetic rack nailed to an unpainted pine wall. Every other night, one of the cadre would do an inspection, making sure all the equipment was accounted for. But on the third evening, the inspector was late or off-duty or possibly absent without leave.

Nobody watched the thin young man with the puffy cheekbone as he took hold of the thin Wusthof 4 1/2-inch boning knife. He slipped it up his sleeve, with the blade under the watchband. An old chef's trick, used for keeping an extra knife for cutting while the hands were busy. The Boy Chef had thought of another application for it.

****

Lew Chun secreted the Wusthof under his pillow at night and hid it under the leather watchband every morning. There were many steel implements on the rack. The big blades were always in their places, he noted, but no one seemed to keep track of the small ones.

That weekend, Sam invited him to a downtown drop-off. The Boy Chef didn't know what to do. To say no was asking for another beating and possibly death. Say yes and it could mean — what? A confrontation with the police, most likely. They would trade his ass for a little peace from the authorities. Maybe. But maybe not. Maybe he was back in Sam's good graces. In any case, now he could defend himself if the worst happened. So he walked to the car with a little more confidence. He felt even more secure when he saw there were no Ketamines in the back seat.

He tried to make conversation as they sped along. "Lucky there's no traffic," he said.

"Dumb bastard," Sam grunted. "In this country, you make your own luck."

That was all he said for the next 15 miles. At the end of the journey, he swerved into a parking garage. The sign said SORRY FULL, but he ignored it, grabbing a remote from the glove compartment and pushing a button. The corrugated steel door rolled up. He drove in, and the door slowly clanged down behind them. The garage was dim and full of cars. No one was in the attendant's booth. An ominous sign, Lew Chun reflected. When they got out, he asked whether the exchange was going to take place here, and Sam said wait and see. Their voices echoed off the concrete block walls and the oil-streaked floor.

"This is the Year of the Rat," Sam said.

"Meaning what?"

"Meaning you been handing us a line. You come to the farm from a French boat. Your father is well-connected."

"My father's dead. Killed by the government. I'm a renegade."

"A renegade with connections."

"What connections? I don't know any cops. I don't know anything. I don't know any*one*. I don't even know where we are right now."

"In a rat trap."

As Sam reached in his pocket, Lew Chun worked his weapon free. He was going on impulse now. Open-mouthed, Sam gawked at the knife shimmering in the half-light. His eyes were still bulging in disbelief as Lew Chun drove the blade into his convex belly. The scream was immediate and deafening. Lew Chun's victim seemed to be mewling, "Not me! Oh, no, not me!" But as with the pigs, there were no words accompanying the sound of misery and shock. For an intense, vivid moment, both men felt this was happening to two other people. Then Sam groaned and clutched at the bloodstain widening on his gray shirt. He sank to his knees on the stone floor, still making a piteous and dreadful sound. He pitched forward and down, bleeding out as the dark red pool widened around his midsection.

Lew Chun bent down and reached into Sam's pocket. A small blued-steel revolver was surrounded by loose $50 bills. The Boy Chef had never touched a gun in his life, and he wasn't going to start now. The bills were transferred to his own pocket. He listened for the sound of approaching feet. Nothing. Sam would have arranged for the garage to be empty so he could do his lethal job in private. After he shot Lew Chun, he would use the office phone and call for others, probably the Ketamines, to remove the body. Well, they would find a different body this afternoon.

Inside the attendant's booth was a black pegboard with an array of car keys. Lew Chun permitted himself a smile. The people who ran the parking garage hadn't thought to lock them up; they must have put a lot of trust in Sam. Perhaps they worked for him. Or he for them.

There was a wide choice of automobiles. Best would be an anonymous-looking sedan, so Lew Chun selected an unwashed gray Ford Escort hatchback. He had only operated his father's restaurant truck, and that for no more than a couple of miles. But he got the hang of the steering right away, creeping up the ramp and onto the street.

An idea came to him as he drove. The angle of the sun said he was going east. With luck, he could drive quite a ways in that direction before abandoning the car.

On the other hand, in a little while, Sam's people — or the cops, if they found the body first — would be looking for the Escort. If they found it at an off-ramp going west, they would assume that the Boy Chef was heading back the way he came, toward California. That way, he could buy some time while he determined how to get from Iowa to Shawn Lin in New York City.

****

The car was abandoned at a mini-mall. It was the first time Lew Chun had seen one, and as he took in the sights of a prosperous disordered country, he formulated a plan. Signs pointed the way to a city five miles distant. He went into a RadioShack, bought a Walkman and a set of folding headphones, and then found a phone booth at the rear of a gas station.

He asked Information for the number of the Greyhound bus depot, called there, asked when was the next bus to...to... and abruptly realized that he knew nothing about the States. He rang off and considered his situation. It would be risky to go directly to New York because it would keep him penned up in a vehicle, easy to find once his pursuers got the scent. He called Information again and got the address of the depot.

En route to town, he turned the Walkman to AM 1010, an all-news radio station. Not a word about Sam. The Ketamines must have cleared the body away. Or it could be that Sam wasn't dead. It could be that he was in a hospital somewhere, unwilling or unable to talk yet but planning his revenge. Lew Chun shook off the thought; his knife had gone in too deep.

Within an hour, he entered the city, and 10 minutes after that, he located the bus depot. A framed map of the States hung from a rear wall, its glass streaked and greasy. He picked a big city not too far away, where he might find a Chinese restaurant, ask a few questions, get his bearings. Still no mention of Sam on the radio as Lew Chun paid cash for a one-way ticket, climbed aboard, sat in the back and went to sleep with the newscaster chatting away about Mikhail Gorbachev, the ayatollah and Salman Rushdie, unrest in Romania, the crash of a crop-dusting plane in Davenport, and a prediction of heavy rain and local flooding. There was zero about a stabbing in a garage.

A pawnshop was visible from the rain-streaked bus window when Lew Chun debarked. He went in and bought a large scarred-up leather suitcase for $35. It wouldn't do to check in to a hotel — even a second-rate one in Columbus, Ohio — without luggage. The sign behind the front desk said they took cash or credit card. The El Dorado fit the requirements. It was dusty, anonymous and quiet — with long-stemmed silk roses in black vases and dark green carpet. On a table were menus of local restaurants. One was called the Hunan Taste. The concierge said it was right around the corner.

The greeter at the door was a reedy adolescent whose name was on his white jacket. Ping was trying hard to be an adult maître d' — too hard, Lew Chun thought. He remarked on the teenager's thinness without saying anything. (When had he ever seen a Chinese waiter who wasn't underweight?) Ping promised that every one of his mom's dishes was outstanding; leave the choice to him. And what was the gentleman doing in Ohio? Working his way across the country, Lew Chun said. Picked grapes in Napa Valley, worked in a pawnshop, sold appliances in a RadioShack. Ping gave him an empathetic look. Eventually, Lew Chun added, he would end up at his uncle's house in Boston.

Then it was Ping's turn to talk. He said his mother had followed her brother Dao from the megacity of Guangzhou, formerly Canton. He had come to Canton, Ohio, because he liked the sound of it. And there he struggled. Too many Chink restaurants for the size of the population, a health inspector told them. He pulled up stakes and moved to Columbus. And here he got on. His sister and her son followed.

In Canton, Ohio, only Asian clientele — and nowhere near enough. In Columbus, Ohio, plenty of *gweilo* — a disparaging Cantonese word for white people. Kind of like ofays, *gaijin* and all the other words for outsiders, nonmembers of the ethnic club. Lew Chun looked around. Ping was right; plenty of Ohio *gweilos*, attacking their chow mein and noodles, eating out at the Chink place with gusto.

By the time Ping went off to the kitchen, Lew Chun had learned where to buy discount clothing, the cheapest places for takeout food and the name of a bus line run by Asians for Asians. When Ping returned with the food, Lew Chun tried him out in English. He did well, as long as he stayed in the present tense. ("Mom cook good. You see. I get your meal now. It taste fine. You happy.")

It was the worst meal the Boy Chef had ever eaten, including the slum food he and his father had tried in Shanghai. The chicken was tough, the sauce over-salted, the vegetables flavorless. Ping's mother must have been trained by veterinarians, he thought. Nevertheless, the waiter was awarded with a big smile and the assurance that the cook was a genius. Lew Chun drank all the tea in the pot so he could cram it with the inedibles when no one was watching, left what he thought was a generous tip and took off with a promise to come back very soon.

The heavy mist followed him into the hotel and entered the room through the slightly open windows. Lew Chun slammed them shut, lay on the bed and snapped on the little color television. His body felt as heavy as a sack of gravel. He had been on the run for days, weeks, escaping from the Chinese government, from the American immigration authorities, from the snakehead network, from Sam, from the Ketamines.

On the screen, a senator from Kentucky was bombinating to the CNN host. He said that politics made strange bedfellows. "No, it doesn't," Lew Chun responded to the image. "Politics makes orphans." He began to cry. Lew Chun hadn't allowed himself to shed tears since the age of 11, but now they came in a flood. He knew why; the son never had a chance to mourn his father. Worse still, he didn't know whether he would ever see his mother again — or, for that matter, his schoolmates or the staff at the Western Lake. They were just faces now, stuck in memory like old photographs in an album.

He was just 23, hated by people he never knew, no roots, no friends, no helping hand, holed up in a strange city in a foreign country. The pillow was wet when he went to sleep, but it was dry when he arose at 7 o'clock. He had made up his mind by then.

The TV was still on, and the early headlines streamed under footage of an interview with a senior officer in uniform, his chest decorated with a fruit salad of ribbons. No mention of violence in Iowa. Even if the police were on the case by now, Lew Chun assumed it would be too small for CNN to bother with. But the Boy Chef wouldn't be too small to bother with, not if the authorities had his name and description.

He washed up and shaved and walked with a slight stoop, trying to look like a nobody as he checked out. The desk clerk didn't even lift his head. Moving deliberately, avoiding eye contact with fellow pedestrians, Lew Chun made a series of brisk visits to the places Ping had recommended. He bought three white long-sleeved shirts, a blue and red striped tie and a blue sharkskin suit off the rack at Danny's Smart Discount Clothing.

A corner deli had all he needed: two oversize turkey sandwiches, two Hershey bars and three bottles of Poland Spring water. At the bus terminal, he visited one of the surprisingly clean men's rooms, packed the clothing and the food in his suitcase, emerged, and purchased a ticket to Akron. He stayed in that city one night, ate at a slightly better Chinese restaurant and bought another ticket to Pittsburgh. There the routine was repeated. The idea was to accustom himself to the States, get used to walking around freely, without showing fear in his face or posture.

Lew Chun might have convinced the waiters and hotel clerks. But he couldn't convince himself. The feeling clung to his skin, to the back of his neck, to the base of his spine — the expectation that at any second, an immigration officer would put his hand on his shoulder and demand to see his papers. Or that a policeman would knock on his hotel door and place him under arrest for murder. So he stopped zigzagging across America and bought a one-way ticket to New York City. *Dumb bastard. In this country, you make your own luck.* Lew Chun had no idea how to locate his distant relative Hsu Dong — now Shawn Lin — or, if he did find him, whether he could gain an audience. But in Chinatown, Manhattan, USA, a place he imagined as teeming with faces and skin like the Boy Chef's, at least he could hide in a crowd. Here he was only a target waiting for bullets.

****

The emperors and the dynasties came and went. So did Chiang Kai-shek, Mao Zedong, Zhou Enlai and Deng Xiaoping. And still the practitioners of traditional Chinese medicine carried on, as unchanged and durable as the Great Wall. Only last winter, his super-rational parents had paid visits to an obscure pharmacy on Guozijian Street. The chemist prescribed wulinshen, a fungus obtained from the nests of termites. It was supposed to provide a deep and dreamless sleep in times of stress and misfortune. Perhaps it did; they swore by the substance.

Lew Chun dreamed about wulinshen on the journey east and wished he had some. The low-slung bus, its suspension shot, rattled and shimmied on the roads between Pittsburgh and New York. Sleep came hard and only lasted a few minutes at a time. China boasted aluminum buildings and 30-mile bridges, and still there were places that sold exotic herbs and the ground horns of cloven-hoofed mammals. But who knew what the Gold Mountain would provide in the late 20th century? Given what the passenger overheard from gawking American tourists, he would have to be content with aspirin.

They pulled in to downtown Manhattan at 2:30 a.m. Five local stops and there was Chinatown. A low hum greeted their ears, and the new visitor thought it came from a machine just out of sight. But no; it was the sound of the city in summer, and as he was to learn, that phenomenon had no "off" button. After a while, you just stopped noticing. Street lamps illuminated groups of people still awake and alert — a few shop owners arranging their windows, men dipping large nets into a hundred-gallon tank and fishing out wriggling sea turtles for tomorrow's soup, four couples strolling and laughing, police walking in pairs. They were all Asian, even the cops, mostly Chinese but a few who looked Korean and one Japanese woman, who was furtively swapping envelopes for money as soon as the uniforms had turned the corner. Lew Chun pretended not to observe the negotiation. The last thing he needed was trouble on this foreign and intimidating turf.

Halfway down Pell Street was a small handwritten sign on a four-story building. It said Eleanor & Peter Wong, Bed & Breakfast. Below that was the most welcome word imaginable — VACANCY. A bald man of about 50 was at the desk, but he couldn't have been Peter Wong because he was white. He rolled a nightstick, conspicuously lying across his desk, and announced, "$200 a night." Before Lew Chun had a chance to say anything, he added, "In advance."

The bills were produced.

"One night only?" the man inquired. It was not a friendly question.

"I think so."

"You think so. You don't know so?"

Lew Chun didn't know what to reply, so he merely shrugged. The desk clerk took the money and issued a steel passkey for Room 4C. Lew Chun walked upstairs alone, found the room and realized that the bathroom was at the end of the hall and that there was somebody in it. The toilet flushed, and a heavy middle-aged Chinese woman in a blue and white caftan and tan suede slippers emerged. She said good evening and waited for his reply. When he gave it, she asked how long he planned to stay. When he said he wasn't sure, she heard the intonations of Beijing, her hometown. She examined this latest guest more closely. Weary, thin, disoriented in every sense.

"You're new."

"I just got in."

"You're very young. Are you in school?"

Lew Chun didn't like questions. Not this late and not from a stranger.

"I hope to go to university here."

She smiled. "You remind me of my son. I'm Melanie Chu. You?"

"Sam," he ad-libbed quickly. "Sam Yung."

"We'll talk in the morning, Sam — before I make my rounds." She rummaged in her kimono pocket and found a little folder. "Take a look. Maybe you'll want something. I sell everything half-price to Chinese. Good night." She waddled off. He washed up and went to bed. Just before he turned off the table lamp, Lew Chun examined the paper Melanie Chu had given him. The front said Global Feng Shui Products. Inside was a list of those items: Electric Fountains, guaranteed to give you peace of mind and help you make sound investments; Lucky Bamboo; Crystals, for protection, health and love; Buddha Image, for harmony and spiritual growth.

Obviously a hustler, but if Mrs. Chu sold to the Chinatown shopkeepers, she might be a good guide to the region. He wondered whether she had ever heard of Shawn Lin. He wondered whether the breakfast would be Asian or American. Then the wondering stopped, and the next thing he knew, light was pushing its way between the slats of the blinds and into the room.

Human sounds were bouncing around the stairwell. Lew Chun opened the door. The words were clearer now. There were two voices, one male, one Melanie Chu's, speaking English — something about the man upstairs. He heard the world "illegal" — as in illegal immigrant, a guy with no documents. Dressing rapidly, Lew Chun searched for an exit. This was a house, not a hotel, and for guests, there would be only one way out — down the stairs and through the front door.

He looked up. At the end of the hall, there was a hinged door in the ceiling. Lew Chun knew exactly what it was; houses have doors like that all over the world. They lead to roofs — the locale of water tanks and ventilators. This door had a big zinc hook-and-eye arrangement, easy to unlock. The door swung down. Lew Chun went back to the room, brought out a chair and his suitcase. The voices became muted. Perhaps they were talking about someone else. But he couldn't take the chance. Shoving the suitcase up and onto the roof, he pulled himself up and out and walked across the roofs of two adjoining tenements.

That put him at the corner of the block. There was only one route from here — down the rust-colored fire escape and onto the street. Lew Chun took the clanging steps slowly, one at a time, as if it were part of his morning routine. People were on their way to work. Some of them looked up. All of them kept going.

The Boy Chef found a cafeteria on Kenmare Street. Sparsely attended and quiet. A good place to think. He ordered tea and a roll from the counter, went to an unoccupied table and took stock of the situation. He had no papers. Anyone, official or otherwise, could have him arrested for vagrancy, jailed, sent back to die in the People's Republic. No doubt there were rewards for turning in an immigrant in the country illegally, which must have been why Melanie Chu had been talking about him in the lobby.

Lew Chun asked for directions to Mulberry Street from people on the sidewalk. He had been told that the men and women in New York were highly salaried, well-dressed, cool, shrewd, confident, their wallets stuffed with $20 bills. But as he hurried along, it struck him that every other New Yorker was crazy. Grotesques were everywhere. Beggars thrust their hands belligerently, as if it were his fault they were broke. Bad violinists played on street corners with their hats turned down so pedestrians could throw in silver coins. People talked to themselves, arguing, remembering. Little men speaking Spanish gathered under shop awnings and made wet kissing noises as pretty girls walked by. Drunks, brown and white, caromed off buildings. None of this would have been visible on the streets of Beijing. It wouldn't have been allowed. Citizens were freer here, but they didn't seem to know what to do with themselves.

Ten minutes later, he stood at 238, pressing a brass buzzer. A peephole had been set at eye level, and it was put to use for a full minute before the green door swung open. A muscular and hostile black man loomed in the little foyer.

"Yes?"

Lew Chun answered in English. "I'd...like to see Shawn Lin."

The threatening figure looked down at this caller and his suitcase. "Everybody'd like to see the Colonel. Everybody'd like to *be* the

Colonel." He gave the young Chinese the full *Star Wars* treatment, basso profundo voice, intimidating posture, furious glare.

Lew Chun didn't know how to respond.

Darth Vader looked down at Lew Chun's suitcase. "Selling what?"

"I'm his cousin."

"Cousin have a name?"

Lew Chun supplied it.

"Wait here."

The Boy Chef stood on the hard rubber doormat for a long time before the man reappeared. He made a motion with his hand. Lew Chun trailed him down a dark hall and into a sitting room. A Chinese man of his own height and build — but with salt-and-pepper hair — sat in a big upholstered chair with a blue silk cover. He was barking something into a phone the same color as the chair. There was something of a military air about him. But he had neither the erect posture nor the quiet confidence of a military-school graduate. Nor did he seem the battlefield commission type, someone with a tough mouth and pained eyes that had seen too much and forgotten nothing. Lew Chun put his puzzlement aside for the moment and checked out his surroundings.

On the table were black-and-white pictures of two young women in gold frames. Lew Chun guessed those were the Colonel's daughters. Their names were at the bottom of each photo. Amy had a sweet, serene affect. The other one, Jade, was a dragon lady right out of a Bruce Lee film — visible from her body language, as well as her formidable don't-mess-with-me expression. Next to their photographs was a book bound in cross-grained blue leather. The first line of gold lettering read "The Art of War." Under it was the author's name, Sun Tzu.

When Shawn Lin finished talking, he waved away the black man, turned to Lew Chun, lowered his voice and tapped on a wooden slat bench with blue cushions.

"Sit, Boy Chef," he said.

Once a flattering title, now a weight around the neck. Shawn Lin knew the identity of his caller. One wrong gesture and Lew Chun was on his way back to Beijing.

"Your father couldn't stand me," Shawn Lin said in their native tongue. "Your mother was ashamed of me. Why are you in my house?"

****

A river of ice floes ran through Lew Chun, and his father's phrase raced around his brain: "It's the cold ones we have to watch for and worry about. These are the dream killers." This gentleman, this "colonel," was as cold as marble.

At the same moment, the marble gentleman was appraising his visitor. This young man was anxious, full of dread, bright, desperate. Shawn Lin had found such greenhorns useful over the years because their gratitude could be cut out in little pieces and traded for favors. Sometimes they would even die for their rescuer. Sometimes. And if not...

"Why are you in my house?" Shawn Lin repeated. His tone was resonant and knowledgeable, like a voice-over in a documentary.

Lew Chun swallowed hard and leapt. "First, sir, I'm not my parents. Second, I thought my life wasn't worth $10, but everybody seems to want it. So I thought I would ask you to help me find the answer."

The Colonel removed his spectacles and closed his eyes. A thoughtful man. Or a sleepy one, Lew Chun thought. He wanted to continue but didn't dare to speak. His voice would surely quaver, and besides, it seemed rude to break into his cousin's meditation or his daydream. After an agonizing wait, Shawn Lin severed the silence. "Why did you leave home? How did you get to this address? And how long have you been in the Gold Mountain?"

When the visitor hesitated, he demanded, "Answer me. And don't leave anything out."

Lew Chun unburdened himself. He disclosed the whole story. The burning of Shawn Lin's letters from America, Tiananmen Square, Ang Chun's murder at the hands of the state, the snakehead procedure, the pig sticking, the stabbing of Sam — he told it all. And in the process, he confessed that he had no papers, that he was a fugitive, an illegal, a criminal.

At the finish, the Colonel closed his eyes again. By now, Lew Chun realized he wasn't nodding off; he was deciding. The Colonel took the *Art of War* on hand, turned a few pages and read aloud: "Opportunities multiply as they are seized."

He looked directly at Lew Chun with a dark, penetrating stare. "Clear?"

"Clear," the young man said. Actually, he thought the words were vague and incomprehensible.

The Colonel was going to read something else from Sun Tzu, changed his mind and pressed a buzzer at the base of the phone. The black man appeared in the doorway.

"C.C., ask Philip to come here."

"Right away." C.C. disappeared.

More silence. A plump Chinese in a chef's toque and white smock entered.

"Colonel?"

"Philip Lau, this is my cousin. He has some experience in the kitchen. Take him below. He will plan and cook tonight's meal."

Shawn Lin consulted his Sun Tzu manual.

"There are not more than five musical notes," he read to the two men. "Yet the combinations of these five give rise to more melodies than can ever be heard.

"There are not more than five primary colors, yet in combination they produce more hues than can ever be seen.

"There are not more than five cardinal tastes, yet combinations of them yield more flavors than can ever be tasted."

He closed the book and looked up. "Prove worthy of my trust, Boy Chef. Then we'll see what to do with you."

"Yes, Colonel," Lew Chun said, falling into the routine.

Shawn Lin waved them away. The Boy Chef followed the official chef out the door and down the stairs. They entered a gleaming kitchen in a finished basement with red walls, two immaculate steel sinks, granite islands, butcher block cutting boards, a Viking four-burner stove and an array of knives and implements hanging on overhead racks. Two sous-chefs, both of them younger than Lew Chun, stood near the sinks. Philip Lau repeated the instructions of his employer. These were followed by a question:

"Well, Lew Chun? What is the menu?"

The Boy Chef was used to giving orders to men twice his age. But that was in the family restaurant. Here he had to walk on the edge of a blade — act authoritatively but with deference, move as if he knew the role of every spice, every meat, every sea animal, every vegetable yet be humble enough to ask questions. He assumed that the pantry held all the required ingredients of Chinese haute cuisine, and he was not disappointed.

Quite a person, this "Colonel" Shawn Lin, with his own cooks and surely a long line of retainers to serve the meals and make the beds and clean the rooms. Was he married? Did he have a family? The newcomer said nothing, hoping that as he cooked, there would be small talk and he could learn things. But no; the sous-chefs were intimidated by the chef, and Philip Lau was all business.

Under Lew Chun's directions, amplified by Philip Lau's commands, they made squirrel-shaped mandarin fish; hairy crab; chicken of the fields — a large plate of spicy tender frog; shining pork, chive and prawn dumplings; soups; side dishes; five different green teas; and cakes. Aromas of oil and ginger vied with bouquets rising from the meats and vegetables. When they were done, Philip Lau said in confidence, "There will be many important people at dinner. Later, I will tell you how it went."

Lew Chun asked what he should do until then. He had no place to stay, didn't know a soul in the city.

Philip Lau tapped one of the senior cooks. "Kai, show this young man the blue room."

Kai led the Boy Chef to a bedroom off the kitchen. Its walls and ceiling were robin's-egg blue. A metal cot took up a third of the floor space. It was covered by a navy blanket. On top of that was Lew Chun's valise. The other amenities included a standing lamp with a light blue shade, a small dresser and a tiny bathroom with a glassed-in stall shower. Before Kai left, he advised, "Nap now. All too soon, you will be awakened."

Lew Chun showered, changed underwear and climbed in. Last year, he and his father had stayed at the Hong Kong Ritz-Carlton. It didn't seem half as luxurious as this narrow, confined space. He fell asleep upon hitting the pillow. Kai awakened him by snapping on the light. Lew Chun consulted his Chinese watch: 3:30 a.m.

"The Colonel will see you."

"Now?"

"Now."

He pulled on some clothes and followed Kai to an elevator.

They took it to the top floor. Kai took the stairs down. Lew Chun knocked on a closed white door.

"Come," said the voice of Shawn Lin.

Lew Chun entered to find him in a room illuminated by a half-dozen red candles. Portraits of a few ancient emperors looked down from the walls. In a large frame were three weapons of Old China. One was a guandao, a plain spear common to all imperial soldiers. Next to it was a qiang, a spear of improved design, with a long staff. To the right of that was a jian. Lew Chun remembered a similar weapon — though not nearly so well-preserved — in the Military Museum of the Chinese People's Revolution. It bore the label "Sovereign of Axes." This was sharper still, with a double blade. Miss your opponent and you could get him on the backswing.

Shawn Lin was seated in the center of a maroon couch, wearing a crimson silk bathrobe, matching pajamas and slippers. At his side was a slender Chinese woman wearing the same shade of silk. Lew Chun sensed that she had nothing on under her robe. It was difficult to tell the lady's age in the dim light, but she was quite a bit younger than Shawn Lin. To the Boy Chef, she looked like a Shanghai movie queen. Both of them sipped from Champagne flutes. An ice bucket sat on an end table, with the neck of a bottle sticking out.

"My wife, Ruby," the Colonel said in English. "This is the Boy Chef I spoke about — the one who designed the dinner menu."

"Ah."

"Ruby and I have been celebrating our fifth anniversary. She has been with me through thick. Haven't you, darling?"

Another "ah" and nothing more.

"You did very well tonight, young Mr. Lew Chun. I believe we can find a place for you in the kitchen."

"Very kind of you, sir."

"Do you have a place to stay?"

"No, sir, I just arrived today." It suddenly occurred to Lew Chun that it was morning. "I mean I arrived here yesterday."

She laughed. He didn't.

"We'll find you an apartment. I have some buildings. Good night, Boy Chef. Come to this room tomorrow afternoon at—" he consulted his watch "—3 o'clock. We'll talk then."

His hand began to explore the treasures beneath Ruby's robe as the embarrassed Boy Chef took his leave.

Lew Chun was exhausted by then, but not too tired to dream about the lady in red silk. He awakened late in the morning, dressed, went upstairs and ran into C.C. at the door. The black man was all smiles now; an hour ago, the Colonel had told him, "This Boy Chef looks

troubled, but he doesn't look like trouble, if you know what I mean."
C.C. knew exactly what he meant.

Lew Chun strolled around outside, grateful to find people who looked like him in daytime New York City. They were going about their business, paying no attention to the young man in wrinkled clothes. He returned to the cafeteria, had breakfast and then found a clothing shop and bought black Velcro-style walking shoes for working in the kitchen, a new pair of black trousers, a white shirt and a black linen jacket. But as he emerged from the store, his blood froze.

Across the street, in profile, Sam was giving orders to two men in dark suits — Ketamine One and Two. They didn't see him — he thought. He hoped. Somehow the tormentor had survived; somehow he had located the Boy Chef.

****

"One more child in my life. As if my daughters weren't a sufficient burden."

"This is an entirely different animal. Harmless. And very likely useful. And grateful."

"You think?"

"This Boy Chef will surprise you one day. This I know."

"You know how?"

"Just a feeling."

"A feeling. Well, feel this. Let's go Corsican-style."

"Can't you be serious for one minute?"

"I'm serious during the day. Not at night."

"That boy won't cause a smidge of trouble."

"Smidge."

"He's so needy it hurts to look at him. All pain and sorrow."

"Not much good to me if that's all he is."

"I didn't mean *all*. He has a brain. He has a body."

"So do you."

"You're not interested in my brain."

"Not true."

"And besides, he's terrified of you. Who isn't?"

"You."

"Only because I know deep down you wouldn't hurt a hummingbird."

"True."

"You'd have someone do it for you."

****

Lew Chun put his head down and tried to move along Mulberry as if he belonged there, working his way back to the house. The Boy Chef panicked; he had no wish to bring trouble to his host. But where else could he go?

It no longer mattered if C.C. was a goon. In fact, Lew Chun hoped he was — and was glad to see him when the big guy answered the buzzer. He took the young man directly to the office. The Colonel was dressed in a chalk-stripe business suit, white tie and blue and yellow tie. He was going through some papers and drinking bancha from a porcelain mug as green as the tea. Two Chinese men, both heavyset and totally without expression, stood at either end of the couch.

"You should be on top of the world." Shawn Lin motioned the newcomer to the chair he had sat in the previous night. "But you don't look on top. You look under."

Lew Chun told him why.

"You said you stabbed Sam." Warily, the Boy Chef looked at the bodyguards, if that's what they were. They might have been carved out of stone. Now there were two more people who knew what Lew Chun had done, but there was no going back.

"Ran him through with a knife," he confessed. "Saw him fall. Saw the blood. I thought he was dead."

"What does this Sam look like?"

A description was hurriedly supplied. Shawn Lin nodded. Lew Chun added, "There's not much else I can tell you, sir. I don't even know his last name."

"I do."

Was this bravado, a lie like his title of "Colonel"? Or did he actually know what he was talking about?

"Neok Eng comes from Harbin," Shawn Lin went on. "He goes by the street name of Sam Steele. Supposed to be a hard customer. Been operating in Des Moines for five years. Everyone there is terrified of him."

"You think he tracked me to Chinatown?"

"He or his employees."

"I don't want to bring trouble to your house."

"Please. Pity is repulsive, and self-pity is intolerable. You remind me of my sons-in-law."

Lew Chun had no idea what or whom he was talking about. "Colonel," he entreated, "tell me where I should run, and I'll go."

"You don't run. This is not Iowa."

"But suppose they come after me?"

"They *will* come after you. Then they will lose interest."

"I don't understand."

"You speak American, but you don't understand American." He poured an extra mug of bancha. "You have sailed in a sampan."

"Yes, sir."

"You know that in a storm, if you let the waves attack from the side, you capsize. But if you head into the waves, you stay afloat."

"Yes, sir."

"Here you never show trouble your ass. You always face it. Now go downstairs and help in the kitchen."

There was nothing to do but obey.

The night was long and restless. Lew Chun kept listening for the sounds of a break-in, wondering whether there was an evening version of C.C. who minded the doors and how far he could wander from the house before Sam or his operatives tracked him down. They wouldn't dare fire a gun on these crowded streets, but a knife?

****

A small black-and-white TV rested on the spice shelf. It was always on in the morning, when the tedious cutting and slicing and sauce preparations took place. Right after the weather, the local news ran footage of a street in downtown Manhattan. Two men spoke briefly to the reporter. They were 40-something, both with low foreheads, big shoulders and cruel eyes set close together. Hunting animals. They were identified as skip tracers, a term Lew Chun had never heard before. These tracers had received a tip about three heroin traffickers from Iowa holed up in an East Village apartment. What they were doing there, nobody knew. No doubt a drug deal had been underway.

According to the tracers, the fugitives started firing with small arms as soon as their pursuers entered the building. The tracers were armed with automatic weapons and returned fire. It was no contest. Two of the men were dropped on the spot, their names withheld pending notice to their families. The Boy Chef thought he would recognize them if he saw the bodies.

The camera moved over the chalked-marked outlines of the deceased. The third Iowan made it to the hospital, a voice said, but the doctors couldn't revive him. The police commissioner appeared. He said there was going to be an investigation; New York City was not the Wild West; bounty hunters were unwelcome here. Lew Chun turned back to the stove. He didn't need details. Sam and the Ketamines were dead, and somehow Shawn Lin had arranged it.

Philip Lau and the sous-chefs did a lot of whispering in the kitchen during the newscast, and then everyone returned silently to work. The Boy Chef sensed that he was not to thank Shawn Lin for taking care of Sam. That would imply he knew that the Colonel had the power to reach far beyond Chinatown, to remove obstacles in his way — or in the way of those he wanted, for his own reasons, to protect.

For the next two weeks, Shawn Lin entertained visitors every night and slept until early afternoon, when the routine started all over again. In all that time, Lew Chun never spoke to him, and the Colonel never sent for the Boy Chef.

All the new arrival could do was attend to his assignments, cutting, steaming, mixing, pan-frying, cooking without complaint, staying close to home, answering politely to Philip Lau and the sous-chefs, and attempting to understand the house and the situation he was in. The staff members were a closemouthed group, but they were human, after all. Gossip is the lifeblood of any kitchen, and Lew Chun tried to listen without listening. No useful hints or implications came his way.

And then, on a Sunday afternoon, after a particularly grueling preparation, the kitchen staff was given a rare two-hour break. One of the dim-sum shops had a map of Chinatown Scotch-taped to the window. Lew Chun checked it for libraries. The nearest one was at Chatham Square, within sight of the Manhattan Bridge. In its files were nine major newspaper stories on his cousin, as well as some shorter articles. Gradually, a portrait emerged.

Hsu Dong had been wholesaling drugs and running three whorehouses in Shanghai. He was about to expand his operations, when a corrupt official sold him some valuable intelligence. An arrest was imminent. Hsu Dong must have used a lot of his savings to get a fake identity card — and a lot more to link up with the most powerful snakeheads in the city. They booked him on a plane to Hong Kong. Next stop, San Francisco. Within a month, Hsu Dong had become Shawn Lin, and he had the ID cards to prove it. It was 1983, the year he learned a bitter truth.

In the Gold Mountain, a provincial Chinese operator would always be a provincial operator. It didn't matter what state he lived in — east, west, south, north; there was zero chance for advancement, because drugs and prostitution and gambling — and just about all other illegal activities — were businesses controlled by ethnic groups. The Russians had a piece of the market. So did the Mexicans and, here and there, some groups from the Middle East. But the center of power and discipline was the mob — meaning Italians.

So how did a hustler from the People's Republic rise in the Gold Mountain of America?

This was as far as the Boy Chef had gotten when he felt a hand on his right shoulder. A chair scraped alongside, and a voice said, "If you wanted to know about me, why didn't you come to me with questions?"

Shawn Lin was alone. Lew Chun didn't know how his employer had found him or what he was doing in the library.

Before an excuse could be stammered, Shawn Lin said, "Nothing wrong with curiosity. Everything wrong with going behind my back. Follow me."

Lew Chun stayed in Shawn Lin's slipstream as he left the library, walking on silently until they arrived at a restaurant on Bayard Street. The proprietor knew the Colonel, gave him a respectful, almost fawning welcome and seated them in the rear, away from the other patrons, every one of them Chinese. Lew Chun knew he was in for a reprimand and perhaps worse. He could get thrown out on the street tonight. If he was lucky.

A waiter approached. He withdrew, walking backward as Shawn Lin held up his hand. "Chinatown is a big spiderweb," he explained in a tone reminiscent of a Beijing school principal. "Disturb one filament, the whole thing shakes. Secrets are not kept from me."

"I never intended to go around you, sir." The Boy Chef looked more like a boy than a chef as he tried to explain. "You were unreachable. And I was curious. Too curious, I guess."

"No such thing as too curious. However, you have already forgotten what I tried to teach you. Don't go around trouble. Face it. You want to know about me, ask to see me. You didn't ask, did you?"

"No, sir."

"Well, here I am. Ask your questions."

He didn't know what to say. If he did ask the questions and the Colonel gave the answers, how could the man afford to let this upstart, this prying cousin, this Lew Chun, this Boy Chef survive?

"Very well," Shawn Lin said with an expression of disappointment. "I'll ask one. Your mother didn't approve of me, did she?"

"Well, I—"

"Don't lie to me, boy."

"No, she didn't approve."

"She is of the Mao generation. Puritanical. Severe. Disapproving. Critical. The fact is, it wasn't so much what or who I sold that bothered her. It was the fact that I abandoned my family. She was wrong about that, as she was about all things. Both my daughters now live here. Did you know that? I sent for them, and they came. Both married Chinese-Americans. Their husbands work for me."

"You're a grandfather, sir?"

"One girl, one boy."

Lew Chun expressed his esteem. The Colonel did not return the compliment. Instead, with the focus of a cutter appraising a blood diamond, he assayed the risk and the value of this illegal alien: *tan bright eyes like mine; jet hair cropped short, as I ordered; slender body; narrow eager face; eager to please, perhaps too eager. Intelligent or merely sly? A good company man or out for number one? If the latter, his piece will have to be taken off the board.*

He would throw out some bait and judge the behavior of the fish. "My sons-in-law," Shawn Lee continued, "a hardship. Trustworthy but no head for business. Fortunately, my daughters do. The difficulty is, Americans are uneasy with women in high places. So the husbands cover for them. But Amy and Jade make the decisions."

Lew Chun found it hard to believe the Colonel let anybody even decide what *shoes* to wear without consulting him. But he merely nodded. Several minutes crawled by before Shawn Lin remarked casually, "Don't think the People's Republic is any better about this. Right now they're killing female children. Or exporting the babies for the adoption market. What kind of planning is that? One day, they'll have villages full of men and no girls to fuck. A recipe for misery. Common sense tells you that."

Lew Chun agreed a little too readily. "Thugs don't have common sense." And instantly regretted it.

But to his astonishment, the Colonel, the thug of thugs, took no offense. He went on as if there had been no reply at all. "There's talent and talent," he said. "I'm sure you don't have business brains, either. Doesn't matter. You have chef brains. I can put them to good use."

"Any dish you desire, sir."

"I don't want you to cook for me. I want you to cook for the world."

****

When the two men returned to the house, Shawn Lin outlined his plans. "I've been looking for someone like you, someone with portable skills," he announced. "A fresh new face. Someone to attract the press, the downtown money." He waited for the bewilderment to appear on this post-adolescent face. Lew Chun rewarded him with a stammering protest. "I'm not — I haven't got the kind of…"

In fact, this reaction was contrived. By now, Lew Chun had grasped what the Colonel was after. He wanted the Boy Chef to be the legitimate face of his shadowy business, to cook for the public in a four-star restaurant owned by the Colonel, to be Shawn Lin's respectable public expression. But even this was too small a fantasy.

The Colonel called on the intercom. Amy and Jade were to come by this evening. He had some breaking news to tell them.

"I'm going to build a restaurant around the Boy Chef." He took a piece of graph paper and sketched the layout. "Not too far from here — Chelsea or the East Village. You know the Lower East Side at all?"

He didn't listen to the answer and had no interest in it. The Colonel was too busy playing with ideas, trying to determine how best to use his latest acquisition.

"You know what you were in China? A novelty. What they call a *wunderkind*. You speak German? You'll learn. But first English. You think you talk English? You don't. You need to learn American, rap, street stuff, jargon. Maybe a few words of Yiddish, Italian. Spanish, definitely. In every high-end restaurant in New York — upstairs, Italians, French, Japanese, whatever. Belowstairs, out of sight —

peeling, washing, cleaning — Mexicans. We can do nothing without them. I'll find you tutors."

There was absolutely no point in protesting. Shawn Lin had saved the Boy Chef's life. Now he controlled it. More details were trotted out. The Colonel was on a roll: "There's a lot to do. Many hands will be out, palms upward. Inspectors, union bigs, extortionists of every kind — these I will handle. The hiring, as well — waiters, busboys, kitchen functionaries. Philip Lau will work under you. Don't worry about it; I'll give him a raise. He'll understand. You'll need a manager and a publicist. Get some rest. Tomorrow will start very early."

The day began as promised, shortly after sunrise, when C.C. banged on the door and shouted a list of instructions. Shower; shave; dress; eat; get upstairs. On the living room table was a printed schedule. Heading the list was: 8:00 Meeting Mickey Wong. Five minutes before the appointed hour, an eager, plump gentleman of about 35 appeared, sporting a black silk suit, horn-rimmed glasses and a hyperthyroid attitude. After a few words of introduction and some chatter about rents in New York, Mickey Wong explained his function.

"There's two kinds of publicists, kid," he declared in loud unaccented English. "Column A: the kind that gets you ink and airtime so people get to know who you are. Column B: the kind that keeps your name out of the papers and TV so no one will bother you."

He didn't have to elaborate. Shawn Lin was column B. The Boy Chef would be column A. A real chore for Mickey Wong, Lew Chun imagined, making an illegal immigrant into a celebrity cook.

Mickey looked at Lew Chun's face and read his mind. "You won't be illegal by the end of the week. We'll sell you as a victim of totalitarianism. You fled the People's Republic after—" he referred to a notebook "—after your father was murdered by Maoists."

Useless to argue, Lew Chun sensed. Still, he needed some answers. "And how did I wind up here?"

"You heard about Chinatown back in Beijing. Got smuggled aboard a military plane—"

"I stowed away on a ship."

"Aboard a military plane," he repeated. "You were rescued by operatives of the American government — CIA maybe, NSA, Navy SEALs, Army Rangers, whatever. I'll finish it up tonight, put in the brushstrokes. Joe Womack will read your life into the Congressional

Record next month. You'll get the required papers, plus a sponsor, and away we go."

"A sponsor? Not Shawn Lin?"

"Not Shawn Lin. He prefers to remain out of sight. So does C.C."

"Yes. Goons are supposed to keep away from the headlines," Lew Chun said, trying out a new word.

"He's not what you think, Lew Chun. C.C. is an Air Force vet. Shot up in Cambodia. He looks like a linebacker, but he's educated, has a lot of skills. Don't sell the guy short. You wouldn't want the race thing done to you. Don't do it to him."

An apology was tendered.

Mickey waved it off. "Anyway, Shawn Lin gets no ink. Ever. All credit and blame goes to Mr. E.R. Yuan. Businessman, real estate, import-export. Get it?"

"Got it." The Boy Chef was catching on.

And that, he remembered, was how it began. At noon, there were English lessons. The teachers tried to get him to memorize poems, but it didn't work. English verse never meant anything to him unless it rhymed. A single couplet was all that stuck. He was to recall it many times over the years.

There is only one way to achieve happiness on this terrestrial ball,
And that is to have either a clear conscience or none at all.

English lessons were followed by instructions on manners, behavior, decorum and how to address women of importance, athletes, show business celebrities and politicians. There was even a tutor who came in twice to lecture on 20th-century history and geography. A Hong Kong tailor was assigned to his case. He took measurements for three suits and a blazer. His assistant calculated what the greenhorn would need in the way of shirts, underwear, socks and street shoes.

There were also lessons in functional Spanish and in elementary bookkeeping, European history and American geography. One afternoon, in the middle of all this, a limo and driver showed up at the curb in front of the house. It took Lew Chun and Mickey to a building at the east end of Union Square. "Now you'll get the *emes*," Mickey said, introducing a little Yiddish into the Boy Chef's vocabulary.

On the top floor were the offices of YFD Inc.: Yuan, Farrar and Dean. The sign on the oak door didn't say what these people did for a living. Whatever it was, they were good at it. The suite was well-furnished and plush; the lighting indirect; the piped-in music classical piano; the receptionist blond and pretty and, as befit the style of the time, with a Heathrow accent.

Mr. Yuan emerged. He was a white-haired Chinese-American with an air of endless patience. He introduced himself, shook hands, dismissed Mickey with a nod and showed Lew Chun into his office. It was a large arena with oak floors, ceiling, desk and walls. A forest had died for YFD. On a far wall, behind glass, was a curious item. Lew Chun had expected a fire extinguisher like the ones in Shawn Lin's kitchen. This was a small sledgehammer. He made a mental note to ask about it but then forgot in the course of things.

"Mr. Mickey Wong has given us the book on you," Mr. Yuan informed him.

"I'd like to read it sometime," Lew Chun said.

Mr. Yuan stared at his brash visitor. "There is no room in my life for irony. In yours, either. There are thousands of young men who would be grateful for the gift Shawn Lin has bestowed on you."

"I am grateful," Lew Chun assured Mr. Yuan. "I just have a feeling it's not a gift."

"Not entirely," his host agreed. He studied a paper and read from it. "Shawn Lin intends for you to become his public face. In a few weeks, you will be presented as an impoverished refugee seeking shelter in the global city of the Free World. It has always been your dream to own a restaurant in New York. Now generous donors have made this possible."

"Generous anonymous donors."

"Ah, now you understand." He buzzed the receptionist. "Marie, are they here yet?"

"Just arrived."

"Bring them."

Marie ushered in two well-dressed young Asians — one slim, the other not — into the office and departed. Lew Chun could guess who they were — the Colonel's sons-in-law. Mr. Yuan confirmed his suspicions when he introduced them: Jimmy and Charlie, no last names.

"We are the management," Mr. Yuan explained. "The three of us will take care of all restaurant business. The only thing you need to do is supervise the menu, take care of the kitchen, give interviews and mix with diners of note. If you're asked questions and don't have the answers, refer the reporter to us. I will provide the necessary information, or these gentlemen will. After all, they're your relatives."

Jimmy said, "You are never to bother Shawn Lin."

"If he wants to talk to you," Charlie added, "he'll send for you. Understood?"

"Understood," said the Boy Chef without comprehending but afraid to ask for clarity.

****

The language lessons persisted, along with memorization of the fictive biography as edited by YFD Inc., plus instructions in manners and dealing with the press. Often Mickey took his pupil to the movies or played some VHS tapes for him, usually crime films. Noirs, he called them. He asked Lew Chun to study the behavior and attitude of the gangsters. He did not elaborate on the purpose of these viewings.

Every so often, a request came in for an interview. *The New York Times* asked, and the *Post* and the *Daily News.* So did *Gourmet* and *Food & Wine* magazines. But either Jimmy or Charlie turned them down; the Boy Chef wasn't ready. They wanted to wait until he was *in situ*, working with Philip Lau behind the butcher block cutting boards of Lew Chun's restaurant, Pan Asian, on 12th Street and Second Avenue.

Twice he was taken to the location. Mr. Yuan accompanied him each time. It was not the most fashionable address in town, he said, but that hardly mattered. With the proper back story and plenty of ink and airtime, the place would be a magnet for gourmets and celebs and wannabes.

Two weeks before the opening, the Boy Chef was summoned upstairs to talk to Shawn Lin. "Are you nervous?" he asked.

Lew Chun admitted that he was.

"Very good. Cooking is one of the performing arts, and all headliners are jittery on opening night."

He was about to elaborate, when C.C. knocked and entered without bidding. He apologized for the interruption and then crossed to his boss and whispered something in his ear. Shawn Lin nodded ominously. He made a call while C.C. waited. "I don't care what Charlie wants," he barked to someone on the other end. "Jimmy handles above Canal Street. He needs help, he can use the orange guy." He turned to C.C. "Get Charlie and the others." The big man vanished.

They waited in silence. A fancy menu for the restaurant had been printed up; Shawn Lin handed it to Lew Chun for approval, kind of a "how do you love it?" gesture, and the Boy Chef responded with over-the-top enthusiasm. After some 15 minutes, C.C. showed up with Charlie and three men dressed in khaki chinos and T-shirts. He vanished again. The men already looked cowed, and Shawn Lin hadn't spoken a word. Then he uttered a lot of words, all of them in Mandarin and all of them directed at Charlie.

"I worked too hard for all this." He gestured around the room, but he meant the house and whatever wealth and power he had. "I can't allow Sicilian-style vendettas. In Chinatown, we operate on a higher level. Anyone, any group, steps on your toes, cuts into the business, you tell me. Never act on your own. Ever. Icing is not a freelance assignment."

Charlie eyed the Boy Chef uncomfortably. Getting chewed out by Shawn Lin was humiliating enough; to have it occur in front of a newcomer was intolerable. The others didn't seem to care. Neither did their leader. The Colonel theatrically raised his voice a few decibels.

"Being Chinese is always an issue out there. Among the *gweilos* and the blacks and the Hispanics. And the establishment. Especially the establishment. If we do better than any other group, if we score off the charts in college, then we're no longer considered a minority. In California, they call the medical school UCLAsian, but it's not said with admiration."

His sons-in-law regarded him uncomfortably but remained silent.

"If we keep to ourselves, we're called secretive. If we encourage our kids to take violin lessons, to succeed in math or science, we're aggressive. If we fail, we're born losers. If we make money, we're hoods."

"You can't win," Charlie said, hoping to please his superior officer.

He did not. "We don't have to win," Shawn Lin disagreed. "We have to maintain. We have to stay in the shadows. We're not dumb like the mob, talking murder on the phone while the FBI wiretaps away. Fools. Imbeciles."

Shawn Lin suddenly stopped. He seemed to notice the Boy Chef in a different way. "I'm sure you have something to do in the kitchen," he said in a chilly voice. No more needed to be said. Lew Chun sprang to his feet, excused himself and exited. C.C. was pounding up the stairs as he descended. They exchanged nods.

Shawn Lin's voice sounded behind the door. A different tone was audible for a few seconds, agitated and loud. "YFD is a corporation, not a family. You married my daughter, Charlie. I would hate to lose you. From now on, nothing gets discussed in front of the kid. Nothing. Got that?"

So, Lew Chun concluded, he was a cousin of the Big Man's — the Colonel, the Idol of Mulberry Street — but "the kid" was to hear nothing, see nothing, know nothing. He was to be the fresh, unlined face of YFD. Legitimate and ignorant was what Shawn Lin wanted him to be. Legitimate, this could be managed. Ignorant, this might not be so easy.

That very night, idly watching the 11 o'clock news, Lew Chun saw the future cold and clear. The lead story concerned a foreign national from Colombia. Rodrigo Torrez was a major drug dealer, well-known to Interpol. They had lost track of him until now, when his body was identified after a hit-and-run driver whacked him on Hudson Street. According to eyewitnesses, said driver was heading for the West Side Highway. Some of the accounts differed, but they all agreed that the car was a tan and dented Plymouth station wagon with no visible plates and that the driver was wearing bib overalls and a baseball cap. They were orange.

****

It was all that Shawn Lin wished, including the late September climate. Still warm and sunny during the day, invitingly cool at night, sharpening all appetites. C.C. and a phalanx of security men maintained crowd control. Mr. Yuan was at the left side of Lew Chun when the doors of the Pan Asian officially opened to the public. At his right were two impeccably dressed white men of middle age. These were Mr. Yuan's partners, Malcolm Farrar and Will Dean.

The Boy Chef eyed the menu one last time. How would Ang Chun have regarded this Pan Asian palace? Would his father have dismissed it as yet another instance of Western swagger over Eastern substance? Or would he have taken some pride in his son, an anonymous nobody yesterday, tonight a rising figure in the Gold Mountain, 8,000 miles from Beijing?

And then there was no more time to wonder, as YFD's A-list crowded in. Mickey Wong guided the Boy Chef around his own place, providing introductions as he worked the room, table-hopping from celebrity to journalist to restaurant reviewer. Marianne Fine was at one of the best tables, flanked by her co-stars Beau Martin and Karl Chase. There were principals from the New York City Ballet; two rock groups, who behaved with unexpectedly good manners; a state senator; a police captain; Liz Smith, Cindy Adams and three other gossip columnists; food and wine critics from the *Times* and the *Post* and *The Wall Street Journal*; reporters from the networks; a lady from an Asian FM radio station; and people the Boy Chef didn't know, had never heard of and never saw again — Asian and Caucasian and the occasional African-American. They all had questions. Mickey Wong overrode Lew Chun every time, glibly supplying a bogus vita printed for the occasion.

The cooks and sous-chefs were well-trained — though not by Lew Chun; he scarcely knew them. The waitstaff, hired by Jimmy and Charlie, was flawless. Restaurant critics made much of the Boy Chef when they were introduced, and he followed the modest, hesitant, grateful-to-be-here line as dictated by Mickey Wong. The results were pretty much as expected; one or two dishes were criticized for being too spicy or insufficiently unique, but the reviews were mostly raves, and the public wanted in. By the second week, patrons had to reserve tables three days in advance.

So Lew Chun was not astonished when on a Sunday morning, C.C. came by and said that Shawn Lin wanted to see him right away. The Colonel was seated at his desk, dressed in a serious navy blue flannel suit. His daughters were sitting in upholstered chairs on either side of him. Both wore high-end Asian silk dresses in a quiet blue pattern with small slits at the knees. The sweet one seemed just as sweet as in her photograph; the dragon lady looked just as reptilian. But they were on their best behavior for Daddy — full of smiles and compliments. Given the atmosphere, the Boy Chef found the courage to ask how the profits were going.

Shawn Lin laughed. "Profits? There won't be profits for a year, perhaps two. Do you realize what I laid out for the place — the rent, the equipment, the salaries?"

"I hadn't thought, sir," Lew Chun said.

The Colonel altered his tone. "Well, it's not your business to think. It's your business to cook. And that you do quite well." The daughters nodded. He grew expansive as he rose and walked around the room. "I realize you can't keep living here like a poor relation. I own a little tenement in the East Village — on Ninth Street, just west of First Avenue. An apartment has become available on the second floor. That was the parlor years ago, when it was a town house. Small, but you'll have a marble fireplace. And the price is right."

"But I don't have the money to pay for any apartment."

"You will. You'll draw a salary of, say, $400 a week. That should take care of the rent and clothing." He twinkled. "Food you get for free. And if you want to take a girl to the movies, the theater, some other restaurant, there should be enough for entertainment now and then."

Jade asked Lew Chun whether he had met any girls yet. He told her it had been all work all the time.

"You have no friends?"

"None."

"We will find you an appropriate companion."

Shawn Lin took a certain pleasure in elevating this youth in front of his daughters. They would see the Boy Chef as a competitor for their father's affection and generosity. Excellent.

He stopped at his desk and riffled through *The Art of War*, thinking to read it aloud to his daughters. But as he regarded them, he wondered whether it would have the desired effect. The Colonel decided against it for now, putting on his gold-rimmed glasses, perusing the book like a scholar searching a text, making the ladies wait in silence until he finished.

The king of Wu whimsically ordered his greatest general to train some 200 concubines into soldiers. The general divided them into two companies, with the king's two favorite women at the head of the each one. When Sun Tzu ordered the concubines to face right, they giggled. Again he spoke the command, and again they giggled. Was that how his orders were obeyed? Very well, then. The two favored concubines would be executed. The king of Wu objected, but his general pointed out that to defy the general was to defy the king, and the concubines were killed on the spot. New women replaced them. From that point on, the female troops performed their maneuvers without merriment — and without error.

The Colonel closed the book and handed the Boy Chef an envelope. Inside were two keys and a piece of paper with a phone number for Trans-Asian Moving Co. and an address. "The movers will take your things to that address. The dark key will open the front door. The brass one will let you in to your apartment."

Smiling benignly, he offered his hand — the signal for Lew Chun to leave. The Boy Chef thanked his benefactor and shook hands with his daughters. "Take a day or two to get settled," he was instructed. "We will expect you at the restaurant on Thursday."

Through the closed door, Amy's voice was barely audible. "Nice-looking boy. Clean-cut."

"Very," the dragon lady agreed. "Does he know?"

"He knows what I want him to know," her father replied.

The Boy Chef wondered how much of that exchange he was meant to overhear. Was Shawn Lin serious about wanting to keep him an innocent, or was he eager to make him an accomplice?

****

Mickey Wong started worrying aloud in late October, not because the reservations fell off but because he and Lew Chun kept seeing the same people. According to Mickey, that was a bad sign.

"A cool 25 percent of new restaurants in the city go belly up in the first year," he declared. "Second year, another 50 percent. Troubles with labor, inspectors, laundries, equipment, food orders. For you, the main thing is to make sure the quality stays on the stratosphere. That means you're on duty a minimum of 90 hours a week. Agreeable?"

"Whatever you say."

"It's not what I say. It's what the diners want. You got a powerful sponsor, but not even Shawn Lin can attract customers if they don't want to come. That's your job."

Lew Chun vowed to supervise the cooking and preparation and plating of every dish, every night, if that's what they wanted. Not good enough for Mickey. The Boy Chef had to be visible, chat up the customers, particularly actors, singers, critics, journalists, politicians, athletes. Lew Chun agreed: "What else can I tell you, Mickey? I'll work 24/7. More than that, no one can do."

No one is asking 24/7, Mickey assured him. Six straight nights would be enough. As for details of management, leave those to Jimmy and Charlie. The Boy Chef knew not to inquire about those details. But he was curious enough to do a little investigation on his own — particularly after Charlie showed up at midnight, took a table at the rear and started arguing sotto voce with a white guy in a black sharkskin suit. He had salt-and-pepper hair, a large belly and shoulders that stretched the fabric of his jacket.

From Lew Chun's position near the wall of the kitchen, he could comprehend most of what was being negotiated.

"You don't want to fuck with the union, friend," the big man growled.

"And you don't want to fuck with Shawn Lin," Charlie replied.

"Who the hell is this Shawn Lin you keep throwing at me? I don't see him."

"He's the principal backer of this restaurant. Ask around. See what you can find out about him, and then meet me here tomorrow."

"I don't have to ask around. I never heard of him, and I hear about everybody. Far as I'm concerned, he don't exist. Now, you going to contribute to the fund or not?

"Not."

"We'll see about that, friend."

Charlie and Lew Chun did see about it. Two days later, the *Daily News* ran a story about the disappearance of Victor Zandt, an executive of the Hospitality Union, Local 12. His wife said he was expected home for a late dinner but never arrived. Police were investigating.

Lew Chun didn't have a lot of time to wonder what happened to Zandt, because when he wasn't on duty, he was sleeping or moving in to his new apartment. Someone had arranged for a cot with an army blanket and a pillow in a starched pillowcase and stocked the refrigerator with basics — such as eggs, rice and a roasted chicken from the restaurant — along with two bottles of Chablis, two of Taittinger and a six-pack of Tsingtao. On Lew Chun's evening off, he was lounging around, when the buzzer sounded at the front door.

Ignorant about security, he pressed the button on the kitchen wall. A minute later came a knock at the front door. He looked through the peephole and saw a dazzling Chinese lady in her late 30s or maybe early 40s carrying a large black leather portfolio. She was definitely not one of Shawn Lin's daughters. He let her in.

"Rose Chen," she said. "I'm supposed to design your place, order curtains, furniture, help you choose the colors, order the paint."

Boss lady type. Lew Chun had seen dozens of female party officials with the same take-charge aura. But they had Mao outfits; this one wore a bone-white cotton pantsuit, a pushup bra and heady perfume that suggested her name. She whisked in and began measuring the walls with a metal extension ruler. Then she sat down on the cot, patted the blanket — indicating that the new apartment dweller was to take a seat next to her — and showed him a brochure full of color swatches.

He didn't know what to select.

"Someone else is paying for it, so choose the top of the line," she advised. "Otherwise, they won't respect you."

He asked who "they" were, and she changed the subject. That was one of her specialties. Another was asking personal questions as she riffled through catalogs of furniture and lamps.

"You were smuggled in from China after your father disappeared. Are you in communication with your mother?"

"Not yet. I tried to get word to her through my sponsor." She wasn't going to say the name; neither was Lew Chun. "He said it was too soon after Tiananmen Square. My mother is probably still in hiding."

"I see." She went through the inventory of furniture, upholstery, paints, lamps, everything that pertained to interior city life. She even suggested a Bose radio and a CD carousel. Indeed, Rose wouldn't stop suggesting until Lew Chun gave his approval to every single item. After that, she folded up the various brochures and said, "Do you mind if I ask you a delicate question?"

"Depends on how delicate."

"Well, part one" she offered, "you're a young gentleman, but you're pretty well-known. Do you have any girlfriends here?"

"I had a couple back in China. Not here."

"Why not?"

"Too busy."

"Yes, I can see that. And now, part two. Have you ever fucked anybody older than you?"

Women didn't talk like that in the People's Republic. Lew Chun didn't know how to respond. Not that it mattered. Rose took over. She had an unusual way of going at the desired object, he found, working up from the cuff of his pant leg rather than using the conventional entrance.

The Boy Chef wasn't very good at retention; nevertheless, he held on, and they got out of their clothes and onto the cot, and he didn't embarrass himself. She knew pressure points he wasn't aware of, and she seemed astonished at his ignorance.

"Didn't you ever have acupressure treatments?" Rose demanded.

He said he was ignorant of traditional Chinese medicine because he was never sick.

"Yes, I keep forgetting how very young you are." The way she said it did not seem flattering.

And so, with all the heavy breathing, it wasn't what either of them would call a joyous occasion. Rose had lovely skin and pleasing legs, but she gave the impression of a woman on assignment. Rather like showing her client the colors and patterns in the catalogs, she was giving Lew Chun a tour of her body, letting him know that there were various choices, positions, attitudes that could be special-ordered.

Eventually, he went to the kitchen and fetched some Champagne lodged in the door of the fridge. They toasted each other and the future. While the Boy Chef was thinking about what this all meant, Rose Chen looked at her watch, sprang up, took a shower and was gone almost before he could say goodbye.

"We'll find each other," she assured him on her way out. "I want to see your place when everything's installed." She dispensed a light kiss and clattered down the stairs. He looked down from the window. A car drove by, and she got in it. The driver must have been waiting for her all evening.

****

He sensed that Rose was a verboten topic; he could talk to no one about her without compromising them both. Perhaps he might talk to Shawn Lin — and immediately thought better of it. But then her name came up unexpectedly late one evening as he wandered through the restaurant checking out the last remaining diners. The Boy Chef was doing his boniface act, smiling and asking whether everything was all right, when a young Asian couple invited him to their table.

The man was lean and elegant, dressed for casual Friday, white chinos, white button-down shirt, no tie, gray blazer with silver buttons. He looked to be about 30 — second- or third-generation Chinese-American, given the way he talked. She had a Eurasian caste, beautiful eyes, shiny black hair with flaxen streaks in it, black pantsuit. She was maybe Lew Chun's age and spoke with a New York intonation, so he assumed she was also the child of longtime residents. Neither wore a wedding or engagement ring.

Her date introduced himself as Frank, no last name. She was Julie Tseng. They said they were here on business. He was a forensic CPA with a master's degree in journalism. She was an intern, a J-school student at NYU working on a feature about the new ethnic restaurants.

The Boy Chef was about to tell them to call Mickey Wong, official liaison between the restaurant and the newspaper and TV reporters. But then he asserted himself. Hadn't he just had a fling with an older woman? Surely, he could sit for an interview without a handler at his side.

Julie's questions were the usual. Lew Chun answered them directly, sticking to the line about leaving the People's Republic, said he wasn't much on looking back, expressed gratitude for his sponsors — plural so he wouldn't have to mention Shawn Lin by name. As they conversed, Rose Chen came in with a couple of *gweilos* in brown sharkskin suits. She gave him a curt nod and directed her companions to sit at the other side of the room. Any farther away, he noted, and they would have been in the street.

The interview went on for nearly an hour. The Boy Chef assumed Rose and company had just come for drinks, because they left before the journalists had finished their interrogation. When they did, Frank got up to leave. Julie remained in her seat.

"I have a few more things to go over," she said. That was fine with Frank; he got out his credit card and summoned a waiter. Lew Chun waved him off. A big thank-you, a genial smile and out the door. When Frank was gone, Julie asked how the manager of the Pan Asian knew Rose. Now the Boy Chef changed the subject.

"Nice fellow, Frank."

"Very." She took another sip of her room-temperature tea. Then she repeated her inquiry. "How do you know Rose Chen?"

"I could ask you the same thing."

"I've seen her around. She's pretty well-known in Chinatown."

"As a designer?"

"Oh, is that what they're calling it?"

Lew Chun tried to steer the conversation in another direction: "Are you and Frank—"

"He's gay," she snapped. "Didn't you know that?" She smiled and patted Lew Chun's hand as if the Boy Chef were her little brother. "Yellow and green."

From anyone else, that would have been an unforgiveable insult. From her, Lew Chun regarded it as a backhanded compliment.

She went on. "I hear you're related to Shawn Lin."

Alarm bells went off. "Distantly," he told her.

She scrutinized his face. "You can't be as naive as you sound. Or, I don't know, maybe you can." She looked around. "We can't talk here." She stood up. "You know Kobe, dim-sum place on 23rd and Third?"

"Never heard of it."

"Well, hear of it by tomorrow morning. Eleven o'clock. I'll be in the back." She shook his hand, glided between the tables and went away. A lady as attractive — and as officious — as Rose Chen, but with more to tell him. Maybe. He hoped so.

****

There was an hour to go before the early-bird lunch; Kobe was only half-full. Lew Chun spotted Julie Tseng in the rear and sat opposite her. Julie had an immediate effect on men, and she enjoyed every nanosecond of it. The Boy Chef couldn't mask his interest; he was manifestly struck, as she had carefully planned, evident from the lustrous eyelashes, the mascara professionally applied, the green linen dress clinging to her body, the matching beaded jewelry. She was cool, modish, provocative, everything the investigative female journalist should be.

After the first few light remarks about the dumplings, Julie asked the Boy Chef whether he was ambitious. For example, could he see himself as the owner of a *string* of restaurants?

"You mean a Sino-McDonald's? I don't think so. One restaurant is all I can handle. And that's with 16 in help." Before she could pose another question, he put one to her. "How about you, Julie? Are you ambitious?"

"Full disclosure: I want to win a Pulitzer. I want to be a network anchor or the author of a big book or all three."

"Then why are you talking to me?"

She gave him another one of her hard, probing looks. "Have you ever heard of the Pizza Connection?"

He was ashamed to admit he had not.

Julie's reply was unexpectedly lenient. "No reason why you should." She beckoned a waiter, ordered tea and continued when the man attended another diner.

"The Connection was the longest trial in U.S. history. Lasted two years — from 1985 to 1987. It was all about the heroin and cocaine market, how it worked, who controlled it. No surprise the mob was in charge, using pizza parlors as fronts for narcotic sales. The big boys laundered the cash, then sent it to suppliers in Sicily. How much do you think the traffic was worth?"

The tea came. Julie dismissed the waiter and filled Lew Chun's cup and then hers. She repeated the question.

"How much?" he replied. "I don't know. $100 million?"

"Guess again."

"200 million?"

"More. Much more."

"500?"

"$1.6 billion — with a 'b.' And that was just for the heroin. Impressed?"

"I guess so."

"You guess so."

"OK, I'm impressed."

"The Pizza Connection trial was heavily reported in the papers. I read every single story when I was researching the trial for my thesis. That's when I ran across the name of your relative."

Lew Chun didn't want to give her the pleasure of seeing him react. Julie was silent. A minute passed.

"Go on," he finally said.

She nodded, satisfied that the hook was set. "The prosecution took down the entire operation. The FBI, Interpol, the Italian and Swiss governments — they were all in on it. They got informers to turn in their comrades. They had an undercover agent — 'Donnie Brasco,' he called himself. The FBI set up wiretaps, pictures of buyers; they located the fields in Turkey and the labs in Sicily. The feds got the convictions and broke the whole thing into pieces."

She stopped talking and ordered *shaomai* — prawns in a thin wheat flour, topped with crab roe — *char siu bao* with barbecued pork filling, some chicken and two pots of green tea. Lew Chun wasn't hungry, but when the food came, he pretended to enjoy it as he listened.

"After the trial and the guilty verdicts," Julie recalled, "there came an emptiness, a loss of central authority. The Italians were done. One day they'll return. They always do — too many associations, too many survivors who dodged the bullets. But for the moment, the field was free. Guess who seized it."

"You're not telling me—"

She signaled Lew Chun to lower his voice. "Yes, I am telling you. It was your — what, cousin?"

"Yes, cousin."

"Your cousin is the biggest bloody wholesale drug dealer in Chinatown — which means one of the biggest drug dealers in the city, which means one of the biggest dealers in the Northeast."

He pondered this accusation for a while, ate in silence and finally demanded, "Then why isn't he in prison?"

"You're putting me on, right?" She examined Lew Chun's face for signs of mockery. There was none. "OK," she said, "you really are what you seem. I think. I *hope.* Otherwise, we could both be assuming room temperature by the weekend."

Julie looked to the side, in front and behind them. Satisfied that the other patrons were absorbed in their own meals and their own conversations, she squeezed her voice down until it was for his ears only. "You know the rich — the really rich — have ways of avoiding taxes, right?"

"So they say."

"Same with corruption everywhere. Don't tell me it wasn't like that in the People's Republic. The little wrongos, the middlemen, they get nailed from time to time. The big mob guys, very rarely. It practically takes an army to bring them down. Until the Pizza Connection, everything went along like butter on a pan. Then they got full of themselves, started bragging to each other on the phones, and the FBI closed in." She spoke Italian. "*Addio ragazzi. Finale.*"

"And they don't tap the phones of Shawn Lin?"

"He isn't dumb enough or arrogant enough to use them." She sat and ate and was silent, considering whether to disclose anything else. When the dishes were cleared away, she breathed deeply and took a leap of faith. "My guess is he does it all in person. He hardly ever leaves Chinatown; are you aware of that? Everything he needs is here. He has a black bodyguard and some white lawyers, but everyone else is Asian, and they all speak Mandarin. I don't think the cops have many operatives who speak Mandarin. Do you? He has a gym in that house, his own kitchen, receives guests, sends out for women — yes, women, including your 'designer,' Rose Chen."

Lew Chun wondered aloud. "Why do you talk about her like that?"

"Because she's an ex-hooker and current madam. Because your cousin also operates a string of whorehouses and she manages them — when she's not choosing your furniture."

If Lew Chun had even the hint of an appetite, it vanished. Time to go. "So, what you want from me, Julie?"

"I don't know that I want anything from you. I suppose I'm just covering my ass. I'll leave a note. If anything happens to me, they'll know the Boy Chef told his cousin an investigative reporter was sniffing around."

"I'm not going to tell him anything. I don't really see him that much."

"The restaurant takes all your time, that it?"

"That's it."

"Did it ever occur to you that maybe you're his beard?"

"I don't know what you mean." In fact, he did. In fact, Lew Chun was catching on with great velocity.

****

On the way home, he considered the testimony. Was Julie playing him? Was her information accurate or an accumulation of rumors and suspicions? Was she trolling for information, giving away a little to get a lot? And what if he was his cousin's beard? So Shawn Lin wants to own a clean, untainted business and Lew Chun's Pan Asian happens to be that business. Where's the harm?

At the same time, now that Lew Chun was running a major dining establishment, he didn't want the Colonel to regard him as the Boy Chef, with the accent on "Boy." He needed to define his role. Notes were sent via C.C. Nothing for a week. Then one morning, when the place was closed and Lew Chun sat working out the menu at his customary table, C.C. sat down opposite him. He didn't have to say anything. A taxi was waiting across the street. The driver took them to the house on Mulberry Street.

Shawn Lin was waiting in the sitting room, along with Jimmy and Charlie. C.C. vanished like an echo. The Boy Chef, feeling unexpectedly juvenile and vulnerable, faced a trio dressed in dark suits and white shirts and rep ties. The air crackled with trouble.

"You wish to find out more about my operation." Shawn Lin pointed to a chair. He watched Lew Chun open his mouth as if to protest the summons that had brought him here without warning — and he saw the Boy Chef abruptly change his mind, ready to listen instead of talk. Excellent; the controls were reasserted, and all was stable. These little rebellions could be good for an organization, keep it lively, on its guard — provided, of course, that they were quelled before they got out of hand. There was only one nucleus; the rest, at best, was protons or electrons.

"I don't know that I blame you." The Colonel sat back and let his benign smile warm the room. "You're a bright young man, and you're curious."

Lew Chun's mind crowded with questions he didn't dare ask. How did the Colonel find out? After all, Lew Chun had merely asked to have his role defined. Did the Colonel have someone follow him when he met with Julie? Her colleague, what was his name, the gay guy — Frank — was he connected to Shawn Lin in some way? Or did Julie herself spill the contents of their conversation to a third party? Anything was not only possible but plausible with these people.

No point in looking for hints from the marble faces; Jimmy and Charlie were not the type to give anything away, and besides, it was clear that they were terrified of their father-in-law.

Shawn Lin tapped the small mahogany box that sat on his desk. Ang Chun had had a humidor shaped like this, full of Cuban cigars he offered to patrons of consequence. But when the Colonel lifted the lid on his box, the Boy Chef saw stacks of red, blue and yellow currency.

"Can you identify these, Lew Chun?" he asked. It was the first time he had used the patronymic instead of the title.

"It looks like hell money, sir."

"Very good. That's exactly what it is." The paper money was issued in primary-colored bills. They bore the picture of Yan Wang, Lord of the Earthly Court, who judged the souls of the dead. No one in the Old Country believed this lore; it was like fortune cookies, manufactured for the tourist trade, or like Lunar New Year parades for those who liked the trappings of tradition without honoring them. But as Lew Chun was to learn, this loot had a different function when Shawn Lin used it.

"You want to find out what goes on here." It was not a question.

"No, sir. The restaurant takes all my—"

"With silence comes enlightenment." He took his beloved manual in hand and read from Sun Tzu: "Be stern in the council-chamber, so that you may control the situation."

The air stood still. He called out: "The Mings."

C.C. opened the door and ushered in two men. The first was an elderly Chinese right out of central casting, maroon and gold blouse, big sleeves, loose black trousers. The younger man was obviously his son — himself at least 50 — dressed in a powder blue American-cut linen jacket and khaki chinos. The Mings stayed on their feet, and Shawn Lin made no attempt to play host.

He addressed them in English. "This had better be critical."

"Colonel," the son began, "we thank you for seeing us. And we deeply regret taking your time."

"Benign and great leader," his father continued, "this matter is of greater significance to us than to you. Still, it may affect your standing in the community."

"I will decide that," Shawn Lin said darkly. "Go on."

"A man has come to our store the past two Fridays at closing time. He says he is an 'independent insurance broker.' He demands an envelope with $500 in it. This is to protect us against fire, theft and damage."

"In other words," Shawn Lin concluded, "an extortionist."

"Extortionist." The word was unfamiliar, but the old man was not stupid. "It would seem so, yes."

"This man have a name?"

"He called himself Mr. Cugine."

"And you paid him?"

"Yes. But we cannot afford to keep paying."

The son took over. "We ask your permission. We wish to take measures."

Shawn Lin motioned them to sit down on a mahogany bench. They looked uncomfortable.

"We would take all the responsibility," the son offered.

Shawn Lin shook his head. "The man is mocking you. Cugine is an Italian word for a young punk. He fancies himself a part of the mob. The mob is a chest of drawers full of antiques."

"But he said his people, they could—"

"He has no people. This Friday, you will give Cugine another $500. On his way home, a van will jump the curb. Many broken bones. The driver of the vehicle will find Cugine's wallet and telephone his family. They will discover the 'insurance agent' at the end of Canal Street. They will not find the $500." He took a sheaf of hell money and held it in his hand. "Instead, they will find an envelope stuffed with these. They will get the message. You will not be bothered again."

With a jumble of bowing and declarations of undying loyalty and gratitude, the Mings saw themselves out. Lew Chun assumed this was the close of business. It was only the commencement.

****

Before the next interview got underway, Shawn Lin put on his gold-rimmed reading glasses and peered again at the Sun Tzu manual. His office was as quiet as a concert hall before the pianist begins. His eyes moved to Charlie and then to Jimmy before coming to rest on the Boy Chef. "Regard your soldiers as your children, and they will follow you into the deepest valleys; look upon them as your own beloved sons, and they will stand by you even unto death."

In the end, more than a dozen people entered, case by case, beseecher by beseecher. These were single men or small families, Chinese, melancholy, needy, cornered. Each received an audience with Shawn Lin. Some cringed in his presence; others tried to act proud but deceived no one, least of all themselves. They knew better than to question Lew Chun's presence; after a quick glance at him, they concentrated on the Colonel.

Most wanted to bring relatives from China to New York — get the name of a reliable snakehead, borrow money for the payment, arrange for papers, legitimate or forged. All were middle-class or lower, store owners or employees of local businesses. Other than paying back the loan — for which Shawn Lin charged zero interest — there seemed to be nothing they could do to return the favor, and the Colonel said as much. Shawn Lin merely waved his hand. He was asking for nothing except the opportunity to administer charity to the needy.

After the Asians were gone, Shawn Lin told C.C. to bring in Mr. Felix Corazon. He turned out to be a fat moist Hispanic gentleman of middle age in a rumpled seersucker jacket, dirty white pants and untied sneakers.

"Do not let Señor Corazon's appearance deceive you," the Colonel informed his young cousin. Jimmy and Charlie smiled but didn't laugh at the guest. "He is a person of great importance and substantial means." Now he addressed Señor Corazon. "Do I exaggerate?"

Felix Corazon took a chair without invitation, delicately fingering his nonexistent trouser creases. "Colonel, I don't think it is in you to exaggerate."

"You are extremely late in your payments. Tell me why."

"Esteemed sir, you and I, we have been doing business for nearly five years. Have I ever been behind in my financial obligations?"

"Never. This is why I am so shocked and appalled. Is there something wrong?" The words were solicitous, but the tone was freighted with menace.

"It is like this." The sweaty man got sweatier as he spoke. "As you know, Colonel, I supply the retailers. They pay me, I pay you. But they have been slow with money. And, " he added hastily, "they have reason."

"And what might that reason be?"

Felix Corazon gave his interrogator a spaniel look. "It is the mayor. He has told the chief of police to crack down on product. So my distributors are lying low. We know this will pass. But for now, we must be invisible."

"I understand," Shawn Lin told him. "I am simpatico."

Mr. Corazon relaxed a bit. "And I am grateful, Colonel."

"Nevertheless, last month, you were very glad to receive many kilos. I did not say to you, 'Wait. Trust me, all will be well. It takes time.' No, you wanted the blow right away."

"I understand, Colonel. So I will pay. With vig. If only you would wait."

"Vig is a Russian expression," Shawn Lin said for Lew Chun's benefit. "Short for vigorish. A mindless euphemism. Used by illiterates." Back to Felix Corazon. "No interest will be imposed."

"Ah."

"But no waiting will be permitted."

"Oh."

Felix Corazon sighed and shrugged and produced his checkbook. Charlie and Jimmy gazed at their shoes. Lew Chun assumed it would be impolite to peek, and he studied the wall. The writer rose and handed the check to Shawn Lin, who pocketed it without a glance.

"You aren't going to look?" Felix Corazon asked.

"Certainly not. It is a matter of trust between businessmen." The interview was over. Felix Corazon left, the back of his jacket dark with flop sweat.

Two minutes later, Rose Chen flounced in, carrying a black leather portfolio and wearing the same style of pantsuit she'd had on the other day, except that this one was the color of a brown eggshell. If she was surprised to see Lew Chun, she didn't show it.

Shawn Lin and his sons-in-law exchanged knowing smiles. "What have you brought me?" the Colonel asked her.

Rose approached the desk, unzipped the portfolio and spread it open. The images jumped out at the audience. Glossies, 8 by 10 inches, of young women stripped to the skin and assuming various poses. Some were waist-up photos; the rest were full-length. Very little was left to the imagination. Shawn Lin turned page after page, nodding his approval. Then it was as if a cloud had crossed the sun. He pointed at the picture of a long-haired black girl seated on a stool.

"Too young," he groused.

"Her Haitian passport says she's 18," Rose told him.

"What her passport says is irrelevant. We all know these things can be faked. She looks 14, 15. Junior high. I won't have it."

"I'll scratch her off the list."

"You'll do better than that. You'll find her parents or her guardian or whoever peddled her to you. And you'll give them $500 and tell them I don't want to see this kid's picture again. Not when she reaches 21. Never."

He looked consecutively at Rose, Lew Chun, Charlie and Jimmy. "In case I haven't made myself clear in the past, with children a line is drawn. A fence is built. A moat is dug. Someone, anyone, in my network sells product to a child, the police are informed. This is our agreement. A trial, federal prison, no parole. Guaranteed. A minor is used as a prostitute, the pimp and the madam are out on the street. *Wanchengle.* Finished." He turned over a few pages and glared at Rose.

"I'll examine this. It'll be returned to you tomorrow. With instructions." He waved her away. She seemed glad to go without any further damage.

Everyone sat still. When the boss dismissed them, the sons-in-law exited in a hurry. Now it was just Lew Chun and Shawn Lin.

The Colonel wasted no time. "You asked. Now you know how I make a living."

"I never asked."

"Not in so many words."

No defense was offered. Satisfied, Shawn Lin resumed. "The restaurant you run, your apartment, your salary, your life — it all comes from this. You don't approve."

No reply. None was expected. "I don't know that I approve of it myself. But here we are. I cannot step back without destroying everything and everyone. What I have to do is maintain."

"It must take a lot of energy," Lew Chun said in an exhausted voice.

"Energy and care and money. A lot of each." Then, after a long pause: "Sometimes it is very tiring."

The confessional tone was the last thing Lew Chun had expected to hear. It was, in fact, half authentic, half theatrical — to give the Boy Chef a glimpse of responsibility, as well as power.

With the same calculated self-drama, the Colonel suddenly perked up. "Do you know why I assumed the title of Colonel?"

"No, sir."

"A leader is always surrounded by generals. The generals often conspire to dethrone the leader. Then they turn on each other. Not so the colonels. When the dust settles, one of them emerges as a man of the people. Gadhafi is a colonel. Nasser never rose above that rank."

He looked far off and then came back to earth. "What I envision," he said grandiosely, spreading his arms wide, "is a series of restaurants. Not a chain, just maybe a half-dozen Lew Chun's Pan Asian restaurants, in various cities — Boston, Philadelphia, Chicago, LA, San Francisco. Eventually, there could be a Pan Asian brand — not only food. We could do cutlery, crockery, clothing. I would like to be entirely legitimate, shed all this other nonsense — the pharmaceuticals, the women."

He called for tea, riffled through some papers, started to make a call and changed his mind.

"Gambling I don't touch," he said suddenly. "A lot of profit in it. The Russians, I know what they do. They launder the money, put it in shell companies, scatter it in hundreds of bank accounts with phony names. If it was only the rich, who cares? But it isn't. It's losers — down-at-the-heels whites, ghetto blacks, Hispanic servants — putting money they don't have on horses, numbers, dice. Digging holes they'll never get out of. Gambling wrecks finances. Ruins families. You don't bet, right?"

"No, sir."

"Don't smoke, either."

"No, sir."

"Even one cigarette makes you a monkey. Same with gambling. Drinking is different. You can have a glass of wine, a beer, something stronger — recreational drugs, say — and you can be healthier for it. Same with hookers. If they're clean, good-looking, what's the harm? My girls save more marriages than they destroy. Believe me."

The tea arrived. A servant poured and disappeared. The two men sat drinking it silently. The phone rang. Shawn Lin paid no attention. Five minutes later, it rang again. This time, he smiled patiently and answered the call, listening and saying yes several times, nothing more. After a few minutes, he was more responsive. "Have him come here. I'm sure this can be worked out. He is to come alone — no, with his wife. Yes, exactly as you say — no problem." He rang off and looked at Lew Chun as if for the first time. He thought to himself: "This child of a woman who disdained me, who looked on me with shame, this flotsam washed up on my shore — could he be the answer? Could he be my salvation?"

"You are without taint," the Colonel declared. "You must stay that way. Will you cook dinner tonight for me, my wife and our guests?"

"Of course, sir. An honor."

"Go and prepare. Tell the restaurant you will not be in attendance this evening. Create an entree that will knock our shoes off."

His guest made ready to leave.

"You are the best part of me," Shawn Lin blurted. No way to buy back the admission now, even if he wanted to. And he was not sure he wanted to. The Boy Chef was equally uncertain about what had just occurred. He bowed out as the Colonel pressed a button on the phone.

****

The dinner was a smash — kudos and air kisses to Lew Chun, introduction to the guests, Teddy Broz, a florid bulky man in a black sharkskin suit, and his obese wife, Milena, wearing gigantic gold hoop earrings, a diamond and emerald necklace, a half-dozen bejeweled gold bracelets on each thick freckled arm, everything as loud as her voice. Mr. and Mrs. Broz were obviously people of importance, and they were lavish in their praise. The Boy Chef felt very accomplished. The sensation lasted for two days.

That Saturday, Mickey Wong was waiting for Lew Chun at the bar as he entered the Pan Asian.

"We gotta palaver, kid," he said in a voice like a glass shard.

They went to the back of the restaurant and down the hall to a little room marked "Private." The staff members were just starting to arrive, and they were too busy to say anything but hello. Lew Chun closed the door. "What's troubling you, Mickey?"

"The Russians."

Mickey was met with a curious, unknowing look.

"Worse than the Italians," he groused. "Worse than the Japs. Worse than us, frankly. They control gambling across the boroughs."

"So? Shawn Lin told me he has nothing to do with gambling. Was he lying?"

"No, he told you the truth. Most of it." Mickey fiddled with a knife and fork at his place. Lew Chun asked whether he wanted something to eat. He said no, he was just nervous. Then he explained why.

"The Russian hoods own the building next door. They run a gambling establishment on all four floors. Sports betting, cards, numbers — you know about numbers?"

"Afraid not."

"Never mind. Not important. The thing is they want to expand."

"Let them."

"You don't understand. That dinner you cooked? It was supposed to soften up the Russian, convince him he could have his joint, Shawn Lin could have his place, and nobody gets hurt. No dice. The son of a bitch wants to buy this building."

"We have to move, that it?"

"We can't surrender to these fuckers."

That was different. Now Lew Chun could see why Mickey was so edgy.

"What does Shawn Lin want me to do?"

"I don't know. I don't think he does, either. There's going to have to be a confrontation. That's for sure."

"But I heard he never leaves Chinatown."

"Who told you that?"

The Boy Chef shrugged.

"He leaves when he has to. And now he has to." Mickey got to his feet. "Look, kid. In about half an hour, this place will be full of customers. Twenty of them will be ringers — heavy hitters with pieces."

"Pieces?"

"Guns. Uzis, AK-47s."

"In my place?"

"Don't fret, kid. Nobody's going to shoot up the restaurant. It's just, you know, peace through strength. The Russians know we're armed. They won't kick up a ruckus. But later—"

"What does that mean, later?"

"It means Chinese fireworks. You got a bed here?"

"There's a cot in my office."

"That's where you sleep tonight."

Lew Chun pressed for more information, but Mickey told him he had said enough. Too much, in fact.

****

Shortly after 8 p.m., Mickey steered Lew Chun around the Pan Asian, both of them assuming a casual air as they checked the tables. Mickey coughed as they passed a group of three white men with faces like fists. The Russians' idea of casualwear was identical brown flannel sport jackets a size too small, white unbuttoned button-down shirts and clip-on black bow ties. The strollers walked by without looking back.

To the side, where they had sat before, were Frank and Julie and a young Asian woman who posed like a tulip in a vase. Her name was Gia, and she was introduced to the Boy Chef as Julie's sister. The blood relation was not surprising; both women broadcast the same combination of innocence and seduction. It would be interesting to meet their father sometime, Lew Chun thought. Julie asked for a follow-up interview. After a token protest, he slid into the fourth seat as Mickey kept moving.

"What do you do, Gia?"

"You mean 'How do you do?'"

"No, I mean *what*."

"Journalism major." She made a head gesture in Julie's direction.

"My sister does everything I do," Julie said. "Only better."

Lew Chun said he hoped so.

Julie did not react. But Gia awarded him with a big warm smile. "Can we speak with you after hours?" This question had all sorts of possibilities, including one that Julie was using her sister as bait. It was worth thinking about, except that Mickey was closing in and there was no time to ponder anything.

"We have a staff meeting tonight," Lew Chun told Frank and the sisters. "How about later in the week?"

"Name the day," Julie demanded.

"Call me. I'm usually here from late afternoon until midnight."

He departed before they could begin their grilling. Mickey led the Boy Chef back to the office and ordered him to stay there until the all-clear signal was given. Lew Chun reacted with indignation.

"What is this, Lebanon? What's going on, Mickey? Tell me, or I swear I'll walk out of here."

"You won't get far, kid. Our guys will bring you back, or their guys will cut you in half."

"Goddamn it, Mickey, I have a right to know."

He considered the situation for a minute. Locking the door, he pulled up a wooden slat chair, turned it around and sat in it, leaning his chin on the back. "You didn't hear this from me."

****

Mickey took his time, unspooling the information like thread. But in the end, he omitted very little, and most of that because he had overlooked it. Shawn Lin had ordered a three-pronged attack. The strikes were to begin at closing time. First victims, that trio of Russian diners. They had been followed from Bensonhurst to an underground parking garage on 14th Street and Third Avenue, and from there to the restaurant. The garage attendants had been paid off by C.C.; he would replace them with his men. When the Russians came back for their Buick, they would be shot with tranquilizer guns. Nothing fatal, just a strong chemical to knock them out.

After they collapsed, they would be placed sitting up, looking for all the world like drunk passengers, breathing heavily, leaning against each other. The sedan would be taken to a construction site on the West Side. There the driver would trespass, thanks to a gate with a conveniently broken lock. He would back the vehicle into a huge mound of soil and broken rock. The material would clog the tailpipe. Fumes would drift forward into the car itself. The driver would exit, leaving the key in the ignition, the windows rolled up and the motor running on a full tank of gas. By morning, when the construction crew arrived, the Russians would be dead of asphyxiation. Of course, the medical examiners might detect the presence of barbiturates, but those people were overworked, and an official verdict of death by misadventure might make their lives a lot simpler.

Second, the house next to the restaurant. Gambling occurred on all levels, the high rollers on the top floor playing stud and draw poker; below, croupiers, 21, slots, craps, everything else. The cops knew all about it. Four times a year, they were paid off. Every so often, there was a raid in which small-timers were rounded up; nobody got hurt.

"But there's two new deputy commissioners looking for ink and airtime." Mickey, never a closemouthed type, was a font of information. "This is an easy one. They get to clean out a gambling den, make some arrests, look smashing in the *Times* above the fold and on all three networks. The papers, the local news on CBS, NBC and ABC, plus CNN, get tipped just before the raid. Too much advance notice, word gets back to the Russians — they got their own tipsters — and they vanish before the uniforms go through the door."

Lew Chun waited, but his informant didn't add anything.

"You left out the third prong, Mickey."

"Ah! That's the Hiroshima part." He went to the door and yanked it open. Nothing. Nobody. The sounds of the kitchen were remote. He came back and sat down again. "There are two guys in white Con Ed overalls right now. They're under a block in Brooklyn. You ever been to Brooklyn?"

Lew Chun shook his head.

"Well, there's a neighborhood, Brighton Beach. They call it Little Odessa. Teddy Broz lives there. Owns four adjoining tenements. Lives in one. It's like a fort, guards at the door, snipers on the roof. But he overlooked something. Underneath the houses are old gas mains. Rusty. Leaky. One of them is gonna blow." Mickey checked his watch. "Right this second, the fuse is burning down. Slowly. Two a.m., people will see the explosion for blocks. Miles."

The Boy Chef slumped in his chair. All this effort, all these attempts at legitimacy and status turning to charcoal. "So, now we're at war."

"There's not gonna *be* a war, kid. That's the point. Peace through strength. I don't know if the Russians'll recover the bodies, but they'll get the message: Don't fuck with the Colonel. The price is too high. We'll hear grumbling, threats, ultimatums. But then there'll be a phone call. They want to set up another gambling scene. Shawn Lin says OK, with conditions. No presence on this block. No interference with his operations or this restaurant."

"And you think they'll agree?"

"Wouldn't you?"

"I don't know."

"Well, I do. Stretch out on the cot, kid. And don't worry. Just be glad you're not living in Brighton Beach." He took a pint of Jack Daniel's from his courier bag.

"Drink?"

"No, thanks."

"You want to stay sharp, that it?"

"That's it."

"You're not gonna see anything, kid — because you're not gonna leave the premises. Shawn Lin's orders."

"Even so."

"As you wish."

"As I wish," the Boy Chef grumbled. "That'll be the day." Mickey retrieved a glass tumbler from the bathroom, poured himself a double and raised the glass. "To hell money," he said, and then he knocked it back with one swallow.

✳✳✳✳

The forecast was accurate in every detail: raid, explosion, dead Russians, Teddy Broz among them. Lew Chun was ordered to stay in place for two days, sleeping over, never leaving the Pan Asian. Someone came by and left extra clothing fished from his closet. He was not surprised. Shawn Lin would have the keys to the front door and the apartment; he would simply hand them to C.C. or some other functionary. After all, he owned the place.

On the third day, Mickey came by with an all-clear signal. He insisted on driving the Boy Chef home, walking into the flat and checking the closets and under the bed. Nothing had been disturbed, except for a pile of newspapers on the night table. After Mickey departed, Lew Chun went through them. The *Times,* the *Post*, the *Daily News* and *The Wall Street Journal* had all run stories about the gas explosion in Brooklyn. It was attributed to a leak in an ancient main. Two dozen investigators were combing through the wreckage. There was no mention of arson.

On Page 5, the *Post* carried an unrelated item about a "freak accident on 11th Avenue." Three men with no ID had left their motor idling and had died of carbon monoxide poisoning. Thus far, the bodies were unclaimed.

The Boy Chef had just about finished washing up and dressing, when the phone rang. Gia.

"You still up for that interview?" she asked.

"Up. Interesting word."

She pressed on. "I could meet you at the Pan Asian." He hardly ever called the restaurant by its proper name; it sounded strange in her mouth. He was about to ask her to meet him at the apartment but stopped midsentence. The invitation might have been considered tacky and off-putting. Not the best way to begin. Still, she *was* beautiful. What harm could there be in dining out?

"OK," he said, trying to sound halfway between interested and indulgent. "Next week? Thursday night?"

"How about sooner?"

"Too much to do."

"Have it your way, Boy Chef."

Patronizing. Talk about not the best way to begin.

"Next week. Thursday. Eight," he repeated tersely. "See you then." And then he rang off before either of them could change his or her mind.

****

Facts began to surface in the news, but only in fragments. The Russians in the car were identified as "perps with long rap sheets." They had been living in Little Odessa. One of the deputy commissioners made the same statement on all three networks: "We believe it's no coincidence that the three men died the same night the gas explosion killed Teddy Broz and his associates." The public was assured that the investigation was ongoing. Three days went by. There were no other bulletins and no leaks.

On Thursday, 10 minutes after the appointed hour, Gia appeared. She was wearing a red Shantung dress that clung to her like paint, and she made a point of walking very slowly to the table. A lot of men turned their heads as she passed by, even the ones with dates. She trailed a faint aroma of peaches. Lew Chun ordered a bottle of pinot noir. They exchanged the customary trivia about the city, about domestic and foreign news, about the food. He asked her to let him choose a tasting menu — a dozen dishes, small portions, guaranteed to please.

"Why not?" she asked. "You always get your way anyhow."

"Not always."

The drinks arrived. She clinked his glass. "You like being a man of mystery?"

"There's nothing mysterious about a shuttle."

"A shuttle?"

"I go from the restaurant to my apartment and back again. That's it, every day."

"Sometimes you don't even do that. Sometimes you stay here all day."

Red flags went up. But he only asked why she would say that.

She took another sip of wine. "Because someone was watching your apartment last week."

"That someone wouldn't be you?"

"No. Anyway, you must have an automatic light, because it goes on at 7 p.m. every night and goes off at 2 a.m. every morning — unless you turn it off earlier, which you didn't for two nights. Which means you stayed at the Pan Asian those nights."

"Clever girl. Is that what you want me to say?"

The first course arrived. *Tofu millefeuille* with truffle sauce. Gia rolled her eyes with delight. "I'm not all that clever," she said between bites. "But I know people who are."

"And they watched my window for a couple of nights."

"From a car, yes."

"And why is that?"

She said she would ask them. The next course came — shiitake-leek spring rolls with three dipping sauces. Gia made no attempt to hide her approval. But she wasn't giving anything else away.

"Well, you tell your clever friends," Lew Chun insisted, "the subject stayed at his restaurant because there was so much work to do. We had three corporate parties in two days, with complicated dishes like you wouldn't believe."

"What I wouldn't believe is that you were too busy to go home, especially on the nights—"

"What nights were they, Gia?"

"You know."

"No, I don't know. Tell me."

But she wouldn't. Her silence lasted through the chicken satay with pureed almond and then the shrimp shaomai.

Lew Chun broke through. "When I listen to you, I hear your voice speaking other people's words."

"I'm not like them."

"Who are you like?"

"I'm like me. Listen, I could tell you things about my sister. And I could tell you things about your cousin. But not here."

He tried to read her face. Julie or Frank — perhaps some other investigative colleague — had been timing his night light; someone was probably watching it now. They might try Gia's place, assuming she had an apartment and not an NYU dorm room. But her bedroom might contain a hidden microphone or one of those tiny cameras they were always writing about in the *Times'* Science section. Trouble, however he handled it. He needed help on this.

Radiating a bogus confidence, Lew Chun assured her he would find a place where they could be alone, excused himself, went to the office and called Mickey. Not in. He left a message asking him to call him at home. Then he returned to the table and informed Gia he was wanted in the kitchen. An emergency; a sous-chef had just quit. Why didn't she stay, enjoy the next dish, oil-poached salmon, and leave him her phone number? He would call tomorrow morning with a time and location.

Whether Gia bought the emergency-in-the-kitchen excuse was impossible to say. She smiled at the Boy Chef and patted his arm as if she understood all things. He told her the meal was on the house; she was free to leave whenever she wanted. Lew Chun had a feeling that about three minutes after he went away, she would go out the front door.

When Lew Chun got home, Mickey was seated on his couch, thumbing through a copy of *Playboy* he had just bought. Lew Chun didn't bother to criticize the intrusion; privacy was a luxury of the past. Mickey had brought a bottle of Johnnie Walker and poured himself a shot into one of the tumblers he had fetched from a sideboard. He offered one to his host. Lew Chun turned him down.

"Don't worry about a thing, kid," Mickey said with a broad gesture. "We had the whole house swept. No devices of any kind."

Lew Chun told him about the observers who had checked out the apartment the previous week.

"Old news. While they were watching you, we were watching them." He knew all about the sisters. "The older one and her fag friend are investigative journalists. The young one is a wannabe. You know the difference between a regular journalist and an investigative one? The regular will sell his mother for a story. The investigator will also sell his mother, but for a cheaper price. And he'll deliver her to your door in a shopping bag."

"So what am I supposed to do, Mickey?"

"Get laid; that's what you're supposed to do. Invite her up here. Have dinner sent in. Candlelight. Champagne."

"And when she starts asking questions?"

"Answer them."

"Really?"

"Really. Answer them with lies, half-truths. Make up stuff. She's young. She'll buy what you tell her." He sang a tuneless couplet: "Under the spreading chestnut tree, I sold you and you sold me."

The Boy Chef asked him where that was from.

"'1984,' kid. Ever read it?"

"No."

"Just as well."

****

Mickey Wong was as bright as a beach and very quick on his feet, but his real gift was his total amorality. He recognized a fellow creature the moment he saw Gia and warned the Boy Chef accordingly. Gia was the kind of little sister who was much more dangerous than the elder one, he observed. She knew instinctively — aided by the journalism professors she had slept with — that getting a story meant doing whatever you had to do. Digging around, trading secrets, exchanging favors. At her age, she lacked power and influence with the right editors and the pliable columnists. But she did have her torso and adjoining parts, and they would compensate for her inexperience.

Gia did indeed make her body a wonderful place to visit. Her sharp round knee fit exactly in Lew Chun's palm, and so did each breast. Physically, she was full of rhymes. Added to that were unblemished skin that smelled like fresh fruit of all kinds and glowing chestnut eyes, especially shiny when they looked up at him from the pillow, her black mane framing her ovular face.

For a while, he heard Mickey's toxins sounding in his head. Then they started to fade out.

Sometimes the Boy Chef sneaked away during the 3 p.m. lull; sometimes they had a real date, went to a movie at the Film Forum, ate dinner at a French or Italian restaurant. It was not too long before he realized they were being watched in those venues and followed when they grabbed a cab. The faces were familiar; they were Shawn Lin's men, making sure that none of his enemies was after the Boy Chef or his date. Or so Lew Chun assumed at first, noodling with Gia in the back seat. But soon he began to worry. Suppose the trackers thought he was selling the Colonel out.

Impossible. They had to know better than that. He was doing exactly what Mickey had advised, giving away no more than an alert researcher would already know, forever vague when Gia asked about Shawn Lin, conceding that the Colonel might have a hidden life but saying there was nothing the Boy Chef would know about; he was a recipient of the Colonel's largesse and nothing more — at which point she would get sharp. "Your cousin is a criminal. Don't you know that?"

"No, I don't know that," he would respond.

"He's a felon. Doesn't matter what his lawyers claim."

"He's never been convicted. You said so yourself."

"I didn't say he wasn't smart."

"I've never seen him do anything crooked."

"You see what you want to see. At least admit he's an influence peddler."

"He has some authority in Chinatown. That amounts to a few streets, a bunch of houses and stores. That's all."

"Right. And Russia is the new playground of capitalism."

Why did she mention Russia? Was she trying to provoke him, or was it meaningless country-dropping? In any case, he didn't rise to the bait. He just changed the subject, and they returned to bed.

But in a few days, Gia would start all over again. "How did Shawn Lin get rich?"

"Real estate, I think."

"You think."

"I heard him making some deals for buildings. That's all I know."

"You mean that's all you're telling me."

"That's all I know."

She would let it go at that for the moment, yielding to Lew Chun's entreaties, wise enough not to withhold the sweets.

That was the trouble. He could feel himself increasingly drawn to her, perhaps falling in love with her. It showed in his body language and in his conversation if people bothered to watch or listen. And as it turned out, they did.

****

Two weeks into winter, Mickey came back to the kitchen and said he needed to talk one-on-one — and not in the office. He looked grim. Lew Chun didn't ask where they were going. He cleaned up and followed Mickey into a waiting taxi. They went south, past Chinatown, past Fulton, all the way to Wall Street, and then turned left and stopped so close to the East River that they could hear it lapping at the concrete boundaries. Mickey led the way into a medium-sized office building, up the elevator to the seventh floor. They entered a suite with gold lettering on the door: The Cathay Society. The lights were on, but nobody seemed to be in attendance.

Mickey hadn't spoken a word in the taxi. Lew Chun took his cue from that and kept his mouth shut. Now that they were seated on the office couch, Mickey seemed ready to talk but uncertain about how to begin.

"Look," he said. "I understand sex."

Lew Chun brought his hands together silently, miming applause.

"I understand love," Mickey continued. "I understand loneliness. All three apply to you and this girl, this Gia."

"And?"

"And I want you to stop seeing her."

"*You* want? Who the hell are you to tell me who to see?"

Mickey held up his hand, trying to calm the situation before it got out of hand. "OK. All right. I'm sorry to break it to you like this. I should have been more diplomatic. The truth is, it isn't me giving the orders."

"No? It looks like you. It sounds like you."

"It's Shawn Lin. He doesn't want you to see her anymore. In fact, he forbids it."

"Why would he do that?"

"You'll have to ask him."

"I'm asking you, Mickey."

He shrugged.

"Screw this," Lew Chun snapped. "Let him tell me himself."

"I will," said Shawn Lin.

****

"I followed you here," he admitted, entering the room.

The Boy Chef got to his feet. "I didn't see anybody."

"That is what you may expect to see when I follow you. Haven't you learned that by now? Sit down." Shawn Lin addressed Mickey. "You have matters to attend to." The obedient lackey did as he was told. An eerie silence settled in.

Shawn Lin cleared his throat. "I take no pleasure in interfering with people's personal lives."

He watched the Boy Chef squirm, his face puzzled as he tried to figure out where the Colonel was going with this. "Of course, you have a right to your own love life, Lew Chun. You're a young man; you're getting prominent. This is attractive to women. The hormones are flowing, and why shouldn't you take advantage of your position — the immigrant making good?"

"Sir, with all respect—"

"This is a monologue, not a conversation."

The Colonel looked for a perceptible head bow and got it.

"Ordinarily, I would applaud your liaison with Gia Tseng. She's a very nice-looking girl, from a good family. Her father is a prosperous wholesale grocer."

Lew Chun knew the monosyllable that was on its way. But.

"But she is a journalist. And you tell her things."

"You had a hidden microphone at our table?"

"I had a lip reader several tables away. That was sufficient. In any case, Lew Chun, Gia is an ally — but also a rival — of her sister. These are dangerous people. They could cost us very dearly."

"Not if you have nothing to hide," Lew Chun heard himself say.

"Don't be absurd. Everyone has something to hide, and I have more than most." He crossed the room to a three-tier metal file, unlocked the top drawer and withdrew a black leather-bound accounting book.

"I didn't want you to see these things, didn't want you to know them. But you leave me no choice." He dropped the book in Lew Chun's lap and returned to his seat. The Boy Chef ran his eyes down vast columns of numbers. They had no significance to him.

"Examine the lists of names and locations."

"Sir, I—"

"Forget the 'sir.' We're blood relatives. Call me Shawn Lin."

"All right, then. Shawn Lin."

"Read the names. Aloud."

Shawn Lin was gratified to see the young man do exactly as ordered.

"Read the locations."

When Lew Chun finished, the Colonel said, "Now you know how I make my living and the people I work with. You saw some of this earlier. But you were ignorant of details. No longer."

"Shawn Lin, there's no need—"

"The first 10 pages cover the receipts from merchants for cocaine. Ten pages later, for crystal meth. Next section after that, heroin." This was said without any expression; he might as well have been talking about varieties of tofu.

"The houses of prostitution are listed in the second section, along with receipts. And then, of course, there is human traffic. Smuggling Asians into the U.S. — Asians with expertise in computer programming, air conditioning repair, architecture, medical fields. After they're here, I supply them with fine-looking ID. The experts who create those papers — driver's licenses, insurance certificates, Social Security cards and the like — are listed on Page 33. In certain ways, it's our most profitable venture."

This was not said as a boast or lament; it was simply a statement of fact. The statement, however, carried a heavy freight. Without showing his amusement, he noted that Lew Chun seemed impressed, as well as terrified.

"By some measures," the Colonel said calmly, "you could call me important. But by other standards, I'm only a small-business man."

"Not so small."

Shawn Lin smiled indulgently. "There are only a few judges on my payroll. I have little political influence. No unions under my thumb the way the mob did. On the other hand, Chinatown is impenetrable to outsiders. And it is easily controlled once you convince its anxious citizens that you can bring them security and prosperity. This I have done."

He waited for a word from Lew Chun. It was not forthcoming. After allowing the Boy Chef to squirm a little, he resumed. "I have been very frank with you. You will do me the kindness of returning the favor."

"I-I don't know what you want from me, Shawn Lin."

There was a tinge of sadness in his reply. "More than anything, I want you to understand. I'm not hard for the sake of hardness. I would much rather read and listen to music and make love."

He read the skepticism in Lew Chun's eyes.

"You know the story of the old Chinese laborer who journeys to the old village wise man?"

"I don't think so."

"Well, he says, 'O Great One, I cannot pee.' The ancient tells him to go in a flask. He fills it completely. The sage says, 'So what's the fuss? You peed just fine.' The laborer says, 'Yes, certainly, if they *let* me.' Well, Lew Chun, they won't let me. They won't let me live my life."

"Who is 'they'?"

"Sometimes the Mexicans. Sometimes the Italians, although not so much these days. Sometimes the Russians. You were told about them."

Lew Chun didn't want to get Mickey in trouble. He said he had read about it.

"Doesn't matter how you learned. These days, you know many things — too many things to be with a journalist. Possibly Gia does want you. But she wants information more. There are plenty of other choices. Not whores. Nice girls. I can provide introductions."

"Shawn Lin, Gia is harmless."

"She is unsafe."

"She's a college student."

"Trust me on this."

"And if I keep seeing her?"

"Bad for you, terrible for her." Shawn Lin didn't wish to go into details. He took a different tack. "But why are we walking on the dark side?"

More silence. Then: "Lew Chun, you have been admitted into the organization. This is a compliment."

"I never asked for admission."

"Doesn't matter," he declared. "You're in." He rose. The Boy Chef took this as his cue to withdraw. The meeting was over.

****

That night, Lew Chun arrived home to find a voice message from Gia. The call was not returned. She left another message the next night. On Sunday night, she telephoned three times, the last shortly after 1 a.m. That time, Lew Chun picked up the receiver. Better to get it done, he told himself.

"Where have you been?" she demanded. "I've been trying to reach you for days."

"Business meetings. Special dinners. New menus. The days and nights got away from me."

"You've met someone else."

The door was open; Lew Chun went in. "I think so."

"You *think* so? You don't know?"

"I...didn't want to say anything yet."

"You figured it might not work out. If it didn't, you could always go back to the runner-up."

"It's not like that."

"Oh? What *is* it like?"

"Gia, I'm sorry about this. I really am—"

"I don't believe you. I don't think you're sorry at all. I think you're glad. I can hear the relief in your voice."

It took a great effort for Lew Chun to reject this self-portrait of a woman scorned. But in the end, he did. It was less about losing a great love and more about missing out on a big career. Gia didn't know it, and he couldn't say so, but she would be a lot safer now. If they continued, that career would be reduced. And perhaps worse — a good deal worse.

****

The van had been white once. Now it was streaked with smudges and rust. The lettering on the side panel read Pasko TV Repair — No Job Too Small. On the face of it, there was nothing unusual about this vehicle — except that it had been in the same locale every day for a week, switching sides of the street according to parking regulations. No repair vehicle would remain idle that long, unless the owner was ill. But Lew Chun thought not. He thought it might belong to Frank or Julie or Gia; they were keeping an eye on his place again.

Passing by, he committed the plate number to memory and wrote it down on a corner of the *Times'* Sports section when he had a chance. That afternoon, he visited the Chinatown headquarters and gave the paper to C.C., along with a note. A couple of days later, he was ordered to return. C.C. was in the room, looming against a wall. Mickey sat on the leather couch to the left of Jimmy and Charlie. Shawn Lin was installed as usual, behind his desk. He motioned Lew Chun to a seat.

"We traced the owner, kid," Mickey said. "We were hoping it was the press keeping an eye on you and the house. No such luck. The car belongs to a Mark Brody. Could be Irish. Could be Russian. Our guess is column B."

"We figured the Russian problem was over," Jimmy said. "They brought a rifle, so we brought a mortar."

"End of story?" Charlie asked rhetorically. "We thought so. Doesn't look like it."

Jimmy added, "Point is, we think they're parked on your block because they're keeping an eye on you. For what, we don't know. But the Colonel has a pretty good idea."

Shawn Lin spoke to Lew Chun. "They could be waiting for the right time to take you off the street, hold you for ransom. It's not their style, but they might be changing tactics. Whatever, we can protect you most of the time, but nobody can do it all of the time."

"I wouldn't ask you to," Lew Chun said. "I can take care of myself."

"With all due respect, you can't. Not without some hardware and some training. C.C., show him what I mean."

The big man reached in his jacket pocket. He produced a small pistol from his jacket. "This is a Smith & Wesson snub-nose. Black grip, steel body. Very accurate revolver up close. Not so good for distance."

"Then again," Mickey pointed out, "this is for self-defense, not attack. It fits in your pants like small change. Check mine." He exhibited his own snub-nose and then put it back. "Or you can keep it in your jacket like C.C. did. Either way, you're protected."

"If we're wrong," Shawn Lin said, "and Brody turns out to be harmless, you can regard it as a souvenir. Until then, you will keep it on you at all times. Under the pillow at night."

Shawn Lin made some gesture they all understood. Jimmy and Charlie filed out, followed by Mickey and finally C.C.

When he and Lew Chun were alone, the Colonel appraised him quietly. The Boy Chef may have acquired the requisite hardness after all. Then again... Perhaps he needed to be provoked yet again. For the troops and the officers, there were never too many tests. "You know and I know that you stabbed a man once," Shawn Lin observed. "You have it in you to be a warrior. I don't ask you to be one, only to act like one."

"I don't know what that means, 'act.'"

"Maybe you're nervous or afraid. Doesn't matter. If you have a loaded side arm, you'll walk differently, speak differently. A subtle thing, but this Brody will get the message."

"I don't know, Shawn Lin."

"I do."

Lew Chun made ready to leave, but the Colonel kept going. "One more thing. I want you to vary your hours and your approaches. Come home at a different time every other night. Arrange for unaccustomed drivers to take you to the apartment by unaccustomed routes. Have them leave you off down the block sometimes. Always make sure they see you unlock the front door and go in."

Again Lew Chun prepared to depart, but there was more to hear. "I will try to protect you, have someone hanging around, but there are always cracks in the wall."

"I'll deal with it, Shawn Lin."

"I hope so, Lew Chun. I hope so."

Arrangements were made with a private pistol range at 11th Avenue and 48th Street, near the docks. Andover Control served private security people, deliberately anonymous men and women in gray uniforms. Like them, Lew Chun wore noise-canceling headphones and fired at paper targets from close up and far away. C.C. supervised. In the beginning, the Boy Chef embarrassed himself, the rounds spraying the targets but rarely approaching their centers. After a dozen sessions, C.C. issued a backhanded compliment; he said this was as good as his student was going to get and that was good enough for all normal purposes.

"How about abnormal ones?" Lew Chun asked.

His teacher affected not to hear.

****

The mesomorph in a peacoat and navy wool watch cap became a conspicuous sight every couple of days. He would skulk around at the end of the block, smoking under a lamppost or leaning against a car and pretending to read a copy of the *Post*. Lew Chun recalled the exchange with the Colonel early on: *"I didn't see anybody." "That is what you may expect to see when I follow you."* And he wondered whether the shadow was an enemy or an impressionist doing Charles Bronson in *Death Wish*.

All guesswork stopped on the night of the blizzard. The taxi service called and said the cab was out of commission; the buildup of ice and snow had made driving impossible. The local news said buses and police cars and fire engines would be running for a short while. Drivers of private cars were advised to stay off the streets. Home wasn't all that far away, so Lew Chun decided to walk.

The wind sang, and the snow was audible as he crunched along, moving rapidly but not running because it was too slippery underfoot. A solitary truck headed north on First Avenue; otherwise, everything was still — save for the sound of another pair of feet not far behind him. Lew Chun slowed his pace. The man in the peacoat slowed. Lew Chun picked up the pace. Peacoat picked up the pace. Was it Brody? Even if it wasn't, even if it was some journalist creep, Lew Chun had to lose him. And it had to happen now, when the weather was foul and travelers could barely see their hands in front of their faces.

The block was largely composed of brownstones and shop fronts. Building superintendents often lived on the basement level; if you wanted to see your super, you opened the wrought-iron gate and walked downstairs. There were no lights in a basement apartment in the middle of the block. Going on instinct rather than reason, Lew Chun descended the icy steps, gripping the rail with both hands. There was a small recess in the entryway. He ducked into that, felt the snub-nose in his pocket and pressed the safety catch to the off position as he had been trained.

"Come out, now," ordered a voice as cold as stone.

Lew Chun was sure the tracker could see the steam of his breath but made no reply.

"OK, Boy Chef, we do this the hard way."

So he knew Lew Chun's identity. Well, Lew Chun knew the name of his pursuer. They were even. He took the pistol from his pocket and waited for Mark Brody to make the next move. When he did, it was lethal. Brody tried to aim his pistol while stepping down on a sheet of ice. He didn't completely lose his footing, but the shot went wild.

He was not given a second opportunity.

Lew Chun pulled the trigger of the Smith & Wesson three times. None of the shots missed their objective. Muffled by the wind and the groans of trucks shifting gears, the sounds dissipated in the raw night air. Brody groaned and fell facedown. Lew Chun mimicked what he had seen the police do on the television cop shows, feeling the victim's neck for a pulse. There was none. The snow kept coming hard, blanketing both of them. Shaking off the cold cover of white, Lew Chun walked up the stairs and down the block. He headed east to Avenue B.

Before he got there, however, he walked to Seventh Street and then made a square journey, returning to the place where he had fired the revolver. This time, he went down the opposite side of the street. Snow had completely covered his tracks, as well as Brody's. If anyone else had traveled on Ninth Street between then and now, the tracks were indiscernible.

Surface travel had slowed to a standstill. Two large sanitation trucks were pushing their way south. There were no buses, no private cars or cabs, no police cars. Lew Chun went directly to the subway station at Astor Place. The trains were still running, but he had to wait a long time for a southbound local. It was crowded and had a heady aroma of wet wool, garlic and Right Guard. Straphangers were talking merrily about the weather. None of them had the slightest interest in the killer among them. A half-hour later, he was on Canal Street, making his way to Shawn Lin's house. C.C. was at the door. He took one look and asked, "What's wrong?"

****

At the finish, C.C. mumbled something about being sorry about the whole incident. He said Shawn Lin would know what to do, but the Colonel was unavailable right now. Lew Chun was pointed in the direction of the shower. A pair of red silk pajamas and a bathrobe hung on the inside of the bathroom door. The unexpected drop-in was expected to stay the night. Or *was* he unexpected?

As he soaped up and inhaled steam, the lethal confrontation replayed as in a dream. The man with the TV repair truck *may* have staked out the block even in the snow. But more likely, he knew exactly when his quarry was coming home. Shawn Lin had cannily advised Lew Chun to stagger his schedule. That he had done. Only one other person knew the new routine — the Colonel himself.

Did this evening go down as planned? Was the Boy Chef supposed to confront Mark Brody and kill him? Who was Brody? Nothing for it now but to climb into the clothes that had been offered, find a bed and wait for an audience. It might take a day or two or three, but Lew Chun was determined not to leave until some answers were forthcoming.

He did not have long to wait. At 6 the next morning, C.C. stopped by with shirt, suit and underwear, all freshly cleaned and pressed. Lew Chen climbed into them and followed C.C. to the office. When they arrived, Shawn Lin gave them a perfunctory greeting; he was on his way somewhere. The Colonel wore a black merino suit, a white shirt and a red and blue rep tie. He was stuffing some papers in a messenger bag as the Boy Chef cleared his throat, ready to begin the litany of accusations.

"You want to know if you were set up," the Colonel said directly. No small talk, right to the point. "Yes, you were meant to shoot Mark Brody. Under other circumstances, he might have survived, but you were too well-trained. He had absolutely no chance."

"And now *I* don't have a chance. That it?"

"The gun was unregistered. It has been removed from your room. It will never be recovered. Nobody knows who shot Brody — nobody outside this building. The police have no clue. The Russians are in no position to do anything. Brody was the last of their hit men, and now he's gone. He'll be replaced by others, *ça va sans dire*. But that will take at least a year. Meanwhile, we grow in strength and influence."

Lew Chun had repressed his fury and his fears for too long. "You told me I was the best part of you!" he exploded. "You wanted me to run a good place, be clean, stay out of the line of fire. Now I'm a killer, just like one of your fucking coolies! You saw an opportunity the day I walked in here. You didn't want to help me; you wanted to use me. No, you wanted to *own* me."

The Colonel permitted himself a smile as thin as broth. When he spoke, it was without a trace of rancor. "I admire your passion. There's so little true emotion in the world. Everybody talks; nobody feels. You mean what you say. I respect it. I really do."

"Bullshit."

"Lew Chun, you're on a tightrope over a volcano. Walk fast; get to the other side; and sit down."

And Lew Chun did sit down. Perhaps it was the subtext in the command: Listen or die. Satisfied, Shawn Lin completed his explanation.

"I wished you to terrify Brody. That's all — truly. He was supposed to go back to his bosses and tell them their cause was futile, that even the Boy Chef was armed. Alas, it didn't happen as we had planned."

"*We* had planned."

"Very well, *I* had planned. Mea culpa. You understand?"

"I think so. You want me to feel sorry for you."

"I don't wish you to feel *for* me. I wish you to feel *with* me. I wish you to come along on this journey. Let me offer you a deal."

Lew Chun squirmed in his seat. The Colonel saw the discomfort. For him, it was an encouraging sign. It always preceded the closing of a favorable negotiation.

"You will complete your studies, earn the degree I never had," Shawn Lin offered. "However long it takes. When you present me with the diploma, I'll have it framed and put on the wall behind my desk. Within a year from that date — two years at the most — you will be the owner and operator of a pair of restaurants. Probably more than that. You will be a recognizable name, not only in Manhattan but across the country. There's going to be a television food network soon. The camera loves you. You'll have your own show. You'll be totally legitimate — and more famous than you ever were back in China or here in New York."

"And in more trouble than I am now."

"You will never be in trouble. I will protect you. Always. This is a vow, an oath, an unbreakable promise. You are a decent person, an honest man, a promising figure. I envy you. I have never been an honest man. But today this is what I want to be. Believe it or not, I want to follow you, not the other way around."

Lew Chun could not hide his doubt and distrust, but the Colonel continued, like a televangelist working on a flock of unbelievers.

"You know how I make my living. I don't hide what I do. Not from you. It got me to this place, to these things. But, Lew Chun, now I want to depart from all that. I want to leave the hookers and the snakeheads and the product. I can't do it overnight. It will take time. It will take three years to get clean. But then, Charlie, Jimmy, the girls — and you, if you care to come along — we'll be part of something new and big. And totally within the law."

Lew Chun hesitated, and that was all Shawn Lin needed.

"One year," he repeated. "Give me one year. If things aren't the way you like them, you can walk. I get the Pan Asian, but you get your rep, with no strings, no debts, no obligations. It's a win-win."

He stuck out his hand. The Boy Chef wavered, teetered and took it.

The Colonel broke away. "I'm behind schedule. Later."

It was as if someone had breathed the verse in Lew Chun's ear.

There is only one way to achieve happiness on this terrestrial ball,
And that is to have either a clear conscience or none at all.

He wanted to recite those lines to Shawn Lin. He was suddenly exhausted, bone tired of this tempter's act, this pied piper's tune, this snake charmer's assurances. But when he looked up, the door had clicked shut. Later, after three-quarters of a bottle of Chianti and a lone dinner in his apartment, Lew Chun decided it was lucky he had not recited the couplet. The promising Boy Chef could be the late Boy Chef by tomorrow.

****

"Everything that rises must converge, you fucker."

The printing was made with a black Sharpie, hand-lettered over a tear sheet from the previous week's *New York Times* Dining section.

The block letters read, "Your erstwhile aficionada." Gia's graduate school education and still-smoldering resentment served as her signature.

The picture showed Lew Chun under the Pan Asian canopy, bidding farewell to Woody Allen, Brooke Astor, Robert Rauschenberg and Yo-Yo Ma. Mickey had spotted the personae at different tables and talked them into posing for a shot on their way out. None of the four was happy about it, but the staff had labored mightily for them, serving up a series of phenomenal courses.

When the photographer had left, the Boy Chef and Mickey repaired to a small back room for a congratulatory drink. Shawn Lin was already there, lying on a cot, very much at home. He sat up when they came in, gesturing to the table, where a bottle of Champagne sat in a silver bucket.

"Colonel," Lew Chun said tentatively.

Mickey tried a technical approach, hoping to elicit a smile from Shawn Lin. "An article like this," he burbled, "it's good for a thousand covers." He was not talking about magazine covers; he was speaking of seats in Lew Chun's Pan Asian. Mickey went on to explain that "cover" meant "paying customer" in restaurantese. The smile was indeed forthcoming, as Mickey thought it might be; the boss loved to hear jargon like that. Lew Chun took the cue, going on to discuss "campers" — diners who overstay their time at the table; "hockey puck" — an overdone piece of meat; "shoe" — an unskilled chef; the "two-second rule" — the time it takes from the moment an entree is accidentally dropped on the floor to its return to a saucepan.

A lot of grins and toasts. And then a dark cloud, as always, made its way onto the scene. "You have your own lingo, and that's a good thing, Lew Chun," Shawn Lin pointed out. "But you're uneducated, and that's a bad thing."

"I've done all right so far," the Boy Chef countered, entering a plea in his defense. "A lot of celebrities come down here. You saw Yo-Yo Ma."

"Yo-Yo Ma was a prodigy."

"I was a prodigy."

"It's not the same. He's a musician. You're a Chinaman."

"Yo-Yo Ma is a Chinaman."

"Yo-Yo Ma is a sophisticated musician. He was born in Paris. He attended Harvard. He has performed on television. You would be at a loss to talk to a celebrity."

"What do you want me to do, Colonel? Take cello lessons?"

"You need to take life lessons. You need to be *quelqu'un*, not just an immigrant who can make his way around a stove. You need to be able to read and write with skill. Have you ever written anything longer than a menu?"

He had lost the argument at "Colonel."

The next day, Mickey drove Lew Chun to the NYU School of Professional Studies. The Boy Chef was not happy about it. "Shawn Lin wants you to go places he can't go. Don't fight it."

All right, Lew Chun conceded, I won't fight it. I'll be what he wants, whatever the hell that is. As they drove, he could see himself as *quelqu'un* — somebody — invited to meet the president or the governor or at least the mayor. "Shawn Lin?" he would say. "Ah, yes, the old guy was quite helpful when I first got to the Gold Mountain. But that was long ago. We hardly see each other anymore. I feel bad about it. But there are only so many hours in the day."

****

There were classes in European history, art history, French, for which Lew Chun received high marks, and classic Greek and basic Latin, for which he did not. In the "Introduction to Writing" class were two men in their 50s — foreigners, but not Asians — and two papery uptown women of a certain age. The rest were a racially and ethnically mixed bag, eager to advance in their chosen fields. Without much success, Lew Chun tried to figure out just what those fields were.

During the second semester, students were asked to submit brief biographies. The Boy Chef wrote that he was a cook and let it go at that. The older men were the overweight, closely cropped Persky brothers, owners of a foreign-language FM radio station aimed at European immigrants of all kinds. Morris and Myron constituted the entire staff of WGK, "The Station That Talks Like You." They were embarrassed by their Eastern European accents and by their inability to write grammatical English for prospective clients and advertisers. The WASP ladies wanted professor Quentin Balston ("call me Cue-Ball") to write a history of their families; they said they were willing to pay for his services. The women had intense discussions with him before and after class.

As is customary in the rooms of higher education, even though they were permitted to move wherever they chose, the students always took the same seats. To Lew Chun's right was a weedy gentleman in his 40s who worked for the U.N. To his left was a flexible brunette with a throaty voice. A publishing executive, her paper said; Doubleday, somewhere uptown. During the breaks, Tina Ross smoked cigarettes in a holder and blinked slowly, trying to look like Audrey Hepburn and, to Lew Chun's untrained eyes, succeeding.

Tina wasn't Asian. In fact, she was Jewish, though like many at NYU — and indeed in the City — not observant. The Boy Chef immediately sensed that any attraction on his part would displease Shawn Lin. This immediately whetted his sexual appetite. It was not an easy romance; every time he approached, Tina would break away, and in the early goings, he never got close enough to inhale her perfume.

As the midterms approached, Myron, the hairier of the Perskys, with follicles in his ears and nose — everywhere but on his head — drew Lew Chun aside during a break. Myron put a paw on his shoulder. "You and this girl." He made a quick movement in Tina's direction. "You're *shtupping?*"

The Boy Chef had been in New York less than a month when he learned a handful of Yiddish words: *schmuck, schlep, yenta, shtick, chutzpah. Shtupping* he had not encountered before, but he instantly knew what was meant and replied no, not yet.

Myron shook his fuzzy head. "Here's the thing, Lew. You don't mind?"

"That's my name."

"To me, this is a familiar type, Miss Ross. To you, she's a shixa. You understand?"

"Not really."

"Of course," he said to himself. "Why should he know?" Back to Lew Chun: "A shixa is a girl who's not Jewish."

"But she *is* Jewish."

"To me, a Gentile girl, a Christian, that's a shixa, To a Chinaman, a Jewish girl is a shixa. Not your kind. Forbidden fruit. You're expected to marry a girl who looks like you, right?"

Lew Chun allowed that that was so.

"So stay away from Ross. You know what a Jewish girl makes for supper?"

"What?"

"Reservations."

"You know why Jewish girls like Chinese food?"

"Why?"

"Because 'wonton' is 'not now' spelled backwards."

He went on like that for 20 minutes. Before this conversation, Lew Chun had never heard anyone deride his own people. When he and Tina went out for coffee, he broached the subject. "Jews are like that," she told him. "It's like, if you insult us, we can be more insulting — and funnier in the process. They were probably telling jokes on themselves at Auschwitz."

"They weren't telling jokes at Auschwitz."

"You don't know that."

"I know what happens when the government draws blood. Nobody laughs; believe me."

"Maybe Asians don't. Jews are different."

"Yes, well, maybe you're more secure than we are."

"Secure?! You think Jews are secure? We walk on ice. One wrong step, back in the Volga."

It was like a Monty Python sketch: "I'm here for an argument." "No, you aren't." "Yes, I am." With Tina Ross, every subject turned into grounds for dispute — college, European and Asian history, personalities, entertainment, life.

As they quarreled, a question kept swimming up in Lew Chun's brain: Why did she mention a river in Russia? Was she working for the Russians in Brooklyn? Fear crept to the edges of his mind, a fear planted by the Colonel and his distrust of anything or anyone new. He shook it off, ashamed of his suspicions and determined to break free from Shawn Lin's influence, from his malignities and manipulations. He had to live his own life, not the one the Colonel had chosen for him. He went out in the hall and made a phone call. Upon returning, Lew Chun asked Tina Ross whether he could buy her dinner, no quid pro quo. Something in his invitation was persuasive; she went against her instincts and agreed.

The call had been a message to the maitre d': Do not recognize me. No special consideration. Treat us like any other couple on a downtown date. Spread the word.

And indeed, when the couple arrived, they were led to a very ordinary table. The waiters vied with one another for the straightest face. The Sancerre kept flowing, and by the fifth course, Tina allowed herself to mellow.

Lew Chun thought he saw some winks and nudges from the staff members, but with great effort, they maintained the charade all through the meal. As it drew to a close, the Boy Chef made his revelation: "This is my place."

Tina had no idea what he meant.

He put it another way. She still regarded him blankly. He told the waiter to bring the sous-chefs and the maitre d' and three other waiters. Her doubts began to melt. One of the men held a framed copy of the *Wall Street Journal* story with the Boy Chef's picture in the lower left-hand corner.

"Do you begin to believe me?" Lew Chen demanded.

She nodded and began to laugh and cry at the same time. After a few more drinks, he poured her into a cab. When they got to her place, she invited him in. They sat close together, and he spoke a bit about his father; she talked much more about hers. Adrian Ross was, in his daughter's words, a deadbeat dad — a term Lew Chun had never heard before.

Adrian and his wife were both souvenirs from the 1960s. He discovered women after he was married and cannabis after he was named a correspondent by a fellow geology professor at Santa Cruz. Adrian ran off with her and was now teaching math at a junior college in Taos. He never called or wrote. Tina's mother had dropped out of society and joined a multiracial commune in Tacoma, from which her daughter bolted when she was 16. Cora Ross regarded Tina as a bourgeois who had bought into the "war machine of Amerika." She did call and write on occasion, mainly to attack the greed and racism that had totally co-opted her daughter.

Lew Chun stayed all night — and the next morning and afternoon. Unwinding like nylon line off a fishing reel, he went into detail about his life in the Old Country and in the Gold Mountain. She cried again when he told her about the Square and the boat and the pigs and the stabbing. He didn't stop until he got to Myron Persky and his routine about Jewish girls. At that point, Tina allowed herself a disapproving smile. Then the smile disappeared. But then she broke into laughter again and started kissing him on the lips and working her way south.

He considered Mickey's advice a girl ago. What would Shawn Lin do? he asked himself. And immediately went the opposite way.

****

At closing time, C.C. appeared. The Colonel wanted to see the Boy Chef. Could it wait? It could not. Very well, Lew Chun was ready to confront the Colonel. He had gone over his declaration of independence many times, recited before Tina, emphasizing the need to maintain clean hands not only in the kitchen but in life, reminding his listener that gratitude was one thing and bondage another.

He and the Colonel did indeed have words that night, but Lew Chun never got to use his. When they arrived at Shawn Lin's office, a meeting was already underway, with Mickey, the daughters, the sons-in-law, Mr. Yuan, two of his employees, C.C. and some Asian men and women who were never introduced. A blackboard was set up on the side, but nothing had been written on it.

From behind the desk, the Colonel addressed the little crowd. "I'll make this simple." He stood up but signaled that the rest should remain seated. "Life has been good — very good. We were all prosperous. We were all in shape. *Were*. Because now we suddenly find ourselves in a life struggle." He made a wide hand gesture. "A conflict that could take all this away from us. Mr. Yuan will explain."

The elegant white-haired Chinese-American gentleman took the stage. "There is far too much money in substances to assume any one group has an exclusive. The Sicilians had great success for a long time. The Russians came along; they, too, enjoyed prominence before they ran into a wall."

He and Shawn Lin exchanged knowing looks, but nothing was said. Mr. Yuan resumed. "These were strong and brutal people, but they are being replaced by a group far stronger and more ruthless." He pointed to Jimmy, who took over.

"They are called the Cartagena cartel. We know about the Medellín and Cali cartels. They're bad enough. Cartagena is worse."

Jimmy approached the blackboard with a stick of chalk in hand. As he spoke, he wrote the assorted designations in big dusty letters.

"Their lowest workers are *halcone*s — falcons. These are street people who spot the police, know the safe drop-off points, the names of the customers."

Lew Chun nodded. He knew all about the falcons; back in Iowa, he was one of them.

"Next highest, *sicarios* — enforcers. They have the arsenal of weapons. They do the extortion, the kidnapping for ransom, the murders to keep people in line or intimidate the competition.

"Then come the *lugartenientes* — the first and second lieutenants. They discipline the enforcers, pay the salaries, distribute the enticements and administer the punishments.

"Last are the *capos*, the real commanders. They're the ones who plan the strategies, make out the hit lists, arrange to have people slain on the streets, on buses, in their homes."

Shawn Lin took over again. "The purpose of this meeting is to decide what to do next. With the Sicilians, it was not hard; the government did the job for us. The Russians we handled ourselves. But the Cartagenas — this is another story."

He grabbed an eraser and removed the Spanish words. "They grow the cocaine in their own country, and they refine it there — no importers needed. Very efficient, very ambitious. They're in Florida right now." He wrote MIAMI, TAMPA and ORLANDO in capital letters.

"We have information that they have big eyes for New York. They will be here soon. Some of their advance men are already in the City. And why not? It's a major market, and to them, it looks wide-open."

With sweeping glances around the room, the Colonel locked eyes with each of them in turn. "How do we stop these people? What sort of tactics do we use? What kind of weapons?" He pointed to the framed spear, called a guandao, and then at the long-handled lance, called a qiang. But his finger came to rest at the double-bladed killer, the jian. "I want ideas from you — jian ideas."

Removing his glasses had the desired effect; as he peered from one listener to another, each squirmed under his cold scrutiny. His expression of disgust was palpable, particularly when the Colonel's eyes briefly came to rest on Jimmy and then on Charlie before moving on. Who could trust his life, his career, to these irresolute underlings? If they were afraid of him, how could they rise to the challenge of the Cartagenas? Indeed of any competitor? Married to my blood but weak, scurrying creatures with eyes on the side like hunted animals, deer, squirrels, hares. We must be hunting animals with eyes in front like wolves and owls. Like...he thought he saw possibilities in the Boy

Chef, but perhaps not. Perhaps it was just a momentary thing, an inapt comparison with the sons-in-law. A female voice broke into his contemplation. Amy, the quiet daughter, was offering a suggestion: "We could hit them on their home ground. Assassinate one of their leaders right in front of spectators, in Colombia."

"Interesting," the Colonel said. "Audacious. But not for us. We don't play away games." He made a head gesture at the Boy Chef. "Hasn't the vaguest idea what I'm talking about. Doesn't watch sports." True enough on the face of it, but Lew Chun read the papers; he knew very well what an away game was.

The Colonel continued. "Cartagena has a big container port on the west and the Núñez Airport to the north. You would be lost down there on their turf. Chances are your body would turn up in the rainforest, eaten by predators and agave worms." A shudder passed through the audience.

Other options were offered. Florida was not exactly an away game; it was in the continental United States, no language barrier, as easy for Shawn Lin's operatives to penetrate as it was for the Cartagenas.

Interesting thought, the speaker replied, stressing the positive. Florida is a pleasant place — except in hurricane season. Smiles all around. And yet not always so pleasant. Grimaces all around.

"We would be tourists in the south of North America, just as we would be strangers in the north of South America. This would make us insecure and nervous. And insecure and nervous people make mistakes. That is a luxury we cannot afford."

Well, how about this? a voice proposed. We find out where the Cartagenas' advance party is, and we move in. Leave one or two alive to take the message back to their masters.

Much is to be said for this frontal approach, Shawn Lin responded in his military voice. Deadly force had its effect with the Russians. But very likely, that was because *they* were the disoriented ones. *They* were the strangers feeling their way on unfamiliar ground. And for how long would this intimidation be effective anyway? These groups are like dragon's teeth. Cut down 10 and a hundred may rise at some future time.

Ideas began to fly across the room, and each in turn was swatted down. Shawn Lin remained even-toned, pleasant, even deferential. But nothing pleased him. Some 40 notions came his way, and not one was deemed worthy of exploration.

The Boy Chef tried to keep himself to himself. It wasn't his affair, this business of Hispanic big shots muscling onto the Colonel's terrain. Yet almost involuntarily, he made his way to the blackboard, speaking as he stepped. "The solution is in front of us. What's the biggest organization, bigger than the snakeheads, bigger than the mob, bigger than the drug cartels?"

He scrawled three letters, USA, and then showed off the education he was receiving at NYU courtesy of their host. "Way back in the Jurassic era of crime, the feds put away Capone and they shut down Murder Inc.

"In our own lifetimes, the top hats in the mob were destroyed when the FBI tapped their phones and persuaded soldiers to cooperate for lighter sentences or for none at all."

Jimmy didn't get it. "What's your point?" he demanded. "You want us to join the Bureau, start wearing white shirts and camel's-hair coats?" He got a smattering of laughs.

Lew Chun ignored him. "We can make the feds work for us. When they come around, we act terrified. We agree to work with them. We become unpaid agents."

Charlie asked, "And why should they listen to us?"

"Because we portray ourselves as tributaries and the Cartagenas as the big river. We give the FBI everything they want — in exchange for being left alone to peddle our two-bit hash. We spill everything we know about the Cartagenas, where they live, where they sell, who they are, top to bottom."

Jimmy enjoyed playing the mockingbird. Winking at his colleagues, he aped the Boy Chef's overenthusiastic timbre. "And we just pick up the pieces, that it?"

"That's it," answered Lew Chun genially, as if the shot had bounced off without leaving a dent. It had not, and he made a mental note for future reference.

"What are we, Lew Chun, the Sanitation Department?" Charlie joined in.

"No negative responses," Shawn Lin reminded everyone in the room. "Besides, there's something to what he says. The government does a lot of trading. Sharks for tuna. Happens all the time. They do it with drug dealers, gambling, contraband." He looked directly at Lew Chun. "Talk to us. What's your proposal?"

"I don't have a proposal," he said. "It was just a…notion."

"Just a…notion." Now it was the Colonel's turn to play the mockingbird. Furtive smiles all around. "Well, you're going to have some more notions, and you're going to have them tonight." Shawn Lin looked up. "This meeting is over," he declared. "Tomorrow, same time, same place." They all filed out, except for Lew Chun. Intuitively, he knew better than to join them.

The Colonel sat silent at his desk after they were gone. Minutes slid by while he made indecipherable notes in Mandarin. At last, he looked up. "Two things. Whatever the girl believes, you are as much a part of this organization as Jimmy or Charlie or their wives or C.C. or me."

The girl. Of course Shawn Lin would know all about Tina, Lew Chun realized. Her background, her address, her shoe size. Her bra size, come to that. Yet no scene was made about her ethnicity. It was as if the fact that she wasn't Chinese had no bearing on all this.

"As long as she's not working against us."

"And how do you know she isn't, Colonel?"

"Trust me." As if the Boy Chef had a choice. Fussing with papers on his desk. Then: "Also, I have some news from Beijing — something you need to know."

"About Mother."

"Exactly."

"Is she safe? Is she well?"

"She's in a village 300 kilometers from Beijing. Being cared for."

"Does she know I'm all right?"

"She knows."

"Can I call her?"

"We will get to that. First we speak of the Cartagenas, about your strategy."

"Sir, there is no strategy. I was only thinking aloud."

"Think some more." A darkness spread across Shawn Lin's face. The voice assumed a new edge, like the blade of the jian. "How do the feds get involved?"

"Well…" Talking fast. "One of your people could find out their official location."

"We already know where that is. 26 Federal Plaza. Not far."

"Somebody could go there, ask to see the head investigator."

"You think they'll see some Chink off the streets? Grow up, Boy Chef."

So it was back to that. Lew Chun tried to put some iron in his comeback. "Very well, he doesn't see No. 1. Could be he sees No. 2, No. 3, No. 12, whatever. And could be he delivers the message."

Shawn considered that for a while.

"And could be you're the messenger."

"Could be."

"Except you know shit about the Cartagenas."

Lew Chun faked a look of disappointment. "Someone else then."

"No," he responded. "You. Only you."

There was a brief pause — and then matters changed forever as Lew Chun slid from observer to insider, from wary innocent to true disciple. He made a token protest: "You're right, Colonel. I don't know shit about the Cartagenas. I don't know the details. I don't really know anything."

And got the answer he wanted. "Ah, that's the beauty of it," Shawn Lin pointed out. "You're ignorant." He stood up and stretched. "Lew Chun, for this task, all you need is survival skills. And time — lots of time. You have no shortage of these things."

****

According to Shawn Lin, the Cartagenas were like the Russians — Neanderthals with a love of glittering objects. That translated into expensive cars, dwellings and women. Yet there was a difference between them. Properly handled, that difference would save the Chinatown operation and all its employees and operatives. Because unlike the guys from Brighton Beach, the South Americans were headed by bilingual smoothies, gentlemen who called you amigo and did a lot of touching your arm for reassurance purposes and hugging when they said adios. In the past, the Cartagenas had slain and plundered recklessly, sometimes bringing whole armies down on their necks. They had killed many and bribed more. But that was the day before yesterday. Today they thirsted for respect.

Accordingly, Shawn Lin instructed his adjutant to play the opponents' game, answering their questions courteously, broadcasting a malaise but not quite a mistrust. The Boy Chef was to be simultaneously fervent and wary — listening to all they said, learning whatever he could and exhibiting a barely discernible restlessness and ambition, as if he were chafing at the restrictions his job demanded.

Ten days later, the first Cartagena came into the restaurant. He was thin, stylish, outfitted in a Louis Vuitton black silk jacket with silver buttons, a blue shirt, a red tie, custom jeans, Lucchese boots. He ate alone. When he finished, he handed the headwaiter a card and requested an audience with the proprietor. Pablo Vélez, Insurance & Real Estate, was ushered into Lew Chun's office. He refused a drink, sat only when bidden and spent the next five minutes praising the cuisine, the ambiance, the décor and the efficient, polite help. The Boy Chef sat meekly while Vélez raved on. When the unction got thick enough to grease a garbage truck, he said, "Señor, I am already insured. I rent my apartment and the restaurant property, and I have no wish to own real estate."

The patron agreed. "Sir, both you and I know that I am not here to sell you anything. The business card is a cover. My real business is import-export. I deal the same sort of goods as your employer."

"Then perhaps you should talk to him."

"*Tristemente*, your *jefe* is impossible to get to. I am informed that you can give him a message."

Lew Chun inquired softly, "And who will this message be from?"

"From *my* jefe."

"And may I have his name?"

"He prefers to be anonymous."

This demanded a stonier reply. "I don't think that will do, Señor Vélez. I'm sure you know the name of Shawn Lin."

"Ah. I see." He hesitated and then appeared to give in. "Very well. My man is Ruben Molina."

Lew Chun knew this information was correct.

"And what is his message?"

Pablo Vélez leaned back and spread his hands. "It is like this. We are not very different people, the Latino and the Oriental. We have the same kind of clients, the same sort of enemies. We have no wish to fight; we wish to share. The pie is large enough for all."

Lew Chun knew this to be total fiction. He nodded nonetheless. "And this is what Señor Molina has to say?"

"Not quite."

"Ah. Not quite."

"You see," Vélez elaborated, "Ruben Molina wishes to emulate."

"Emulate." The amusement could not quite be hidden from the speaker.

The spiel went on undiminished. "Your boss, he has a legitimate side." He gestured to the walls. "Lew Chun's Pan Asian and who knows what else? Well, we, too, would like to open our own place, a South American cuisine, high-end, with many exotic entrees and a great chef and sommelier."

"And what is to stop you?"

"A lack of experience. We have so little information of the food service business." The salesman reached in his shirt pocket and consulted a list of handwritten items. "We require advice about budgets, waitstaff, linens, glassware, liquor licenses, sanitary inspections, garbage disposal — all the things that you know so well."

"And what would be our reward for this advice?"

Vélez was relaxed now; he thought he had heard an unspoken "yes" woven into the reply. "We can provide you with the better product — and at great discounts. We can offer also fresh markets. There are new clients all the time. We cannot handle them all. There is much room for two organizations in this city of opportunity."

The Boy Chef ached to laugh in the man's conniving face. There was room for two organizations like there was room for two heads on the same neck. But the assignment was only to listen and to nod thoughtfully. When the sales pitch ended, Lew Chun promised to convey the information to his *jefe* and, putting on a long face, said he must now part from his new friend and return to work.

With elaborate courtesy, the señor said he understood, recited the telephone number on the business card and made ready to leave. Lew Chun escorted him to the front door. A minute later, five occupants of a round table rose and exited. The Pablo Vélez bodyguards. They paid by credit card but left an extremely generous tip in cash.

****

Lew Chun had not overlooked Gia Tseng, but apparently she had overlooked him. She had completely vanished from his orbit, and he knew why. She was, after all, a student with courses to complete and papers to submit. But that was not the main reason. She stayed away because the Boy Chef had told her outright the most recent time they had met that he was not going to furnish the material for a Pulitzer Prize and that he had become involved with another young lady.

So it was something of an astonishment to see her pop up one evening. The table had been reserved for a Mr. Frank Alba. (So that was his name.) A few weeks ago, the Boy Chef's line about seeing someone else was pure fakery, a way of getting rid of her according to instructions from above. Now the excuse was real. He wished Tina were present as proof. No such luck.

They invited Lew Chun to join them. He wanted to protest that it was a busy night, that he couldn't get away just now. But he had learned that journalists are stubborn creatures; they would make a habit of showing up until he sat at their table. Better to get the unpleasant business over with now.

"Thank you for coming." He ordered three glasses of Dom Perignon.

Gia made a token fuss — "Champagne, no less. You didn't have to do that."

"No, I didn't."

They exchanged a look. Then Gia speculated: "You must want something,"

"I do. I want you to stop being reporters when you come in here."

"'Check your hat, coat and vocation, ma'am'?"

"If you wish."

"I don't wish."

He grinned pleasantly. Gia wasn't getting anything out of him, and she knew it. But then Frank took over. "I know Pablo Vélez was here. He saw you."

"A lot of people saw me."

"He saw you about setting up his own restaurant, yes?"

"You're doing the talking, Mr. Alba."

Lew Chun could see he didn't like being addressed as "Mr." That put a partition between them. But Frank Alba was not to be stopped that easily. "Pablo Vélez also presented possibilities," he said. "Markets, cheaper product and so on."

Lew Chun tried to look inscrutable.

Gia broke in. "Lew Chun — please, *please* listen. Don't do this to yourself."

She tried to read his face. He gave her the kind of bewildered look a cat gives a juggler.

Frank Alba resumed: "Let me give you a little background. My name sounds Italian, but it's Spanish. I was born and raised in Carta.

These *caballeros*, these operators, they're people I grew up with. The head of things, Ruben Molina, his father was my teacher. He comes from an educated family. He went south, got involved with criminals. He became an animal. But Ruben is a smart animal and a hungry one. He will eat your boss the way you eat an egg roll."

"Well then," Lew Chun returned blithely, "the thing is hopeless. Have a good evening."

Frank Alba realized he had misplayed the meeting. "Wait." He grabbed Lew Chun's sleeve — and immediately pulled back. "Gia and I, we're not working with the Cartas. We're working against them. Look, Ruben, he thinks I'm a CPA. Harmless. He talks to me, sooner or later something will slip out. We use that, along with whatever you can give us, the sky falls. You don't get touched. We don't even mention you."

"And Shawn Lin?"

"We can't protect everyone. But he'll be given a light sentence, two years, three at the most. Meantime, you become the downtown prince."

"Meantime, I have a kitchen to look after."

The Boy Chef looked directly at the pair, shifting from Frank Alba to Gia. "*Under the spreading chestnut tree, I sold you and you sold me.*" He was pleased at their puzzlement. As he departed, he threw a last remark over his shoulder: "I think I better tell Shawn Lin about this meeting before he learns it from someone else."

****

But the Colonel already knew. Whether he had a hidden microphone or spies on the staff, which was more likely, Lew Chun never learned. What he did discover was that Shawn Lin had the book on Frank Alba, as well as on Gia Tseng. Those connections to the South American hustlers were not an invention. Frank really had gone to school with the Big Cartagena.

In Shawn Lin's view, however, that only made things worse. For Frank was not only a certified public accountant but also a forensic auditor. If he got some hard facts, some inside intelligence, he and Gia could wreck everything — throw the Colonel's plans on the floor like a crate of eggs, bring the feds down on all of them, not just the South Americans. Result: bankruptcy, disgrace, a trial, prison. And, it went without saying, a Pulitzer.

For the first time, Lew Chun could see some confidence draining out of Shawn Lin.

"Something must be done," he told the Boy Chef. "Which means you have to do something. You have any ideas?"

"Not really."

"Well, I do. You request to meet this Molina. You insist on it. Say you have something for him — something that could destroy all of us."

"He won't see me. To him, I'm nobody."

"Right on the first count, wrong on the second. He will indeed refuse to see you one-on-one. But you're not nobody. He'll send the same delegate." He consulted his notebook. "Pablo Vélez. And you can tell him."

"Tell him what?"

"That Frank Alba is nosing around, trying to find evidence about our operations, that the CPA title is just a cover, that he's selling us out, all of us, the Hispanics and the Chinese."

"And if they believe me?"

"They'll know what to do. I would."

Accordingly, a message was left with Vélez's secretary, a contralto with a Colombian accent like his. Lew Chun waited for the response. Two days later, it came.

This time, he and Vélez convened at a place of the Cartagenian's choosing — a jumping Puerto Rican venue on West 14th Street. It was noisy, and the food looked plentiful and nourishing, but they weren't there for the entrees. The sound provided a cover for Lew Chun's information. He confided that Shawn Lin was ready to cooperate — in a limited manner.

"Limited how? What does this mean in English?" Vélez demanded over the din.

"It means I show you a breakdown of costs for running a restaurant, give you some points about real estate. Manhattan might not be the right place for you. Maybe start in one of the outer boroughs."

"We did not come from Cartagena to open an eatery in Brooklyn."

"It's your call," Lew Chun replied in what he hoped was a combination of amiability and toughness. "Another thing."

"Go on."

"Shawn Lin says no prying."

"What does that mean?"

"You got a guy nosing around my place. We don't like it."

"We got no guy doing nothing."

"You ever heard of Frank Alba?"

"*Maricón.* Little faggot hangs around the business office. He's nothing. Went to school with my boss. Molina feels sorry for him. Alba talks big, knows zip, zero, nada."

End of subject. Lew Chun attempted to reintroduce the subject of the CPA, but Vélez wouldn't hear of it. In the end, they agreed to meet at the same Puerto Rican spot next Monday. Lew Chun would hand over some financial records of the Pan Asian. These would give an idea of costs and taxes and the other details of maintaining a restaurant in the City. Such a venture is expensive, he warned; then again, Pablo Vélez's *jefe* would surely have deep pockets.

****

The phone rang at midnight 10 days later. Lew Chun had just arrived home and thought it was Philip Lau calling to remind him of a kitchen obligation. But it was Gia, and she was screaming. "You son of a bitch! You motherfucker! You murderer! He's dead! He's dead, and you cocksuckers did it!"

She cried on in that fashion, defamatory and loud. He put the phone where he could hear the music but not the lyrics. By and by, her screams dissolved into uncontrolled weeping.

"Gia, tell me what happened. Go slow."

"Frank Alba was stabbed to death tonight."

"My God,"

"Yeah, right," she snuffled.

"Where was this?"

"Near the Chelsea Piers. They're reporting it as a gay-on-gay crime. He was supposed to have been killed by a French sailor, someone from off the ships."

"And you don't believe it."

"You're goddamn right I don't. Frank was in a committed relationship — with a *librarian*, for Christ's sake. He wasn't a cruiser. He hated those people. It was a setup. He was murdered by your kind."

"My kind doesn't have people killed." Lew Chun found himself choking on the words. Yet he couldn't believe that Shawn Lin would have Frank Alba iced. The man wasn't a threat; he was a nonentity *pretending* to be a threat. And then, as he tried to mollify Gia, it all came to him. Lew Chun had mentioned Frank as an irritant, a pebble in the shoe. That was enough for the South Americans. They decided to show some muscle in New York. He listened to Gia's wails, responding with sympathetic monosyllables until she was too exhausted to go on.

As Gia had said, the media treated Frank Alba's death as a sex-related murder. He was portrayed as a troubled cruiser, and his killer as a foreign unknown. The police called in a sketch artist; he made some drawings based on street scuttlebutt. A couple of arrests were made, but the evidence turned out to be inconclusive. The accused *marins* were allowed to return to the Aquitaine. The battleship weighed anchor two days later.

It took almost a month for Lew Chun to get face time with Shawn Lin. He was prepared for evasions and denials, not for outrage. Shawn Lin swore lengthily and stridently that he had nothing to do with the killing; the room seemed to shake as he shouted, "My hands are as clean as a surgeon's! So are yours! I mean, come on, dropping a name at a lunch, who knew the Cartagenas would reply with violence? *If* they were the ones who ordered the hit. Maybe Alba *was* the victim of a queer crime after all. Ever think of that?"

There were times when Shawn Lin thought he had missed his calling. He believed he would have made a great defense lawyer. For decades now, he had negotiated with upright authorities and outright scoundrels, high rollers and lowlifes, and he had always won them over. Sometimes this was accomplished with bribes or threats or worse, but far more often, it was with his unique amalgam of acumen and charm. Here the Colonel had started with theatrical wrath, but now, as his argument gained force and momentum, he gave the Boy Chef a forgiving smile. Why are we arguing, was the subtext, when we're on the same side? He could see Lew Chun was visibly wavering, wanting, *needing* to believe his benefactor regardless of the evidence. Shawn Lin ended the summation before the jury of one could change its mind.

****

Woody Allen and Soon-Yi Previn. John Lennon and Yoko Ono. And switching sides, Bruce Lee and Linda Emery and Yo-Yo Ma and Jill Horner. Mixed Asian and Caucasian, and not a cataclysm in sight.

Lew Chun collected items about these mixed-race couples when, after a year of appeals and dates and experimental weekends together, he found himself getting very serious about his Jewish shixa. He listed her liabilities, which were few, and her assets, which were bounteous. He planned to enter them in evidence when he saw Shawn Lin. But when the Colonel summoned him, the subject was not Tina Ross. Not initially. Topic A was genetics.

"Ever heard of DNA?" He answered his own question before Lew Chun could stutter a reply. "Deoxyribonucleic acid. All our traits, all our characteristics are in there. We're smart, we Asians — maybe too smart. We don't want to make the mistake the Jews made."

He waited for that to register. "Celebrity is intoxicating. My fault, building you up. Nothing we can do about that now. But I want you out of the papers, out of the scene. Take care of business. Run the restaurant. Get married—"

Lew Chun leapt in. "To Tina?"

"Why not to Tina?"

"But she isn't Chinese."

"Lew Chun. I have two daughters and two sons-in-law. I have you. I have a small, loyal Asian staff. That's all the DNA I need. Who you take as a bride is unimportant, as long as she stays in the background."

"In other words, out of the scene."

"Those are the other words."

One more put-down. Lew Chun prepared to leave.

"Now," the Colonel said, "you want to talk about visiting your mother?"

He waited for a reaction — gratitude, bewilderment, something. But the young man stayed impassive.

"I have worked out a way to get you into the Republic," he continued. "And better still, I have worked out an exit strategy."

"What's the catch, Colonel?" Lew Chun demanded impatiently.

"There is a quid pro quo, if that's what you mean. Complicated, but I think we can pull it off — if you cooperate."

The Boy Chef had taken enough dictation. Maybe later, he heard himself say. He made a curt farewell and left. C.C. saw him rushing out and went to the Colonel.

"Anything wrong? You want me to follow him?"

"No need," said Shawn Lin in a calm, amused voice. "He'll be back."

A half-hour later, Lew Chun, after finding Tina's home, called on her uninvited, made love to her on the couch and proposed. She called her mother. It was hard to tell whether Mrs. Ross was pro, con or undecided. Bride and groom were married quietly at City Hall the following month — no relatives, no announcement, no ceremony.

That was sufficient for Lew Chun, but Tina insisted on going to the Colonel for his blessing. "He's your boss, and he's your cousin," she reminded her new husband. "You know what Yiddish Alzheimer's is? It's when you forget everything except a grudge. Don't do that. Be Chinese for a change." Lew Chun let her drag him to Shawn Lin's without an appointment. They were ushered in immediately. It was almost as if Tina had called in advance.

The Colonel was joyous, embracing them both. There was no hint of past unpleasantness. He called for Champagne and, when C.C. fetched it, toasted the couple, insisting on throwing a party in their honor.

Lew Chun remonstrated: "You just said I wasn't to attract attention. I was supposed to go back into the woodwork, run the Pan Asian unobtrusively, stay out of the media."

"That's precisely what you need to do," he responded. "Eventually. But if this marriage doesn't have a celebration, all that happens is more buzz, more inquiring journalists, more prying noses. This way, we have a big blast, inviting everyone, and then it's over. Trust me on this."

"*'Trust me on this,*'" Lew Chun repeated when he and Tina were alone. "Like I would trust him to tell me the weather when they were selling umbrellas on street corners."

"Oh, give it a rest, darling," she told him. "Let the man show off. He's proud of you. He loves you. Can't you see that?" She ran her knuckles through his black hair. "Boy Chef can't see anything."

"I see you. That's enough for me."

They went on a brief honeymoon to the Mohonk Mountain House in Ulster County, about two hours from the city. The building was once the property of a wealthy Quaker family, catering to the rich. Now it served anyone with enough money to afford two adjoining rooms with a fireplace — and every suite in the place had one. That weekend, the house was playing host to a convention of crossword puzzle addicts.

The newlyweds sat in the last row, watching the competition. Three crossword champions, two puffy young men and a thin middle-aged lady, stood before the audience. A man with a microphone moved among the aisles. When onlookers raised a hand, he went to them and allowed them to submit a term. The contestant had to identify it before the other competitors did.

"Maldives," said a white-haired woman sitting in the aisle in a wheelchair.

"An island nation of 26 atolls in the Indian Ocean," said the thin lady.

"Correct." The man with the microphone moved on.

"Cotard's syndrome," shouted a teenager in one of the front rows.

"A mental disease," answered the younger of the male contestants. "The sufferer believes that she or he is dead or imaginary."

"Right on the money," said the emcee.

Tina tugged at Lew Chun's sleeve. "These people know everything."

"We'll see about that," he whispered. Then he stood up and called out, "Hell money."

"Chinese spirit currency," chirped the third cruciverbalist, "to be used in the afterlife. Except it's all recent; the Chinese never heard of hell until the missionaries introduced them to it."

These people *did* know everything, Lew Chun acknowledged over dinner by the fire — Diana Wynyard, Spanky McFarland, movie stars from more than a half-century ago; the names of Alaskan bridges; who really wrote Purcell's *Trumpet Voluntary*; the life span of a flamingo; and just about anything else one could name. But it was hell money that got him. How could a *gweilo* know about such a thing?

There was plenty of hell money at the wedding party. The affair was quite a public occasion, especially for a man who was supposed to vanish into the kitchen and become anonymous. Tina's colleagues at Doubleday attended, as did her mother (declaring to Tina in a stage whisper that it was good she married out of her imperialist race, but couldn't it have been a Black Panther?).

The entire Pan Asian staff, to a man and woman, was on hand. The truth was Lew Chun had no intimates, only colleagues, and the employees served as stand-ins. Philip Lau ran the occasion with the smoothness of a Beltway host. He saw to it that each guest received a walletful of phony currency, and there were many recipients. All of Chinatown seemed to be in attendance, people Lew Chun had seen on the streets or in the restaurant but whom he had never actually met, police brass in and out of uniform, columnists, TV anchors, camera crews, children, parents, grandparents, Asian, African-American, white, Hispanic.

The last category was the one he found the most compelling. Shawn Lin had invited the Cartagenas, and five of them showed up. Three were *toros* — large musclemen with foreheads by electrolysis. Ruben Molina spotted the Colonel, and his guards forced a wedge through the crowd, bringing their boss to meet his host. The two men shook hands with graceless formality, like middleweights before round one.

But Molina's deadpan lasted less than 10 seconds. His bulls nodded to him, and he to them. Satisfied that he was secure on this foreign turf, the *jefe* assumed his cordial persona, patting Shawn Lin on the shoulder, grabbing his arm, congratulating him on the lavishness of the affair and, at the same time, praising his good taste in furnishings, food and company. In turn, Shawn Lin pressed drinks, food and hell money on his Cartagena guests. The duplicity was thick enough to walk on.

Even so, each man got what he wanted. No hostile remarks were exchanged; no threatening body language expressed. Smiles and consumption of food were the order of the day, along with a surprisingly modest intake of wine and liquor. No one misbehaved; the plainclothes security force had nothing to do, and nobody stayed late. Lew Chun and Tina even got Cora to her plane in plenty of time. She had thoughtfully brought her suitcase to the party so that she wouldn't have to go back to the bourgeois suite at the Plaza they had paid for.

The couple returned to an empty restaurant in the hands of a cleaning crew, vacuuming, sweeping up, deodorizing. Yet something remained: a strange aura that reminded Lew Chun of something one of the history teachers had discussed — the Phoney War, which occurred from 1939 to 1940, before the real one broke out and the massacres began.

****

There are many shortcuts that keep a restaurant afloat — and in demand. As instructed, the Boy Chef disclosed a great many of them to Pablo Vélez. In return, he received the names and addresses of drug wholesalers in seven states. The Carta had no notes and took none. He recited all of his contacts from memory as Lew Chun entered them into a ledger, the information disguised in a simple code. Lew Chun knew very well what Vélez was doing; if the feds ever got hold of the evidence, it would be in the Chinaman's handwriting. The Cartagenians would have clean fingers. Smart.

The information was relayed to Shawn Lin. He had Charlie and Jimmy check it out. All was as promised; the product was first-rate, the price cut-rate. Everything seemed to be working according to plan. And then came the evening when Philip Lau called in sick. He had cracked a molar chewing an ice cube. A root canal had acted up. The endodontist would take care of it tomorrow morning. Interesting excuse — one that Lew Chun had never heard before. It was too late to find a substitute. The Boy Chef was forced to do three jobs — administrating, cooking and, when an assistant to the mayor and his party arrived late, explaining the wide choice of appetizers and entrees. He retired to his office to notify Tina; it was going to be one of those 3 a.m. closings. When he looked up, he saw Shawn Lin in the doorway. Charlie and Jimmy were flanking him. C.C. stood in the background.

"Philip," he said flatly.

"What about Philip?" Lew Chun asked.

"How well do you know him?"

"I don't know him at all. He was here when I arrived. I assumed you hired him. Why ask me?"

"I did hire him. He came highly recommended. I didn't check his credentials closely, and neither did anyone else. Didn't need to, we thought. He worked well, went home to his family in Queens, never objected to overtime, never asked for a raise."

"Sounds ideal."

"Too ideal. I assume he never gave you any trouble, either."

"None."

"Well, he's about to."

"Meaning what?"

"We have been watching Philip Lau for over a month. Most of the time when he's finished work, he takes the GG to Queens. But on Tuesdays, he takes a detour. He gets off at Jackson Heights."

Shawn Lin waited to see whether the Boy Chef was impressed. Satisfied, he resumed. "At Jackson Heights, Philip Lau goes to Rensalier's jewelry store on Steinway Street. This is known to us as an unmarked office of the FBI."

"How do you know—"

"Never mind how."

"You think he's an agent?"

"More likely an informant."

"Are you sure? He seems so—"

"They always 'seem so' — so hardworking, so willing to please. That's what makes them so dangerous."

"What do you think he's told them?"

"My guess is not very much. Otherwise, we would have been raided by now. He is probably stringing them along, seeing how high he can raise the ante."

"So what are you going to do about it?"

"It's what are *you* doing about it?"

"Me? I don't know how to handle this."

"I do." He consulted a paper. "On Friday night, Philip is scheduled to close up. You will be on the premises when he does."

"But Tina and I—"

"You will be on the premises when he does."

"And if I am?"

"You will confront him with the evidence."

"What evidence? I haven't got any evidence."

Shawn Lin handed Lew Chun a blue folder. "You have now." The folder contained six photographs, all of Philip Lau going into or leaving Rensalier's. As Lew Chun examined them, further instructions were issued.

"When Philip returns to work, you will notify us. That night, after hours, as you and he are going over the receipts, you will introduce the subject of informing. He will, of course, deny everything. You will show him the pictures."

"And then what?"

In turn, the Colonel gently tapped the faces of his sons-in-law. "We will take care of the rest."

****

"The tooth doctor, that man is a genius." Philip Lau pulled back his lower lip to show the Boy Chef a gleaming molar. "Pain completely disappear." He promptly went to work in the kitchen, humming, tirelessly preparing and cooking dishes for the next six hours. Not until the customers and the staff had gone did Lew Chun hand the puzzled chef the blue folder.

Philip Lau scrutinized its contents. "So? Proves nothing."

"Not according to Shawn Lin. He says you're an informant for the feds."

"The which?"

"The FBI — Federal Bureau—"

"I know what FBI is."

"Well, Shawn Lin says—"

"He says shit," Philip protested. "Doctored photographs. Fakes."

The chef's increasing volume and the quick, defensive movement of his hands gave him away. Now Lew Chun had to keep him on the premises until the militia arrived — C.C. and some like-minded thugs, he guessed. What they would do to Philip he preferred not to know.

"I quit," Philip Lau said suddenly. "I'm leaving. I don't want to work for you anymore, Boy Chef. I'm twice the cook you are. Three times."

Lew Chun tried to block the exit, backing toward the stainless steel meat locker. "If you believed that, why did you stay?"

"Let me go."

"Answer the question. Why did you stay here if you resented me so much?"

"Pay was good."

"Pay is still good. How come you want to leave?" Lew Chun demanded in a louder voice, stalling as best he could. *Where the hell were C.C. and his boys?*

Philip Lau moved forward. "Step aside."

As he did, it came to Lew Chun that the classes he had been taking were all about culture. Not one session with a martial arts instructor. Shawn Lin didn't think that was important; there were trained security guards and police, on- and off-duty, to deal with malefactors. Except there were no trained security guards now, no off-duty police — only the Boy Chef and a man who could bring down Shawn Lin and all that went with him.

With the exception of a pharmacy, no place has more deadly material than a kitchen. Philip Lau's eyes searched for a weapon as the Boy Chef backed up. He grabbed an eight-inch Global cleaver. It caught the gleam of the bluish fluorescent lights as he advanced with great confidence, which he had for good reason; with this very steel, he had dismembered many a heifer in five minutes.

Lew Chun inched backward, wildly searching for a knife he might use in his defense. Nothing was near, and he knew that if he turned his back and ran, Philip Lau would throw the cleaver and split him in two. He reached the door of the meat locker, felt for the handle and yanked it open with all his strength, magnified by adrenaline. It smashed against Philip Lau's face. The sudden crunch and the painful exhalation were the noises of ruin.

Lew Chun pulled back the door. Philip Lau was disoriented but still clinging to the cleaver. Once more, Lew Chun pulled the door back and slammed it against his potential killer. Philip Lau groaned harshly, dropped the cleaver and went down, half-conscious, wavering. Groaning at the bulk, Lew Chun shoved him into the locker and slammed the door shut. There was no handle on the inside. The semiconscious butcher would be stuck there freezing until Lew Chun released him, and that would not happen until help came. He thumbed the numbers for Shawn Lin on his bulky new cellular phone.

And then something unforeseen occurred — something the Boy Chef could never overlook or forgive.

****

Seconds after Lew Chun punched in the numbers, steps sounded in the distance. Seconds after that, in walked C.C., with Jimmy and Charlie in his slipstream. Behind them: Shawn Lin.

"We had your back." C.C.'s rolling bass was meant to be assuring but reminded Lew Chun of wind in a tunnel.

"Some back. He could have killed me."

"Well, he didn't," Shawn Lin said. "Stop feeling sorry for yourself. There are a thousand things to be done."

"Like getting Philip Lau out of the locker before he freezes to death."

"Au contraire. He's going to give new meaning to the phrase 'out cold.'" The Colonel gave a disturbing, mirthless laugh. At that moment, the Boy Chef could visualize himself in the locker alongside the man he had, quite by accident, defeated.

"You're going to have to exit New York for a while, Lew Chun."

"Philip Lau stays in the locker until he freezes to death, that it?"

Shrugs all around.

"And when the FBI misses their informant, they'll come here and start digging around. Instead of one missing chef, there'll be two. They'll come looking for me, and that'll take the heat off you."

"Don't be absurd. They'll assume you and Philip were both done away with. And they'll come after me."

"So why don't *you* get out of town?"

"There are good reasons. Go home. Tell Tina you'll be away for a while. Our cover story is you're going back to the People's Republic — to see your mother."

"And am I?"

"You are."

"How will I get there?"

"It will be arranged."

"How long will I be gone?"

"I don't know."

"You have to know."

"Don't ask so many questions."

"Come on, Colonel. I need to know. Tina needs to know."

"Very well. A month, perhaps."

"A month."

Darkness spread across three faces. Shawn Lin demanded, "Boy Chef, will you simply do as instructed for a change?"

"Or won't you?" Charlie asked.

"Do I have a choice?"

Jimmy gestured to the locker. That was the other choice, he indicated wordlessly.

Lew Chun did as instructed.

****

Tina Ross Chun understood why he had to make the long and hazardous journey. His mother was ill, the messages said. She might be dying. What she couldn't appreciate was how long her new husband would be away from home.

"A month?" she kept asking between crying spells. "A whole month?"

Each time, he said, "Worst-case scenario. My guess is 10 days, two weeks at the most." And each time, he knew he was spinning a yarn to keep her calm. The length of the sojourn was going to be determined by Shawn Lin, not by the Chinese government or the American one — and certainly not by Lew Chun.

"How will you get there? You can't just fly into Beijing."

"There are ways."

"Are you going to tell me what they are?"

"No."

"Why not?"

"People are going to come around asking questions. It's better that you don't know. That way, you won't have to lie."

She dug in. What kind of people were going to come around? Criminals? Cops? G-men? Lew Chun said he really didn't know. Shawn Lin—

"Shawn Lin. The Colonel. That wrongo."

"That wrongo pays for everything, the restaurant, the apartment — our lives, if you want to know the truth."

"Yeah, right, an apartment for two, except only one person is going to live in it, a restaurant you're supposed to run but you won't see for a month. Newlyweds that just about get the bed warm, and he has to go — to China, no less."

These exchanges resulted in long bouts of heated quiet, followed by Lew Chun's pleas for understanding, followed by a small thaw and brief, intense lovemaking, before the painful routine began anew.

So it went until a call came in with explicit details. Lew Chun was to leave in the middle of the week in the middle of the night. By that time, worn-out by arguments, he was almost glad to leave, get this misadventure over with so he could reclaim his life. A Town Car double-parked at the specified time and place. The Boy Chef emerged with a small overnight bag — the only luggage he was permitted. Toothbrush, shaving kit, underwear, shirts, pants, socks and nothing else. He would be met at his destination by a man with ID and instructions. From the car window, he waved farewell to a window in the apartment. No reaction. Then Tina appeared, but only to wave indifferently. She gave her husband a hurt expression for the thousandth time and withdrew into the dark.

C.C. was driving. Lew Chun expected him to go to JFK. Instead, they went further east than that, cutting through the dark for three hours, losing traffic until they arrived at a boat basin. A sign said they were two miles from Amagansett, at the eastern end of Long Island.

Driver and passenger hadn't talked much in the car and didn't speak at all as they waited on the darkened shore. Then, without warning, C.C. started to move the car onto a pier. As the sky lightened, there surfaced the oddest ship either man had ever seen, even in films about fantastic seagoing vessels.

It was not exactly a submarine. Up close, the object appeared to be more like a narrow steel boat in the shape of a tube, but with two hatches on top. C.C. approached the captain. He was a gruff unshaven Hispanic man in jeans, a denim shirt and a dirty white ship's officer's hat of no known navy. He and C.C. spoke. Money changed hands. The captain motioned Lew Chun aboard. They were not introduced. C.C. turned around, waved backward and walked to his car. The Boy Chef was on his own.

As soon as he found a seat, the hatches were closed, and then the ship went below the surface. Tiny portholes revealed nothing but dark water. It occurred to Lew Chun as the sea closed around him that rich or poor, all his life had been spent in confinement — in a school, in a restaurant, in a plane, in a slaughterhouse, in another restaurant. He had become familiar with cities, but he was ignorant about nature. About the world, he acknowledged bitterly. Not because it was incomprehensible but because he hadn't been curious enough. And now he was paying for that detachment. It was as these events, one after another, were happening to someone else, someone experiencing his last day on earth.

There was hardly any room to breathe, let alone turn around. The only light came from dim battery-powered lanterns on shelves. Five other sailors, all Hispanic, sat on both sides of Lew Chun. They were as grungy as their boss. One of them, a fat sweaty seaman who reeked of onions, spoke broken English.

"You sell?" he inquired.

Lew Chun told him no.

"You buy?"

"Not that, either."

"Then why you here?"

The captain yelled at the underling in an unfamiliar Spanish dialect, very different from the way the kitchen help talked to one another. He turned to Lew Chun and spoke in English.

"You are aboard a narco-sub." He saw that the Chinaman had no idea what he was talking about. "We take cocaine powder — yayo — from Ecuador to wherever."

"Under the water?"

"Better than *over* the water. This here is not a real submarine. We just duck under the waves, out of reach of the radar. Your cousin can tell you."

"Tell me what?"

"Everything. He is one of our best customers. For him, we endure diesel fumes and the stink of each other for days when we cannot rise to breathe the sea air."

Lew Chun took a chance. "But the money is good."

"If you live through the journey, yes, the money is exceptional. But not everybody makes it. I saw a boat like ours sink itself before the Coast Guard could get to it. They arrested the crew, but two tons of cocaine sit on the ocean floor."

He laughed. "The sharks got high." He translated this witticism for the sailors. Dutifully, they hooted, snorted, repeated the words and laughed again.

There was not enough oxygen below deck, and Lew Chun joined in mindlessly: "How about a halibut with a habit?" he inquired to no one in particular. "And a jellyfish junkie?" The captain closed his eyes in disgust. Only one person was allowed to be funny on this ship. Before he completely zoned out, Lew Chun asked where they were going.

"Away." The captain's eyes remained shut.

"Far away?"

"Far enough."

Lew Chun attempted to keep his own eyes open, but it was impossible to fight off the lack of air. Briefly, he wondered who was steering the boat. Then the grinding of the engine and the overpowering stench of the toilet gave way to blackness. The crewmen ransacked his clothing while he was unconscious. They found exactly what Shawn Lin wanted them to find — nothing.

When Lew Chun awoke, he checked the clock on the wall. Three hours underwater. Thinking became an impossible feat. Hallucination took over. They all died and were now drifting in limbo. Before the fantasy could go on, the vessel began to rise. Sluggishly, inch by inch, they came to the surface for some air. The boat stayed up less than an hour, but it was enough to refresh the brain. Lights from a far-off ship appeared on the horizon. There was concern in the faces of the sailors and anger on that of the captain. The hatches slammed down, and the non-sub sank beneath the waves once more.

The day and night underwater had made Lew Chun a brother to all those countrymen who came to the Gold Mountain in steerage. He was going back the same way. Hope had long since given way to despair when they resurfaced, this time in blackness. The clangs of buoys sounded in the warm wind, and far off he could make out the illumination of a harbor. A scow came alongside.

"Get in," ordered the voice of another native Spanish speaker — though he had a different accent — and Lew Chun did as he was told. The ship that had brought him backed away, dived down and vanished in a cloud of bubbles. The scow went toward the shore with as much noise as a dandelion seed makes floating to earth. Directly into Lew Chun's ear, a sailor whispered, "They don't go much for contraband here. You could be in prison for your lifetime."

"Where the hell are we?" he returned.

No answer. They put him ashore under a harbor light that kept sweeping the bay. Spanish was in the air. More money changed hands; Shawn Lin had not stinted on the dinero. Still, Lew Chun reasoned that he couldn't have been taken to South America — not this quickly. Or Central America. Even Mexico was farther than they had traveled.

And then he saw the sign on the store, and it all became clear. The words were worn but legible in the meager illumination. They read CAYO COCO. He had seen it on a map in one of the NYU history classes. They were on an island off Cuba, linked to the mainland by a causeway visible on the left.

A male figure emerged from behind an unpainted wood-frame shack. "Follow me," he said. Lew Chun might have hesitated, except that the words were spoken in Mandarin. As he came closer, Lew Chun recognized the type. He was probably from Harbin, unusually tall and spare. He wore a drab olive uniform and carried himself like an officer. The traveler was invited inside a plywood shack.

"You will obey me and me alone. I am Shen. No interrogations. Understood?"

Lew Chun asked his customary question: "Do I have a choice?"

Shen waited until Lew Chun assumed a contrite expression. Satisfied, he resumed. "Impossible to get on a plane and calmly fly to

Beijing from JFK. So your cousin has devised a roundabout method. I am your controller. You comprehend?"

"Yes."

"There are many of us here in Cuba."

"Chinese, you mean?"

"Communist Chinese. There is much traffic between Beijing and Havana."

"And I'm supposed to be one of you."

"Correct. You will speak only when addressed by the authorities. These are your papers."

He handed over an envelope. Lew Chun was used to the drill by now. Innumerable papers had been forged over the years — for smugglers, refugees crossing Nazi borders to escape the Gestapo, Russians fleeing the czars or the commissars, people fleeing Cambodia, Laos or Vietnam, perhaps spies or terrorists entering the U.S., Canada, Mexico. The maker of false documents was a threat to every government, a lifeline for every fugitive. And now Lew Chun was one of those fugitives, all over again. His father's words rose up. *When fate throws a dagger at you, there are only two ways to catch it: by the blade or by the handle.* Lew Chun could visualize the metal whirling though the summery Caribbean atmosphere.

✳✳✳✳

They boarded a bus to the international terminal at the José Martí Airport. In the waiting room, Lew Chun was given documents printed in Mandarin and Spanish. To his dismay, they concerned the production of nickel, a subject about which he cared little and knew nothing. But he examined them slowly and thoroughly, in case undercover Cubans were keeping an eye on this unknown Asian. According to the literature in his hands, Minmetal of the People's Republic owned 49 percent of Cubaniquel. The state-run mining company had the controlling stock.

The Air China flight was delayed, and he napped several times, never deeply — not with all the loudspeaker sounds announcing departures and arrivals and delays in Spanish and French and English. Between naps came endless examinations of credentials. Every time he took them out for the same two officials in fatigues, he imagined himself being cuffed and hauled off to jail. Once in a while, the examiners would exchange a glance, but they made no hostile moves. It occurred to him that Shawn Lin had probably paid these men off, as well. No reason Cuban communists should be any less corruptible than American capitalists.

At noon, five hours behind schedule, they were airborne. Lew Chun and Shen sat near the bulkhead in a three-seat arrangement. A portly Cuban sat by the window and gave them a porcelain smile but, assuming that both men spoke only Chinese, had no small talk. Once the plane reached cruising altitude, Lew Chun slept so deeply he was unaware it had touched down twice before it reached its final destination, Beijing Capital International Airport.

More examination of documents followed, but Shen proved to be an excellent Sherpa; they were permitted to leave in less than the customary two and a half hours. A dark blue Dongfeng microvan waited for them at the curb, its tiny motor idling. There was barely room for a driver and one passenger. The military-looking occupant got out, and Shen assumed the driver's duties. Bending a bit, Lew Chun occupied the passenger's seat. A city had risen during his childhood, but it had dramatically expanded since then, and today the monstrous capital seemed to reach out to the planets. It had intimidating gray buildings, larger and more ambitious than those in Manhattan, and streets that seemed to have no beginning and no end, groping toward the world outside Asia.

Shen drove to a spot on the outskirts of Beijing. There he gave Lew Chen some Chinese currency, ordered him to wait for the bus and, for the first and only time, mentioned the name of a town. The American was to debark there. Without any further instructions, he sped off. Lew Chen sat on a wooden bench until the long green bus came. It went over absurdly long bridges, wandered past big white brick buildings, acres, miles of urban sprawl, farms and outlying districts with thousands of tiny structures. When he got off, alone, a bent old woman appeared to be waiting for someone. She addressed him in Cantonese.

"You are Tsung Dao Pei?"

That was the name on his papers. He nodded.

"Now the real name," she insisted.

He had come this far. If she couldn't be trusted, all was lost anyway.

"Yes, I am Lew Chun."

"The Boy Chef."

"That's what they used to call me."

"Come."

She walked with slow, painful steps, down two narrow streets, along an alley and up to the wooden steps of a shanty with green blistering paint. "I will leave you here," she said without another word of explanation. Lew Chun watched her limping along until she turned a corner. Only one move remained: He knocked on the door. Another old woman in faded plum-colored scrubs opened it. She looked him over and waved him in. He followed her to a bedroom. At the back, sitting up in a leather chair, was his mother. She looked older than he remembered — and unwell. Tears ran down her sallow cheeks. "You never got to say goodbye to your father."

Lew Chun wept with her. They embraced and started talking over each other. Her nurse kindly withdrew.

"I wanted more children, but they only let us have one," she reminded her son. "And it had better be male." She had said this many times before. "It was wicked, what they did, killing tiny girls or putting them out for adoption. Did they believe women would go along with the Leader with never a question?"

More lamentations. "Systems die. Instincts remain," she said.

The nurse returned after a while. She induced Lew Chun to come out into the hall, where they could speak privately for a moment. "Your mother has had a difficult time. She is ill, and there is trouble with her memory."

Lew Chun said he felt that actually might be a mercy. Looking at his mother's seamed face, lightened with the appearance of her long-vanished son, he could guess what had happened since the time of Tiananmen Square.

"This was a clever woman, well-educated for her time," he told the nurse, simply to put the facts on record. "And now, because she is the widow of a counterrevolutionary, they made her a nonperson, no longer a part of Chinese society. Hidden in the shadows of some provincial slum. Forgotten and afraid."

"But she is still sweet," the nurse reminded him.

"Yes, true. My father had some of that sweetness, along with his energy and skills."

"And so do you."

"No, I did not inherit that gene."

Why was this? he wondered when he returned to his mother's side and held her hand, chatting about nothing, careful to omit any bad news. Why did he have no generosity of spirit or fellow feeling? It was as if these emotions had scattered, left on the sides of the Gold Mountain. And now they were irretrievable. Lew Chun went into an elaborative tale: He was on vacation, and the governments of the United States and China had both allowed him a visit to her for humane reasons.

It was impossible to say whether she believed any of this. She rocked back and forth, hummed a little tune and fell into a shallow sleep.

Presently, the nurse returned. A small man in fatigues accompanied her. He did not introduce himself.

"I have lodgings," he whispered. "You will be safe with us."

"Who is 'us'?"

"Friends."

"How safe?"

"Away from the military. No one knows you're here except for your mother and a few trusted friends."

"How trusted?"

"Questions. Always questions. Put it this way. If they weren't dependable, you would now be under arrest — or very possibly dead."

"Point taken."

"Follow me. Stay behind by about 50 feet."

And Lew Chun was in flight once more, this time in the country of his birth, a place run by men and women he didn't know but who would no doubt lock him up if they learned his whereabouts — and perhaps have him extradited back to New York. There he would be tried for the disappearance of Philip Lau. At this point, the crime surely involved the NYPD, the FBI and who knew how many other initials.

"Will you get a message to Shawn Lin?" he asked at the door.

"He will get a message to you," said the man he identified as Mr. Anonymous, and they were off.

****

They put Lew Chun up in a one-room flat above a garage. The bathroom consisted of a toilet, a sink and a homemade shower — a garden hose attached to a faucet, with a sprinkler on the business end.

Food was brought on a tray, just as if he were in prison or hospital. Banging went on during the day; mechanics in dirty brown overalls were fixing dents. Occasionally, they would run into the stranger who lived upstairs. The workmen stared with eyes that looked past him. Lew Chun assumed they were part of the group providing cover, and he never tried to engage them in conversation.

Any talking was done with his mother on the days he was permitted to see her. She spoke exclusively of the past, her husband, the restaurant, the Boy Chef, the prosperous days. The rest of the time, Lew Chun stayed in the flat. There was a radio, prattling state propaganda, and sometimes Mr. Anonymous would bring a newspaper of incomparable dullness, all self-congratulation about the New China. When a local school structure collapsed because of sleazy materials, the scandal was only reported on the first day. Twice he heard the mechanics talking about strikes and bread riots in the south. But the information consisted of rumor and gossip, nothing substantial. No names or locales were given, and he didn't dare to let his curiosity show.

After a week, Mr. Anonymous came by with some sheets of paper. He said Shawn Lin had sent a message.

"I have decoded in English," he said proudly.

"I didn't know you spoke English," Lew Chun replied.

He switched to that language. "With great fluency I speak it. I was in my class at university top third."

Lew Chun didn't ask what university.

Mr. Anonymous began to read the dispatch. "You must lie—"

"That's all I've been doing, lying."

"Kindly allow me to finish. He says, 'You must lie *low*. Very dangerous here. Do not write or call.'"

"That's the message?"

"That's the message."

"Nothing about Tina? Nothing about my wife?"

"Nothing about either woman." He flashed a knowing smile.

"It's the same woman."

"Ah. I see. Nothing in any case."

After a few more days, Lew Chun demanded to get a note to Tina.

"The word of a visitor is not law," said Mr. Anonymous, slipping back into Mandarin.

"I'm not a visitor. I'm a fugitive."

"Could be worse," Mr. Anonymous pointed out. "You might be in a real jail. They are much worse than this place. And there the food is garbage."

"This is my wife we're talking about. I have to tell her I'm all right."

"I will see what can be done."

"And tell Shawn Lin I want to know what's going on, when I can come home."

"I thought China was your home."

"It was. Not anymore."

Mr. Anonymous gave this strange Chinese-American a quizzical look and got a hostile one in return. After he departed, Lew Chun turned their conversation over in his mind. *What did he mean he thought China was my home? Did Shawn Lin intend to dump me here, blame Philip's murder on me, set Interpol on me? But that would be like setting fire to his hair. I owe him my restaurant, my good fortune, even Tina. But I don't owe him my life.*

The following week, Mr. Anonymous was ebullient.

"I bring news." He showed off his gold teeth in a wide grin.

"Give me the bad news first."

"No bad news. Only good."

Lew Chun leaned back and waited.

"First, you have a job. Right downstairs. Banging out dents, painting scratches."

"That's not good news. Good news is I'm going to New York."

"Not quite yet. This will be explained in a letter from your cousin."

He gave Lew Chun a white envelope with American stamps on it. The letter was in garbled English in capital letters, with words like SCORKTAVY and PSUDJAMNIZ.

"It's in code," he explained.

"No shit," Lew Chun said.

Mr. Anonymous took back the paper and deciphered it. "Your cousin says the following: Rest easy."

"Yeah, right. Rest."

"He also says, 'The federal police came looking for the chef. They did not say why. I said I did not know what had happened. They looked for you. I said I was worried. They said they had searched Philip Lau's apartment. If they found anything, they didn't say. Then they got Tina to let them into your apartment. She said she knew nothing, and they found nothing.'"

"So? Why can't I go back the way I came?"

"Shawn Lin goes on: They sent your picture to all their bureaus. So you are being hunted. This will pass in time."

"He say how much time?"

"He says everything can be fixed — except the time it takes to fix it."

Mr. Anonymous handed over the paper. It contained a series of scrambled letters, along with Roman and Arabic numerals, like a child's puzzle.

****

After breakfast the next day, Mr. Anonymous explained the next move.

"While you're waiting," he said, "you will make yourself useful in the garage.

All the men have been bought and paid for by your cousin. Totally dependable."

"How do you know that?"

"No one has come by to arrest you, have they?"

"Not yet."

Mr. Anonymous brushed off an imaginary fly. "They'll show you how to fix dents and dings, eliminate scratches, that sort of thing. You'll wear stained overalls, look like everyone else. Report this afternoon to Bo."

Bo was an oversize frowning no-nonsense type, familiar to anyone who has ever worked under a factory foreman or the head of a wrecking crew. It had been a long time since anyone had contradicted him without regret.

On the first day, a forklift ran over Lew Chun's right foot; the pain was sharp but temporary. After that rite of initiation, the men taught him a few tricks with a rubber mallet and how to heat up the metal with an open flame before applying the touch-up paint. He was off and limping.

Unlike those in the U.S., these repairmen didn't have their names stitched to their overalls. They kept their distance, instructing the new man on the fine points of automobile mending but never introducing themselves. So Lew Chun identified them by characteristics: Stutterer, Fat Man, Thin Man, Clown, Loudmouth. They always ate lunch together, the food supplied by a teenager. The youth dropped off the soup and dumplings — barely edible — from a truck. He never stayed. The men chatted and ate. Sometimes they played kampung blackjack, a variation of twenty-one — five-card maximum, doubling down if the player believes he has a hot hand. For three days, they talked among themselves and didn't issue an invitation to Lew Chun to play blackjack. On the fourth, they asked him to take the role of dealer, customarily the designated loser. It hardly mattered; he had the money and needed the company.

Late on certain afternoons, two young women entered the garage without notice. They also had no identities. Lew Chun privately referred to them as Patience and Fortitude, the names of the lions in front of the public library on Fifth Avenue. When the pair showed up, a couple of men peeled off and went to a back room. When they were finished, the next johns followed. The American was not invited and took no offense. He was in love with Tina and felt that any excursions with hookers would be a betrayal. He hoped she felt the same when someone hit on her — a certainty back in New York.

So on those days, Lew Chun retired early, grabbed something from the little dorm-sized refrigerator, had a beer or two and went to bed. But he would often come to consciousness in the small hours and think of Tina. Questions broke into the night. Did she know his location? Did she wonder whether he was in trouble? For that matter, did she wonder whether he was alive? Shawn Lin would be useless. He would stay far away from her, and if she appeared at the restaurant or his office, she would be told he was away, gone, unreachable. Had anything been discovered about the fate of Philip Lau? Was Tina being watched? Could her husband get word to her? But how was that even possible when his sole contact with the outside world was the totally uncooperative Mr. Anonymous?

And then an entirely different subject matter arose. They were in the middle of a kampung blackjack game with Patience hovering above them, when Clown mentioned a vehicle on the hydraulic lift. "Rear-ended," he told Thin Man. "Looks like a rhinoceros's ass after it backed into a propeller."

Loudmouth asked who owned the wreck.

"Some Beijing big man. Always bringing one of his cars in for repair." Patience inspected the damage. "Many's the time I bounced in that." She and Clown and Loudmouth went in back, laughing uproariously.

When they were out of sight, Stutterer said, "Huh-her and half the gug-girls in her house. Li Dao huh-had them all." Li Dao. Lew Chun knew him by another name, *Fēngxiàngbiāo*, the Weathervane, the man who had killed Ang Chun — or had had him killed. No surprise that he was still around — or that he drove a big car. He would *always* be around and always in a position of authority. The Weathervane was not a survivor; he was a thriver. That afternoon, a small daydream was born. It grew to full size over the next fortnight. Instead of vaguely fantasizing about Tina, Lew Chun began to work out a specific plan for balancing the world, doing to *Fēngxiàngbiāo* what the Weathervane had done to his father.

****

In Lew Chun's view, the strategy had no downside. Even if it failed, the Colonel would be forced to bring the Boy Chef back to the States before he did further damage — the kind of damage that couldn't be repaired. Now the hours were no longer a procession of noisy rubber mallets, spray paint machines, card games and empty chatter. Now exile had a meaning.

Any number of scenarios came to mind. In one, Lew Chun would somehow get permission to take Wednesday morning off. The Weathervane was too important to pick up the car himself; he would send an enlisted man. Before the flunky took the wheel, Lew Chun would secrete himself in the back, between the seat and the floor. The car would be driven to a reserved space in a military parking lot.

When the big man came to drive himself to a meeting or to his home, Lew Chun would have a choice of instruments for the homicide. A rubberized extension cord could serve as a noose; several sat on shelves at the rear of the garage. There were also industrial knives on another shelf. The Weathervane's throat could be slit with one of them.

Alternatively, portable nail guns hung on the side walls. These were not lethal, but in three seconds, Lew Chun could fire five little spears in the back of his victim's head and finish him off with a chokehold.

But as Wednesday morning came closer, he recognized that all this was fantasy — like imagining himself as a black-belt sensei. Even if the assassination were successful, how long would it be before investigators traced the weapon back to the garage and to the Boy Chef?

After eliminating the choices one after another, he realized that he was a total amateur at using garage tools of any kind and a professional at using kitchen equipment of all kinds. The Boy Chef knew how to prepare fowl, hare, steer, vegetables, soups, appetizers, entrees, desserts. He knew how to find herbs in the wild, even in backyards. He could tell the difference between *Volvariella volvacea* — the "paddy straw" mushroom, which gives depth to roasts and stews — and the rare, nail-like fungus *Trogia venenata*, which causes paralysis and death.

That particular mushroom had always been a nightmare for Chinese forest managers. After years of trying nicotine spray, Agent Orange and petroleum-based toxins, they found the little white mushroom impossible to eliminate. The fungus kept cropping up after rains, hiding in the stumps of rotting trees, under rocks, at the edges of ponds. The best the workers could do was warn mushroom hunters and keep the poison centers on alert. According to the paper, this year there had been only three incidents. Lew Chun determined to provide them with the fourth — if he could secure the cooperation of a prostitute.

He kept agitating for an introduction. At first, the men greeted him with backchat and mockery.

"I thought you were married." Clown indicated the gold band on his left hand.

"Yeah, well…" Lew Chen put on an abashed smile.

The others were equally sarcastic and unwilling to share. But after a few days of ragging — and the aid of many Harbin beers he had brought in and paid for — the mechanics came around. When they were done with their mockery, they let him make a choice. He selected Fortitude. She was in one of the back rooms lying on a large cot, looking up as if he were making a delivery and waiting for a tip.

"What can I do for you?" she asked impudently.

He tried to sound knowing. "What you do for the others. Only more."

"Can you pay?"

"Whatever you ask."

Lew Chun refused to feel guilty about this negotiation. After all, it wasn't about sex, he told himself; it was about information. And he couldn't get one without the other.

Fortitude knew tricks that he had never seen, even in the bluest of movies — things with her tongue and long fingers with carefully sanded nails. In addition, she had snapper organs, and as the men had whispered, one could stay in her a long time. But eventually, even this fake passion came to a conclusion.

Lew Chun thought he had performed pretty well; at least he hadn't embarrassed himself. However, to this lady of the evening, morning, afternoon, weekday, weekend, one john was the same as another. If she liked him, she gave no indication.

But then, as they were in the process of post-coital relaxation, she asked him who he was and where he came from. Assuming she had been briefed by the others, he admitted to his American background and said he'd been accused — unjustly— of a crime. Vigorously maintaining his innocence, he told Fortitude about his New York lawyers, men who said he could be railroaded, convicted, sent to prison — which was why he had jumped bail and returned to the land of his birth.

She looked skeptical. He changed the subject: "Could I take you to dinner?"

The laugh worked its way out of her throat. It was not a pleasant sound.

"If I need to dine, I have a man to take me," Fortitude said.

"I have money," Lew Chen assured her.

"You have money, but you have no power." He assumed this was a sexual put-down, until she went on: "You have no political presence. You know nobody. You *are* nobody."

"That doesn't mean I can't take you to dinner."

"At the White Table? Don't be stupid, dear one. You couldn't get past the awning."

"And you can?"

"I can in the right company."

He took a chance: "And when did you last eat at that restaurant?"

"Tuesday. I eat lunch there every Tuesday. Table five, dear boy."

Dear boy. Boy Chef. Always the kid. Nothing he could do about that, not without wrinkling the covers in every sense of the words. So they went on chatting about nothing until he showered Fortitude with little fens and big yuans, Chinese currency that meant little to him, and she went off to who knows what assignations.

Over the next few days, the idea truly took shape. Lew Chun knew the White Table. It was a rival in the old days; faceless owners but very competitive. They had greased many official palms, which Ang Chun refused to do. Nevertheless, their food was outstanding. Name an exotic dish and they could make it. Better than the Western Lake? He didn't think so. But as good as? Very possibly. Or so Lew Chun was told; the Boy Chef was never allowed to go there. Bad for business to be seen dining at a competitor's. But next week, at long last, he was going to put in an appearance — although under very peculiar circumstances.

The outline was simple enough. On any given Tuesday, Fortitude would be dining with her best customer — at least the one with the most sway in this part of the city. Chances were that gentleman was the Weathervane.

Three big roadblocks stood in the way of vengeance.

First, Lew Chun had to borrow or steal one of the cars in the garage, drive to a place where the lethal mushrooms grew, collect the proper amount and cook them.

Second, he had to get them into the Weathervane's lunch.

Third, he had to flee back to the U.S. before the authorities figured out how *Fēngxiàngbiāo* met his end.

Lew Chun weighed the odds. Any one of these was difficult. A trifecta would be the longest of shots.

****

Three days of threats had the desired effect. Ultimately, Mr. Anonymous realized that if he didn't connect Lew Chun with the Colonel, this American hothead would give himself up to the authorities. The very next day, he took the Boy Chef for a slow drive on Chang'an Avenue. Satisfied that they were not being followed, he handed over the car phone. Shawn Lin was at the other end. His words were scrambled by a coding machine, but to make doubly sure of privacy, he spoke in Mandarin.

Lew Chun told the Colonel he intended to get even with the Weathervane for what that monster had done to his family. He was not specific.

Shawn Lin ignited. "Are you crazy? Is this the way you repay me?"

"Repay *you*? For sending me to China?"

He wasn't listening. "Trust me, you're in the safest possible place right now."

"But I *don't* trust you. And if you don't bring me home, I promise you I'll go through with this."

"Time to stop being a boy, Lew Chun. You're a grown man. You're married."

"Yeah, with a wife I can't talk to."

"She's here."

"Here where?"

"Sitting beside me."

"Let me talk to her."

There was a pause, and then, just like that, he heard Tina's summery voice, also scrambled but in English.

"Lew Chun, darling, is that really you?"

From the sound, he could tell she was on a loudspeaker.

"Yes, it's really your husband."

"Are you all right?"

"As all right as I can be 7,000 miles from you."

"Shawn Lin says you can't come home right now."

"Shawn Lin is wrong."

"Lew Chun, he told me everything."

"He couldn't have told you everything. He doesn't know everything." She was interrupted by a grinding electronic noise. Then: "He says it's better if you stay there — for a little while longer."

"How long is a little while?"

Shawn Lin broke in. "Two months. At the outside. Perhaps sooner."

"One week."

"Don't be stupid."

"One week." Lew Chun was so loud Mr. Anonymous winced. He changed lanes and took the next exit.

"You're a fool. Tell him he's a fool, Tina."

She started crying. "Your cousin says they could execute you if don't do what he says."

"Bullshit."

"Oh, Lew Chun, we both want what's right for you, that's all."

"What's right for me is to come home."

As they talked, Mr. Anonymous took an auxiliary road, dipped under a bridge and re-entered the highway in the opposite direction. He was returning to the garage.

Silence greeted Lew Chun on the American end, and he declined to fill the dead air.

More indecipherable sounds of sobs, barely audible words of consolation. In the end, Shawn Lin yielded, either to Tina's tears or to Lew Chun's intractability: "Very well. One week. You will retrace your steps. In the meantime, keep your head down."

"Thank you," wife and husband said simultaneously.

"Did you hear what I said?" Shawn Lin bellowed.

"Yes."

"This will cost you."

"Yes."

"When you receive my orders, you will follow them to the letter."

Wondering what that cost might be, Lew Chun switched to a humble, conciliatory tone. "Without a doubt. Absolutely." He attempted to continue, but the connection broke, and Mr. Anonymous either couldn't or wouldn't get it back. As he pulled into the spaced reserved for visitors, he voiced seven monosyllables: "I will tell you when to pack."

No further details were offered, and none was requested.

With one week to go, Lew Chun felt Tina pulling on his left sleeve. *Why bother with moves that could destroy his life and hers?* Simultaneously, his right sleeve was being pulled by obligations to his dead father and his disabled mother — and just possibly, he told himself, to China. He fished around in a pocket and pulled out a renminbi coin with a number on one side and a water lily on the other. The flower would represent Tina. He flipped the money in the air and let fate decide.

****

Nobody wanted to part with wheels that morning — not while there was so much bad weather around. Not until Lew Chun proffered three cases of beer. Clown made a show of reluctance before indicating a dented bottle-green hatchback with new tires. The car had to be back by lunchtime. It was clear by Clown's smirk that he believed the visitor was going to see Fortitude. He was indeed correct, but not in the way he imagined. "Two hours," Clown shouted as the car backed onto the road and into the rain.

Lew Chun stopped at a store specializing in uniforms for servers. Paper bag in hand, he drove toward a park remembered from the past, windshield wipers slapping the big drops around. The place was still there but much better appointed, like everything else in downtown Beijing. No one was on the grass; the storm saw to that. He walked around alone, turning over stones and newly fallen branches. Nil. He drove on, hoping to find another park. But all the old properties had been developed, white and gray high-rises everywhere, getting slick in the rain. There were no opportunities to find what he sought for almost an hour. He was in unfamiliar territory by then. A narrow two-acre lot, looking forlorn and neglected, sat in a valley. He drove to it and got out and started kicking mounds of wet leaves. And there, under an old rotting log, sat the *Trogia venenata*, as full of death as a hospital.

With work gloves, he uprooted the mushrooms, secreting them in a plastic bag. Lew Chun knew that was the easy part, and he drove back to the city in a state of tension, forcing himself to drive below the speed limit. It would not do to attract attention so close to the finale. He tried to appear purposeful and professional — a garage mechanic in brown overalls and a hard white hat on his way to work.

The rain collaborated. Traffic dispersed. A car pulled out from a parking space two blocks from White Table. People ran for cover. The windows kept getting streakier and steamier as the Boy Chef cooked the mushrooms in a stolen pan over a stolen can of jellied petrol. As the little white mushrooms sizzled, he changed into the clothes purchased at the shop — waiter's starchy jacket, cap and pants. The shoes were inappropriate, but at least they were black. The dirt would wash away as he walked under his stolen umbrella.

The White Table's kitchen opened onto an alley, and the door was ajar to let the steam escape. Lew Chun backed in, trying to blend with the staff. Every restaurant in the world is hysterical at lunchtime; he counted on the waiters to assume he was a new cook and the cooks to mistake him for a new waiter.

Each outgoing tray had a note on it. That way, the server knew its destination. One was marked No. 5. It sat unattended on a granite ledge, waiting for the chef to hand over the entree. In the midst of the chaos of waiters and chefs, Lew Chun lifted the steel top on one of the black mushroom soups. He dropped in the payload. This was pushing his luck. In for a fen, in for a yuan, he figured, and pushed it some more. Grabbing a piece of paper from one of the trays, he scribbled "Li Dao" and put it under the soup bowl. Only then did he withdraw.

Dark thoughts accompanied the power walk to the car: What if the contents of that tray were *not* going to Li Dao and Fortitude? Or what if they *were* going to them but Fortitude got the *Trogia venenata*? Lew Chun would be not only a murderer but the killer of an innocent hooker who wanted nothing more than the chance to rub elbows — and some other moving parts — with an urban power broker.

Clown was nowhere near as angry as Lew Chun expected him to be when he pulled in three hours behind schedule. That night, he discovered why. Without warning, two large Chinese men in khaki forced his door open and clomped in.

"Get up," the first one ordered.

Lew Chun saw it all clearly: Someone had spotted him in the kitchen and told the Weathervane, and *Fēngxiàngbiāo* had dispatched two of his goons for payback. No arrest, no trial, just an execution here and now. The second one said, "You packing? Going on a trip?"

Those were the last words he would hear for some six hours. The last rays of the sun made the dock look pink as he came to consciousness and peered around. Lew Chun was on the deck of the Henri Brun II. He was surrounded by seamen doing their jobs and a French *gendarme militaire* with a pistol conspicuously displayed in a brown leather holster. The latter looked down at the new passenger with something like contempt. Then he walked on by, certain that this Chinaman wasn't going anywhere. The sailors continued to work boisterously, arguing, boasting and kidding around in French.

It wasn't hard to unravel what had occurred. Lew Chun's abductors were following orders from above: no trouble from the Boy Chef. Ergo, they sapped him when he was bending down to pick up a garment bag. Safely comatose, he was conveyed to this freighter, currently rocking in the swell. The crew would know when to heave him overboard, preferably dead, alive if the waters were invested with predators.

Lew Chun probed his pockets. The wallet was gone. Likewise the roll of bills. He was nauseated, but not enough to contribute anything to the bay. With a lot of noise and commotion, the ship up-anchored. Nobody mentioned a destination.

An atmosphere of dread seemed to envelop the ship and its crew. Lew Chun was confined to a cabin with a locked door, a small porthole, a cot, a sink, a toilet and little else. Assuming somebody would come by and bring him on deck at any moment, he fought sleep as long as he could, but he eventually succumbed. However, he remained undisturbed until sunrise, when an adolescent in a crisp white uniform dropped off a tray of scrambled eggs, toast and coffee. He said good morning in French; the passenger answered in kind. The steward didn't seem eager to engage in conversation.

After the adolescent left, Lew Chun moved the eggs around, drank the coffee, washed up and got dressed. His head still smarted from the knockout, and food still had very little appeal. When two raps sounded sharply at the door, he assumed it was the man coming to collect the dishes and yelled, "*Entrez, s'il vous plaît!*"

A bearded middle-aged gentleman in a uniform came in. "I am your captain, Maurice Platte," he said in French. This was a real ship's officer, complete with a braided cap — not a bit like the felons in the pseudo-sub plying the waters around Cuba. "Freighters are allowed to have 10 passengers. You are the 11th."

Lew Chun motioned Captain Platte to a chair. The officer remained on his feet, standing in a parade-rest attitude. "You will remain in your cabin until further notice, so as not to arouse curiosity of the other passengers."

"Sir, may I ask who those other passengers are?"

"Five American couples, returning from a tour of China. Their ship suffered from severe engine trouble. It needs extensive repairs. Rather than wait, they hired the Henri Brun II. It was an inconvenience, but they paid well, you understand."

Lew Chun understood: M. le Capitaine was not likely to give his prisoner anything but misinformation and commands. "Our cargo is machine parts. We will make several ports of call. You will remain here throughout."

Futile to seek permission for a stroll on deck. It seemed insane, but when Platte departed, Lew Chun got down on the floor and did pushups, just to stay in some sort of shape until they came to get him.

A picture began to take shape in his brain. He had blown the attempt to get back at the Weathervane. Someone in the kitchen had spotted him. The mushrooms were never served. The bogus waiter was traced back to the garage. The rest was easy. The thugs threatened the mechanics, entered his room and did what they did. It would not be surprising if the Weathervane himself was aboard, waiting to knock off the murderous son, just as he had the troublesome father.

A blue-uniformed mess boy came in a couple of days later, black, singsong Caribbean accent, cheerful. He identified himself as Manny. Lew Chun thought he might work on the lad. "Where we going next?" he asked in French. "The usual," Manny replied guilelessly. "Shanghai, Ningbo, Hong Kong, Yantian."

All in China. It wouldn't do to escape in any of those locales, even if Lew Chun could get over the side and into the water.

Manny mentioned two other ports: Klang—"

Malaysia. Maybe there.

"—then San Diego."

"And after?"

"Then home." Needless to add, sans Chinaman.

When Manny moved on, Lew Chun weighed his chances. Port Klang it would have to be. After that was the open sea, where they would want to ditch their captive.

Shanghai could be heard and seen from Lew Chun's little round aperture on the world — grumbling shouts of dockworkers, forklifts rolling around unloading heavy cargo, shrieks of pulleys, gnashing of gears and always the *cree, cree* of gulls arguing over garbage scraps. It took about eight hours all told. They up-anchored at dusk.

It was the same thing at Ningbo. Hong Kong was different. Save for a skeleton crew, everybody got shore leave. It was too foggy to see faces, but mobile bodies could be discerned. Sailors became day-trippers. Passengers turned into rich tourists, Nikons and American Express gold cards emerging from their luggage as they went down the gangplank to be fleeced by expert shearers.

At Yantian, a couple of unfamiliar white and surly mess boys dropped off meals and picked up the empty trays. They were accompanied by a shore patrolman with a .45-caliber pistol on his hip and a white SP band on his arm. Not a good sign. If the Weathervane showed up at Port Klang, the execution would follow close behind. Lew Chun knew he would be dead. There was no way he could overpower Li Dao and the military cop.

But why not try? Why not make a bloody scene? The customary choice in life-and-death matters is fight or flight. Here it would be fight *and* flight. Still, if Lew Chun somehow managed to escape, how would he get back home? Perhaps he could make his way to the U.S. Consulate, seek asylum there — if there was one in Port Klang. And if there wasn't? Who knew? First break out, he told himself. Then worry about consulates.

He would have to go on offense; that much was inarguable. Weathervane, mess boys, SP and all. There were no weapons in his tiny cabin; the dining utensils were plastic. The ceiling had nothing but lightbulbs. The porthole glass was small, thick and marked shatterproof. The chair was made of cheap white pine, about as sturdy as a tongue depressor. The only solid object was the cot, and that was composed of a solid iron frame and a metal-spring mattress. Or was it?

Sometimes the feet of a cot were made of two pieces. He got under and felt around. The feet were separate, attached by nuts and bolts. And the threads on one of the metal bolts must have been worn through; he could spin it with his fingers. The other three were attached by bolts that needed work. He undid them over the next few hours, protecting his fingers with a thin washcloth. When it was done, Lew Chun lifted up the frame and removed the leg. It was some 18 inches long, cold, black, a comfortable fit for the right hand. He returned the leg to its place, got up and tried to live the next few days as if resigned to his fate.

The porthole allowed the entrance of white gold daylight, followed by a purple and salmon-colored sunset and then pure darkness punctuated by silver stars and then a pink sunrise before the motors slowed. Peering out at an angle, Lew Chun could make out the prow of the Henri Brun II putting into port. Soon the loading and unloading would begin. It was breakfast time. He went to the couch and detached the weapon that would set him free or get him annihilated.

When all was still, a single pair of footsteps echoed metallically down the corridor. They went on by. He waited. And waited. The scheme took on the aspect of a surreal cartoon. In his skull cinema, Lew Chun saw dinosaurs flourish and perish, giving way to little furry mammals. Hominids became humans. Dynasties rose and fell…

The steps sounded again. This time, they stopped at his door. A key was inserted. Lew Chun stepped back on the hinge side. Very well, he said under his breath, *Fēngxiàngbiāo*, here I am. Let's both go to the inferno together. The door opened an inch or two and then widened, admitting a fan of light. He raised the black metal bar and stared at the face of his antagonist.

"God, you *are* the world's biggest fool," jeered Shawn Lin.

****

The ambush was not without precedent. Lew Chun thought back to that time in the library when Shawn Lin had come up behind him an eon ago. He was about to stammer an apology for the makeshift weapon, for the hostility that must be radiating out of his face and body. But four syllables changed all that:

"Put down your toy."

Lew Chun sank onto the cot.

Shawn Lin took the chair. "Seasick?"

"I was."

"Keeping things down now?"

"Yes."

"Good. Let's talk about *Fēngxiàngbiāo*."

"The Weathervane."

"Yes, him."

He waited for Shawn Lin to disclose the information. After a lengthy, dramatic pause, he spoke. "Dead. They believe the Weathervane succumbed to mushroom poisoning. Or so my friends inform me. I assume you were behind it."

Lew Chun withheld nothing.

The Colonel listened without giving anything away. Then he said: "No one has been arrested. Officially, it was an accidental death. However, they're tracing the mushroom distribution all the way down to the wholesalers and farmers and beyond."

Lew Chun thought of his father's story. *"You* ate *them? Those mushrooms were not for eating! They were for buying and selling!"* But he stayed as expressionless as a carp.

Shawn Lin walked around the little room. "The man in the freezer."

"Philip Lau."

"Still missing. So are you."

"Not anymore, I guess."

"No," he agreed ominously. "Not anymore."

The future opened before Lew Chun like a chasm. The Colonel was going to turn him in, not for murdering a Chinese officer but for whacking an FBI informant. The Boy Chef would take the fall for his cousin's criminal activities, leaving Shawn Lin in the clear.

"So," Lew Chun concluded. "You're going to see me into an orange jumpsuit, that it?"

"Not quite. *Ça va sans dire* you have seen the passenger list."

"*Ça va sans dire, non.*"

"Surely, the captain informed you about the other passengers."

"Ten American tourists. I didn't believe a word."

"Clever boy."

After all he had been put through in China — to say nothing of Chinatown. Smart boy. Not smart man, not smart fellow. Just a kid you could send anywhere and he would have to go.

"Do you want to know who they really are?" Shawn Lin inquired.

"If you want to tell me."

"We'll meet at the evening mess. Now that we're no longer subject to inspection, I can let you stroll on deck."

When Shawn Lin left, Lew Chun expressed his dissatisfaction by refusing to get up from the couch. The Colonel didn't seem to notice. An hour later, Manny arrived with a clothes bag. Inside was a navy blazer and white duck pants. A note was pinned to the hanger. "Now that you're back in the fold, dress the part." Lew Chun inquired when dinner was served, washed up a half-hour before, climbed into the new made-to-measure outfit from his New York tailor, and showed up five minutes early.

Shawn Lin was already there, spiffy in seersucker cords. He regarded his cousin with an amalgam of amusement and pride. This Lew Chun, this Boy Chef, had grown up under his umbrella. Experience had sanded away the splinters and knots. He carried himself differently, with an understated authority. Not quite there yet, but admirable in his ability to absorb his formal lessons and, more importantly, his life lessons. Now he must learn the art of compromise. That would come in time. Not that there was much to spare. He waved at a waiter, who took a bottle of Moët & Chandon from an ice bucket and filled two glasses. These were placed soundlessly on the red and white checkered tablecloth. The Colonel thanked him and waved him away.

He sipped the Champagne. "Colder than the souls of men." He sat back and surveyed the room. "The others will join us in a moment.

Now that your inner ear has settled down, I want to talk to you beforehand."

Lew Chun said he was all inner ears.

"What? Ah, I see. Inner ears. Most amusing. Now listen closely. What we've worked out is that you and Philip Lau were seized—"

"Seized?"

"Abducted. Kidnapped."

"No way."

The Colonel was not finished. "You and Philip were taken by truck to an undisclosed location for debriefing. You were held and interrogated until your escape."

"Escape," Lew Chun echoed flatly.

"Philip, unfortunately, was disabled by his captors and could not flee."

"And these kidnappers were?"

"Cartagenians, of course."

Lew Chun stared at his cousin in disbelief. Such a bright man and such a dumb declaration. "Colonel, no one's going to buy that story."

"They will when you tell it. You'll describe the abduction, the truck ride, the place they held you all this time."

"Yeah, right. And when they find out there is no such place—"

"Ah, but there *is* such a place. This you shall see for yourself."

The Colonel refilled their glasses and tried a warm, indulgent approach. "This is a great deal for you to absorb. One needs time and sleep and nourishment."

Lew Chun studied the carte du jour.

"Might as well shred that." The Colonel seized the paper. "Complete balderdash. There is no such thing as a fine meal on a boat. Oh, the stabilizers can neutralize the pitch and roll, but one cannot dine properly when a room is in motion. Same thing in planes. First class is the same the world over, food — even filet mignon — microwaved to extinction. Salads unforgivably cold, vegetables will all the flavor removed. The desserts a travesty. The wine is superb, good year and all that, but used as a screen against ennui, terror and the whoosh of the jets."

He raised his glass again. "No, to eat well, one has to be on land and in one's own place."

For weeks, Lew Chun had imbibed nothing but beer, and as Shawn Lin discoursed on taste and refinement, he could feel the alcohol doing its work. His host suddenly rose and beamed.

"And here they are."

In glided Jade and Amy. They both wore designer dresses in a snakeskin print, Jade in a color that matched her name, Amy in blue. Jade had a necklace of reptile teeth; Amy went for white pearls. Lew Chun got to his feet. When the sisters sat, so did he. But the Colonel moved on, walking past the bar and out of the room. A waiter came over, filled two Champagne flutes and presented them to the ladies.

Looking after Shawn Lin, Lew Chun held his glass aloft. "To absent friends."

"Oh, he'll be back." Amy sipped her drink.

Jade agreed. "He's just seeing to Ruby."

"Is *she* here?" Lew Chun asked.

"He doesn't go anywhere without her," Amy said.

Jade, with just a hint of the bitch within: "Ruby doesn't travel well. He has her stashed away in their stateroom."

There was a long silence. The Boy Chef broke it: "Next stop, San Diego."

Amy yawned. "Been to California?"

"Once."

"I see."

Then dead air. No attempt at conversation. Depression was about to settle in for the afternoon, when a file of new people entered the room — a mixed group, Asians and whites, all in good suits, white shirts and rep ties. Lew Chun recognized one of them. Mickey tossed him a salute and started to the table.

Shawn Lin chose that moment to return. Retreating to the bar, Mickey ordered a Dewar's and soda and watched everyone's reflection in the big mirror. The Colonel resumed his seat, assuming his all-is-well smile. He gave his daughters a quick visual appraisal. Good-looking women but too self-satisfied, too smug. Were they really up to the next move? Or had they become like their husbands, competent — albeit not first-rate — reliable followers but inadequate leaders? He addressed the table. "Enough small talk. We have business to discuss."

He nodded to Jade, who reached into her black Coach bag and gave him a map neatly folded in quarters. He placed it before Lew Chun.

"You're going to commit this to memory. I'll test you for the next several days, until we land. By that time, you'll know everything they want to hear."

"They?"

"The FBI."

Lew Chun found this weird and discomfiting, spilling this scenario before Jade and Amy. But the sisters seemed at ease, as if they knew what their father was going to say before he said it.

"You wanted to come back well ahead of plans," the Colonel reminded the Boy Chef. "You were stubborn. You were intransigent. And in China, you were criminal. One word from me and you could be in a lockup in Beijing or New York. One word."

Not an empty threat; of that, Lew Chun was convinced. He listened with respect.

"We were forced to make accommodations. Now it's your turn. Let me go over this slowly so you understand. The FBI doesn't give a shit — pardon me, ladies — what happened to Philip Lau. He was not a federal employee. He was an informant."

"Then why are you putting me through this?" Lew Chun indicated the room, but he meant the whole business of getting shanghaied aboard the Henri Brun II, as well as all the other humiliations.

"Because," he explained, "they can't abandon a case that's on the books. They need a story with conclusion, even if it leaves some details hanging. The tale is as follows. You were taken against your will to a house in California. You escaped, got word to me, and I came out to bring you back."

"And when they can't find that house?"

"Ah, but they will. You will lead them to it. That is the purpose of the map." He unfolded the paper.

A circle of red surrounded a neighborhood on Collins Avenue in Oakland.

"No. 42 is ours," he said. Lew Chun had no reason to doubt him. The Colonel probably had properties all over the country, the ownership so heavily laundered it could never be traced to Shawn Lin of Chinatown.

"The Cartagenas held you here at Collins — with armed guards — for weeks."

"And how did I escape?"

Jade broke in. "One evening, a guard went out for food. You overpowered his partner."

"And how did I do that?"

The Colonel took over. "I'm not sure. You might have used one of your shoes to knock him out. Or perhaps he fell asleep and you hit him with the base of a table lamp. Which do you think is most plausible?"

"The lamp," Amy said.

"The shoe is more believable," Jade insisted.

"No, I like the lamp," Lew Chun heard himself say — and he was in the bag, just the way Shawn Lin wanted. The rest of the trip was taken up with false memories of the night he had been kidnapped, the long truck ride, the voices of his abductors and, finally, the house where he had been kept.

By the time they docked, he had the catechism down by heart. Mickey drove them across the Golden Gate Bridge, passed through well-tended suburbs, run-down areas and bleak scruffy neighborhoods, and eventually pulled up at the chosen house. In adjoining easy chairs, the sisters questioned Lew Chun intensely as Shawn Lin looked on from behind a rosewood desk. Mickey perched on a piano bench. Sitting cross-legged on a blue and ecru Persian rug, Lew Chun noticed that they all wore cotton flesh-colored gloves. He could guess why.

Jade began. "How many interrogators? And what were their names?"

"Three. They never called each other by name. I called them Groucho, Chico and Harpo, but only to myself."

"What did they look like?"

"Hard to tell. They wore stocking masks. Denim pants. Blue shirts."

"All the time?"

"All the time they were with me. I would guess they were in their 20s. Average build. Not tall, not short. Leathery hands. Black, unwashed hair."

"They ever let you alone?" Amy asked.

"Never. Not when I slept, not when I ate. One of them always went to the john with me."

Jade: "And they had a boss?"

"Diego."

"Talk about Diego."

"He was thin, smallish, salt-and-pepper hair, very well-dressed. Pinstriped suits. Elegant. Pencil mustache."

"And where was Philip Lau all this time?"

"In another part of the house. I heard his voice at night sometimes, moaning. They kept saying I was next."

After two hours of this recital, Lew Chun inquired, "You really expect to get away with this?"

"You *will* get away with it," Jade said. "You're very convincing. "

Amy went along with her. "Something about that unlined face. There's times when he looks 12 years old."

"Just pretend I'm not here, why don't you?" he said.

The Colonel had enough. "I realize it's too much to expect gratitude from you. After all, we only brought you back to life and wife."

"And where *is* she?" he demanded.

"Tina is at your apartment. She knows you're back. Do not call her. You understand? You will be watched, and your hotel phone tapped. You two will be together soon enough."

Lew Chun did not react with the appropriate joy.

"I hardly expected applause," Shawn Lin remarked testily. "Still, you might mumble a *xiexie* sometime."

There was no way Lew Chun would give the Colonel what he really wanted — abject fealty. Nevertheless, the Boy Chef did say "thank you" in Mandarin, to show he wasn't entirely ungrateful. The resentment was kept offstage.

****

That evening, the Colonel and his family dined out. Mickey stayed on, attending to details. Lew Chun was to touch all sorts of items — tumblers, chair backs, tabletops. Mickey kept the flesh-colored cotton gloves on. The FBI would find only two sets of prints — Lew Chun's and those of Philip Lau, carefully selected from the kitchen of Lew Chun's Pan Asian and brought 3,000 miles west.

Grudgingly, Lew Chun went over the story yet again. When Mickey saw no profit in yet another repetition, he capitulated. "OK, kid, you're ready for prime time. Let's go."

"Go where?"

"Hotel. I booked you a room. All part of the plan."

As Mickey drove the rented red Taurus, he imparted a little information. "You're moving up, kid. You're escalating. The Colonel doesn't show it, but he has a new respect for you. Because you pushed back."

Obviously, he expected the passenger to be delighted with this news. But Lew Chun shut his eyes and made a snoring noise.

This didn't stop Mickey. He maintained his irrepressible verve while dodging in and out of bridge traffic. "Shawn Lin wants the daughters to get to know you better."

"What about Charlie and Jimmy?"

"What about them?"

"Aren't they supposed to get to know me better?"

"Those schlubs? Nobody gives a fuck what they think — least of all the Colonel. They're window dressing, kid. The real cogitation is done by Amy and Jade. Mostly Amy."

"I thought she was the timid sister."

"That's what she wants you to think. She's as tough as sharkskin, that one."

When they pulled up at the hotel, Mickey opened the trunk and pulled out a Samsonite suitcase on wheels.

"All the clothes a boy could want," he said as a valet put away the Ford for the night. "You'll need 'em."

They went to the front desk and checked in. Nobody was in the elevator as they ascended to the 11th floor.

"You want a nightcap, kid?"

"No, thanks."

"Good. Morning'll come fast enough. The feds get up early."

"They come to me, or I come to them?"

"They'll show up here, strafe you with questions. Stick to the script, you'll be fine. We got your back."

"How about the front and the sides?"

"What? Oh." He gave Lew Chun a tolerant smile as he got off. "Call me tomorrow — after they've gone."

****

The inquisition was not so harsh or full of traps as he had feared. There were two interrogators, both around 50, graying, both an inch or two above six feet. Lew Chun had been told what to expect, and the inventory was not very different from the outline Mickey had furnished. Weary, hard faces, camel's-hair coats, blue suits, white shirts, blue ties, hair oil, pistol harnesses that showed when they opened their jackets to produce their green plastic-coated IDs.

One of them placed a tape machine on a table. The other one turned it on. Everything was for the record. Lew Chun acted precisely as Mickey had instructed, describing in detail how he had been taken from his place of work in New York, along with a chef named Philip Lau. They had been blindfolded and separated. Lew Chun had been tied up and driven cross-country in a series of trucks. Periodically, he had been taken out of one vehicle and forced into another. This always had taken place at night, when no signs or towns had been visible. Except for shouted orders, nothing had been said to him. He had always been in shackles. Three men — Groucho, Chico and Harpo — had played poker and pinochle and hearts. They had spoken Spanish with one another. He didn't think he could identify them, but he would love to try.

They liked that line, but not enough to stop asking questions. Lew Chun kept offering the men instant coffee; they kept trying to shake his story. They didn't get anywhere. After two hours, they thanked him, said he would be hearing from them and went wherever G-men go.

Lew Chun assumed his hotel phone had been tapped. So he ordered a sandwich from room service and watched black-and-white reruns of *I Love Lucy* and *The Honeymooners* until Mickey showed up in midafternoon, launching into a loud routine about missing tea bags. As he did, he felt under tables, chairs, light fixtures and kitchen appliances. There were no visible eavesdropping devices. He shrugged and broadcast the news that they were going on a tour of the city.

On the road, Mickey felt safe enough to speak openly.

"Can't be too careful. These guys will try to trip you up. Remember: Don't wander from the road we paved for you. Keep in mind Philip Lau was a stoolie. They used him, but they disrespected him."

"In that case," Lew Chun demanded, "when can I go home?"

"Shawn Lin says tomorrow."

In his peripheral vision, Mickey could spot the doubt and disbelief.

"Why not, kid? If the feds want you, they'll find you. Believe me."

"You going back?"

"Not for a day or two."

"Shawn Lin? The sisters?"

"Same thing. It wouldn't look good for you to be traveling with the Colonel and the girls. You're on your own." Mickey consulted the rearview mirror and growled, "Feds. On my back." He slowed down to the speed limit. "I'll drive you to the airport. Buy a ticket. Take a cab back to the hotel. Stay there until I call."

Lew Chun did as bid, returning to his room with a one-way American Airlines noon flight from SFO to JFK. There was nothing to do now but pack and wait. At 5:30 p.m., Mickey phoned with fresh instructions: Come down promptly; the car is sitting at the curb. He neglected to mention that he was no longer driving the red Taurus. Now Mickey sat behind the wheel of a white stretch limo.

"Who's getting married?" Lew Chun asked jauntily.

"Get inside."

Jade and Amy were on the jump seats. Shawn Lin sat comfortably in the back.

"They can't tap limos," he said. "Not yet." The Colonel patted a place next to him. Mickey moved the long car out of the driveway and onto the street. Shawn Lin went on. "We're going to have a business meeting. This is how we'll have to conduct our affairs for the nonce."

He implied that the new conditions were the fault of his protégé. "While you were…out of the country, we did not sit still. We're opening two new restaurants. One in Philadelphia. Amy and her husband will be in charge of that. One in Boston. Jade and her husband oversee that one."

Lew Chun wanted to ask about New York, but the Colonel was way ahead of him. "You will return to Lew Chun's Pan Asian. Everything will go on as before."

The ladies simmered in silence; this was old news to them. Now that their father had gone public with his plans, however, it was real and irrevocable, and Lew Chun could see the covetousness in their faces. Shawn Lin told Mickey to return to his hotel. When they arrived, the trio exited. Amy and Jade wished the Boy Chef a safe and pleasant trip, but there was nothing safe or pleasant in their voices.

Shawn Lin didn't utter a word. The family went into the lobby. Mickey stayed at the curb. No valet approached. In a couple of minutes, the Colonel emerged and got back in the limo.

"Drive around some more," he ordered. The Colonel turned his attention to Lew Chun. "Their resentment should be obvious."

"It is."

"How does that make you feel?"

"Terrible, if you want to know. I just acquired two more enemies, and it wasn't my doing."

"They were always your enemies. You didn't know that?"

"No, I didn't."

"Well, now you do. Charlie and Jimmy are all right in their way, hardworking if I ride them, relatively honest. But not bright, not original. They navigate by staring in the rearview mirror. We can't go forward by looking backward."

"What about your daughters?"

"You know better than that, Lew Chun. Very often, women are more astute than we are — my own wife included. But they are not leaders."

"You never heard of Indira Gandhi?" Lew Chun asked. "Golda Meir?"

"Mrs. Gandhi was slain by men she trusted. Mrs. Meir had to be rescued from her own folly when her country was attacked. We cannot afford such events."

Looking back, Lew Chun compared the next hour to watching the rerun of a plane crash on the 11 o'clock news. The audience is all-knowing but powerless. The Colonel opened his everlasting Sun Tzu manual. "It is the unemotional, reserved, calm, detached warrior who wins, not the hothead seeking vengeance."

He regarded the listener with a penetrating scowl. "Without me, you would have had China and America and Europe hunting you down. How long did you think it would take them? What were you thinking?"

"I wasn't thinking," Lew Chun admitted.

"Well, if you want to go back to the Pan Asian, if you want to be my No. 2 man, you're going to have to think. Hard."

"The thing is, Shawn Lin, I don't want to be your No. 2 man. I just want to resume my old life."

"You cannot have one without the other."

Simple. Unsubtle. Direct. The Boy Chef would be a player — a major New York City restaurateur — or a face on a WANTED poster, a fugitive with the life expectancy of a mayfly. The Colonel had made his point. Lew Chun resolved to acquire his own copy of Sun Tzu's *The*

Art of War from the library. The '90s were about to end. He was not going into the new millennium unarmed.

****

Behind, night and stars. Ahead, a red sunset.

The flight from California to New York offered hyper-saline snacks and the predicted tongue-burning, merit-free meal. On the other hand, it offered lots of time to ponder. Perhaps too much.

Shawn Lin had been quite specific about Lew Chun's new role. Yes, he was to be the principal maker of menus, the official boniface of the Pan Asian. But he was also to be the Colonel's adjutant, meaning that if someone encroached on company turf, and there would always be intruders, strategies would have to be worked out — according to Sun Tzu, no doubt. And Lew Chun would execute those orders. Would "execute" be the operative word?

Other queries accompanied that one. Did the Boy Chef want the restaurant and all that came with it — the celebrity, the money, the life? Or did he want to get hold of Tina and run someplace, some small town where nobody knew them, start all over again?

As the plane began its descent into JFK, he asked himself still more questions. *What's so terrible about the place you're returning to, with its luxuries and its advantages and pleasures? Shawn Lin said you could consider yourself on holiday until he got back. A beautiful young woman waits for you at the end of this journey.* And as he filed out with the rest of the passengers, there she was.

Next to Tina were men Lew Chun recognized as part of the Colonel's household staff, plus C.C., a black colleague of similar burl and a white-haired gentleman wearing a dark, subtly striped bespoke suit and a homburg. He had the look of a Brit — one of those all-business, take-charge people — but nobody seemed to acknowledge his existence.

Least of all Lew Chun. He was too busy grabbing Tina and kissing her and allowing the staffers to hustle them into the back of a big Buick, where they could make up for lost time. In the excitement, Mr. Bespoke was forgotten.

****

Bloody adolescent, he is — nursemaid to the stars, that's yours truly — travesty I call it — not to their faces, of course — not a fool — know what side of the scone is buttered.

The formally dressed gentleman swallowed his resentments and assumed an air of bland elegance, a distracted Oxonian visitor to the Colonies. He walked far behind the object of his attention but never lost track of him. The follower was middle-aged, with receding blond hair turning to a distinguished white around the temples. He was dressed in a black chalk-stripe Turnbull & Asser suit, Savile Row in appearance and demeanor and well aware of his affect.

An ardent reader of W. Somerset Maugham, he fully subscribed to the Old Party's observation that money is like a sixth sense, without which one cannot make full use of the other five. To that end, he was willing to do whatever was required of him. Over the years, this characteristic had proved attractive to his employers. But it was his other skills and attributes that made him invaluable. He was familiar with the vagaries and loopholes of double-entry bookkeeping. Better still, he knew tax laws in Europe and the U.S., how to disguise profits and exaggerate losses, how to prevent hostile takeovers, and how to terminate with extreme prejudice those who got in the way.

****

For almost a week, Tina and Lew Chun holed up, taking the phone off the hook, turning off the cellular phones, making love and catching up with life. They dined out only once, and then at a Greek delicatessen two blocks away. But there were omissions. Even after the most intense sessions, when they were both lying in their own juices, Tina was careful not to ask too much about where Lew Chun had been and what he had done. To equalize matters, he didn't ask how his young wife had spent her off hours. There would be time for all that.

Late in the week, they received individual summonses. Tina had to report to work on Monday morning; Lew Chun on Tuesday afternoon. That was agreeable to both of them. Tina wanted to catch up with friends and office scuttlebutt; Lew Chun was eager to see what, if anything, had happened to the Pan Asian. Things looked the same, aside from a fresh paint job (gold doorframes and wainscots and, predictably, Chinese red walls). Same waiters, more or less, same cooks. But a new head chef had taken Philip Lau's place, an older Korean named Hyun-soo Park. He had been the main attraction at Doran's in San Francisco, Lew Chun was informed, brought here by Shawn Lin for big bucks. Hyun-soo Park was the real thing; diners could tell that the minute they inhaled the entrees steaming away on the Garland stoves.

The very night Lew Chun returned to duty, Gia and Julie reappeared. His initial instinct was to slip back into the kitchen. But no, it was better to go through this hill than around it. He glided to their table, greeting them cordially. "Word gets around."

Gia nodded. "We heard you were back." Not a word about Frank, and Lew Chun was not about to introduce the subject.

Julie said, "Where were you?"

"Away." Cold silence. He added, "On business. We opened two new Pan Asians, one in Philadelphia, one in Boston."

"And that's where you were."

"Some of the time."

"You didn't take your wife."

This to let him know they had kept an eye on the apartment. Instead of reacting with rage, which is what they seemed to want, he asked how they liked the new chef. Outstanding, Gia said. As if it had just popped into her mind, she asked, "What happened to the old chef?"

"He got a better job overseas."

"Where overseas?"

"You'll have to ask my cousin."

"So you'll be returning to your old job."

"Again, you'll have to ask Shawn Lin." He excused himself from their company and worked the room for a while. They stayed another half-hour and departed without a farewell.

"Who are they?" asked a waiter, watching them go.

"Trouble," the boss answered.

"What kind trouble?"

"Journalist trouble."

He looked puzzled.

"Great pain."

That he understood.

****

The restaurant practically ran itself. For more than two months, the staff did the cooking and the heavy lifting; Lew Chun oversaw the meals, mixed with certain guests, wrote checks for unpaid bills. Twice he was summoned to Center Street to give lengthy depositions. There he traced and retraced the abduction to California, describing the gang and the sounds of Philip Lau under duress.

The interviews were conducted by the same federal investigators with the same tape recorder. It was all very businesslike. Lew Chun stuck to his story, but not too rigidly. After the last grilling, they released him with a warning not to leave town. Leave town, he mused. If only they knew.

During this period, Lew Chun found it difficult to read anything except books about China. No newspapers, no magazines. He kept trying to understand what had happened to his father, to Shawn Lin, to himself. But that was only a fraction of his off hours. Most of them were devoted to Tina, the woman he still thought of as his bride. They spent many evenings at the movies or at Broadway musicals. When they dined out with others, it was uptown, mixing with Tina's colleagues at the publishing house or with two of Tina's college classmates at Columbia's medical school. The women were always in scrubs, taking a break from the inhuman hours put in by doctors and nurses in training.

One night, after the interns returned to the hospital and Tina and Lew Chun were on their way home, he said he would gladly change places with them.

"Don't you like the restaurant anymore?" she asked in that soft way she had.

"I did when I cooked."

"And now?"

"Now I administrate."

"I know you don't like me to ask you about work—"

"I never said so."

"Well, others did."

"What others?"

She changed the subject. "What does that mean, 'administrate'?"

"It means I sit around, look things over and wait for Shawn Lin to show up."

"Which is when?"

"I think next week."

"You think."

"Nobody knows."

He knew Tina wanted to dig a little deeper. But she didn't want to alter the climate of the evening. So she brought up their favorite pastime: "As long as he's out of town, let's play."

And play they did, walking out late and window-shopping and fantasizing about a more spacious apartment, a more spacious life. Toward the end of summer, they had reason to dream: Tina was pregnant. From then on, anything they talked about was phrased in the future tense.

On an afternoon in early September, Lew Chun watched five waiters setting up the covers as they always did. He pitched in as if one of the troops, folding crisp linens, lining up bottles at the bar, arranging the gleaming glasses and silverware. As they made arrangements, the man he had seen at the airport, the formal one in the London suit, entered and went directly to the Boy Chef.

"Mr. Lew Chun?"

"And you are?"

"Eric Bern." He spelled it. "As in the city in Switzerland. Some — most, actually — address me as Professor. Shawn Lin asked — look in on you — smooth the way."

He affected a pip-pip-old-boy British manner right out of a Sherlock Holmes movie.

"Well, look on, Professor," Lew Chun responded, deliberately paying more attention to the napkins than to him.

"Told to be sure you arrived safely — need to be sure you stay that way."

Lew Chun beckoned the Professor to a chair and sat across from him. "If you don't mind, what else do you do for the Colonel, besides looking after me?"

"Not at all — Colonel's CFO. Chief financial—"

"I know what CFO stands for."

He shook off the belligerence. "Emeritus Prof. Economics — Baruch — student had been a beneficiary of Shawn Lin's generosity — brought us together — Colonel needed a financial manager, checked me out — signed on without hesitation."

"And you still teach."

"I wish — no time — too much to do right here right now — three restaurants — numerous real estate holdings — fiscal complications."

Lew Chun could imagine what those complications entailed but just played with the napkin and hoped the Professor would get to the point.

"Lew Chun — may I? — your cousin — extraordinary figure — you don't, you *can't*, realize — even I didn't appreciate how exceptional — up from nothing — Asiatic — rejected everywhere — now key player — phenomenon."

"Yes, well," the Boy Chef said, pushing his chair back, "we have a lot of work to do before the diners start arriving."

"Quite — don't let me interfere — catch you later."

He didn't get up. Lew Chun wandered around, went backstage, peeked out and saw him talking to a waiter. Pretty soon, tea was brought to Eric Bern's table, along with an appetizer. The Professor had settled in. Was he only a CFO? Or did he have other duties? Was he also a bodyguard? A snoop? Was he armed? Didn't look it, but you never knew.

Eric Bern vanished in the chaos of a busy night. He wasn't there at closing time. Lew Chun caught a cab at 2 a.m. When it pulled up to his building, a couple quietly sauntered by, holding hands and stopping to kiss every few feet. As he mounted the brownstone steps, a call sounded: "Good night, Mr. Lew Chun." It did not come from the lovers. No point in turning around; he knew who had spoken.

It was like that for the rest of the week. Worthless to confront Bern; he'd say he was following the Colonel's orders. Lew Chun would wait for Shawn Lin to return.

He did so the following Monday, striding into the Boy Chef's little office without knocking. The Colonel extended his hand.

"Don't blame Eric Bern. I asked him to watch over you."

Lew Chun couldn't let it stop here. "What is the Professor besides your CFO? My guardian angel?"

"Guardian demon more like." He went to the urn, poured himself a cup of sencha and sat down. "Look, Lew Chun. You've moved up. More money, more sway but also more exposure. If they want to get me, they'll go after you because you're out there."

"Who's 'they'?"

"Whoever wants what we have. "

Wearily, Lew Chun reminded Shawn Lin that he had never asked for this. Not once.

The Colonel expressed sympathy. Whether it was genuine or calculated was impossible to tell. "I know. But here it is. I want you with me. And I want you and your wife safe. Bern will see to that. Don't let the academic manner deceive you. He's carbon steel inside."

"Mob guy."

"Nothing of the kind. He's an intellectual. And you know how intellectuals are attracted to violence."

Lew Chun said nothing.

"Ever read any Norman Mailer?"

"Some."

"Jean-Paul Sartre, Herbert Marcuse?"

"Mentioned in class."

"Clean fingernails fascinated by dirty hands. Eric Bern is one of those."

"Dangerous."

The Colonel shook his head. "Useful." He drained his teacup. "You have nothing to fear from the Professor. He'll take care of you — and Rita."

"Tina."

"Yes, sorry, *Tina*. I've been away too long."

"Likewise."

The Colonel prepared to leave. "Go home. Spend more time with your lovely wife. Meet me at YFD Monday next. Five p.m. Some issues have arisen."

"Do we have a problem?"

"Many. Nothing you can't handle."

Vacation was over.

****

Amy, Jade, Jimmy, Charlie. Mickey was there, as well, content to unfold a steel office chair and sit near the wall. Lew Chun joined him there. In front, on cognac-colored leather chairs with decorative brass nails, were an Asian and two Caucasians. The first was Mr. Yuan; the others were his partners, Farrar and Dean.

C.C. perched restlessly on the rim of a matching couch alongside the other African-American linebacker type Lew Chun had seen at the airport. Both chewed toothpicks and radiated attitude. Close to the mahogany desk was Eric Bern, and behind it sat Shawn Lin. The walls were lined with matched-set law books behind glass covers. A few middle managers were scattered in the back; at a hand gesture from Mr. Yuan, they exited and closed the office door behind them.

"I will make this short, if not sweet." With a mechanical smile, the Colonel consulted his manual. "Opportunities multiply as they are seized." His eyes swept the room. "We are at war, ladies and gentlemen." He closed the book and recited from memory. "The point is simply to win the siege with as few losses as possible. Thus, we must know our enemy."

Mickey tossed a softball question. "And who is the enemy this time?"

"'This time' is the right way to put it. There is always an enemy. There always will *be* an enemy. Success breeds envy. Envy breeds assaults. Not so long ago, we were beset by the Russians. Recently, it was the Cartagenas. Now we have a new group who want what we have."

After a theatrical pause, he spoke. "Our old foes the Chinese." He squeezed every cubic centimeter out of the silence that followed.

Then: "I hear you say, 'But *you're* Chinese, Colonel.' Yes, I am. So are others in this room. But I'm not talking about us. I'm not talking about Chinese-Americans rising in American society. I'm talking about China-Chinese — people who have no interest in living here, in making it here. They want to smash our hive and carry the honey home."

Nobody reacted. Everyone looked to the leader.

Shawn Lin elaborated. "I'm here to tell you that they will do no such thing. Any comments? Any suggestions?"

The temperature in the room dropped a couple of degrees.

"Well then, let me tell you what Sun Tzu says: 'Though we have heard of stupid haste in war, cleverness has never been seen associated with long delays.'"

Mr. Yuan spoke up in a calm, firm tone. "We can hardly be clever until we know more about the enemy than this."

"Very true," Shawn Lin responded. "Let me give you a brief history lesson." He got up and perched on the desk. Sweeping the room with his penetrating hazel eyes, he gave a lecture on China as a major source of acetic anhydrate, ephedrine, pseudoephedrine. "The Professor will elaborate."

Eric Bern took the floor. "Cocaine, heroin, crystal methamphetamine — illegal in China — 50 grams of heroin — punishable by death — public executions — one televised — whole cities watched — and yet … and yet — ever-expanding demand."

Shawn Lin resumed. "Why is this?" He answered his own query. "Because the consumption is too pleasurable and the production is too profitable."

The Professor amplified the point. "Millions at first — billions by the '80s — now, trillions."

Lew Chun suspected that everyone in the room knew this. They registered awe anyway.

"So." Shawn Lin returned to his seat behind the desk, where he could preside in comfort. "Now we know who the enemy is. He looks like some of us, and he thinks like *all* of us — shrewd, single-minded, ruthless. Solution, ladies and gentlemen?"

In about as long as it took to spit out his toothpick, C.C. said, "Be shrewder, more single-minded, more ruthless."

"Precisely. But how?" Back to Sun Tzu's *The Art of War*. "Just as water retains no constant shape, so in warfare there are no constant conditions. We must modify our tactics in relation to our opponent."

He reminded the group of past foes and old victories. "We beat back the Russians because they were fighting on unfamiliar turf and because, as C.C. points out, our hearts were harder."

C.C. permitted himself a small speculative grin.

"The Cartagenas needed more imagination. It was not a matter of force alone. We enlisted the American government. It did what we could not."

Bern again: "Government won't work against the Chinese — diplomatic issues — stepping on hands — war by other means — United Nations committees — complicated — could end up with both sides against us."

Shawn Lin wrapped it up. "I need solutions, people. Strategies. Within the next 24 hours, drop off your ideas through the mail slot in the front door. I don't care how ridiculous they may seem. I want to hear them. *Within the next 24 hours.* Company dismissed."

Every listener's face registered a kind of hopeless confusion. How could any of them invent a strategy when Shawn Lin himself was empty of ideas? Lew Chun appeared to be as bewildered as the rest. Yet he did have an idea hidden behind the mask. It might be effective.

Or it could destroy the whole complicated structure the Colonel had so laboriously built — and everyone in it.

****

But there was no meeting in the next 24 hours. Or the next week. Or, in fact, for about four years. Tina and Lew Chun happened to be looking out the window of their apartment when the first reverberations shook the building. Then the secondary noises began. They knew not what had taken place, only that under a brilliant late-summer canopy, the city had caught fire.

In the next few days, they and the rest of the world learned what implacable hatred could accomplish using the element of surprise. Sun Tzu never knew anything like this — immense silver planes plunging into stone and metal towers, thousands screaming, jumping to their deaths, burning alive. Whatever had been stirring in the Colonel's mind had been obliterated by the suicidal gesture of the executioners. Or so Lew Chun believed when the meeting was indefinitely postponed.

Like everyone else, he and Tina groped for meaning in those days, a purpose in this obscene celebration of death. Raised in post-Confucian society, he had no faith in faith. And Tina — who had only the residual Jewish sympathies of her parents, who never went to synagogue, even on the high holy days — was just as bewildered by religion, let alone fanaticism.

They went on numbly, uncertain and afraid like the rest of the city. And then, one afternoon a year later, a local urgency joined the national ones. Tina felt a new life kicking inside her. Every day, the Chuns could see the aftermath of loathing, the stink and pollution saturating the air. What kind of world would their child face? Two world wars had been fought in the past century. Was this the beginning of the third one, the one that would drown civilization in a sea of fiery aggression and insane vengeance? There were weeks when Lew Chun and Tina cried together at breakfast, at dinner and in bed.

And still... Lew Chun could never recall who it was who said humans can adapt to anything. Some truth teller in one of his textbooks. As the weeks rumbled on like a subway running late, there was a powerful effort to recover the regular, the normal, the average common rhythms of life in New York City. There was little to do at first. The Pan Asian suffered a sharply diminished take, and there was very little money coming in from the Colonel's other holdings. At least that was what Eric Bern claimed when they met in the half-empty restaurant. The Professor said Shawn Lin would carry the full staff nonetheless. He believed that the bad times would slowly pull away like the neap tide; patience was the key.

Lew Chun thought it was all a lie to keep the lid on the employees until the Colonel could get rid of them one by one. In fact, Eric Bern was not lying, nor was Shawn Lin. Sooner than New Yorkers dared to think, fear stopped walking behind them. They learned all over again that not every police or fire siren was a portent of catastrophe — that once more, vapor trails over Manhattan were the signs of commercial jets flying safe routes. Everywhere they walked or rode or wandered, there were cops in blue uniforms and camouflage outfits; Army reservists with helmets and AK-47s guarded the tunnels and bridges. People griped about the encroachments on their privacy, about the intrusions of government, about removing shoes and getting X-rayed at airports. But they started to dine out again. And young couples counted down the days when they would welcome a new member of the family.

Lew Chun returned to work, going over accounts paid and unpaid with Eric Bern. In the process, he saw in detail where the revenue came from. Handsome intake from all three restaurants, with Lew Chun's Pan Asian in the lead, amounted to a fraction of the income. None of this was discussed as they went through the books. Lew Chun didn't bring up the subject, because he didn't want to confront the reality that lay behind the grosses. And Bern had been instructed to stick to the numbers and forget about the letters — the identities of clients, the names of chemicals and the factories that produced the product.

Tina and Lew Chun called their son Aaron, a name inspired by their Jewish and Chinese heritage; the last two letters were the Mandarin word for "peace." They urgently needed to believe in *on* during the winter of 2002. Even if it was the self-deception that believed the lie, they clung to it. For two weeks, Lew Chun wrote a letter to his mother every day, charting Aaron's weight, his growth, the dazzle in his pecan eyes, the fuzz turning into hair. Pictures were crammed into the envelopes and handed to C.C. when he dropped by. He promised to give them to the Colonel personally.

There was no way Lew Chun could check on this; Shawn Lin stayed out of sight, more rumor than person. So the Boy Chef was surprised and pleased when, at the end of a fortnight, he received a letter from China. His mother had in fact received the news and the photos. She went on and on about her late husband, about how delighted he would have been to be the grandfather of a boy, about her own happiness. She confessed to a growing infirmity; travel would be impractical. And anyway, getting a visa to visit America would be next to impossible — something about Lew Chun's activities.

The letter ended with one of the sayings people have written in China since the days of Confucius. Despite the re-education camps, the Central Committee could not expunge them: "If your plan is for one year, plant rice. If your plan is for 10 years, plant trees. If your plan is for 100 years, educate your child."

That Lew Chun would do. No chance Aaron would be like him — speaking with an accent, bewildered by a country he pretended to understand, working for someone who could end a person's life and have a condolence card sent to his family.

Actually, the Colonel became quite benign when he granted the Boy Chef an audience. A trust fund had been set up so that Aaron's education, from kindergarten through college, would be paid in full. Lew Chun would have refused money outright, but everyone knew what school fees were in the city. He promised to pay back every cent. Shawn Lin nodded with half-closed eyes.

The young parents worked out their reply to current events: They would answer annihilation with life. Aaron had barely passed his first birthday when Tina's belly became noticeably swollen with child. On the birth of their daughter, Lew Chun phoned the Colonel, failed to get through and left a message: In gratitude, they would name their second-born Lin in his honor.

That got him. "This is well," he said when the call was returned. "But on one condition."

"Anything."

"Doubtless you intend to spell her name L-I-N."

"Yes."

"You are to spell it L-Y-N-N."

"As you wish. But why?"

"It will sound American. It will look American. Too late for me to assimilate. Too late for you, as well. Not too late for your children. Look around you, Lew Chun. Look around."

"At what?"

"Ah, the Boy Chef is still a youth. I will explain before the next meeting. Be here early Thursday — noon."

****

Save for the Colonel, the room was empty. The *house* seemed empty. No C.C., no secretary. Lew Chun took up his regular position and listened.

Shawn Lin resumed exactly where he had left off, as if there had been no days and nights and months between conversations — or, to be more precise, monologues. "In America, acceptance, tolerance, goodwill — these are illusions. All that talk about freedom, economic opportunity for all? Guano. Bird shit. The truth is, the people who run things, they don't want you to be yourself. They want you to be them."

"And we can't be them, can we?" Lew Chun played along, hoping the Colonel would reach the end of his goddamn lecture, let him go back to work and play.

"You married a Jewish girl. You could learn a lot from her people. I did. From day one, the Jews understood what this country is all about. They didn't change their names, didn't alter their looks, most of them. They kept their heads down, didn't attract attention, scored in school, seized their chances, rose in the American world. We have to do the same."

"I'm trying," Lew Chun said.

"So I have observed."

The Colonel returned to his little book and turned the page, seeking a passage. The day's newspapers lay on a little table; Lew Chun flashed on headlines about the war in Iraq until he couldn't stand the images on the pages or in his head. He stared out the window at the repairing city.

Indistinguishable conversation occurred in the hall. Seconds later, C.C. opened the door, wished them good morning and informed Shawn Lin that Mickey was here. Lew Chun barely had time to read the op-ed section before Eric Bern's arrival was announced. Then came Jade and then Amy, unaccompanied by husbands. When Mr. Yuan arrived, C.C. ushered them all in. He stayed.

There was the customary polite chatter. Everyone found a seat, and Shawn Lin began. "I have some bad news and some worse news."

He consulted his desk calendar. "You will recall, I asked for ideas to help us survive the next battle. Then history intervened. Now we are back on that page. There will be a battle after all. This much is certain." He waited for the buzz to stop. "Now the bad news and the worse news. I received two letters yesterday. One was from Dr. Qin. He is my cardiologist. I will have to have a bypass. Four arteries are blocked. I will be out of commission for more than two months."

Little broken cries of distress from the daughters, sympathy from the men. The Colonel wasn't having any of it. "While I'm recovering, someone has to take over this desk and its responsibilities."

Everyone looked around. He went on. "I have decided on that person. My cousin Lew Chun. You all know him." Grins of solidity from Mickey, who would smile at a virus if Shawn Lin told him to, and from C.C. and Eric Bern. From the ladies, rigid faces and arctic eyes. Lew Chun tried to convey with expression that he didn't seek this promotion, in fact detested it. But there was only so much he could convey without speaking, and in any case, the sisters clearly believed he had only one distinguishing characteristic: blind, fierce and implacable ambition. Their father had finally found someone as ruthless as he was.

Jade broke the frost. "Daddy, this is insane."

Amy was more explicit. "You're panicking. He's too young. He doesn't have the experience."

"OK, we're females. We know our place," Jade wheedled. "But why not Charlie? Or Jimmy? Or both?"

Shawn Lin consulted his manual. Jade's voice dropped an octave. "Oh, please, for God's sake, not that old general and his fortune cookies."

It was like striking the high priest at his altar. Outraged, the Colonel raked them up and down. He spoke of respect, told them that every cent they had was the result of his generosity. He reminded his daughters of a few things. He had brought them here, paid for their schooling, their wardrobes, their weddings. He had offered their husbands careers, put their pieces on the board, granted them the ability to keep their kids well-housed, well-fed, well-clothed. And what was the response? Tantrums from overindulged brats.

As dressing-downs go, Mickey confided to C.C., it had to rate among his top five. When the Colonel dismissed his daughters, the sisters exited without a backward glance, walking with small deliberate steps, their heads held high as they tried to retain a shred of dignity. It took him a few minutes to settle down. When he did, in a calm voice he thanked the rest for coming. They took this for a dismissal and started for the door. Eric Bern never left his seat. Shawn Lin said, "A few words." He was looking at the new appointee. Lew Chun wondered whether they would be bad words or worse words.

****

"My time is restricted," he said when the three of them had the room to themselves.

"Listen, Colonel," Lew Chun burst out, "these bypasses — only last week the Science section had a story about how fast people recover. A month and they're back at work. They just have to take it easy for a while. No late hours, booze. But you don't drink much, so there's no—"

He laughed. "What operation? I'm not having an operation."

"But you just said—"

"I said many things. One of them was, let me put it politely, an exaggeration. My heart is strong. I wanted to leak misinformation about the terrible thing that happened to the leader. With my girls, by the weekend the entire East Coast will believe I'm a walking cardiac."

"But why?"

"When the Chinese dealers and distributors hear I have serious medical issues, they'll make their move. These are the enemy, Lew Chun. Unlike any others. They'll think they have an opportunity, and they'll seize it. Then we take our countermeasures, with you as navigator."

"Navigator? Why me?"

He held a bunch of papers in his hand. "In what seems an eon ago, I asked everyone in the room to submit a plan. You thought by now I had forgotten."

He held the papers at arm's length. As he spoke, he fed the ideas into a shredder. Each contribution made a high ripping noise, like a big animal digesting a small animal.

"We can blow up their building and make it look like an accident."
Shred.

"We can turn them over to the FBI and get out of the way."
Shred.

"We can get hold of their tax records and give them to the IRS. That's the way they got Capone. Tax evasion, not murder."

Shred.

He addressed the two listeners, alternating from Lew Chun to Eric Bern and back again. "These Chinese, I know them. They're not like our other competitors through the years. These people are out of reach. Their operatives are here, but their laboratories are halfway across the world. They can get to us, and we can't get to them."

He reached into a drawer and pulled out a piece of stationery folded over twice. From across the room, Lew Chun recognized it.

"That is," he continued, "we couldn't get to them until this paper came across my desk. It contains an idea so original, so bold, so audacious it might well deter our Chinese rivals, not just now but for a long time to come."

"Has to," Professor Bern predicted. "Done right — dead cert."

They turned to the inventor of that dead certainty. He sputtered, "But, Shawn Lin, this was just a wild fantasy. I handed it in as a kind of joke."

"A joke?"

"All right, a dream. There's no way it can happen. We're not an army. We're a small band of — of what? Merchants, I suppose."

"Merchants. Yes, why not? Like all merchants, we have buyers. And those buyers will go elsewhere if they can find better products for lower prices. Fair enough; I believe in a free market. The mob didn't. The Cartagenians didn't. Neither did the Russians, and neither do the Chinese. They want to obliterate everyone who stands in the way of their cartel. We will not permit that to happen."

He handed Lew Chun his own letter.

"Aloud," he demanded.

The Boy Chef swallowed hard and read his own words.

****

He got home early that night. By now, they had steady help, a middle-aged Caribbean couple, Billie and Trevor Le Sueur, vetted up, down and sideways by the Colonel, C.C. and his crew. Trevor's face bore a close resemblance to a fielder's mitt, dark with use, creased and flexible. The Chuns were assured that he was a black belt in something aggressive and that he was armed with several weapons, all of them licensed.

When the Le Sueurs went to be in the spare room that was no longer spare, Lew Chun and Tina kissed the sleeping children and loved away the night. He asked her again, as on other occasions, whether it bothered her that like most Asian men, he had so little body hair.

"You mean like those hominids who have to shave their backs?" she asked.

"Well — I mean, does it make me any less masculine?"

"Baby," she said, "men like you are more evolved. If I wanted a yak, I would have married a yak."

"I'm sure there were many yaks who wanted you."

"Whole herds of them."

It was like that all the time. He wanted no other, nor did she. No incidents disturbed them that month or for several months to come. He learned later that Shawn Lin had people keeping an eye on the building 24/7.

But if things were the same or better at home, things were different and ominous at work. The vital customers, the politicians, the police captains, even the press people began to speak to him and of him with a deference mixed with respect and fear.

Pondering this over the course of weeks, Lew Chun began to understand. It was because of that letter he had submitted. Not a word of its contents had leaked out; what did escape, however, was news about the exclusion of the daughters and of Jimmy and Charlie. The Boy Chef hoped that after a few days, the Colonel realized how ludicrous the idea was and simply hadn't gotten around to saying so.

Less than a week later, Julie showed up solo. Rather than duck her questions, Lew Chun floated over to her table. She was in tangerine silk, breathtaking and well aware of her effect.

"You're much too beautiful to dine alone."

In a cold sotto voce, she responded, "I'm on assignment."

"Where's Gia?"

"In school."

"Night school?"

No answer. He ordered two glasses of Champagne.

Julie demurred. "I don't want any."

"They're both for me," Lew Chun explained.

"I hear you're colossal," she said without awe. "You give the order to swim and everyone asks, 'How far out?'"

"Julie, that's so ludicrous I don't know where to begin. I'm the boss here, period. Shawn Lin's daughters and sons-in-law run the other restaurants, and they're a lot closer to him than I am."

"By blood maybe." She leaned in as the bubbly arrived, changed her mind and took a sip. He offered to clink glasses, and she responded. Then it was all business again.

"Come on, Lew Chun, word is you've kissed a frog and become a prince."

"Whose word is that?"

"A source. Let's leave it at that."

"Your source is wrong, Julie. Everything is just the way it was. Nothing has changed. I still work a 12-hour day, and the customers still come to eat what we serve."

"Look, it's no secret your cousin wants to go legit. Are you maybe helping him open a chain of restaurants? I promise it'll go no farther than me. That's not what I'm after."

"What *are* you after, Julie?"

She looked around. When she was satisfied no one was looking or listening: "They never found Frank's killer. That's what I'm after."

"Can't be all you're after. When we first met — you and your sister and Frank were after something else. Something to do with South America, remember?"

"Yes, I remember. We've moved on, you and I."

"What does that mean?"

"What I said. Your cousin obviously found a way of dealing with the competition. Good for him. I just hope Frank wasn't part of that way."

"He wasn't."

"You don't know that."

"I know Shawn Lin."

Julie's lovely face turned unlovely. She fished around in her purse for money or a credit card. There was no way Lew Chun could confide in her or even talk to her. He said good night, wished her luck and let her pay her own check. If it was going to be a war from now on, he was not about to fund Julie's "sources" and underwrite the hostilities.

That night, he left word on Shawn Lin's private phone. Some people were nosing around — he didn't mention names — and there was very likely a loose tongue somewhere in his organization.

****

Eric Bern called the following day and said he wanted to drop by over the weekend, some time when Tina was out with the kids and they could talk alone. That wasn't hard to arrange. Aaron had been agitating to revisit the Bronx Zoo; this time, his sister would come along. As an added enticement, Tina would bring their foldable two-seat stroller. The Le Sueurs would meet them at the seal pool and wheel them to their favorite animals.

The Professor arrived at 10. Lew Chun introduced him to the family. Tina disliked him on sight, a feeling she made no attempt to hide. A car and driver were already arranged; Lew Chun would join Tina and the children in the early afternoon. With much laughter, they agreed to meet at the monkey house at 1 p.m.

When Tina and Aaron and Lynn left, the Professor asked Lew Chun to join him at the window. They watched everyone get into the limo and take off for the Bronx. Ten seconds later, another limo pulled away from the curb and followed. "Our men," Eric Bern noted. "Staying discreetly behind — keep an eye on them at the zoo."

"You think of everything," Lew Chun said, deadpan.

"Colonel does — amazing figure."

"Yes, quite." Lew Chen mocked the Englishman's affectations, but the Professor went rushing on, austerely refusing coffee, tea and cake.

"Came here to talk, not eat — much to discuss."

They sat across from each other at the butcher block table in the kitchen.

"OK," Lew Chun said. "The floor is yours."

"Nutshell-brief — tested your ideas."

"Tested how?"

"More accurate to say intensely researched."

"And?"

"Fantastic, *impractical*, loony — what you thought, correct? In point of fact, quite practical — going ahead with them."

"Holy shit."

"Exactly."

Lew Chun had to stop and think about the implications, what they meant, how dangerous and, for all he knew, fatal this could be. From the look on Eric Bern's face, he could see there would be no U-turns ahead. He tried to stare the Professor down, and the words tumbled out: "Who the hell *are* you?"

"No secret — Colonel gave you my curriculum vitae."

"Well, then what the hell are you?"

"In a plane — navigator. Here on earth — tactician. Others dream." He pointed to Lew Chun. "I work things out — three dimensions. Your idea, your theory — I make it throw a shadow."

"You still haven't answered my question."

"Swiss citizen — Eric Bern not my true name — trained engineer — twice-divorced, intelligent, flawed, drawn to money, drawn to power. But — a big but — absolutely loyal to my employer — know no other fidelity. Sufficient?"

"Not really. What about before you met Shawn Lin?"

"Adviser — Emirates — countermeasures."

"What does that mean, 'countermeasures'?"

"Arranged for their self-defense — surveillance, ordnance, certain aircraft. And so on. "

"What kind of 'and so on'?"

He made an empty-handed gesture. "Told you I was loyal." But then he disclosed a little. Not enough but something that could be dissected.

"Arms trade — going on for decades. Dealers change — grade of weapons moves up — essentially the same thing. Nations, republics, sometimes significant individuals — all need to protect their property — citizenry, families. If they have the means — dealers aren't hard to find."

"You know this how?"

"Was one. Once. Shelf life very brief — too many colleagues took 'early retirement.'" He drew a finger around his throat. "Became a broker — put weapons sellers in touch with prospective clients. Both sides pay well — yours truly included in the final negotiations sometimes — or not. Their choice, not mine."

"And this is one of the times you're included."

"More than a broker to Shawn Lin — planner, as well — seeing this operation through till completion."

"Very selfless."

"Not altruism — fealty. Don't mind taking risks — reward worth it many times over. Think I will have that coffee after all — get you one while I'm at it?"

While the Professor fussed about, Lew Chun recalled that ominous meeting a few days before. It was as if he were the director, the cameraman and the actor all at once. A waking nightmare.

****

"You asked what we can do against a powerful enemy," Lew Chun's shattering letter had begun. "This enemy doesn't have the backing of mainland China, but business is business. The People's Republic will never use military force against these manufacturers and dealers of illegal drugs. Not as long as they're peddled overseas, away from the Homeland. Not when China can be given a major slice of the profits.

"These drugs come from all over — China, Turkey, Afghanistan, even Africa. But they are all refined and packaged in one place.

"Indonesia.

"I have gone to the library, gotten the maps out, found out what I could about the Chinese factories for manufacturing high-grade heroin, crystal meth and all the rest. Their main refinery is located on a small, heavily guarded island."

"Miabu is 10 miles across at its widest point. There are two main ports. Freighters are said to pick up cargos of plywood and textiles. That they do — along with illegal substances. No doubt these are taken below decks and well concealed, in case of inspections.

"We can't hope to fight such competitors with arms. They're too well defended. We can't infiltrate their personnel. The men and women are all Indonesian, apparently from the same villages, so they all know each other. A stranger would be detected immediately.

"What to do?

"If we were a nation, no problem. We would invade.

"But we're not a nation, not even a city-state. We're just an enterprise.

"However, we have what the financial managers call Discretionary Income. If we carry out this plan, we'll need it. A lot of it. Multiple millions, would be my guess."

Shawn Lin interrupted him. "You don't guess. You *know*."

"Very well," Lew Chun conceded. "I know." He continued to read from the letter. "On the island of Miabu is a phenomenon peculiar to a lot of Indonesian islands. It has a volcano. Naga Kecil. Small Dragon. It hasn't been active since 1877. Even then, it erupted for only a few days, and the lava did more damage to outlying structures than it did to the few island dwellers. But that was more than a century ago.

"Today Miabu is populated almost entirely by workers in the Chinese factories and packaging plants.

"For an effective attack on our competitors, we need three things.

"A) Unity of purpose.

"B) The element of surprise.

"C) A large explosive device.

"Not the kind of bomb that will destroy a small village. This would not impress the Chinese, nor would it stop them from their work. Repairs would be immediate. And soon enough, they would reply with a device of their own.

"But what if we were somehow to acquire a bomber? And what if this plane were to drop its payload not on a village, not on a plant but in the mouth of the volcano?

"There's a very good chance that it would trigger a major eruption, with explosions, air black with cinders, lava pouring out and cascading across the stone sides, setting fire to the island and the wooden buildings on it. And what is the likelihood that those buildings — every one of them — are made of cheap local lumber?

"Of course, this would not be Krakatoa. That was a massive eruption. Back in 1872, it darkened the skies of Indonesia for weeks and colored the brilliant sunsets of Europe for months afterward.

"Nothing like that is possible from a man-made catastrophe.

"But it could show how far we can reach and what earthly forces we can unleash.

"Very truly yours, etc."

The silence was broken by Eric Bern's applause. He kept it up for quite a long time, making Lew Chun uncomfortable but clearly giving pleasure to Shawn Lin. Then the Colonel spoke.

"This is a suggestion so outlandish and foolhardy it would be laughed out of any meeting of sensible men. And women, for that matter. That's why I kept my daughters away — and everyone else but the three of us.

"This outline you have sketched — it demands work, long hours and a massive investment of time and cash."

"Then we shouldn't—" Lew Chun began. But it was like trying to hold back the rain. The Colonel brought out his cherished manual and pointed to a passage. Sun Tzu had already shown the way: "Open confrontation will trigger overpowering resistance. Thus, the key to victory is surprise." Shawn Lin looked up. "Except for the delivery system," he declared, "warfare remains the same over the millennia. Surprise is always in season."

✳✳✳✳

From then on, Shawn Lin scheduled strategy meetings at all hours, and his new appointee was forever inventing new reasons for leaving abruptly. One weekend night, as soon as Aaron and Lynn were asleep, Tina's long-suppressed rage bubbled over. This had gone far enough; Lew Chun had to get out, leave the Colonel's wretched and illegal organization. He had to save himself and his family, open a new, independent restaurant place away from New York, far from the Colonel and his devious schemes, whatever they were. She would help her husband, do the paperwork, borrow money, anything to get out from under the monster that had no name, a great evil thing with secrets a man couldn't share with his wife. When Lew Chun promised to think about quitting, she rolled her eyes in theatrical disbelief. The clashes intensified.

"If it was anyone but you, I'd say you were seeing someone."

"You're the only one I'm seeing, Tina."

"Well, you're not seeing enough. Of me. Of the kids. What the fuck is really going on? Tell me."

"Nothing's going on. We're all just working overtime. That's all."

"What kind of work? You were never like this before, all knotted up, jumping every time the phone rings, tossing in your sleep. *When* you sleep."

"I sleep fine. You're the one who twitches in the middle of the night. You're the one who's restless."

They would circle around the unnamable with accusations, counter-accusations, attacks, excuses, until both were too exhausted to go on. Passion was not an answer. No matter how intense, it was temporary.

Tina was just as angry afterward as beforehand, and Lew Chun was increasingly defensive, jittery, quarrelsome.

The next week, it got worse, ending with a "get out," followed by an "all right, I will." An hour and a few beers later, Lew Chun came in sheepishly and apologized, and so did Tina, and they made it through the night and then the week ahead.

But the marriage was fraying. It didn't help when Lew Chun accepted a late drink from Julie. She didn't act surprised or grateful, didn't ask questions, simply waited patiently for him to crack open.

Two truths were known to him. A) From any angle, in any light, Julie was so beautiful she made his throat constrict. B) She was not — and never would be — trustworthy.

That they wound up at her place was expected. That she would try to mine him for information when they were lying back on overstuffed pillows was unsurprising. What *was* startling was how much she already knew. Not about the marriage but about the business.

"Your cousin's supposed to be kicking around something big."

"I told you what it was."

"You said real estate. This is not real estate."

"You know that how?"

"Doesn't matter. I know it."

"Well, you're better informed than I am."

"Please don't give me that crap, Lew Chun. You want to protect Shawn Lin, fine. But don't tell me you don't know what's going on."

No words from him.

"I'll find out another way."

"Is that a threat, Julie?"

No words from her.

So the night came to a rapid conclusion, with subdued rage on both sides. Julie's because even with all her wiles, she couldn't get Lew Chun to spill anything. His because Julie made clear that there would be no stopping her on the way to a Pulitzer. Bad stuff all around and nowhere to go. So he went home. Tina didn't say anything when Lew Chun came in the door with roses and apologies. She didn't have to.

****

"I need to speak to you."

"Of course you do, boy." Boy. Shawn Lin had shifted back to patronizing mode. He waved at an empty chair. As expected, Eric Bern was already in attendance. The surprise was C.C. Lew Chun no longer cared. He didn't intend to withhold anything from anybody. He brought up old resentments, as well as new ones, complained about confusion of purpose, misery at home, guards and security people who made privacy and independent movement a thing of the past. He spoke of edgy nerves, of plans that seemed to be nothing but talk, of Julie and what she knew or implied she knew.

All three of them listened politely and intently. But as always, it was only the Colonel's reaction that counted. When Lew Chun finished, Shawn Lin closed his eyes for a moment, as if meditating on the weight of the world, and then opened them and said, "You're absolutely right." That was the signal for the other two to regard the Boy Chef with sympathy and understanding.

Shawn Lin wasn't finished. "You have been open, and I have been closed. Not a way to do things." But he wasn't through. He wagged a finger. "Sleeping with the enemy is bad; sleeping with the curious is intolerable."

Lew Chun writhed in his seat, furious with the Colonel for telling the others about his indiscretion but angrier with himself. "I should have known I would be followed that night, all the way to Julie's place — and, for all I knew, inside her bedroom."

This impertinence went unacknowledged. "Journalists are woodpeckers," the Colonel continued. "They never stop hammering with their sharp little beaks. Haven't you learned that by now?"

"I was having trouble at home. Julie Tseng got me at a difficult moment. It won't happen again."

"No, I don't believe it will." Shawn Lin shifted the subject before the Boy Chef could add anything. With Eric Bern's aid, he took a large heavily embossed paper from the center drawer of his desk and Scotch-taped it to the wall.

"A more compelling view than the one of Oakland."

Even from where Lew Chun sat, he knew what it was: an ordnance map of the island of Miabu. The maker's name was obliterated, but it had an official look, like something from a U.S. Army survey or possibly an Indonesian one.

The Professor spoke: "Kicking this around for years — arrangements, how to requisition what we need — no waves, no chatter. Don't want to awaken our Chinese friends — don't want to arouse the world."

"The plane is not an issue," Shawn Lin explained. "This does not have to be one of those jumbo jets with bomb bays the size of a Mercedes. We will requisition the needed aircraft at the appropriate time."

Lew Chun hesitated. He knew the smart play would be to remain mute, let the Colonel reveal the weakness of his plan. But he couldn't stop himself. "Then what's the hang-up?"

"The weapon. In your own letter, you mention it. Or have you forgotten?"

"A bomb, I suggested."

Eric Bern said, "Unspecific."

"I don't know anything about bombs."

Shawn Lin pointed out, "This much you should know. A quiescent volcano usually has a cap at its peak. The cap is made of cooled lava. It isn't as hard as a rock; it *is* a rock. A standard military bomb would bounce on it."

"Hopeless, then."

"Don't be absurd." He signaled for the Professor to take the lead.

"Saw what happened in Desert Storm — right? War in Iraq — rapid advances — why? — because NATO air forces employed bunker busters — laser-guided bombs — vast destruction — light payload — 650 pounds max."

"And you're going to buy one of those bunker busters."

"Hardly," Shawn Lin broke in. "For one thing, they're stored in Army forts, guarded by battalions. Secondly, even if we could get hold of one, it would be overkill. We don't need anything so powerful. And traceable. Interpol would be on our doorstep in a week."

He enjoyed Lew Chun's bewilderment.

"I sent you to school to learn a little history. Ever hear of World War II?"

"Yes, I've heard of World War II."

"We had three enemies. They comprised the Axis. Identify them." He winked at C.C. and Eric Bern.

Lew Chun surprised him. "Germany, Japan, Italy."

"Excellent. Most of the imbeciles out there say Russia. They forget the birthplace of fascism. Now, can you identify Barnes Wallis?"

"There you have me."

"He was a weapons designer during World War II. Wallis invented the bouncing bomb that skimmed across the water. There was a movie about it."

"*The Dam Busters.*"

"Bravo."

"Turner had it on TNT. Colorized."

Shawn Lin pantomimed applause. "Wallis also invented the earthquake bomb."

Eric Bern picked up the story. "Missile with a tail — picked up speed — spun furiously. Dropped from five miles up — broke the sound barrier. Explosives cased in steel — bomb punched through metal two feet thick. Ate through *15* feet of concrete bunker. Then the blast — indirect — at the side or underneath the target — devastation followed."

"That was 50 years ago," Lew Chun pointed out.

"Precisely, boy, precisely," Shawn Lin stated. "Ancient history. Obsolete. Nobody cares about such ordnance anymore. Which is why those earthquake bombs are not so well-guarded. One of them, in fact, has been…lifted from a storage place outside Glasgow."

"And you know where it is."

"Not exactly. It will take a substantial amount of time and money to find the location. And it will take a more substantial amount of money to purchase the thing."

"How long and how much?"

"All of a sudden, you're very inquisitive," Shawn Lin observed.

"Not so sudden."

With slow, almost formal movements, Shawn Lin got up from behind the desk, drew up a chair near his adjutant and spoke as if no one else were in the room.

"I appreciate your situation. I don't want to wreck your marriage. Things are difficult enough for you two as it is."

No counterargument from Lew Chun. He was too curious to interrupt the Colonel mid-presentation.

"If you come in, boy, you take a long shot. This is bold, this operation. No one ever attempted anything like this before. It could go bad. Very bad. Or it could make us so powerful we can sell the business for billions and live legitimate, privileged lives on an island somewhere."

"How about Manhattan island?"

"If that's your choice, why not?"

"And if I don't come in?"

"We'll go ahead without you. From this point on, you will revert to restaurant manager."

"In other words, I'll be shut out of my own idea."

"Perhaps it's better that way."

"I don't think so," Lew Chun responded before he knew what he was saying — and abruptly realized that he wanted to know the plans, the procedures, everything.

"Once you're committed, there is no illuminated exit sign over the door like in the theater."

"Get out now or stay forever, right?"

The Colonel didn't need to answer. If the Boy Chef ever doubted the outcome of this meeting, he knew it now. Had he wanted out, he would not have made it past C.C., who was sitting by the door.

"I'll stay," he answered.

"Splendid." Eric Bern handed him two spiral notebooks. The temperature of the room went down. Everyone relaxed. For a self-dramatizing moment, Lew Chun imagined the ground opening under him. It vanished as quickly as it came. He knew only too well that he was not Dante and Shawn Lin was not Satan and Eric Bern was not Virgil. They were just four American gentlemen on an autumn afternoon, planning the end of the world.

****

Tina could see his dodges and evasions, but she couldn't see through them. Lew Chun kept maintaining that things were exactly the same as before, and she kept insisting that he was hiding something, covering up for criminals.

Long before their parents acknowledged it, Aaron and Lynn sensed that Mommy and Daddy were not getting along. They acted out, became querulous and hostile to each other, and went at the source of their insecurity.

Lew Chun began to seek any excuse to stay late at the Pan Asian. On a slow night, Gia showed up — the first time in months. She was alone. He passed her table, looked down and said, "May I?"

She pointed to the chair opposite her.

He ordered the now-customary Champagne and asked how her sister was.

"We were going to ask you the same thing."

"We?"

"The people I hang with. Colleagues, friends."

"Journalists."

"Some of them."

"Most of them.

"All right, most of them."

"Well, they know more than I do, Gia. I haven't seen her in weeks. She used to come here now and then. Not recently."

"She's been missing for those weeks. Julie sent me an email, said she was going away for a while. Then nothing. All this time, not a message to me, to any of us."

"Maybe she eloped."

"She's not the eloping type. Even you could see that."

He didn't respond. She was a stressed-out, worried young woman, and Lew Chun would make a convenient piñata for her to whack.

Gia leaned over and asked, "You really have no idea where Julie is?"

"Clueless."

"She's been out of touch before. But not like this."

"Tell the cops. They'll make her a missing person."

"I would, except—"

"Except?"

"She'd kill me if she's on a story somewhere."

"There's your answer. She's out there in some undisclosed location, with a notebook and a tape recorder."

"Well, if she is, the story is you and your cousin. That's all she talked about when she dropped out." Gia hesitated and pounced. "Would you take a lie detector test?"

"What kind of question is that? You think this is an act? You think I know where she's hiding?"

"You afraid to take it?"

"No."

"Well, then—"

"Where's the machine? Police headquarters?"

"There's a polygraph at the J-school. They use it for training. Don't worry. It's not admissible in court."

"I'm not worried."

"I bet."

"Try me."

In one of NYU's offices, a reedy student posing as a forensic psychologist administered the test. Straight face, closed door, very official, with a two-way mirror. Strap-on devices on the arms and chest to measure blood pressure, heart rate, physical and emotional status. Gia said she was going for a coffee break, but Lew Chun was pretty sure she lurked behind that mirror, watching his verbal and physical replies.

They were straightforward and to the point. The interrogator started off with harmless questions. What was the subject's name? Where did he live? What was the name of the place where he worked? Where did he buy his clothes? Was he married? What was his wife's name? Did he have children? What were their names? Interspersed with those queries, more probing ones were introduced. Did he know Julie Tseng? What did he think of her? Did he believe she was curious or nosy? Did he find her attractive, pushy, quarrelsome, hot, cold, frigid? Did he know where she was now? And then came the expected flurry of punches: Is Shawn Lin a relative? Do you work for him? Do you think *he* knows where Julie is?

Lew Chun stayed calm, answered with the appropriate noes and yeses. The student finished and removed the straps. About five minutes later, Gia came in with two lattes in big paper containers. Lew Chun thanked her, said he was late for work, invited her to come by the restaurant anytime. She dismissed him with a cold glance and made some entries in a notebook. On his way out, Lew Chun looked back. She was already poring over the polygraph findings.

As he walked to the restaurant, he wondered how he had done. Truth be told, he didn't care for Julie Tseng; she was lovely to look at, but she was pushy and determined in the wrong way. That much must have been registered by the polygraph. The truth was, though, that he truly had no idea of her whereabouts. Surely, this must have shown, as well. What may have leaked out, the Boy Chef feared, was his ambivalence about the Colonel. When he got to work, he put in a call to Shawn Lin's office and asked for an appointment. Four days later, they got back. Lew Chun could be squeezed in after breakfast tomorrow for 10 minutes.

Admitted to the inner sanctum, he wasted no time on niceties. He spoke about the missing Julie Tseng, her sister, the lie detector. Shawn Lin exhibited no emotion at all, nor was he the least bit interested in the test.

"Why should I care about a reporter on the make?" he asked, expecting no reply and getting none. "You think such a hustler could get past the front door here? You believe her sister has the slightest idea how to investigate a story? These are entry-level snoops, amateurs in every sense."

He gestured with his right hand, waving the subject away. "They've been sniffing around since Frank Alba was shot, both of them. Will Dean is all over this. One lawsuit and they'll be lucky to get jobs writing Stop & Shop flyers. Now, as long as you're here, let me bring you up to speed…"

Lew Chun hardly heard what he said; the charts and maps went by like glimpses of the countryside seen from a train window, because thoughts kept caroming around in his brain: Why would the Colonel want to know about Frank Alba at all? If Julie Tseng was so insignificant, why was Will Dean "all over this"? But to think that way was to be irrational. Shawn Lin had to be above such considerations. He fought Russians, Colombians and now Chinese operations. Why would he bother to swat a couple of gnats?

****

He saw it coming but failed to duck.

"Lew Chun, it's not working. We have to split. We have to live separate lives."

The image of the family fractured, the children beyond reach for days at a time, was too gloomy to contemplate. Apologies, regrets, promises followed. He swore to change, to reform, to make any accommodation to avoid a separation. She hesitated. He entreated. They reconciled — and then the arguments resumed, the shouts growing louder, followed by tears, recriminations, accusations, threats.

The morning after the worst day they had ever spent under one roof, with neither of them speaking except to present a calm and entirely bogus front to the kids, Mickey phoned with the Colonel's latest order. A so-called emergency meeting had been scheduled for 10 a.m. at the Colonel's office. Lew Chun showed up an hour early just to get out of the house. Even so, he had been preceded by Eric Bern and C.C.

They were admitted to the inner sanctum but told to keep quiet and watch as Shawn Lin distributed favors to his Chinatown supplicants. A young man was standing before him, flanked by his elderly grandparents and his father.

"My boy wants to join the Army. The National Guard," the father said. "As you know, we have only a little money from the store and many bellies to fill. My father and mother, Ming himself." He pointed to his son. "Plus Ming's small brothers and their smaller sister."

"I want to be an art director, sir," Ming explained. "I think there is a future in this. Making television backgrounds, creating commercials, designing electronic games."

"So, what's stopping you?" Shawn Lin asked.

Ming was abashed. "Well…money…"

"Get a scholarship."

"With respect, Colonel, my grades are outstanding in art but not good enough in English composition and social studies."

"So you thought to go into the National Guard for a couple of years and then go to college with Army money."

"Yes, sir. But my family is afraid for me."

"I agree with your family."

Much relief on their faces.

Shawn Lin continued. "Ming, the Army, it's all volunteers. This works out to about one percent, perhaps less, of the population. No one cares for the military except the military. You may be sent to dangerous places, with no guarantee of safety. You may come back wounded, in the body or, worse still, in the head, and no one to thank you for your service except a few officers and some political nobodies in Washington."

"But, sir—"

"You need money. I will find the money — if you can find acceptance at a college. Agreed?"

"Sir, it seems to me—"

"State or private, I don't care which. Have you been accepted?"

"I-I haven't tried. I thought the Army—"

"Think again. Return when you are admitted."

The family melted away in a chorus of gratitude.

"Anyone left?" the Colonel demanded.

"One." The voice came from the corridor.

An obese Chinese-American gentleman entered, beaming.

"Joe Din," he said, unnecessarily identifying himself. He was evidently familiar to everyone except Lew Chun. He carried a sheaf of papers and went into his jacket to produce some more.

"Good morning, Colonel," he said brightly. "Good morning, all."

Shawn Lin checked his watch. "And what can I do for you this morning, Joe?"

"You can die."

There was a gray glint, and then pandemonium took over. Joe Din had a pistol in his right hand and fired it directly at Shawn Lin. Without pausing to aim, he spun around and squeezed off two shots at Eric Bern. Lew Chun found himself staring at the barrel of the blued-steel gun. It never went off. C.C. brought down the shooter, firing twice with his own Colt.

Three men were on the floor now, bleeding out — Joe Din, Eric Bern and Shawn Lin. C.C. dialed 911. It was obvious that Joe Din had been hit in the head and chest and that he had no chance of survival. Lew Chun and C.C. rushed to the remaining two. Just then it was impossible to say what their chances were, why they were shot and what was behind the surprise attack. It was the very kind of attack that Sun Tzu kept warning about, yet when it happened, his great disciple was unprepared.

****

He had seen patients in extremis on cop shows. But nothing prepared him for the real thing — someone who was powerful yesterday, now at the mercy of the medical establishment. Tubes everywhere, inserted in Shawn Lin's nostrils and both arms and under the sheets to a catheter. An oxygen device feeding him air inside a clear plastic enclosure. Visitors limited to five minutes.

Lew Chun started to say something, but the man in bed shut him up, deliberately closing his eyes, letting the Boy Chef know that he had no interest in anything he had to say. Shawn Lin wanted him to listen, not speak.

"Here's the irony," he muttered in what was half monologue, half groan. "I thought an attempt on my life, on my enterprise, would be made by some outliers — Colombians who didn't give up, a lone wolf

Russian. But no, in the end it was one of our people, an Asian, a Chinese, a familiar. Somebody got to Joe Din. C.C. killed him, right?"

Lew Chun nodded.

"We don't know who that somebody is. But we can make a guess. The important thing is not to slow down on the project."

"Shawn Lin, you have to heal. We can deal with the project later."

"No. Don't you see? We show the slightest hesitation, we retreat one inch, they take advantage. They overwhelm us. We have to show them. Things are in place."

His breath came in broken gulps. Glancing at the wall clock, he asked, "Eric Bern — he's all right?"

"He was struck by one bullet. Missed all the vital organs. He's supposed to be in pretty good shape, considering."

A pained choking sound. Then: "Better shape than I am."

"I think so."

"You have been to see him?"

"Not yet. He's down the hall, they said."

"When they kick you out of here, find him. He'll fill you in. Take this to him." He held out a black and white covered notebook, the sort that every schoolchild has in his backpack. Lew Chun gently took it in hand. A fine disguise, he acknowledged, the data hidden in plain sight.

He peeked at a few inside pages. A doctor, an intern and a nurse entered. Shawn Lin stuck out a weak hand. The Boy Chef took it.

"Go," he ordered, and then he began to make choking noises.

The corridor was filled with private security men in gray, vetted and hired by C.C., plus the customary city cops in blue. They stood in pairs, chatting in low voices as he passed by. Shawn Lin was in a room by himself. They had fixed his bed so he could sit up and look out the window at the East River. Whereas Professor Eric Bern had to share his room with another patient. That elderly gentleman was being wheeled out for X-rays as Lew Chun came in.

The Professor and the Boy Chef shook hands. The Professor said, "Bad news — for us — for them."

"'Them' meaning who?"

"Microphones — never know — best to be discreet." He assumed a confidential tone. "I have a seller — merchandise under the table."

The merchandise being an earthquake bomb, Lew Chun assumed.

"Borrowed — convenient euphemism — borrowed from a Scottish concern."

Meaning stolen from a fort outside Glasgow. That much had been picked up from his conversation with Shawn Lin.

"Town by town — mile by mile — made the overland journey — destination Wales. Sits in a garage — not large — not radioactive. Safely stowed — invisible to passers-by — covered with tarpaulins — behind a metal garage door. Smashing."

"And they want to sell it to us."

"For a price."

"How much?"

"Trio — three ways."

"How much?" Lew Chun repeated.

With a matter-of-fact tone, the Professor informed him. "Three million."

"Dollars?"

"Pounds."

"Why don't they ask for three private yachts while they're at it? And three villas in Tuscany and three Bentleys and three chauffeurs to drive them?"

"Lower your voice — nurses all down the hall. Payment authorized — Shawn Lin himself — if the object is authentic."

Lew Chun mulled that over. "How will we know?"

"I'll know."

"You going to go over there, take a look?"

"We are."

"We?"

"You — me — Colonel can't travel."

"You're in no shape to go anywhere."

"One week — recovery powers of a yak — start packing."

"I can't leave my family right now."

"Bring them — they stay in London — we go down to St. Davids."

It would have been insane to negotiate with him. Lew Chun promised to think it over and got out fast. The next day, he visited Shawn Lin in the afternoon. The oxygen apparatus was gone, but the tubes were still in place. He confronted the Colonel with the idiot notion of traveling overseas in the company of a man he didn't know and didn't trust.

Shawn Lin was having none of it. His pain could not be concealed, but his mind was lucidity itself. He argued, "If we're looking for nice, Eric Bern is not our man. If we're looking for reliable, he is. He and I were shot at the same time by the same man. Doesn't that tell you something? I trust him."

"Right. And you trusted Philip Lau."

The Colonel grimaced and waited more than a minute to go on defense. "It's not that I trusted Philip Lau. I didn't think about him, which is worse. But I've thought about Eric Bern, examined him every way. This man is a genuine intellect, with the advanced degrees to prove it. His main liability and his principal asset are identical. He's obsessed by influence and hungry for money. I will shovel the gold to him — if he comes through."

"And if he doesn't?"

No answer. Lew Chun sat there wondering whether his benefactor was dying or crazy or too full of pharmaceuticals to think straight.

"When you talk to Eric Bern, boy, you talk to me. Follow him to the place overseas. Take the family. You'll be safe, all of you. This I guarantee. Examine the merchandise. If it's good, return here, and we'll decide on V-Day."

Shawn Lin closed his eyes. He didn't talk any more. He didn't need to. Lew Chun knew what was being communicated.

V stood for volcano.

****

In terms that would have shamed the advertising agencies for airlines and cruise ships, the all-expenses-paid trip to London was described by Lew Chun. The best was saved for last: The children were to join them. Second honeymoon, opportunity for husband and wife to heal and start over. And for brother and little sister to see another nation, another culture. The Le Sueurs would complete the entourage, at Shawn Lin's expense. They would all fly first class to Britain and back, also courtesy of the Colonel.

Tina wasn't buying. "Your boss got himself killed almost. Are you next? Am I? Are the children?"

"Honey," Lew Chun pushed on, "the guy who shot Shawn Lin was a disturbed coolie from down the street, nothing to do with business. A lone wacko blaming the Colonel for a life falling apart, store going under, family leaving him. He's dead. C.C. shot him. Self-defense, totally cleared with the police."

He kept at those fabrications day after day, concocting an elaborate, plausible tale. He was going overseas to interview major English chefs, enticing them to the Pan Asian restaurants for higher salaries and better working conditions in the Big Apple. Never would he leave Tina's side — not for a single night. After consulting Frommer's and Fodor's guides, he assured her they would have the very best meals, theater tickets, trips to the British Museum, the London Zoo, the Tate, the Royal Festival Hall, the toy shops off Shaftesbury Avenue for the kids.

She gave in after a siege of almost two weeks. Tickets were purchased. Tina packed four trunks, as if they were leaving for a month. Eric Bern agreed to take a separate flight and check in to a different hotel. He stopped at the Connaught. The Chun family had a suite at Grosvenor House, with an enormous room for the youngsters and another for the Le Sueurs.

Tina had been in London before. She led her troops everywhere, newly energized. They had not only their own couple in service but also their own bodyguards. Two men, always a pair, often different, shadowed them everywhere, hanging around the hotel lobby in the mornings, sitting outside in a car when they were in for the night. As the Chun family trekked across the city, the protectors followed at a discreet distance. Lew Chun spotted them after a couple of days; no one else caught on — Tina because she was too merry, the children because they were too distracted.

Four days and nights into their hegira, the family dined at a high-end Indian restaurant. Lew Chun excused himself to wash up in the loo. Stepping outside, he dialed Eric Bern from a red booth on the corner. The instructions were concise. The following weekend, Eric Bern and Lew Chun would fly to Wales and check out the merchandise.

As he was finishing the tandoori chicken, Lew Chun casually mentioned that he would be making a quick visit to Cardiff. There, he would interview a beer maven. That seemed plausible enough, he assumed — brew and Britain and all that. He offered to take everyone along. Tina threw him a look that could have been interpreted as doubt, cynicism or just weariness with his palaver — or possibly all three. She wiped her mouth, checked her lipstick in a pocket mirror and said she'd prefer to stay in London. He could book a table at

Simpson's in the Strand for Monday night. From the airport, he could grab a cab and meet them there.

Saturday traffic was bad, and it took over an hour to get to Gatwick, more time than it did to fly to the Welsh city. The Boy Chef and Professor flew to Cardiff, where a large black Vauxhall awaited. A light blue car, less pretentious, trailed them. When they got to St. Davids, they hung around, jingling coins in their pockets, pretending to window-shop. Presently, a tweedy 50-something Briton crossed the street and introduced himself. He bore a fleeting resemblance to the British actor Harry Andrews — tall, balding, big stick-out ears. Mr. George, as he called himself, asked whether the gentlemen were from America.

Lew Chun and Eric Bern identified themselves, producing papers from their jackets. Mr. George poked around in each one. Then he frisked both of these unfamiliar Americans. Satisfied, he led the way to his vehicle, another Vauxhall, this one maroon and dented in the front. His smallish partner acted as chauffeur. Mr. Joseph was a dark-haired cockney with a tweed cap pulled down to obscure his features. He drove around some winding streets to confuse the passengers and to lose any and all who might be tracking them.

They pulled up outside a small Tudor house with a closed garage. Although Mr. George had a key to the front door, this was not his home. That much was clear by the tentative way he walked through the place. The quartet entered the garage from a side door off the kitchen. Instead of a car, there was a large wagon with two levels. On top lay a half-dozen oak barrels bearing the white stenciled letters DEAN'S EDINBURGH STOUT. On the second level was an unpainted pine box. Inside that was the prize. The earthquake bomb was spray-painted in a cartoonish glossy black.

Out of Eric Bern's briefcase came a bunch of small tools. He removed the lid and went over the bomb, while Lew Chun sat on a wooden sawhorse. He appraised what he could from the ignoramus's point of view. If this bomb was the goods, it had been smuggled out of a British army fort at high risk and great cost. Hence the price. Hence the three-way split. These two felons had to pay off someone in uniform, probably a bribable quartermaster.

The wagon rode on inflatable rubber wheels — meaning that it could be driven, presumably at night, over local streets, many of them cobblestoned, without causing undue alarm. If the driver was approached, he could pull back the canvas tarp to show the barrels. They would be making a racket. Ale, they would say, straight from the brewery. You know how it is, constable.

Messrs. George and Joseph remained standing. Every so often, one of them would hover over Eric Bern's shoulder to examine the examination. It took the Professor close to an hour to complete his inspection. "This is satisfactory," he concluded.

"You bet it's satisfactory, matey," Mr. George grunted. "You got the price?"

"As agreed. Half now, half when it's loaded."

"Loaded where?"

"You'll be informed."

Mr. Joseph said, "And when will we be informed?"

"Few days — understand you want to get on with your lives — want to get on with ours, as well."

"We can't afford to wait, matey," Mr. George said.

"Want these or not?" Eric Bern flourished an envelope.

"Lemme see."

The two men looked at the documents — bearer bonds worth a million and a half dollars.

"This is satisfactory," said Mr. George, mocking Eric Bern's tone. "Have the rest by the day after tomorrow latest."

They drove the Americans back to the original meeting place.

"How are we going to get that thing out of Wales?" Lew Chun asked when he and the Professor were on the road and no one could eavesdrop.

"No 'we' — take care of transportation myself — you return to wife, offspring, etc."

"But where are you taking it?"

That clearly made Eric Bern uncomfortable. But after many miles, he began to talk.

"You're not to get too close to this — Colonel's instructions — extremely fond of you, he is."

Lew Chun uttered a noncommittal sound.

"Wants you to be ignorant ergo innocent — so no details — entitled to some, one supposes."

They sped past farms and sheep, past pine forests and sycamore- and oak-lined roads. These faded into the background as Eric Bern spoke and Lew Chun listened, trying to make sense of this excursion.

"Payoffs and bribes — almost endless. Mr. George and Mr. Joseph will hand over the earthquake bomb to yours truly — lined up two associates — indispensable fools — truck drivers who believe they're transporting drugs."

"And they'll drive it where?"

"Lamprey — private airport near Gwynedd — local flights pretty much — not all that closely examined — merchandise loaded onto a Cessna 207 equipped with floats — tricky part — finding calm open water — landing on it."

"Open water where?"

"Cannot disclose to you — absolutely verboten — Cessna sets down on the sea — vessel awaits — if all goes well."

"Always the 'if.'"

"Our freight will be transferred from plane to ship. Now you know everything."

"Now I know nothing. Where will the ship go? What happens when it gets there? What kind of timetable are we talking about?"

No reply.

"I have difficulties with this, Professor."

"You have difficulties — I have orders — clandestine, the Colonel — knows all, reveals nil — to you, he might."

"To me, he will."

Driving back to London, they took turns behind the wheel. The Professor wasn't going to talk any more, so Lew Chun clicked on the car radio and listened to the BBC's jabbering about a world far away and irrelevant.

At the outskirts of Bristol, he called Tina; he was on his way to Simpson's, might actually get there early. He did — and spent the time arranging for a table for four and working on a single malt and water. When Tina and Aaron and Lynn arrived, tensions evaporated, with everyone talking at once, laughing at their own disjointed accounts. Lew Chun invented all sorts of tales about the beer men he had interviewed. Then the children took over. With great enthusiasm, Aaron told him about the Burlington Arcade and Harrods and the toy soldier shop near Green Park and the costume shops on Shaftesbury Avenue and the other places they had been and the things they had bought. It was a wonderful evening — until they were put to bed and the adults faced each other in the sitting room.

"I don't care if you lie to me," Tina said. "Just don't lie to the children."

"Why are you so hostile? What sin did I commit this time?"

"When you left for the airport, I looked out the window. I saw the driver. It was that Eric what's-his-face."

"Professor Eric Bern. I know you can't stand him, so I didn't mention his name."

"You didn't go to Wales to interview beer mavens, did you?"

He admitted that he hadn't.

"Then why did you go? Why are you working with that creep?"

"It's a project for Shawn Lin. Extremely confidential."

"So confidential you can't share it with me. So confidential you have to invent stories to cover your tracks — stories that fool your children, but not your wife."

"I know how you feel, sweetheart—"

"Sweetheart me no sweethearts. You don't know how I feel."

"Well, tell me."

"Held at arm's length."

He reached out to her.

"That's not what I mean," she retorted. "And you know it."

"Tina, if I keep you away from company stuff, it's because I don't want you or the kids to be compromised, endangered maybe."

"Oh, but it's all right for you to be compromised and endangered."

He didn't know what to say about that.

She did.

"Lew Chun, either this is a marriage and a partnership or it's a fraud. And I won't live a fraud."

"You want to examine the books? You want to know every detail of Shawn Lin's enterprises?"

"I only want to know what you're doing. I can see what it's doing to you — to us."

Lew Chun vowed to include her in his business life, as well as their life together. With her help, he would leave Shawn Lin completely and never look back. But he needed time; it was an enormous, wrenching decision.

Unhappy with this indefinite offer, Tina began a rebuttal — and then abruptly sank back in her chair, too exhausted to continue. They retired to the luxurious queen-size bed. But the loving was different now. Fatigue had something to do with it, but disappointment and distrust were stronger ingredients. The marriage was on course to crash and burn upon their return to New York. In the middle of the night, however, that course changed. The phone jangled in the insistent, two-beat British manner. Crackling and static were followed by a loud shaky voice identifying itself as Mr. Yuan.

"You need to come back."

"What's happened?"

"Shawn Lin. One of the bullets is closer to his aorta than the doctors supposed. There will be a procedure. On Thursday."

Lew Chun consulted his backlit watch. "It's Tuesday morning."

Tina rolled over unhappily, neither awake nor asleep.

"You must return today," Mr. Yuan insisted. "There is a ticket in your name. British Air. First class. Nine a.m. flight." He rang off.

Lew Chun told Tina the contents of the call. She rang off, as well, turning away, pretending to return to dreamland. He stayed up, dressed and packed. At 5 a.m., he had the hotel call for a cab and then went in and kissed Aaron and Lynn. The sleeping children were like objects seen underwater, magnified and distorted. He wanted to wake them, tell them he had to go, but knew they would only be alarmed and befuddled. Explanations would have to be left to Tina.

He wondered — always the wondering — what she would tell them, whether she would turn the kids against Daddy, lay the groundwork for a separation. Not necessarily, he allowed himself to hope. This current crisis with the Colonel — with any luck, she might put a lid on the tureen. Might be convinced to stay a while longer. Might yet understand how determined he was to extricate himself from Shawn Lin's lures and enticements.

****

It was an opera without an orchestra. Dressed in a blue hospital gown, the patriarch sat up on pillows in his hospital room, his wife washing his face with a small white towel dipped in rubbing alcohol, the room filled with roses and orchids, relatives and friends.

"My deathbed," Shawn Lin said. This was followed by a chorus of denials. Among the voices were two sopranos, Amy and Jade; a basso, voiced by C.C.; and a mix of baritones and tenors, including Mr. Yuan, sons-in-law Jimmy and Charlie, Eric Bern, and Lew Chun.

"Or not," the patient addressed the entire room, his eyes roving from person to person. "I have no wish to be morbid. But the truth is that tomorrow morning, quite early, they're going to take out a bullet lying near my heart. I could stay; I could go.

"If I stay, then I'll kick ass, same as before." Forced laughter. "But if I don't awaken or if I'm disabled, certain papers have been drawn."

Mr. Yuan handed him a manila file crammed with documents. The Colonel selected a few and put the others on a white blanket covering him from the waist down.

"I'm well aware of your…dissatisfaction with the way I do things. Yes, you, Jimmy, and you, Charlie. So I have provided compensation in the way of money and stock. Amy, Jade, you are my children, my blood. I want the best for you and your families. After all, they are blood, too."

Lew Chun could see the anticipation of bad news in the way the women held themselves. It was not long in coming.

"The fact is," their father continued, "that you're beautiful, chic, smart. But neither of you are forceful or inventive enough. Nor are your husbands."

Jimmy and Charlie visibly chafed but listened in silence.

"All that I possess, all that we have, could vanish overnight — unless we act with *chòngjìn er*. He translated the term in English for the *gweilos*. "Dash. Verve. Audacity. None of you will be surprised by what comes next. All of you have been anticipating the official word. Well, here it is."

He turned to his adjutant. "This boy, this runaway I saved from jail or worse. He has repaid me. Us."

Now he addressed the two couples. "Don't resent him. He doesn't want this. He doesn't want to be the director of this company. And with any luck, he won't be for years yet. But for now, he is my choice. I do not ask you to agree with this. Only to give Lew Chun respect. Are there any among you who disagree?"

The Boy Chef didn't dare look at Jimmy and Charlie, let alone their wives. The Colonel went on to praise the new restaurants, which were showing strong profits, to thank C.C. for saving his life and, rather jauntily, Mr. Yuan for saving his money, and the others for their loyalty and commitment during this difficult time.

Painfully, he shifted his position in bed, and the little audience understood the visit was over. But as everyone wished him good luck, the Colonel requested a few moments with Lew Chun and Eric Bern. When the others were alone, he told the Professor to close the door.

"These are things you must know, Lew Chun. Yuan, Farrar and Dean handle the investments, the real estate, the holdings, the money. C.C. is more than a bodyguard. He is an adviser. And he gets things done. You will obey him when he instructs you. *Wǒ míngbai?*"

"Understood."

"Here is more for you to understand. This man," he explained, indicating Eric Bern, "has also earned my trust. And therefore yours. We will proceed with our battle plan as outlined. The details are in his possession. If this succeeds, our enemies will know that we can destroy them in imaginative ways no matter where they are. Do I expect a total surrender? Of course not." He fumbled for his trusty manual and repeated a favorite observation.

"'Though we have heard of stupid haste in war, cleverness has never been associated with long delays.' Stick to the schedule I have laid out, and move forward immediately, if not this week, then this month — no matter what happens or doesn't happen to me."

He thumbed through the pages and found another passage. "To fight and conquer in all your battles is not supreme excellence. Supreme excellence consists in breaking the enemy's resistance *without fighting*." He took the Boy Chef's hand. "*Wǒ míngbai?*"

"I think so, Colonel."

"Very well. Now go."

The visitors disobeyed his instructions for the first time, sitting at his side until the nurse and doctor made them leave.

On the street outside the hospital, Eric Bern asked a surprising question. "Straight out — believe in the afterlife?"

"I don't see any reason why I should."

"Ah — like the atheist who dies — meets God face to face. 'Well,' He says, 'here I am. Why didn't you believe?' 'Because,' the man tells Him, 'you didn't give me enough evidence.' How much is enough — evidence of God all over the earth — just have to know where to look. Evidence of life after death — ghosts everywhere — spirit of Bach haunts pianos — Shakespeare hovers over stages — your father, you think he's gone? With you now — inside your head."

He looked a little deranged just then but absolutely devoted to his beliefs and to Shawn Lin and his young cousin. Lew Chun didn't know how to respond to this half-religious outburst and made no reply. Discomfited, the Professor dismissed his own musings: "Idle talk." Yellow lights shone on the roofs of cruising taxis. He hailed one and took off, both men wishing the same thing: a speedy recovery to the Colonel.

Lew Chun walked south on the city streets. He needed to be alone to think about what lay ahead. It was not too late, even now, to duck out. But it was better to think about a successful procedure, the bullet removed, Shawn Lin recovering quietly at home, surrounded by attendants and family, convalescing quietly, issuing orders as he did only a short while ago, the whole burden of leadership lifted from the Boy Chef's inadequate back.

The Tina at the door was very different from the one he had left a few hours ago. The voice that greeted him was softer, and the eyes no longer glared; she seemed to understand how much stress had weighed on her husband — and therefore on the entire family — the past month. But she also exhaled a defeated air, as if she saw something that Lew Chun was unwilling to face: No matter how skilled the physicians, no matter how slow the finale, the assassin had done his job.

****

The phone rang at noon. Aaron and Lynn were at school. Tina had made it her business to go shopping and leave Lew Chun to grind out the hours on his own. It was C.C., but he was no longer the surly, dangerous presence. Tears ran down his voice.

"He's gone. They tried everything. I'm the same blood type, B positive, but they said it wouldn't do any good. The bullet went too deep, too close."

Lew Chun asked whether there was anything he could do.

C.C. exhaled brokenly. "He told Ruby he wanted no service, no memorial, no obituary in that tiny type in the *Times*. Cremation. She says the Colonel wished you to keep his ashes on your desk."

"Anything I should do?"

"Not yet. There's a long roster of people to inform. I'll get back to you this afternoon. By the way, the patrols around your place are doubled."

When the family returned, they were told the news as gently as possible. Daddy's boss is very sick, and he would have to go to the office. When the adults were alone, things got real. Even though there would be no service, Lew Chun would surely be called on to attend a memorial meeting. Perhaps several meetings.

Tina was unsettled by all this, evidenced by her quick, nervous conversation about nothing. On one hand, she was relieved that the terrible influence on her husband was gone. On the other hand, he might be called upon to fill the vacuum, and this would mean — what? She couldn't say. It would change the man she married, and not for the better; that was a lock. Lew Chun tried to convince her otherwise; he would help Shawn Lin's company regain its footing after the loss of its prime mover, but in the end, as in the beginning, he was a family man. Together, they could start anew in a different place in a different city.

She wasn't buying. "I'm all out of slack to cut you," she informed him. When the children were asleep, the fire resumed. "Your cousin ran a major drug ring. Don't you think I know that?" Tina said in a loud whisper. "How naïve do you think I am?"

"He was going to abandon everything," Lew Chun insisted. "He wanted to remake the company entirely, operate a chain of restaurants like mine — like ours — all over the country."

"Oh, yes, the big shots with the dirty hands all want to be immaculate, scrupulous businessmen. Only not now. Never now. Always in the future tense. And the future never seems to arrive, does it? How many times have we heard and read this garbage about going legit? And you still believe it. You act like a man; you make love like a man. But deep down, you're a boy, the same bewildered greenhorn who hasn't learned a damn thing since he left Beijing."

"Honey, this is totally unfair. Shawn Lin hasn't been gone 24 hours, and already you put me on defense."

"I don't mean any disrespect," Tina said quickly. "But he's gone, and you're here. I don't want you to become another self-styled Colonel — another major dealer with a string of enemies and no way out because he's gotten used to the money and the power."

"I have enough money. I have enough power. I just have to see this thing through."

"What thing?"

He hesitated. There was no way Lew Chun could tell her about the Indonesian proposal. On his deathbed, Shawn Lin might very well have forsaken it or handed it over to Eric Bern. If only.

"Let me work this out," he entreated. "I'll walk away as soon as the dust settles. This I swear to you."

This was met with icy doubt.

"Honey, I have to do this. There are a lot of employees, people who depended on Shawn Lin for their livelihoods. I can't just say *bonne chance et adieu*. Give me a month, two months at the outside. Allow me to show the flag, make sure the company doesn't go under. Then I'll walk away. No matter what. If I don't get to keep the restaurant, we'll start over in another region — New England, the South, California, I don't care where as long as we're all together. Tina, I have to do this."

She didn't say no; that was all he could reasonably expect. Three days passed by and then five and then an entire week without an argument, without ominous pauses or recriminations. On the eighth day, Lew Chun was summoned to the place where he had first met Shawn Lin a career ago.

He knew what was going down before it was stated by Eric Bern. C.C. and the Colonel's widow, Ruby, dressed in a dark navy blue suit, were the only other people in the room. She looked pale but defiant, like someone who is angry and disappointed but has no tears left. She handed Lew Chun two packages. One was wrapped in gray paper.

"These are his ashes," she said. "You know what he requested."

"Yes." He took them, standing as long as she remained on her feet.

"And he wanted you to have this."

He gratefully accepted the Colonel's copy of Sun Tzu.

"I'm going home," she said. "I must do this."

"Of course. I'll come for a visit this afternoon."

She corrected him. "Not that home. My family's home. In Oahu. I grew up there. My mother and sister are there. I will die there. I had hoped otherwise. It was not to be." Anticipating what the Boy Chef was about to say, she went on. "I wish you well, Lew Chun. He loved you. Not like a father. More like a sage with a favorite student."

He didn't know what to say. He asked whether she needed anything and immediately felt inadequate and immature. But her expression remained undisturbed.

"Shawn Lin left me well-provided-for. I will lack nothing. Nothing except my great love."

She exited with the posture of a statue in motion, head held high, queenly and beautiful in grief. There was absolute quiet after she had gone. Eric Bern broke the stillness. He had been quite busy these past few days. Mr. Yuan and the others would be deliberately kept ignorant. That way, they would have plausible deniability — in case the whole thing blew up in their faces and Interpol started sniffing around.

In exactly one week, three men would be bound for Indonesia — the Professor, C.C. and… Lew Chun's cheeks reddened, and his voice went up a dozen decibels. Didn't they realize how superfluous he was? He offered nothing of value. Wasn't that evident? Granted, the plan was his. But he had no clue how to implement it. None. Zip. Zero Nada. Weren't two men enough? Two men who knew what they were doing?

"I'll be flying the plane," C.C. said.

Eric Bern pointed to his own chest. "On board — make sure mission is accomplished," Eric Bern said.

"So what am I?" Lew Chun answered himself. "Excess baggage. In the way, all the way."

"You're the CEO," C.C. snapped.

Eric Bern chimed in. "Your design — outrageous, unpredictable, off-the-wall strategy. Endorsed by the late, much-lamented — no question — you heard the widow — designated replacement."

Lew Chun went at the subject another way, appealing to their human sympathies. "My marriage is breaking up. I took everybody to England, trying to reclaim what we'd lost. I go away again, this time by myself—"

"Invent something — business trip — talent hunt."

"Tina won't buy it. Not after all the deceits I've thrown at her."

"She'll forgive — woman's specialty."

"Says the man who isn't married."

"Not now I'm not. But the third time around—"

Lew Chun had him backed into a corner. "And what drove you apart?"

"Nothing. She died."

Before the Boy Chef could apologize, the Professor took advantage of his position. "Your wife wants this marriage to work — you, as well — children involved — real mess, divorce. Don't believe in no-fault — always someone at fault — usually both parties."

"You said it," agreed C.C.

Eric Bern closed in for the sale. "Keep her in the dark for 10 days — then free to do what Shawn Lin always wanted — head up a chain of restaurants — break away free forever."

"And a day," Lew Chun said.

C.C. asked, "What's that supposed to mean?"

"It's the way fairy tales end."

****

"Here's how it works." The Professor assumed a voice of authority, as if addressing a classroom of graduate students. "False IDs — traveling as Australian nationals."

Lew Chun asked for clarification. It was already getting hard to follow, and the instructions had barely begun.

"Barred from flight to our destination — post-9/11 airport security too thorough — travel by train to Seattle — no examination of documents on passenger trains — taxi to Jennings Harbor — board a freighter bound for Singapore — skipper taken care of."

"And how much time does this take?"

C.C. broke in. "We should be in transit the better part of two weeks."

"That's one month I'll be away."

"Give or take."

"So I'll tell Tina what?"

"We've thought about that. Your mother is still alive, no?"

"Barely."

"That's it then. Tell Tina your mother is fading fast. You're going to China to see her."

"Been there, C.C., done that."

"Well, goddamn it, do it again." He shook his head and presented his palms in a gesture of incomprehension. "I shouldn't have to remind you, I'm an adviser here, a counsel." He forced a smile. "True brown. Do anything for Shawn Lin. Do the same for you. Stop being negative. Let's get this done."

"Until the next time."

"There won't be a next time. No one will dare to challenge you after this. Not for years. By then, you'll be doing what Shawn Lin always wanted for you."

"Providing high-end Asian meals across the country?"

"Exactly."

"Yeah, right."

"Don't say that. This is the last time for all time. That's why the Colonel needed to get it done. He didn't want you to pay the dues he did."

Lew Chun asked whether he could be alone in the office for a while, think things over. Without hesitation, Eric Bern slipped him a handwritten timetable and left the room. Lew Chun looked it over and then fed it to the shredding machine. C.C. departed without any further warnings or advisories.

Lew Chun quickly rummaged through Shawn Lin's files, searching for anything on Frank Alba or Rose. No use asking C.C. or Mickey or Mr. Yuan or Eric Bern. If they knew anything, it would never be disclosed to the Boy Chef.

The hanging files were incomprehensible. There must be a secretary somewhere, yet he never had seen one on the premises. He smacked his forehead. Of course; Shawn Lin wouldn't have anything incriminating here, where it could be uncovered by investigators — city, state or federal. The evidence would be at the offices of Yuan, Farrar and Dean. Particularly Yuan. He would have the answers to a lot of things. Lew Chun leaned over the desk, picked up the phone and made an appointment.

****

"He is just driving me up the wall, the ceiling, the roof."

"Go back to sleep, babe."

"Can't. I'll just have more bad dreams."

"Take something."

"No. I need to have my head clear."

"Well, at least stop jumping in and out of bed. Sit up. Read. Watch a movie."

"I don't want to keep you up."

"Too late for that."

"I keep thinking about how far the Colonel took us — all of us, not just you and me. Lorrie's in Colgate. Jamal starts at Stanford this fall. You think student loans would have covered all that? Plus this house, these clothes?"

"I know, babe. He was a wonderful man, but he's gone. He passed. You have to make adjustments."

"The kid's not ready. I don't know if he'll ever be ready. What if Shawn Lin's daughters are right? What if we got ourselves a triple-A ballplayer never going to make the majors?"

"You don't know that."

"No, nobody knows that."

"The boy needs your help. He doesn't need your misgivings."

"I don't know, babe."

"Well, I do. Go to sleep, C.C."

****

Sheaves of papers awaited his signature. A notary witnessed and stamped each one in turn, from power of attorney to a series of corporate documents, bond issues and tax certificates. The ordeal ended with five books of paychecks.

Lew Chun's hand was beginning to cramp at the end. As the notary went out the door, he remarked, "Looks to me as if we have a couple of hundred employees."

"Try 518," Mr. Yuan corrected him. "Some on the books, some off. Those we pay in cash."

"Expensive."

"Quite the opposite. The wages are high, but we don't pay benefits or overhead. And they don't pay taxes. Everybody's happy."

"And what do these happy people do to earn their wages?"

"Tasks."

Tasks. It might have been better to leave it at that, but Lew Chun couldn't stop himself. Not now. He mentioned Frank and Julie. Mr. Yuan frowned a bit too hard and said he knew very little about them. Journalists, weren't they?

"Shawn Lin didn't like journalists sniffing around, did he, Mr. Yuan?"

"Certainly not. No businessman does. And Shawn Lin was particularly secretive."

"One of those journalists was murdered. The other disappeared."

This was met with a cool Buddha smile. "And?"

"And I wondered if you knew anything about that."

"Not a thing."

It wouldn't do to confront such an august figure head-on. Lew Chun casually asked whether he might look over the files, familiarize himself with all aspects of the business.

"That will take months," Mr. Yuan replied. The Buddha was not so cool now.

"I'll start somewhere," he was informed. "And I'll start now."

"As you wish," he said primly. "Come this way." He led the new CEO to a room lined with white metal file cabinets. Another sledgehammer hung on the wall. Lew Chun was about to inquire, when Mr. Yuan announced, "Our office manager, Mrs. Buchanan, will help you."

He ushered in a fireplug of a lady with a gray cement permanent, in a brown and green print dress. She was of late middle age and didn't care who knew it. "Call me Mrs. B" were her first four words. She had few others. Lew Chun told Mrs. B he would call her if he needed anything. She made no attempt to hide her displeasure, leaving the door open as she retreated.

He went through six double-banked drawers, three on each side, the files neatly marked with words such as Taxes, Distributors, Sales, Properties, Rents, Maintenance, Receivers, Merchandise. They might have been written in Choctaw. Merchandise, for example, was broken down into sub-files of Cereal, Lumber, Aluminum, Textiles, Textbooks. Surely, these were euphemisms, he assumed, possibly for drugs, perhaps for clients. Lew Chun sat at the desk, pondering the next step. The Apple icons stared at him. He pressed a few keys. Nothing. He pressed a buzzer to his right. Mrs. B materialized.

"Sir?

"I need a password."

"Of course you do. Hell money. Two words, all caps."

He thanked her and entered HELL MONEY. Up came all sorts of information, but just as indecipherable. If FBI agents ever got ahold of the hard disk, they'd never be able to decode it. Very wise of YFD. But *somebody* had to have that code. *Somebody* had to know the sources of income, who bought what, who owed what, who lived where, who was loyal and who couldn't be trusted, who was a real threat and who was just noise.

Lew Chun exited that office and entered Mr. Yuan's without knocking. The executive was in deep conversation with Mickey. They stopped talking when they saw their visitor.

"I can't make heads or tails of the files," he reported, settling down on a dark leather couch. It hissed as he lowered himself onto the cushions.

The smiling Buddha was back. "That's the intention. Without the code, no federal investigator can tell what they signify."

"I'm not an investigator. I'm Shawn Lin's protégé."

"Just so."

"I need the code."

"As you wish. Do you need it now?"

"I haven't got time now. I have to go away in a few weeks."

Mr. Yuan shook his head vigorously. The Buddha was gone again. "Don't tell us any more about it."

"Plausible denial, right?"

This time, it was Mickey who said, "Just so."

Rattled, Lew Chun confronted them. "You don't approve of the Colonel's selection, do you, gentlemen?"

"Not our role to approve or disapprove," Mickey replied.

"But you have criticisms of the Colonel's choice."

"Well…"

"Tell me what they are."

"People," Mr. Yuan began, "enemies, of course, but also colleagues, were terrified of Shawn Lin. They are not afraid of you."

"Not yet."

"Not yet." Mr. Yuan sat back in his big mahogany chair. It squeaked slightly.

"Old," Mickey explained in a lighter tone. "Needs oil."

Mr. Yuan appraised Lew Chun hesitantly. "You don't object to advice?"

"Not at all, sir."

The "sir" got to him. He continued in a warmer manner. "The cadre, including me, don't really know who you are, how you will handle this new power. Most think of you as a restaurateur, not as a leader."

"Frankly, that's the way *I* think of myself. "

Mickey shook his head. "That's not what your people want."

"My people?"

"Yes, your people," Mr. Yuan agreed. "Your employees. Your clients. Your lawyers. Your colleagues. Politicians. Police."

"But I only know a few of them — and then only because I was in Shawn Lin's company."

"'Company' in every sense." Mickey put in. "Military and civilian. Never mind. They'll come to you, every goddamn one of them."

"At which point," instructed Mr. Yuan, "you must show two seemingly contradictory qualities: A) You are not ungenerous. And B) You are not soft."

"Meaning?"

"You must listen to your neighbors' wails and the demands of those in power. Use your influence. Give them aid when they deserve it. And say no when they do not."

"How will I know the difference between the good requests and the bad ones?"

"Kid," Mickey began, but then he decided this was disrespectful. "Lew Chun. You learn as you go. Seat of the pants."

The Boy Chef didn't want pants, didn't want to be the heir, didn't want anything except a regular life with a regular family. Not that these men would believe him. They could turn life upside down if he made a scene. Best to sit in Shawn Lin's chair, he thought, fake the humility and the appreciation for all they did to prepare me for Job No. 1. Best to fly away as planned, see the mission through. Now is not the moment to resign. Timing is everything.

****

Poring over some hard-to-decipher receipts, Lew Chun was startled when C.C. rapped on the door and entered unannounced. He closed it behind him, pulled up a chair and drew close.

"I hoped this wasn't true."

Now what have I done? the Boy Chef wondered. But it wasn't about his missteps; it was about Charlie's.

"This is coming to me from two separate sources." C.C. could lower the volume of his rich bass voice, but not its timbre. "The shooter, this Joe Din, was in the pay of the Chinese drug group."

"We knew that."

"What we didn't know is that he was being paid by two sources."

"The Chinese and who else?"

"My people tell me…" He was barely audible. "Shawn Lin's son-in-law."

"Which one?" Lew Chun asked quickly. "Jimmy or Charlie?"

"As far as we can tell, Jimmy is clean. Charlie spent two days conferring with men from Canton. Known merchants."

The calculation was not hard to do.

"If that's true, I'm No. 2 on the list."

"Very likely."

Lew Chun needed time to ponder the next step. But there wasn't time.

"What do you want me to do?" C.C. was ready to act on the moment.

"Drive me to Philadelphia."

It was the middle of the day; they were over the George Washington Bridge, on the Jersey Turnpike and into Philadelphia less than two hours later. C.C. put the car in a lot on Locust Street and stayed far behind, as discussed on the way over. Lew Chun entered the Pan Asian III. Patrons were scattered about in the customary manner. Groups of two and three talking among themselves, consuming a late lunch or an early dinner. A young woman was operating the cash register. The visitor asked for Charlie, and she indicated a room in the back marked "Private."

"I'm his brother-in-law," Lew Chun told her. He opened the door and walked right in.

Charlie was on the phone. He put it down when he saw the drop-in. Shock gave way to a Day-Glo grin.

"Hey, Lew Chun, what brings you to Philly?"

"You do."

"Sit down. Make yourself homely."

"I'll stand."

Charlie needed no further provocation; he got right to the point. "You came here for a reason. You going to tell me right out, or are we going to dance for a few steps?"

"Why did you go after the Colonel instead of me? I'm the one you resent."

"I don't resent you. He liked you best. So be it."

"You not only resent me; you detest me. Did you detest Shawn Lin more?"

"What the hell are you talking about? Shawn Lin gave me all this. Plus our house in West Chester, good money, easy life."

"But he didn't make you the heir. Jimmy, either. He in on this?"

"Jimmy has his head up his ass." Charlie's gaze intensified. "In on what?"

"On Joe Din." Lew Chun pantomimed a pistol with his thumb and forefinger.

"You think I arranged for the Colonel to be shot?"

"You were seen talking to drug guys from Canton."

"It was about supplies for the restaurant."

Charlie's face was genial, the eyes cruel and devious, assuming he could make his sale with a confident grin. Lew Chun didn't call him on it. At the door, he bade his farewell: "Charlie, every Chinese waiter says the same thing when he sets down the dish."

"What's that?" he demanded.

"Enjoy."

Lew Chun never looked back. He knew now that Charlie had arranged for Shawn Lin's death for his own reasons and that if his luck held, the Boy Chef would be next.

C.C. was waiting in the car.

"We have to do something about him," Lew Chun said as they started off. C.C. kept his eyes on the road and drove very slowly, as if he was reluctant to leave Philadelphia. "The Chinese need to get a message."

No comment. After a few blocks, C.C. asked: "Like what?"

"You tell me."

More silence. More streets and traffic lights. Then: "You don't want to know."

"Leave me at 30th Street Station," Lew Chun told him.

Three days went by. Nothing on television. Nothing in the *Times*, *The Wall Street Journal*, the *News*, the *Post*. C.C. didn't answer his cell. Lew Chun left query after query about a delivery he was trying to track down. On the fourth day, he did receive a message, brought by Mickey. Lew Chun was advised to send someone to the out-of-town newsstand in Times Square and pick up the Philadelphia papers, but Mickey had thoughtfully brought them along.

Charlie made the *Inquirer*, way back on Page 11. A holdup in North Philadelphia had ended in violence. A few suspects, nothing definite, arrest promised within days. The third murder that month. In this latest incident, the owner of a popular restaurant in the city had been shot and killed on a side street. Possibly the result of a holdup gone wrong. Used syringes were uncovered in a nearby dumpster.

The memorial service took place at the end of the week, held in a nondenominational chapel. Sparsely attended, mostly by Charlie's employees and a scattered group of neighbors. Many benches were empty. Lew Chun sat in the back, listening to a couple of friends giving their recollections of their late neighbor. Amy spoke, her eyes narrowing as they fixed on the Boy Chef. He stared right back at her, and eventually she looked away. Someone spoke after she finished. As soon as the event concluded, he made his way to the large brass-finished doors. Amy had anticipated him. She stood at the exit, and as Lew Chun walked by, she hissed like a cobra. "You erased him like a number on a blackboard."

"I wasn't even in your town when it happened, Amy."

"Oh, your fingerprints aren't anywhere to be found. I know that. But you did it. You coldblooded prick. He had children."

"So did Shawn Lin," Lew Chun reminded the Colonel's daughter.

****

During this troubled time, Lew Chun reached out to his wife in a new way, entreating her to come to the office, see for herself how he spent his days. Eric Bern's statement had been on the money; Tina didn't want to split any more than her husband did.

The charity work touched and astonished her; Lew Chun had barely mentioned this part of the job. For three days, a parade of the needy trooped in single file, in pairs or, when an entire family pleaded for favors, en bloc. There were those who needed loans for college, startup ventures, night nurses' and doctors' fees uncovered by Medicare. There were graduate architects with no prospects, grandparents who wanted someone to buy their souvenir stores, eligible women who, having abandoned their search for true love, were in pursuit of dowries to attract a husband of any age, no limits.

And, always at the end of the day, there were retailers threatened by gangs of extortionists. These cases were referred to C.C.; he promised the petitioners that the young thugs would no longer bother them. He didn't explain what he would do, and they didn't ask. Nor did Lew Chun. Nor, in fact, did Tina.

She did inquire why C.C. couldn't protect all who were pushed around by punks — not only here but in the slums of Harlem, Midwood, Staten Island and everywhere else in the city. C.C. said he and his "associates" were like the army of a small country. They could protect the turf in Chinatown, but only up to the border. She pretended to understand.

Once a day, Mr. Yuan came by to ask for the CEO's signature. The air was thick with mentions of zipper clauses, ad damnums, chattel, kick-out claims, Yellowstone injunctions and similar jargon. These were supposed to smooth the way for favorable court decisions. "Actually," Lew Chun confessed to Tina in a whisper, "the words are used to snow the great unwashed. I know; I'm a charter member." It got a suppressed laugh, followed by a commandment disguised as a suggestion.

According to Tina, the answer was simple: The man in charge needed a woman in charge — no, not his wife but an experienced lady who could determine priorities, clarify muddy items, bring order to the chaos all around them. Never mind that Shawn Lin never had such a manager; there was a new marshal in Dodge City.

Tina spent hours poring over the classifieds, made numerous calls to headhunters and, after intensive research, furnished her husband with a list. He faxed it to Mr. Yuan, who vetted the candidates, and one morning they passed in review, one at a time. All were Asian. All were free of compromising connections. All had office experience and glowing letters of recommendation. Five were in their late 20s and lissome; the sixth was 54 and married with two daughters, one at Barnard, the other at the Fashion Institute. Mrs. Ng was strabismic, dumpy, humorless. She was signed up straightaway. When the new hire learned the salary, she floated down the stairs. Mickey called Lew Chun that night. "Tina is now locked in. Officewise, she knows there will be neither hanky nor panky. Very up move."

That accomplished, Lew Chun prepared for a very down move: informing the children that he would be leaving them — not for long, just long enough to see Grandma in China. She was in a bad way, very sick. He would be back soon, with souvenirs for everybody. Aaron protested. "Can we go?" "Why can't we go?" "How long will you be there?" And on into the night and morning. Tina was of great help here; she calmed the children down, explaining the situation with patience and cheer. Instead of encouraging Lew Chun, this aroused new uncertainties. Had she really bought his story? Or was she gearing up for a major confrontation when he returned?

****

Lew Chun had never seen so many well-dressed passengers and such orderly children at an airport. Nor had he seen so many attractive ticket agents with such radiant tans and dazzling white teeth. With good reason. *Travel + Leisure* magazine was shooting a commercial. Tina mentally separated the overplaying actors from the real voyagers. Was there anyone she recognized? She thought not. Lew Chun didn't think so, either. There were major hugs and kisses and vows and promises. The couple waved vivaciously until she melted into the crowd.

When he landed in San Francisco, Lew Chun went to carousel six and looked for an Asian holding a cardboard sign. On it would be scrawled "H M IMPORTS," the H M standing for Hell Money. Two minutes later, a drab young man came by. "Mr. Weng?" he inquired as he appraised Lew Chun with a series of quick insulting glances. He led the way to a black Lincoln waiting at the curb and vanished into the scramble of debarking travelers.

Without turning around, the driver handed Lew Chun a thick envelope. It contained false ID, credit cards and club memberships. As they moved on, a cellphone rang. It was lying on the back seat. "For you," the driver said. The caller was Eric Bern, who had vital information. As long as they were in the city, the Professor would answer to the name of J(ames) P(eter) Kern; he had morphed into an importer of Swiss goods.

As for Lew Chun, he was now Christopher Weng, an arbitrageur based in Hong Kong. He had no idea what an arbitrageur did for a living and hoped no one would ask him. Presently the driver stopped at a small building in Chinatown. The scene was far more colorful and bigger than its New York counterpart, complete with a painted entrance and gaudy advertisements. They moved on to a drab dwelling with a tiny lawn and paper lanterns hung in the doorway.

"Safe house?" Lew Chun inquired.

No answer.

"If it isn't safe, I'm dead."

Still no answer.

"Maybe I'm dead anyway."

The driver finally let two sentences escape his lips: "Leave your luggage in the car. Mr. J.P. Kern stays on the top floor." In the two days Lew Chun lived there, Mr. J.P. Kern never tried to contact him, although he must have been the one who ordered meals delivered on a tray outside the apartment door.

All Lew Chun had with him was his carry-on. However, someone had kindly supplied the closet with two suits in the proper size, plus some underwear, socks and a pair of white cotton gloves. He was to put them on immediately and wear them day and night. After he departed, someone — no doubt the same someone who left the suit and underwear — would wipe the place clean of fingerprints and DNA. Eric Bern was a great planner of little things.

The Big Thing was another matter. Lew Chun tried not to think about it. But this was like the ancient Harbin cure for a headache. Go around the house *not* visualizing a white rhinoceros; pretty soon when you close your eyes, an albino rhino is all you can see.

****

Keeping their distance, Lew Chun and Eric Bern took separate buses to San Diego and separate flights to Maui. There was nothing incriminating in their luggage or on their persons. An airport taxi conveyed the Boy Chef to Koki Beach. From there, he walked to a cottage less than a mile from the shore. The front door was open, but no one was home. He searched the drawers of a small chest. They were all empty. In the unplugged refrigerator were several bottles of warm beer and a laptop. Lew Chun used the computer to Skype Tina and the children, deeply ashamed as he continued the tale of the dutiful son journeying to the People's Republic.

The images of Aaron and Lynn jittered and then came into focus. He wondered whether there had ever been a Eurasian child who didn't display the best of both sets of genes. They were effusive and affectionate; Tina was terse. When they signed off, he lay on the bed and looked at the ceiling, with tears blurring the overhead fixture. Three airline mini-bottles of Jack Daniel's sat on an end table. Self-pity drowned the evening in a tumbler of Tennessee sour mash whiskey.

Without being told, he knew how he and the Professor would reach their destination; water, conspirators' friend, is ever willing to provide pathways to destruction. Three nights later, a message was slipped under the door: Pack every item in the oilcloth backpack. Leave not a stitch behind. Flush this note down the toilet. Wait at the curb.

At 9 p.m., a black Toyota Corolla would convey its passenger to a pier in the north harbor.

When Lew Chun arrived, J.P. Kern was already in evidence, acknowledging him with a curt nod. Dressed in denim overalls, the Professor-turned-importer sat on the rough wood platform for almost three hours, watching the gulls leaving the spars, wheeling about and returning. His younger colleague paced around. Few words were exchanged. A skiff came by shortly after 10 p.m. The Professor roused himself and talked to the skipper. Information was exchanged, as well as money, before the boat took them to another, larger vessel. That one in turn sailed to a third, more spacious ship. According to Lew Chun's calculations, they were less than 800 nautical miles from the obscure island of Miabu.

But they were not going to reach the main objective by sea. A rocky outcropping slowly appeared in the miasma. A rowboat took the co-conspirators as close as it could without running aground, and from there they waded ashore in sneakers and rolled-up pants. A basso profundo laughed in the dark.

"Welcome to the sovereign state of Indonesia," C.C. said. He put big widespread hands on the shoulders of Lew Chun and the Professor and then beckoned them to follow him. A quarter-mile down a dirt road, the trio came to a splintery pine shack. C.C. lit a Coleman lamp. It illuminated his patronizing smile.

"I know what's in your head before you do," he said.

"All right," Lew Chun countered, omitting the "smartass" he yearned to add. "What am I thinking?"

C.C. grinned wickedly. "You're thinking, 'This black guy has street cred — up from the ghetto, good man with a gun maybe — but he's basically a hulking urban *schvartze*, so what the fuck is he doing in the Indian Ocean?'"

It would have been folly to admit how close he came, so Lew Chun kept his own counsel. C.C. rambled on uninterrupted.

"Well, Man Chef, let me give you a slice of bio."

He stopped to listen to the night. Insects, water lapping, the occasional cry of a gull.

"It goes like this. Second-generation military. My daddy was an Army quartermaster. Master sergeant. Thirty-year man. We got stationed everywhere, Germany, Korea, Alaska, Egypt. I joined the Air Force right out of Penn. Yes, Penn. Not cum laude but close enough.

Ace in math, not good in languages. Funny, since we were in all those foreign countries. But the military kids on the base always spoke English, and we were never permitted to wander off post."

He extinguished the lamp and led the way back to the beach, following the line of receding water, three pairs of feet crunching in the sand.

"I passed the test for officers, passed the test for pilots. Not a lot of African- Americans in there with me. Learned how to fly the heavy stuff. Never did get a crack at the fighter jets. Flew a lot of materiel all over Eastern Europe, Iraq, Afghanistan and across the States, LA, Seattle, Atlanta, Boston. Never let my kids wander off post, either. Retired after 20 years because they thought I was too old to fly. Wanted me to be an instructor. No, thank you, not Mrs. Cozort's little boy."

So that was his surname. Lew Chun wondered what the first C stood for. It was not a propitious time to ask.

"What I was thinking was, become a commercial pilot, move freight across the country. Didn't work out that way, because a great man crossed my path."

"Shawn Lin."

"That's the man. I was the one who gave him the title of Colonel. You know that? I was headed for the coast, auditioning for a job with Boeing. Then I saw an ad in *Aviation Week* looking for a licensed pilot with heavy cargo experience."

He slowed his pace. "Well, you know your cousin. Strutting, ramrod-style, tough, calculating, unpredictable. He accompanied me on a couple of flights. I didn't ask him what was in the hold. That impressed him. After a year, he knew he could trust me. Up went my paygrade."

Lew Chun's shoes got colder and wetter as he squished on, making the occasional interested grunt.

"The Colonel had this wild idea of flying around the world in his own plane, setting up an office inside the fuselage, sending for clients to visit him there."

C.C. squinted, sensing rather than seeing the doubt.

"It took six months to disabuse him. Fuel costs, for one thing. More importantly, I would have to file a flight plan. That meant the authorities would always know where he was and how he got there, making him very vulnerable to probes by investigators and attacks by—

What shall I call them? Competitors is the best word, I suppose. You understand, Lew Chun?"

"I do."

"After a couple of very believable death threats, he shut down the aviation part of the business. From then on, he rarely left his defensible space."

"Chinatown."

"And why should he? He had more money than God, a beautiful wife, associates who brought him whatever he wanted. The Colonel was going to sell the plane; instead, he found a place to store it. 'You never know,' he told me. 'One day, we may want the damn thing.'" C.C. assumed a chocolate baritone, streeting it up for his small audience. "Well, dat day have arrive, my man. Dat day have done arrive."

A few more yards and they went up the beach, over a small dune, over a larger one, and there it was. Under a spread of stars and a thin white moon, the aircraft sat on a runway of deteriorating tarmac. Colorless weeds pushed through the cracks. C.C. identified the machine as an obsolete Convair from the 1950s. When they got up close, the new paint job was apparent: dark blue and black in a camouflage pattern. This prop plane was meant for night flight. Indeed, someone had secretly flown it here — C.C., presumably — and somebody had had to light the runway when he landed the Convair. Yet no one was around. They might have been on the surface of Jupiter.

"We take off tomorrow, 2100 hours," C.C. announced. "Nine p.m., to civilians. All three of us will live aboard the plane tonight. There are air mattresses and a john. In the morning, I check the fuel lines, props, the works. You two stay inside. You don't go out for anything. We cool?"

He didn't wait for an answer.

"I got two guys working for me. I pay them for the last time tomorrow night. They illuminate my path with kerosene torches. When we're airborne, the flames are extinguished, and our helpers quietly return to their homes in Jakarta. Any questions?"

Lew Chun consulted his calendar watch. "Why are we flying on Sunday?"

"Because it's a day of rest. No one will be on the qui vive."

"Indonesia isn't a Christian nation."

"But they keep Western hours. Besides, Sunday is historic. Pearl Harbor happened on a Sunday, when no one was paying attention. Krakatoa occurred on a Sunday. Our mission is in the great tradition. Day of Judgment, crack of doom and all that. Any other questions?"

Lew Chun could think of plenty. But midflight seemed a more appropriate time to inquire about what happened to Frank and Julie. If anyone knew, C.C. did. Up in the air, he could hide, but he couldn't run.

****

C.C. had supplied everything required for survival — and nothing else. Inside the fuselage, fans ran on dry-cell batteries, circulating the stale air. Meals consisted of room-temperature San Pellegrino, canned albacore and canned kidney beans, the latter of which were opened with a device on C.C.'s Swiss army jackknife.

While the pilot obsessively checked the plane inside and out — tapping on the dials, taking a dipstick to the oil and fuel reservoirs — Eric Bern played endless games of solitaire. He wanted everyone to try a little stud poker to pass the time, but C.C. was too busy, and Lew Chun detested card games. Accompanying his father on a buying trip, he had seen a magician on Nanjing Road in Shanghai. The wizard, dressed all in white, asked the boy to select a card and sign it. He chose the two of diamonds and returned it to the deck. Some ornate shuffles followed. Lew Chun was then presented with the deck and ordered to count the cards. There were 51. The two of diamonds was missing. The hustler removed a wallet from his jacket and unzipped it. Inside was the chosen card, complete with signature.

He was wary of all conjurors after that; manifestly, the skilled ones could manipulate a deck the way he could flip an omelet. Was Eric Bern another kind of trickster, a con man with fast hands and a faster tongue? Yet if that were true, would he have agreed to take this risky voyage? Was something else going on here between these two? Was this some conspiracy to get rid of the young prince, take over the business? But then, why come all this way? They could have iced him back in New York, and no one would have been the wiser.

At around 7, they synchronized their watches like men on a mission in a World War II movie. C.C. unpacked flame-resistant flight suits he called zoombags and made his passengers put them on. They didn't have to ask why.

The constellations had a mean glitter in the black sky. Scorpio looked down; the Scorpion Lew Chun knew from schoolbooks — the Scorpion that stung Orion to death because the hunter had boasted that he would kill every animal on earth.

Precisely at 2100, lights sporadically appeared on the tarmac. Eventually, they were lit every 50 yards for a half-mile. C.C. settled into the pilot's seat. Eric Bern sat next to him. Lew Chun sat behind them, looking over their shoulders. A black leatherette hassock served as a seat, with no safety belt and no in-flight magazine. He reminded himself not to get airsick.

C.C. turned on the plane lights and clicked four switches. The motors coughed on cue, and the propellers turned with increasing speed until they looked like circular blurs. The Convair taxied down the bumpy makeshift runway. Lew Chun bounced up and down like a package and then realized that he was no longer attached to the earth. They were airborne, aimed for devastation, theirs or the Chinese drug factories. Or both.

****

Craning his neck, C.C. looked back and smiled. He was pleased to see his discomfited passengers. "All planes used to be like this," he shouted over the irritating engines. "Hitting air pockets, subject to wind shear, unable to climb above the weather. Not a lot of us left who know how to handle these buckets."

There were times when he seemed to pursue storms; lightning flashes appeared on both sides of the plane, and there was a loud crack midway to their destination, when the Convair was hit by a bolt, although C.C. managed to maintain speed and altitude. As they went on, he explained what was going on. Prop planes are noisy, so he had to fly high, hoping to avoid notice. Most of the people below would be sleeping, but you never knew what kind of observers were in what kind of towers on what kind of Indonesian islands or, for that matter, on what kind of Indonesian ships, bobbing in what kind of harbors. No radar in the vicinity, he assumed, but you never knew even in the remotest part of the globe.

After one spectacular dip and reverberation, Lew Chun screwed up enough courage to put a question to the pilot.

"C.C."

"Uh-huh."

"Two people I know met bad ends after they started investigating Shawn Lin."

"Yeah? And?"

"One of them was named Frank Alba. Investigative journalist. I think money laundering was his thing."

"I know that name. Gay. Cruiser. Murdered."

"That's what they want you to believe."

"You know different?"

"The other person was Julie Tseng. Eager, ambitious journalist."

"Julie Tseng," he repeated. "And what bad thing happened to her?"

"I don't know. I thought you might have some information."

Did a flicker of emotion register on C.C.'s posture? Or was it the Boy Chef's fantasy?

The flyer peered out in the night. "My man, there's no question Shawn Lin hated people poking around in his business. He had no use for reporters. But he wasn't reckless enough to go to war with people who buy ink by the barrel."

"No, *he* wouldn't. But maybe someone—"

"What someone? Who someone?" C.C. snapped.

Then came another series of air pockets and then a storm to get over or under, and the conversation ceased.

Despite the bumps and terrors, Lew Chun faded out. Eric Bern's voice jarred him into consciousness several hours later. "Three o'clock," the Professor was shouting, but he didn't mean the time. He meant the location of the island of Miabu, below and to the right. Ten minutes later, they could make out all four floors of a square-shaped building. Light shone from 20 large factory windows. Even at this hour, there was a shift refining dope.

C.C. banked left and began moving away from the island. "I got one chance to do this," he explained. "One only. Our crate is jury-rigged with a single bay. Inside is one lone device — the bomb from Wales. It has to go directly into the throat of the volcano. I miss and it clatters down the side, creates a lot of noise and does no harm."

"But if you hit the mark," Eric Bern offered, "we get one in the win column."

"Possibly."

"Possibly," Lew Chun echoed flatly. "We came all this way for 'possibly.'"

"Your idea," C.C. reminded him.

No conversation followed. No one knew whether the Convair was being tracked, including the pilot. When crackling escaped from his headphones, he turned off the receiver. Whatever the speaker was saying, he didn't want to hear. Early that Sunday morning, the only boats in the little bay were skiffs and junks with colorful, inconsequential sails. Every one was anchored for the night. C.C. circled around and climbed a few hundred feet. Pushing through clouds, he leveled off to take a final survey — and then went into a sharp dive. Through tight lips, the Professor spoke for both riders: "Innards in the ether."

"Yell," C.C. advised. "It'll help."

From some crease in Lew Chun's brain came a 1-to-10 counting song from childhood. He did as ordered: "Yi! Er! San! Si! Wu! Liu…"

A raw, angry sound issued from the rear of the aircraft. The projectile was released, and C.C. banked to the east. All three men watched the bomb jitter downward as the engines made noises of relief, rid at last of the burden they had been keeping airborne for hours. Picking up velocity, C.C. maneuvered upward and broke free of the clouds.

"Look back," he bellowed. "Keep track of the damage."

But there was none to see. Had the missile gone off course?

The darkness was pierced by a few more bright spots appearing on the ground, street lamps turned on by factory workers or watchmen. Three minutes later, the timing device kicked in. The British thieves had not let Eric Bern down. The lights of an explosion outlined the small mountain, purple against a background of white sparks and crimson fire. The eruption built to a crescendo. A roar was followed by a louder roar — and another. And then the mother roar. Sulfurous gray, orange and yellow vapors issued from the volcano. The airborne trio could feel a series of shock waves in the surrounding atmosphere. Below them, the water — flat and calm only a few seconds before — turned wild. The waves developed whitecaps and reached up to the flickering sky.

"Naga Kecil has been violated," C.C. remarked, "and now she's blowing her brains out."

The flow of orange lava was already visible for 20 miles.

****

C.C. ventured another guess. "I know what you're thinking." Before Lew Chun could reply, he answered correctly: "What do we do next?"

He nodded at the camo suits. "Grab the tubes on each side. Take the air in your lungs, and transfer it to the mouthpieces. When you're fully inflated, plug up the tubes. I'm going to land this thing in the drink. As smoothly as possible, but nothing is guaranteed. We could go down very fast. What you're wearing will either save your life or end it."

Having inflated his own vest, he returned the pilot's seat to an upright position and stared straight ahead in the dark. Fingers of sunrise were beginning to appear in the east. It didn't take a member of the Joint Chiefs to understand C.C.'s timing. He had to get rid of the plane — crash it, for all the world knew — somewhere in the Indian Ocean before the world had its pants on.

"There could be a minor tsunami coming because of what we just did," C.C. warned as he feathered the motors and began their slow descent. "That's why we had to go this far from land. The waves are still normal here. Grab the sides of your seat, and put your head down. Couple of minutes, we'll be going into a controlled crash. Either of you praying men?"

"I used to be," Eric Bern said.

"Well, be again. How about you, Lew Chun? You religious?"

Mao abolished religion, the Boy Chef told him. Or tried to, with limited success. He remembered his grandmother praying at night. In this tense atmosphere, it rushed back to him like an aroma from her kitchen.

Evil karmas I have done with my body, voice and mind are caused by greed, anger and delusion, which are without a beginning. Before Buddha, I now supplicate for my repentance.

Lew Chun kept repeating the words under his breath. Eric Bern's lips moved, as well, mouthing a prayer from his own childhood. C.C. produced a string of beads from his shirt and began reciting the rosary. "The Amazing Hulk — Roman Catholic," the Professor murmured. "Who knew?"

As the seconds wore on and terror took over, Lew Chun mimed a sequence of curses, beginning with himself. How had he come to this suicide mission, a journey that had begun with an idiot notion of squashing Shawn Lin's brutal competition — and then as a self-destructive act of vengeance for a cousin he had never loved or really even liked all that much? It was the power that had attracted him; he admitted this before Buddha now. And what good would power be if he ended up under the waves, the sharks picking his bones, Tina and Aaron and Lynn mourning and then forgetting as the memories receded and other males rose to take his place?

As the Convair skimmed the surface, these tormenting thoughts were displaced by something Shawn Lin had said long ago: Pity is repulsive, and self-pity is intolerable. There was no one to blame but the Boy Chef grown into a Little Colonel. And he knew it.

****

C.C. tapped the glass on his instruments one last time and examined his landing field, the Indian Ocean. The plane might have been a great flat rock spun by a colossus, taking big, arcing bounces on top of the swells until the motors shut off and the lights went out and the air stank of oil fumes.

After five agonizing minutes of creaking and yawing, the Convair came to a dead stop and slowly began to go under. C.C. used his considerable strength to unlatch the exit door, competing with the sea for every inch. He pushed Lew Chun out and then Eric Bern, following them onto the starboard wing. The trio blinked at the illuminating sky. On the count of three, they dived into the black waves and swam away from the wreck before its vortex could drag them down.

The water was cool but calm, and the inflated vests kept the three men safely bobbing in place. But that didn't ease the situation for Lew Chun; he was busy obsessing about sharks and stingrays. What creatures were plying these waters, he speculated, hungry for human viscera, thirsty for blood? Before embarking, he had read about the Indian Ocean, home to 17 species of sharks, including the great white, along with killer whales and giant squid. And there were the human predators to consider — pirates or, worse still, angry, well-equipped survivors of the volcanic eruption, airborne maybe, bent on retaliation.

These anxieties were punctuated by the sounds, all imaginary, of far-off boats coming to rescue the hopeless.

The Boy Chef was visualizing a chopped meat dinner, with him as the entree, when weary, grunting dim sounds did make their way across the water. Whatever produced them stayed well out of sight even though the day was in full fig. Was it another of those aural mirages? The sounds increased in volume, and soon he could make out the shape of a power catamaran. Such craft used to be anchored in the Beijing port when he was a youth. Fishing boats, allegedly, but too powerful for that. Military craft, he and his friends surmised. Equipped with machine guns under the tarps. But no one was suicidal enough to speculate aloud.

Minutes dogpaddled by. In no hurry, the boat slowly circled around the survivors three times before pulling up. Phrases were uttered in heavily accented English. Two Javanese men operated the boat, negotiating with C.C. all the way. One of the crew extended a hand to Lew Chun. He clambered aboard and then the Professor and finally C.C.

Under the hot light of midmorning, they pulled up at a little boat basin, nine miles east of the island they had just attacked. The sailors pulled up the anchor. They watched these peculiar Americans get in up to their waists, holding their satchels on their heads, wading ashore and walking on the wet sand. The Javanese took off for parts unknown, occasionally looking down to count their money and then back at C.C. and shaking their heads.

By now, the sun radiated intense heat in a sky of China blue. A faded red and white striped beach tent lay directly ahead, its door flap jiggling in the wind. The travelers went inside, sat on the dry sand and reconnoitered.

C.C. fetched a map from his backpack. As he was about to speak, Lew Chun was struck by an unexpected pang of conscience.

"I have to talk to the family," he said. "It's been days. They'll wonder what happened to me."

"Can't they wait a few more hours?" Eric Bern demanded. "We're stranded here."

Too much stress had accumulated over the past few days, and Lew Chun blew like a volcano.

"No, they can't wait," he shouted bitterly. C.C. made a keep-your-voice-down motion, but it was too late.

"The Colonel named me as his successor," Lew Chun exploded. "I came up with this idea of putting away the competition. And the result is I'm not even a waiter. I'm a busboy. Cleaning up. Following directions. Staying in lockstep. Bringing up the goddamn rear."

"You want to fly a plane?" C.C. rumbled. "You want to get us out of here?"

"I don't know how to fly a plane, and I don't know how to get out of here. I just want to talk to my family. If I'm going to lead this— I don't know what it is. Company? Organization? Consortium? If I'm going to lead it, I'm going to allow myself some exceptions to the rules. Or I'm going to make up some new ones."

He stomped out of the tent. As he did, he saw C.C. and Eric exchange a glance. It registered concern and, he hoped, fear. For in that loud interlude, Lew Chun had declared his independence and, indeed, his takeover of something shapeless and undefined — something he never fully understood. Whatever its substance, now it was something he wanted.

****

There was no time to enjoy this brief assertion of will. Lew Chun swiftly contacted Tina and the children on the laptop and went through his litany of lies. He told them he was at a seaside in China, noting that they could see the dunes behind him through the window, like the backdrop on a tourist's postcard. The children made the expected sounds of wonder and appreciation. Before he could go on, Aaron announced that two of his guppies had died, both with colorful tails. His voice was very sad.

"Those are the males," Lew Chun reminded him. "We'll go to the Pet Palace and buy two more. Maybe four more." As he spoke, he knew it was the wrong thing to say and that Tina would inform him privately that not everything was replaceable.

Aaron asked whether China had beaches like the ones in Riis Park, within an hour's drive of the apartment.

"Ours are nicer."

"How is Grandma?" the child went on tactfully, prompted by his mother.

"Better. Thank you, son," Lew Chun said, feeling like a leech.

"How about you, honey?" Tina inquired a little too theatrically. "Are you better?"

"Much." He tilted the laptop so she could see for herself. "You look terrific. Miss you. Miss me?"

"Come back and I'll show you."

"On my way."

The tent flap opened, and C.C. emerged.

Lew Chun hastily concluded. "Service here is terrible. Next time, I'll tell you what plane I'm on." He made kissing noises and clicked off.

"Satisfied?" C.C. inquired. "Everything all right now?" In his wake came Eric Bern, wearing a neutral I-just-work-here face.

"Let's get out of this place," Lew Chun said sharply.

"We can't get out just like that," C.C. began. His face was still reminiscent of a catcher's mitt, but the belittling tone had vanished. "We board a motorized skiff in about half an hour. It goes out past the bay to an old Piaggio P.135. Amphibious. Picks us up on water, deposits us at Hang Nadim International Airport on the Riau Islands."

Lew Chun nodded, acknowledging privately that the man really had thought everything out and that he was a dedicated and loyal figure — the Colonel's right hand in every way. And now he, and no doubt Eric Bern, would be waiting for the Boy Chef to assume command. The best way to do that, Lew Chun realized, was not to have another tantrum. It was to be big enough to cede the sandy floor to C.C. and allow him to outline the schedule.

"While you were out here talking to your family," the big man said, "I was inside listening to shortwave. I picked up two floating dispatches about the volcano on Miabu. Nothing about a bomb yet."

An approving word from Eric Bern. "Bravo."

"Not a lot of survivors."

"*Molto bravissimo.*"

"However, an eyewitness said he saw a plane just before the eruption. So there's a half-assed investigation. I don't think they'll find much, but don't bet the house."

C.C. turned back to Lew Chun. "The voyage home will be the most unpleasant part of the journey."

"As if the voyage out was a holiday."

"Hang Nadim has holes in its security. We get smuggled into an outgoing Javanese 747 carrying furniture for high-end chain stores. We debark at Newark and find our way home."

"And all this costs how much?" Lew Chun said. It was not an interrogation.

"All told, close to four mil." C.C. read Lew Chun's expression. "There's nothing money can't do if you have enough of it."

"And do we have enough?"

"How much is enough? Bribes cost. Transportation costs. Security costs. Shawn Lin gave his permission; Mr. Yuan unlocked the safe. Anything else?"

It was time to reassert authority. "Yes, there's something else. From here on, I don't get informed after the fact. I get informed before the fact."

C.C. exchanged a look with Eric Bern. "Very well. The whole thing takes a day in the air. We'll arrive tired and unshaven. There's always the chance of a slip-up. We could get interrogated, possibly arrested."

"And if we do?"

"That's YFD's department. The A team of lawyers. They'll figure something out. They always do. Chances are we won't need them. You know the drill; there are at least 15 people at the restaurant, the office, the community ready to swear we were in Chinatown for the last few weeks."

"Yeah, well my wife won't be one of them."

"Wife can't testify against her husband. Besides, I thought you two—"

"We're fine. But she won't lie for me."

"She won't have to. As you saw, this thing was not exactly Krakatoa. There was no tsunami after all. Just a lot of atmospheric disturbance."

"And some casualties."

"Plenty of those." Before Lew Chun could comment, C.C. jogged his memory. "We're in a war. Shawn Lin knew that. We know that. You know that."

Eric Bern chimed in: "In a war — not who's right — who's left."

Lew Chun opened his mouth to reply but then shut it. With good reason. The son of a bitch, he told himself, was correct.

****

The container stank. The carrier reeked. So did the passengers. It was a lengthy, grinding flight, and they couldn't relieve themselves in the regular toilet because it would have revealed their location. The three men were riding deadhead, unreported and undocumented, in heavy cardboard packing cases stenciled THIS SIDE UP. Having destroyed their forged papers in a fire back at the beach, they had no identity at all. According to the packages, they were teak chairs.

Their section of the jumbo jet was unheated, and not all of the furniture was properly secured. It slid from east to west, north to south, depending on the direction of the craft, and the three men were forced to travel with it. "A slam or two from becoming ground round," C.C. muttered.

Hours later, they felt a welcome noise — the reversal of the jet engine — followed by an unexpectedly gentle landing. "Home," Lew Chun said, daring to speak over the enveloping noise of the engines. C.C. disabused him; consulting his watch, he determined that they were still hours from New York. They were probably refueling at a major hub. Atlanta was a likely airport.

The carrier sat on the tarmac for a long time. Overhead and at the sides were clangs and feet stomping followed by more insistent clangs.

"Listen," the first teak chair whispered, "why don't we get out the rear door, work our way to Manhattan by train or rent a car or something? Even a bus would be all right."

"Why don't we just get out with concentric circles on our backs?" hissed the second teak chair. "We don't know what's going on out there. Airport searches go on all the time. They could be looking for some contraband and stumble across us."

The third teak chair remained speechless.

The wait was interminable, but in the end, no inspectors came to the rear of the plane, and some four hours later, the takeoff occurred.

Well behind schedule, the plane landed at Newark. Voices could be made out as the doors swung open and the packages were unloaded. A forklift took the furniture boxes one by one to a flatbed truck near the long-term parking lot. Inspectors looked over the shipment, poked around one of the larger containers and greenlighted the driver. As the refugees bounced along a ramp to the turnpike, Lew Chun got hold of his little Opinel kitchen knife. It had served him well at the restaurant, but it had never been so handy as now. He liberated himself from the crate. Already loose, C.C. was in the process of freeing Eric Bern from his drywall prison.

They dropped off the truck when it slowed at a toll. The driver spotted the three joggers in his rearview mirror. "Who are you?" he shouted. "Who the fuck *are* you?" But he kept going. To stop and talk to the cops would mean at least an hour delay for him, and like every other trucker on the road, he had a deadline to make. The trio walked briskly to the dry grass berm. Nobody honked or rolled down a window to yell anything else. Stumbling downhill, they came to a drab little mall and marked the location.

C.C. made a cell call. Then Lew Chun made one. Trevor and Billie Le Sueur were at his place. According to Trevor, Tina was out, due back any minute. Everybody was fine, he reported. And how was the world traveler? Good but in a hurry. He was on his way in, would be there this very afternoon. On the heels of that call, Lew Chun made another, this one to Mr. Yuan. Lew Chun said he needed a personal shopper and ad-libbed a list of gifts for Tina, Aaron and Lynn. Mr. Yuan said he would put Mrs. B on it right away.

The fugitives entered a franchise eatery, used the toilets and washed in the sinks, cleaning their unshaven faces. Then they trooped outside to eat on splintery benches. That way, their odors wouldn't be inhaled by anyone except the server. All three men ordered giant cheeseburgers and coffee. In their minds and palates, it might have been haute cuisine at La Grenouille dished out by a black-jacketed Frenchman instead of a scrawny gum-chewing Jersey waitress in a white and orange uniform.

Almost two hours later, the limo pulled up. By then, they had run out of talk. Lew Chun sat by himself, thinking about everything and nothing. He wanted to see the children and hug them to his chest, yet he didn't want them to ask any questions because he would be forced to tell them more falsehoods. He wanted to see Tina and ravish her, yet he wanted to sleep for two days and not say where he had been or what he and his colleagues had done. He couldn't wait to walk in the door, yet that moment hung over the afternoon like a judgment.

With each mile, the pain intensified. By the time the driver dropped Lew Chun at the house, his legs felt as if they belonged to someone else, someone 150 pounds heavier and 30 years older. He climbed up the stairs and got out the key. Someone had left a bunch of boxes in various sizes. They all had the distinctive YFD sticker on them. The personal shopper had been very swift. He grabbed the boxes and let himself in.

No one was there — a much-needed break in the action. A string was taped from a bookshelf to a wall, and on it were white scalloped letters from a stationery store. He had seen them before at many children's parties where they spelled HAPPY BIRTHDAY. These said WELCOME HOME DADDY. Lew Chun unwrapped the boxes and took a walk down the hall to throw the YFD evidence down the garbage chute. That done, he returned, set out the gifts and then took the shower he had been dreaming about. The cloud of guilt was beginning to disperse when he stepped from the bathroom freshly shaved and wrapped in a blue terry bathrobe. Distant whoops were issuing from the living room. The kids had discovered their presents. He emerged to greet his family. Then the Le Sueurs entered, bearing large red helium-filled balloons.

The couple excused themselves with many declarations: Mr. Lew was back where he belonged. They were going to visit their son in Parsippany, New Jersey, returning in the morning. As soon as the Le Sueurs left, there were embraces and shouts and hugs and kisses and ringing choruses of "thank you, Daddy."

Getting the children to bed was a long, uncomfortable process. Lynn wanted three books read to her, and Aaron wanted to hear a detailed description of the 30-mile bridges in China. Eventually, their eyelids grew too heavy to support. Lynn nodded off, and Aaron followed five minutes later. Lew Chun was tempted to fall into bed with his son. But he forced his own lids to stay open and plodded into the kitchen, where Tina awaited him.

Even one single malt would have been excessive, and he had two in rapid succession. They went off to the bedroom. Tina was welcoming, and Lew Chun tried hard to satisfy her and himself as he had done countless times before. But the foreplay was clumsy and the lovemaking perfunctory and over quickly. He fell asleep in the middle of an apology.

The sun was too intense to ignore, even with a pillow to block out the rays coming in between the curtains. Lew Chun pushed himself into an upright position and saw that Tina had left their bed. How long ago was impossible to tell. He looked at the Sony radio clock. The digital screen read 1:17 p.m. Aaron and Lynn would be at school. Tina must have made them tiptoe and mouth their words. That way, Daddy could go on sleeping. Daddy had traveled many miles, and he was very tired.

Lew Chun heard the clink of dishes and came to full consciousness. Not at his best last evening, he recalled. But at least he and Tina would have time alone. He washed up and went to the living room, where she sat with a pot of coffee, some toast and a jar of strawberry jam. She looked as edible as they did.

He kissed her and sat across from her, where he could look at her. She was even more beautiful than he remembered. "Sorry about last night."

"Long trip."

"Very."

"It's all right. Gives us a lot of time alone."

Lew Chun indicated the bedroom. "Shall we pick up where we left off? Where I left off?"

"Let's talk," Tina said. It was not the response he was hoping for. He had a sudden dark premonition. He tried to shake it off. It would not go away.

She gazed at the presents, the latest "Donkey Kong," "Pac-Man," Nintendo — all the electronic devices on the wanted list that year — and her Vera Wang dresses and suits and the diamond Van Cleef & Arpels brooch.

"Things," she sighed.

"Everything is a reproach with you."

"Why shouldn't it be?" she countered. "Every damn movement you make deserves reproaching."

"Like giving you presents?"

"Like trying to make me forget who you are, what you did."

"What did I do? I inherited a business. Is that a sin?"

She took a deep breath and let it out slowly. "Your mother lives in a village called Gad Shan. In the mountains."

"I know where Gad Shan is."

"Yes, well, we talked about the beaches in the background."

"By then, I had left Mother."

Tina wasn't listening. "I combed the papers every morning while you were gone. One day, the *Times*, way down on Page 15, reported a volcanic explosion on a little island in Indonesia. There was a picture. It looked familiar. In fact, it looked just like the background on Skype."

"Tina, do you know how deranged you sound?"

"The early reports said it wasn't a natural eruption. Some witnesses believed the volcano had been bombed."

"Some witnesses," Lew Chun said derisively.

"There was an official investigation."

"And it petered out, didn't it?"

"I couldn't find any follow-up, if that's what you mean."

"Because there was no evidence. The investigators decided the incident was natural."

"I don't know what it cost to buy them off."

"Honey, you don't know what you're talking about."

"People were killed in that 'incident,' Lew Chun."

"Drug packers."

"Well, what are you but a drug packer?" Her voice edged into shrill territory. "And what was so important people had to die for it?"

"I wouldn't know. I wasn't there."

"Is that your story?"

"That's all I know."

"Well, all I know is we've had it."

He reached for her. She slammed down her coffee mug. "You're not going to fuck your way out of this, Lew Chun."

"So you're saying what?"

"I'm saying divorce."

That was an unexpected kick in the scrotum. "Look, I'm sorry about last night, but I was exhausted—"

"This has nothing to do with sex. You're a perfectly fine lover. That's not what's wrong."

"Then what *is* wrong?"

"I never in the world realized how ruthless you are, Lew Chun. I thought you were just caught in your cousin's web. I thought when he...passed, you'd get loose. I thought we really would sell the restaurant, get away, start over. I thought you felt as trapped as I did."

"If that's what you want—"

"It's what *I* want. It's not what *you* want."

"How do you know what I want?"

"I feel it. I've been feeling it for a long time, just never acknowledged what was in front of my nose. Amy says you don't want to be *like* Shawn Lin; you want to *be* Shawn Lin."

"Amy's crazy, Tina."

"She's crazy with grief. We talked."

"Did she tell you Charlie is the reason Shawn Lin died? Did she tell you Charlie was doing business with drug groups in mainland China?"

"So he had the Colonel killed, and you had him offed. Where does it end, Lew Chun? Where does it end? With you crumpled up in the street bleeding into a sewer? And me a widow?"

"A rich widow."

He took a step toward her. She pushed her chair back, and that froze Lew Chun where he stood. He tried a new tack, insisting that she wasn't giving him a chance.

"A chance for what?" she returned. "For conning me again? No, thank you. You've been a stranger to me for over a year and a stranger to the kids for longer than that."

"Work kept us apart. Like a lot of other couples."

"Some work."

"That's going to change."

"Change how?

"I'm the top guy now."

"Hand-picked by the Colonel himself."

"So? He's gone. I'm here."

She shook her head slowly. "Too late."

He pressed on. "OK, OK, he was into some shady deals. But they're all going into the dumpster. This time next year, we'll be in the restaurant business, and that's all we'll be in."

"Oh, puh-leeze." Now Tina got up and started moving around. She looked out the window just as Lew Chun had. Was there someone down there waiting for her?

"Honey." He tried to keep the tone of desperation from entering the scene. "I hated what we were doing. But that's over."

"You bet it's over. The curtain is down." She mimicked a radio announcer. "Thank you for coming. Drive safely."

Tina didn't slur her words. She was steady on her feet, eyes focused, memory sharp. Nevertheless, the intoxication showed. Lew Chun asked whether she had maybe a shot or two before he woke up. Tina admitted that she had.

"So," he tried to lighten things up. "What will you want when you're sober?"

"The same thing I want now. Out."

"Anything else?"

"I don't want your money, if that's what you're worried about." Suddenly, the tears came in a flood. "Oh, Lew Chun, we're surrounded by thugs in a thuggish business. Aaron and Lynn can't be part of that. *I* can't be part of that."

"They're not thugs, Tina."

"Eric Bern is a goddamn Nazi."

"He's not old enough to be one of Hitler's children."

"Don't be literal. He's a cruel bastard. I can see it in his face. He was born to serve the master. And C.C.—"

"C.C. is smarter than you think. He's a goddamn licensed pilot. Did you know that?"

He instantly regretted giving that information away. And she seized on it.

"You don't understand what I'm talking about, do you? Because you don't want to understand. People died in that explosion." The tears were flowing now.

"I didn't kill *anybody*."

"You had them killed. What's the difference? They're dead. I don't know how you can live with that. I can't."

She got out a compact mirror and started working on her eyes. "We'll get through today, put a good face on everything when the children come home."

"But?"

"But I want you gone tonight after they go to bed. From then on, we'll meet in neutral corners and decide what to tell them."

Lew Chun knew better than to argue when she was in this state. He made a pot of coffee, and they waited silently until Aaron and Lynn returned. Their parents' smiles were as bright as a flight attendant's when a plane has to make a forced landing. How the children felt was indiscernible, but the adults knew things were different — different in a bad way. Lew Chun and Tina saw it in their faces and heard it in their tentative voices. After they were put in bed, Tina saw her husband to the door.

"They're onto us," he observed.

"You bet they are."

"Sweetheart, isn't there something we can do for them?"

"Yes. We can do something life-changing for them. We can split."

****

Alone and rootless, Lew Chun took a cab to the Colonel's house and got buzzed in by C.C., who was kind enough not to ask questions. He retired to his old room and rose early the next morning. By 7:45 a.m., he was at the YFD suite before the executives and employees. That gave him time to put on his game face. The first to arrive was Mrs. Buchanan, precisely at 8 o'clock.

"Sir?" She looked down at Lew Chun in dismay. "Why are you sitting on the rug?"

"You don't provide chairs for your guests."

"We do inside." She unlocked the door and showed him to an oversize leather divan.

"I don't need a throne, Mrs. Buchanan. Don't you have anything simpler?"

Her mouth looked like the top of a duffel bag pulled tight as she ushered him into Mr. Yuan's office and pulled up a straight-back chair. Mrs. B prepared to leave, but Lew Chun called her back and let her stand there for a moment.

"As you know, I've been away," he said. "Now I'm back. Things are going to change. I want someone to walk me through all the files, decode them and clarify what needs clarification. If you can do it, fine. If not, I'll need someone who can."

She chewed on that for a while and then swallowed hard. "Is that all?"

"Let me know when Mr. Yuan arrives."

Mrs. B was not used to receiving orders from people she regarded as intruders on her turf, but confrontation was not her style. That would wait until her boss came in. She returned to her lair with short quick steps.

Mr. Yuan entered at 8:45. They were early risers here. One minute later, Mrs. B came in with two mugs of coffee. He was served first. Lew Chun was not given a choice of cream or sugar or both. He took it black.

"Welcome," the executive said with a professional smile. He hung up his fedora on a rack, put his briefcase down and sat behind his large uncluttered desk. "Not a lot for you to do today. But I can have someone walk you through the papers and so on."

"Mrs. Buchanan is unhappy," the visitor commented. "And she's about to become unhappier. I want to know everything that's been going on here. By everything, I mean every single transaction, aboveboard, below-board, overboard."

Mr. Yuan didn't even blink. He was a man used to commands. Part of the job. And he earned a fancy salary while he did it. How much of a salary would be interesting to learn, Lew Chun mused. He had made a mental list of pending items. First among them was the location of his office.

"I thought you would take over Shawn Lin's rooms in Chinatown. Much more defensible than midtown."

"Yes, well, you saw how defensible they were a few weeks ago."

"That was a lapse in security, not an assault by hostile force."

"Hostile force. Like Injuns on a cavalry post."

Mr. Yuan made no reply.

Lew Chun pushed on. "I thought our little overseas mission was to prevent such an assault."

"I cannot respond to that remark. I have no information about such a mission. Nor does anyone here. There are a large group of employees prepared to testify that you and C.C. and Mr. Bern were on the premises for the last several weeks."

"My wife knows otherwise."

"Your wife—"

"I know. Can't testify against her husband. But there are others who could."

"Young man." Mr. Yuan interlaced his fingers and peered benignly over his rimless spectacles, an Asian codger out of a Ying dynasty woodblock. "Whatever you did was neatly accomplished. Word has come in from — how shall I put it? — back channels that China is willing to abandon its plans for a hostile takeover. Too much trouble, too dangerous. There are no visible challenges at present."

Before Lew Chun could present his case, he had to know what Shawn Lin had been into. Only then could he extricate himself and restore his marriage, handing the whole enterprise to Yuan, Farrar and Dean. He wanted enough money to do what Tina wanted, open a big restaurant in Chicago, say, or Seattle, away from here. Far away. But that was all he wanted. Surely, Mr. Yuan would understand. Quite possibly, he might be delighted with this decision.

The rest of the day was spent examining the books, figuring out the basics. Much remained a mystery to Lew Chun, but the outlines became increasingly clear. The Colonel had been the CEO of 11 corporations. Some were public; some not. Each one owned stock in the other. A hostile takeover would have been impossible. He and the boys at YFD managed real estate properties, as well as restaurants and their suppliers — food, alcohol, dishes, linens, dinnerware. These were publicly listed and taxed accordingly. However, they amounted to less than a quarter of the overall business. The other corporations were privately held in various trust arrangements.

The IRS had audited those entities from time to time. Investigators had found nothing. To them, Shawn Lin was just another corner-cutting New York power broker, nobody worth raising flags or arousing concerns. It was what they didn't see that made Shawn Lin so powerful. He and his minions dealt with a well-concealed world of drug dealing, prostitution, illegal immigration and, on occasion, weapons smuggling. Everything but gambling and booze, the two sins Shawn Lin didn't commit or permit. This material was all in the files, heavily encoded and, according to one revealing note, easily destroyed if the occasion presented itself.

Now Lew Chun understood what those sledgehammers were for. If search warrants were ever issued, YFD's hard disks could be pulverized beyond restoration, destroyed in a matter of minutes. With the Colonel's connections, there would be someone to warn him the feds were on their way, and there would be time to take the mallets to the computers.

At 6 o'clock, Lew Chun returned to Mr. Yuan's office and told him what he had learned. The executive smiled. There was a Chemex on his desk. He filled both mugs.

"Splendid. And?"

"And I want out."

The Buddha expression remained in place.

Lew Chun explained. "I don't want the business. I don't want to be the new Shawn Lin. I just want whatever you think is a reasonable payout. Then I'm gone. Whatever's there belongs to you and your partners."

"Ah, well, if only things were that simple," Mr. Yuan sighed. "When the Colonel designated you as his successor, the word went out. It's not just that Chinatown knows who you are. *They* know who you are."

"They?"

"The Russians. And the Mexicans, the Afghans, the Chinese…"

They both took sips of coffee. Mr. Yuan leaned forward. "Don't you see? You have not only replaced the Colonel; you *are* the Colonel."

"I'm not going to listen to this, Mr. Yuan."

But he was unable to turn away. Mr. Yuan purred on: "Lew Chun, you have the power Shawn Lin had — with extortionists who don't dare strong-arm the Chinatown merchants. With precinct captains who can compromise without being compromised, if I make myself clear. With investigators who can be misdirected. With politicians who need the local votes. With celebrities. With criminals whose presence is useful at our restaurants. With the right kind of journalists."

"Like the kind they have in Singapore."

Mr. Yuan ignored this impudent comment. "And most important, with people from the neighborhood. Unfortunately, this engine is not equipped with a reverse gear."

"The hell it isn't." Lew Chun put his hands on the desk and tried to stare Mr. Yuan down. After a long, interminable pause, he lowered his eyes.

"Listen, young man." Finally, the smile melted away like sweat. "If you back out of this, not only are you dead but your wife and children, as well."

A negotiating maneuver or a statement of fact? Pondering the answer, Lew Chun took another slug of coffee. "You just said there were no more challenges."

"Not today, not as long as you stay in place. Exhibit the slightest sign of weakness and they'll take everything — including lives. This is the road map, Lew Chun. Prosperity lies on one side. Annihilation on the other. And a wasteland between."

"Suppose I choose the wasteland."

"Don't mistake YFD for the Witness Protection Program. We cannot provide you and yours with new identities. You are who you are."

At that moment, Lew Chun knew this was not a scare tactic. Mr. Yuan was laying out the truth.

****

There was no way Lew Chun could take Shawn Lin's place in the firmament; that he knew going in. To make the necessary decisions, he had to have help without seeming to need it. Two days after the interview, he appeared at YFD unannounced but not unexpected.

"Could I speak to you, Mr. Yuan?"

"Why, of course. Anytime."

"I don't know exactly what to do or where to go. You see, my wife…"

All at once, everyone sought to help him in his days of need. The corporation owned 15 buildings in Manhattan and quite a few tracts in Queens — houses, malls, storage structures. YFD suggested a sizable, recently empty apartment on East 9th Street between avenues A and B, in Alphabet City. But this, the Boy Chef was assured, would only be for a brief period.

Until the East Village place was ready, he lived in Shawn Lin's house. During that time, a routine established itself, conducted by C.C., with Mickey whispering from the wings.

Three metal detectors were installed, one at the front door of the house, one at the back door, the other at the entrance to the office. No visitor ever made a suspicious move or uttered a hostile word. Early in the week came the needy, the wheedlers, the supplicants, all deferential and embarrassingly grateful for the handouts, the influence, the counsel. Usually, it was about college loans or a second store or the down payment on a co-op or an adoption by the childless or aid to a relative or a trip to the West Coast or to the People's Republic, where barriers against visitors were rumored to be eroding.

When the cause was deemed worthy, a sign was thrown to Mickey, and he arranged for a cash advance. The successful supplicants referred to Lew Chun as the Great Giver or Golden Sir or Bringer of Happiness. If the appeal sounded like a con or if it was badly presented, the Bringer learned to refuse softly but inflexibly. The turndowns were greeted with suppressed groans and crestfallen faces, but the faces showed a new respect. It wasn't hard to read the thoughts behind them: One cannot merely flatter the Colonel's young cousin and expect a reward. With his new influence has come a new remoteness. How must we approach him? How will we petition him to grant a favor? He has so much; we have so little.

He sat, and they stood, so they were all taller than the man they were petitioning. But somehow, Lew Chun was always looking down. "Now you got it," Mickey burbled after one turndown. "You're not Colonel Chun yet, but you're on the people mover." Mickey knew that the boss could cut through this banana oil anytime he wanted. But he also knew that Lew Chun couldn't run the place without him.

In the middle of the week came the pols. Never the mayor or any of the borough presidents, never a state senator in person. They were always represented by some eager law clerk or young executive in a dark Ralph Lauren suit and a shirt with a white collar and striped body. All presenting good teeth and good hair and goodwill, somehow managing to mention en passant that they were graduates of Wharton or the Harvard Business School.

According to their testimonies, they were here simply to meet the new CEO, as they did all new directors of real estate companies. Nothing was promised on either side. But it was understood that if Lew Chun required someone to cut through the red tape for a license, an inspection, something official, these were the men to see. In turn, he might perhaps bestow a favor or two should the occasion arise. Nothing specific. It was the same with the police lieutenants and the reporters. Particularly the reporters. Bogus smiles. Closed faces. "My job is to snow them," Mickey confided. "Their job is to expose you. Be cautious with them at all times. Listen. Nod. Never ask questions." Lew Chun thought of the sisters and of Frank and moved on.

The biggest surprise was the appearance one afternoon of Jade, Shawn Lin's daughter — the reptilian one. She asked for an audience "*à deux*," as she put it, and Lew Chun granted her wish, keeping an eye on her leather bag in case she had somehow fooled the metal detector and concealed a revolver.

When they were alone, she said, "I want to tell you something."

He gave her the opportunity. She paused, as if a script were about to arrive with the required lines. She started to speak, paused and began again. "Husbands can be so weak — especially mine."

Lew Chun said he appreciated her candor.

"I don't like you. I never have."

Again he expressed his esteem.

That seemed to encourage her. "What I want to say — we didn't want things to turn out this way."

"Neither did I, Jade."

"I think you are more of a player than I know — perhaps more than *you* know. But it's done. It was my father's wish. I honor this."

"And Jimmy?"

"He has no say in the matter."

Lew Chun believed that and said so.

Jade tried out her dragon lady face, but it was no good now. She couldn't hide the terror, even though she tried to make it look like respect. The whole thing was suddenly and sadly apparent. Jade had arranged this visit to preserve Jimmy, the dumb one, the innocent one, the loved one. "We give you our approval," she concluded. "One letter changes everything. Once our chef. Now our chief."

They didn't kiss goodbye. It wasn't done in the old Chinese tradition. She gave a little bow. Lew Chun intended to give one in return and then realized she didn't expect or want it. And she was gone, back to Grand Central Terminal and the Acela to Boston.

Sitting alone and thinking about what had just occurred, he envied Jade. Shawn Lin's daughter would no longer have a say in the business. But she and Jimmy would have a thriving restaurant and, better still, a paid-up house to live in — a place they wanted, a place they loved. Was it so impossible for the Boy Chef, with all his new money, with all his new power, to enjoy the same reward? He thought not. So for the next six months, with the aid of YFD and Eric Bern and C.C. and with Mickey chattering in his ear at every turn, the tenants of two 9th Street town houses were persuaded to live elsewhere.

Under the new owner's direction, the adjoining buildings were merged into a single unified dwelling with a garage behind wrought-iron gates. Alarms were installed, along with built-in cameras to surveil the place 24/7. The design and reconstruction must have totaled almost $2 million. Yet in all that time, a bill never presented itself. YFD took care of everything. Lew Chun's Amex and Chase credit card bills were sent directly to headquarters. The only time he needed money was for taxis.

Without an immediate threat, the companies could pursue their goals quietly, and for a time, things ran the way any large enterprise does in the City. There were dealings with civil servants who liked to make the powerful wait their turn — until the word went out that Mr. Chun and his staff were to be let alone. There were likewise the building inspectors. There were also health department functionaries, insurance companies, forensic tax men.

Yet one matter grew more aggrieved with the week. Tina was demanding custody of the children. Lew Chun asked Mr. Yuan to look into it. His message was carried by Mickey. "Your frau has a diesel dyke lawyer. Where Augusta Lortel walks, a weed grows. And the thing is, the judges like her style. Well, maybe not like but respect. This is gonna be major trouble, boss."

Boss, Lew Chun noted. The kid was no longer on the premises.

"What are we going to do, Mickey?"

"Why not share custody? See the kids every other week, show 'em the coast, Europe, Disney World."

Negative.

"Why? Tina can't possibly give 'em what you can. No contest."

"Because she'll spend every waking hour running me down — telling them I'm a criminal, a villain. No kid can stand up against that. Not for long. I won't have it."

"Well, boss, you may be a powerhouse down here, but go a few blocks south to the courthouse and you're just another father pleading for justice, up against one of the most aggressive attorneys in the city. Why don't you and Tina talk it over amongst yourselves, come up with something you can both live with?"

"What part of 'no' don't you understand, Mickey?"

"The part where you convince the court a father is a better parent than a mother."

"Some fathers are."

"Not in New York. You can put up a squawk, maybe cut down the payments, get a weekend or two extra, but that's all she wrote."

"Mickey, this is just like any other battle. You're thinking Dao. I'm thinking Jang."

"Which means exactly what?"

"I'll tell you exactly what after I talk to Tina."

"She won't speak to you, not without Lortel in the room."

"Fair enough."

"And the room is her office."

"Fine."

That answer surprised Mickey, and the boss had bigger surprises in store, depending on how the meeting went. Mr. Yuan had prepared a brief with some interesting items. Lew Chun was curious to see how Tina and Augusta Lortel Esq. would handle them.

The preliminaries were common to all law conferences — long mahogany table with legal-size yellow pads and sharpened Mongol No. 2 pencils, introductions reminiscent of boxers shaking hands before the fight, glass coffee mugs brought in by a young secretary, frosty looks from Tina, brief, hostile statements from the opposition. A male stenographer, young and balding with wire-rimmed glasses and his head down, recorded the negotiations in shorthand. Mr. Yuan brought out a small voice-activated tape recorder and set it up.

Lew Chun expected Augusta Lortel to be a gruff fireplug type in a chalk-stripe pantsuit and New Balance street shoes. Far from it. She could have been a model in her youth, which may have been 30 years ago, but this was a body that had spent many hours in the gym. Her white Armani suit did great things for the blond highlights in her auburn hair. She had a fortune in cheekbones, and her short, fashionable cut showed them off.

Counselor Lortel stated the date, place and attendees, and round one began. Their father could have the children every other weekend, except for one month in the summer, either July or August. That was when they and their mother would go on vacation to Europe or the Hamptons. He would pay for their education and allowances until they reached the age of 25. Talking of allowances, in addition to underwriting Tina's wardrobe and rent, he would grant her a monthly sum amounting to nearly $1 million per year for life.

When the opposition's lawyer was through with her litany, she looked up from her papers. "Those are our terms. I trust you find them satisfactory."

"We find them absurd," Lew Chun told her.

"I assure you," she replied, "we are not being frivolous."

Mr. Yuan broke in. "Nor are we, counselor. We intend to ask the court for custody of Aaron and Lynn Chun, visiting rights, of course, to be granted to Mrs. Chun, along with a fair sum of money."

"Let's take the safety off the trigger, shall we?" inquired Augusta Lortel, warming to her cause. She turned away from Mr. Yuan and toward his client. "We are conscious of the ways in which you accrue your money. We do not feel this is a salubrious environment for adults, let alone children. Far from granting your wish, the courts, should my client testify, might very well forbid *any* extended visits by their father."

"I don't know what your client has told you," Lew Chun replied in a soft voice, "but my companies have no trouble with the Internal Revenue Service, the FBI or the New York Police Department. If you have evidence to the contrary, let's see it."

"We have evidence that will be used at our discretion."

This was supposed to freeze his blood. He didn't react, except to inquire whether that was all.

"No, it's not all. I omitted to mention, for example, your trip to Indonesia, at which time—"

"What trip to Indonesia?"

"You deny visiting that country?"

"Never been there."

"We have evidence to the contrary."

"Hearsay evidence," Mr. Yuan interjected.

"Furthermore," Augusta Lortel continued, now directing her remarks to Mr. Yuan, "we have evidence that your client was involved in hostilities that could be interpreted as an act of war."

"No doubt you have contacted Interpol and the State Department," Mr. Yuan interjected.

"We shall if necessary."

"Well, if necessary, counselor, we will introduce evidence that is not hearsay — evidence about your client's indiscreet behavior, hardly conducive to the moral education of children."

The eyes of Augusta and Tina met for a nanosecond and then went their separate ways.

Mr. Yuan warmed to *his* task. "On three separate evenings, Mrs. Chun played host to a gentleman at her apartment."

"Corey Seaton is a senior editor," Tina protested. "Those were business meetings. We were discussing a biography of William Faulkner. They were friendly dinners, for God's sake, nothing more."

"Really?" Mr. Yuan retorted. "They must have been intensely friendly. On two occasions, the gentleman in question — married by the way, with three children — left after 1:30 a.m."

That got Tina. "You bastard." Her response was directed at her husband. "You total fucker. You had my place watched." She turned back to Augusta Lortel. "They probably have photographs." Back to Lew Chun. "You are the absolute lowest." She teared up, furious at Lew Chun but also at herself for getting caught.

Her lawyer handed her a couple of Kleenexes. Augusta Lortel was a model of restraint. "My client is visibly upset. This meeting is over. We will resume at a time of our choosing."

That was fine with Mr. Yuan. He and Lew Chun took their leave aware that they had scored a point or two late in the game. They were also aware that those points were not enough to win. Nowhere near enough.

****

"It's a standoff," Mickey declared.

He played the tape two more times. Mr. Yuan listened without saying anything. His partners were equally silent as they all sat in upholstered leather chairs scattered around in Dean's enormous corner office. C.C. listened on the sidelines. So did Eric Bern.

"Not a standoff to me," Lew Chun said. "A major hazard."

"Which, the lawyer or the wife?"

"Both."

Mr. Yuan assumed a voice of reason. "Let me negotiate with Augusta Lortel."

"We're through negotiating."

The attorney tried again. "I'll ask for a private audience. Just the two lawyers. Given time, these things can often be resolved to the satisfaction of both parties."

"Time is on their side," Lew Chun pointed out, "not ours. The more they threaten the more we worry. I don't know what goods they have on us."

"They can't have much," Mr. Yuan theorized, "or they would have trotted it out."

"We don't know that. We could wind up indicted. Convicted. Jailed."

Mr. Yuan protested. "Really, I don't think—"

"I do. Something has to be done."

"What would you suggest?"

Lew Chun pondered that. "What would Shawn Lin have done? What would he do now if he were sitting here?"

No answer. "Well," he addressed the small group. "Think about what the Colonel would want. I don't have to remind you how much is at risk."

"You really want us to take action outside the court?"

"Far outside."

C.C. would know what to do. The boss looked at him and nodded.

"YFD cannot be a party to any details," Mr. Yuan announced, presumably for the record, though nobody was taking notes. He put his hands on the table and prepared to rise. The others made similar motions. Lew Chun went out first.

****

"Lew Chun?"

"Who's, what's—"

"You butcher. You fucking bloody killer."

He consulted the digits on the Sony alarm radio. 2:25 a.m. Should have gotten rid of that landline, he grumbled. Hardly anyone uses it, including me. The cell was the way the staff got hold of him. It had caller ID so that, like everybody else, he could ignore the unwanted.

Not the case now. It was Tina, and she was hysterical, screaming at him for being a liar, an animal, a mass murderer.

"What are you talking about?" He tried to remain calm, get the lady who was still legally his wife to keep her voice down. She had the kids; nobody could remain sleeping if she was this loud.

"Augusta Lortel is the matter," she said. "You homicidal manipulative fucker."

"Will you dial down the volume for a minute, Tina? Will you just make a little sense before you go into *j'accuse* mode?"

"She had a brain aneurism last night. They don't think she's going to make it."

"Babe, this is the first I heard of it."

"Babe me no babe, you bastard. You killed her."

"You think I can reach into your lawyer's head from here?"

"I think you can do just about anything if you want it badly enough."

"I don't even know where she lives, for God's sake."

"You don't have to know. You have people to know for you. Medical people. Lawyer people. Felonious people. Am I next, Lew Chun? Do you want me off the stage, too?"

He was fully awake now. "Tina, what is it you want?"

"I want to live. I want my mother to live. I want my children to live. And prosper."

"They'll prosper with me. I know what they need."

"You don't know them. How can you possibly know what they need? Are you aware that Aaron is failing in just about everything? Even arithmetic? It used to be his favorite subject. Did you know that Lynn hates school so much she throws up in the morning?"

Lew Chun was genuinely appalled by this revelation. Was it true, he wondered, or was she taking over for her lawyer, using the old reliable weapon of guilt?

She got louder. "It isn't that you need to beat your wife. You need to do a victory walk over her."

"Tina, will you stop talking trash for a minute?"

"You want Aaron and Lynn under your roof, not mine. True?"

"All right, yes. I don't want you filling their ears with this garbage. And I want them safe."

"With security people in the school?"

"If necessary."

"Do you know how sick that is? Little children with bodyguards?"

"Lots of kids have bodyguards — presidents' children, movie stars' children, zillionaires' children. Grow up, will you, Tina. The real world's a goddamn nasty place."

"How about me? You want their mother safe? Or am I in the way of your scenario?"

"You want security people?"

"Chosen by you?"

"You want to hire your own guards? Send me the bill."

"All this doesn't mean I can't visit my son and daughter now and again, right?"

"Don't be a fool. You'll have all the visiting rights you desire."

A long, long pause. The line crackled. Lew Chun thought maybe she had rung off. Then: "I don't know who you are anymore. But I know *what* you are."

He didn't need to fill in the blanks.

"All right," she sighed. "Augusta's partner will meet your Mr. what's-his-face."

"Yuan."

"And we'll…settle. I don't want anything bad to happen to me or my relatives or my friends."

"Tina, will you stop now? Will you just stop?"

"Yes, I'll stop. But you won't. This is just the beginning for you. One way or another, you're going down. Not now. Perhaps not for a long time. You'll be ever so cautious, you and your people. But one day, maybe five years from this minute, maybe 10…"

Lew Chun put the phone under the pillow. Wound up like that, she could go on for an hour, and he had no intention of lending her any more ears. When he picked up the receiver after breakfast, it was dead.

At 8:30, he called Mr. Yuan and reported the conversation. "The monologue, actually," he said.

Mr. Yuan replied, "I forget who said couples don't part on the best of terms because if they were the best of terms, they wouldn't part. That gentleman was correct. If it was a gentleman. Perhaps it was a lady." Lew Chun had a feeling he had said this to many other husbands over the years.

****

The call from Tina had occurred early on a cold Tuesday morning. Late on a warmer Friday, Rose Chen appeared at the office with folders and papers.

"Exquisite timing," she remarked as he perused the documents. She sat across from him, letting her skirt ride up. Lew Chun kept his eyes locked on hers when they communicated and did precious little of that going over the entries.

Impressive, he could see. She brought in big money from sites all across the tri-state area. The places were identified as fitness centers or alternative medicine groups. Nothing as blatant as massage parlors or models for advertising and promotional material. No problem with raids or complaints. Manifestly, Shawn Lin had never had to tell her anything twice. No client had been threatened; none of her girls had ever been brutalized by anyone, john or pimp. Everyone was of legal age. Everyone was clean. Everyone was satisfied. So Rose said, and so it appeared.

"How long can this go on?" he asked when all the grosses were recorded.

"As long as you let it."

"The police might have a little something to say about that."

"Not if you don't want them to."

He smiled at her confidence. "I'm not that powerful."

She smiled at his diffidence. "I think you are. I think you can get anything you want. Or anyone."

No comment. He handed her back the papers.

As she loaded her Coach bag, she put on a concerned face. "I hear your marriage broke up. Very sorry to hear it."

"Your condolences are appreciated."

"You must be quite…forlorn."

"I am."

"If you ever need company, I have an open schedule."

"I'm not that forlorn."

"It can be very lonely in the penthouse. You don't even have a cat."

"I'll go to Bideawee tomorrow."

She went to the door without comment, opened it and said, "The Colonel's cousin is all gwowed up."

"I might need a pussy," he told her. "I don't need a kitten."

Rose had a comeback; he could see that in her hard China doll face. But she thought better of it and left, closing the door behind her with a light click. No slamming for the madam.

It began to snow, the flakes turning into wet dirty water as they hit the windows. Over the next hour, phone lines two and three lit up several times. Mrs. Ng headed them all off; nothing for Numero Uno to be concerned about. At 6:30, she poked her head in the office to see whether the boss was ready to wrap up the day. He nodded. One by one, the staff members took their leave. Mrs. Ng bid him a fond good night.

"You want the door open or closed, sir?"

"Closed."

"Good night, sir."

"Good night. Stay warm."

Only C.C. was out there now, waiting to drive him home whenever he chose to go.

Then it got truly desolate. A button lit, indicating that somebody from the outside wanted him on line three. Lew Chun waited; he had nothing but time. The light went off. He flipped open the *Times* to the Arts & Leisure section. The newspaper pages rattled in the still air.

An idea stirred. Why not get the Le Sueurs to rustle up something and then go out to a movie? Well, for one thing, there was no one to go with. Plus, it was going to get colder and wetter. Besides, there was nothing worthwhile at the Angelika on Houston Street. Further north than that, he would need a car and driver — meaning C.C. or some of his people. Not worth it.

He gazed at his old diploma and mused about Aaron and Lynn. If the boy was failing arithmetic (whoever heard of a Jewish Chinese kid falling behind in math?), a tutor would have to be found. The papers were full of ads. Couldn't be that pricey. And what if it was? By the time Aaron graduated from college, all this shady stuff would be gone, sold or liquidated. The young man could be a professional with two or three degrees. Or if it suited him, he could work alongside his father, operating a chain of restaurants nationwide.

As for Lynn: Very well, she hated school. So had her old man. He would find another establishment for her. An exclusive one. The fees would be like Harvard's, but what else was the money for? For them. For the next generation. And for protection. The wealthy would always need protection.

Another bleak evening lay dead ahead. He looked down at the shiny streets and the windshield wipers of the cabs going uptown, examined the files yet again and searched for something better to read. Shawn Lin's legacy, *The Art of War* — creased, dog-eared, well-thumbed — lay in the outbox next to his urn. Lew Chun had absently left the book there yesterday, intending to take it home and put it on the headboard. He picked up the manual and riffled through the pages. One after another, the ancient Chinese truths still applied — especially the last nine words.

"To know your enemy, you must become your enemy."

He could hear the Colonel whispering them from the ashes.

About the Author

STEFAN KANFER is the author of 15 books, many of them national and international best-sellers, including the biographies *Groucho*, *Ball of Fire* (Lucille Ball), *Somebody* (Marlon Brando), *Tough Without a Gun* (Humphrey Bogart), *The Last Empire* (the story of the De Beers diamond company) and *A Journal of the Plague Years* (a history of the show business blacklist).

****

Hell Money
is also available as an e-book
for Kindle, Amazon Fire, iPad, Nook and
Android e-readers. Visit
creatorspublishing.com to learn more.

° ° °

CREATORS PUBLISHING

We publish books.
We find compelling storytellers and
help them craft their narrative,
distributing their novels and collections
worldwide.

° ° °

www.ingramcontent.com/pod-product-compliance
Lightning Source LLC
Chambersburg PA
CBHW022157260626
47155CB00019B/3068